Daphne
du Maurier
Don't Look Now

PENGUIN BOOKS

PENGUIN BOOKS

UK | USA | Canada | Ireland | Australia
India | New Zealand | South Africa

Penguin Books is part of the Penguin Random House group of companies
whose addresses can be found at global.penguinrandomhouse.com.

Penguin
Random House
UK

This collection published in Penguin Classics 2006
Published as a Pocket Penguin 2016
001

Set in 10.36/12.8 pt Haarlemmer MT Pro
Typeset by Jouve (UK), Milton Keynes
Printed in Great Britain by Clays Ltd, St Ives plc

A CIP catalogue record for this book is available from the British Library

ISBN: 978-0-241-25972-6

www.greenpenguin.co.uk

Daphne du Maurier

Born 1907, London, England
Died 1989, Cornwall, England

This collection was first published in 1971.

Contents

Don't Look Now   I

Not After Midnight   58

A Border-Line Case   III

The Way of the Cross   183

The Breakthrough   257

Don't Look Now

'Don't look now,' John said to his wife, 'but there are a couple of old girls two tables away who are trying to hypnotise me.'

Laura, quick on cue, made an elaborate pretence of yawning, then tilted her head as though searching the skies for a nonexistent aeroplane.

'Right behind you,' he added. 'That's why you can't turn round at once – it would be much too obvious.'

Laura played the oldest trick in the world and dropped her napkin, then bent to scrabble for it under her feet, sending a shooting glance over her left shoulder as she straightened once again. She sucked in her cheeks, the first tell-tale sign of suppressed hysteria, and lowered her head.

'They're not old girls at all,' she said. 'They're male twins in drag.'

Her voice broke ominously, the prelude to uncontrolled laughter, and John quickly poured some more chianti into her glass.

'Pretend to choke,' he said, 'then they won't notice. You know what it is – they're criminals doing the sights of Europe, changing sex at each stop. Twin sisters here on Torcello. Twin brothers tomorrow in Venice, or even tonight, parading arm-in-arm across the Piazza San Marco. Just a matter of switching clothes and wigs.'

'Jewel thieves or murderers?' asked Laura.

'Oh, murderers, definitely. But why, I ask myself, have they picked on me?'

The waiter made a diversion by bringing coffee and bearing away the fruit, which gave Laura time to banish hysteria and regain control.

1

'I can't think,' she said, 'why we didn't notice them when we arrived. They stand out to high heaven. One couldn't fail.'

'That gang of Americans masked them,' said John, 'and the bearded man with a monocle who looked like a spy. It wasn't until they all went just now that I saw the twins. Oh God, the one with the shock of white hair has got her eye on me again.'

Laura took the powder compact from her bag and held it in front of her face, the mirror acting as a reflector.

'I think it's me they're looking at, not you,' she said. 'Thank heaven I left my pearls with the manager at the hotel.' She paused, dabbing the sides of her nose with powder. 'The thing is,' she said after a moment, 'we've got them wrong. They're neither murderers nor thieves. They're a couple of pathetic old retired schoolmistresses on holiday, who've saved up all their lives to visit Venice. They come from some place with a name like Walabanga in Australia. And they're called Tilly and Tiny.'

Her voice, for the first time since they had come away, took on the old bubbling quality he loved, and the worried frown between her brows had vanished. At last, he thought, at last she's beginning to get over it. If I can keep this going, if we can pick up the familiar routine of jokes shared on holiday and at home, the ridiculous fantasies about people at other tables, or staying in the hotel, or wandering in art galleries and churches, then everything will fall into place, life will become as it was before, the wound will heal, she will forget.

'You know,' said Laura, 'that really was a very good lunch. I did enjoy it.'

Thank God, he thought, thank God . . . Then he leant forward, speaking low in a conspirator's whisper. 'One of them is going to the loo,' he said. 'Do you suppose he, or she, is going to change her wig?'

'Don't say anything,' Laura murmured. 'I'll follow her

and find out. She may have a suitcase tucked away there, and she's going to switch clothes.'

She began to hum under her breath, the signal, to her husband, of content. The ghost was temporarily laid, and all because of the familiar holiday game, abandoned too long, and now, through mere chance, blissfully recaptured.

'Is she on her way?' asked Laura.

'About to pass our table now,' he told her.

Seen on her own, the woman was not so remarkable. Tall, angular, aquiline features, with the close-cropped hair which was fashionably called an Eton crop, he seemed to remember, in his mother's day, and about her person the stamp of that particular generation. She would be in her middle sixties, he supposed, the masculine shirt with collar and tie, sports jacket, grey tweed skirt coming to mid-calf. Grey stockings and laced black shoes. He had seen the type on golf-courses and at dog-shows – invariably showing not sporting breeds but pugs – and if you came across them at a party in somebody's house they were quicker on the draw with a cigarette-lighter than he was himself, a mere male, with pocket-matches. The general belief that they kept house with a more feminine, fluffy companion was not always true. Frequently they boasted, and adored, a golfing husband. No, the striking point about this particular individual was that there were two of them. Identical twins cast in the same mould. The only difference was that the other one had whiter hair.

'Supposing,' murmured Laura, 'when I find myself in the *toilette* beside her she starts to strip?'

'Depends on what is revealed,' John answered. 'If she's hermaphrodite, make a bolt for it. She might have a hypodermic syringe concealed and want to knock you out before you reached the door.'

Laura sucked in her cheeks once more and began to shake. Then, squaring her shoulders, she rose to her feet.

'I simply must not laugh,' she said, 'and whatever you do, don't look at me when I come back, especially if we come out together.' She picked up her bag and strolled self-consciously away from the table in pursuit of her prey.

John poured the dregs of the chianti into his glass and lit a cigarette. The sun blazed down upon the little garden of the restaurant. The Americans had left, and the monocled man, and the family party at the far end. All was peace. The identical twin was sitting back in her chair with her eyes closed. Thank heaven, he thought, for this moment at any rate, when relaxation was possible, and Laura had been launched upon her foolish, harmless game. The holiday could yet turn into the cure she needed, blotting out, if only temporarily, the numb despair that had seized her since the child died.

'She'll get over it,' the doctor said. 'They all get over it, in time. And you have the boy.'

'I know,' John had said, 'but the girl meant everything. She always did, right from the start, I don't know why. I suppose it was the difference in age. A boy of school age, and a tough one at that, is someone in his own right. Not a baby of five. Laura literally adored her. Johnnie and I were nowhere.'

'Give her time,' repeated the doctor, 'give her time. And anyway, you're both young still. There'll be others. Another daughter.'

So easy to talk . . . How replace the life of a loved lost child with a dream? He knew Laura too well. Another child, another girl, would have her own qualities, a separate identity, she might even induce hostility because of this very fact. A usurper in the cradle, in the cot, that had been Christine's. A chubby, flaxen replica of Johnnie, not the little waxen dark-haired sprite that had gone.

He looked up, over his glass of wine, and the woman was staring at him again. It was not the casual, idle glance of someone at a nearby table, waiting for her companion to return, but something deeper, more intent, the prominent, light blue eyes oddly penetrating, giving him a sudden feeling of discomfort. Damn the woman! All right, bloody stare, if you must. Two can play at that game. He blew a cloud of cigarette smoke into the air and smiled at her, he hoped offensively. She did not register. The blue eyes continued to hold his, so that he was obliged to look away himself, extinguish his cigarette, glance over his shoulder for the waiter and call for the bill. Settling for this, and fumbling with the change, with a few casual remarks about the excellence of the meal, brought composure, but a prickly feeling on his scalp remained, and an odd sensation of unease. Then it went, as abruptly as it had started, and stealing a furtive glance at the other table he saw that her eyes were closed again, and she was sleeping, or dozing, as she had done before. The waiter disappeared. All was still.

Laura, he thought, glancing at his watch, is being a hell of a time. Ten minutes at least. Something to tease her about, anyway. He began to plan the form the joke would take. How the old dolly had stripped to her smalls, suggesting that Laura should do likewise. And then the manager had burst in upon them both, exclaiming in horror, the reputation of the restaurant damaged, the hint that unpleasant consequences might follow unless . . . The whole exercise turning out to be a plant, an exercise in blackmail. He and Laura and the twins taken in a police launch back to Venice for questioning. Quarter of an hour . . . Oh, come on, come on . . .

There was a crunch of feet on the gravel. Laura's twin walked slowly past, alone. She crossed over to her table and stood there a moment, her tall, angular figure interposing itself between John and her sister. She was saying something, but he couldn't catch the words. What was the accent, though – Scottish? Then she bent, offering an arm to the seated twin, and they moved away together across the garden to the break in the little hedge beyond, the twin who had stared at John leaning on her sister's arm. Here was the difference again. She was not quite so tall, and she stooped more – perhaps she was arthritic. They disappeared out of sight, and John, becoming impatient, got up and was about to walk back into the hotel when Laura emerged.

'Well, I must say, you took your time,' he began, and then stopped, because of the expression on her face.

'What's the matter, what's happened?' he asked.

He could tell at once there was something wrong. Almost as if she were in a state of shock. She blundered towards the table he had just vacated and sat down. He drew up a chair beside her, taking her hand.

'Darling, what, is it? Tell me – are you ill?'

She shook her head, and then turned and looked at him. The dazed expression he had noticed at first had given way to one of dawning confidence, almost of exaltation.

'It's quite wonderful,' she said slowly, 'the most wonderful thing that could possibly be. You see, she isn't dead, she's still with us. That's why they kept staring at us, those two sisters. They could see Christine.'

Oh God, he thought. It's what I've been dreading. She's going off her head. What do I do? How do I cope?

'Laura, sweet,' he began, forcing a smile, 'look, shall we go? I've paid the bill, we can go and look at the cathedral and stroll around, and then it will be time to take off in that launch again for Venice.'

She wasn't listening, or at any rate the words didn't penetrate.

'John, love,' she said, 'I've got to tell you what happened. I followed her, as we planned, into the *toilette* place. She was combing her hair and I went into the loo, and then came out and washed my hands in the basin. She was washing hers in the next basin. Suddenly she turned and said to me, in a strong Scots accent, "Don't be unhappy any more. My sister has seen your little girl. She was sitting between you and your husband, laughing." Darling, I thought I was going to faint. I nearly did. Luckily, there was a chair, and I sat down, and the woman bent over me and patted my head. I'm not sure of her exact words, but she said something about the moment of truth and joy being as sharp as a sword, but not to be afraid, all was well, but the sister's vision had been so strong they knew I had to be told, and that Christine wanted it. Oh John, don't look like that. I swear I'm not making it up, this is what she told me, it's all true.'

The desperate urgency in her voice made his heart sicken. He had to play along with her, agree, soothe, do anything to bring back some sense of calm.

'Laura, darling, of course I believe you,' he said, 'only it's a sort of shock, and I'm upset because you're upset . . .'

'But I'm not upset,' she interrupted. 'I'm happy, so happy that I can't put the feeling into words. You know what it's been like all these weeks, at home and everywhere we've been on holiday, though I tried to hide it from you. Now it's lifted, because I know, I just know, that the woman was right. Oh Lord, how awful of me, but I've forgotten their name – she did tell me. You see, the thing is that she's a retired doctor, they come from Edinburgh, and the one who saw Christine went blind a few years ago. Although she's studied the occult all her life and been very psychic, it's only since going blind that she has really seen things, like a medium. They've had the most wonderful experiences. But to describe Christine as the blind one did to her sister, even down to the little blue-and-white dress with the puff sleeves that she wore at her birthday party, and to say she was smiling happily . . . Oh, darling, it's made me so happy I think I'm going to cry.'

No hysteria. Nothing wild. She took a tissue from her bag and blew her nose, smiling at him. 'I'm all right, you see, you don't have to worry. Neither of us need worry about anything any more. Give me a cigarette.'

He took one from his packet and lighted it for her. She sounded normal, herself again. She wasn't trembling. And if this sudden belief was going to keep her happy he couldn't possibly begrudge it. But . . . but . . . he wished, all the same, it hadn't happened. There was something uncanny about thought-reading, about telepathy. Scientists couldn't account for it, nobody could, and this is what must have happened just now between Laura and the sisters. So the one who had been staring at him was blind. That accounted for the fixed gaze. Which somehow was unpleasant in itself, creepy. Oh hell, he thought, I wish we hadn't come here for lunch. Just chance, a flick of a coin between this, Torcello, and driving to Padua, and we had to choose Torcello.

'You didn't arrange to meet them again or anything, did you?' he asked, trying to sound casual.

'No, darling, why should I?' Laura answered. 'I mean, there was nothing more they could tell me. The sister had had her wonderful vision, and that was that. Anyway, they're moving on. Funnily enough, it's rather like our original game. They *are* going round the world before returning to Scotland. Only I said Australia, didn't I? The old dears . . . Anything less like murderers and jewel thieves.'

She had quite recovered. She stood up and looked about her. 'Come on,' she said. 'Having come to Torcello we must see the cathedral.'

They made their way from the restaurant across the open piazza, where the stalls had been set up with scarves and trinkets and postcards, and so along the path to the cathedral. One of the ferry-boats had just decanted a crowd of sightseers, many of whom had already found their way into Santa Maria Assunta. Laura, undaunted, asked her husband for the guidebook, and, as had always been her custom in happier days, started to walk slowly through the cathedral, studying mosaics, columns, panels from left to right, while John, less interested, because of his concern at what had just happened, followed close behind, keeping a weather eye alert for the twin sisters. There was no sign of them. Perhaps they had gone into the church of Santa Fosca close by. A sudden encounter would be embarrassing, quite apart from the effect it might have upon Laura. But the anonymous, shuffling tourists, intent upon culture, could not harm her, although from his own point of view they made artistic appreciation impossible. He could not concentrate, the cold clear beauty of what he saw left him untouched, and when Laura touched his sleeve, pointing to the mosaic of the Virgin and Child standing above the frieze of the Apostles, he nodded in sympathy yet saw nothing, the long, sad face of the Virgin infinitely remote, and turning on sudden impulse stared, back over the heads of the tourists towards the door, where frescoes of the blessed and the damned gave themselves to judgement.

The twins were standing there, the blind one still holding on to her sister's arm, her sightless eyes fixed firmly upon him. He felt himself held, unable to move, and an impending sense of doom, of tragedy, came upon him. His whole being sagged, as it were, in apathy, and he thought, 'This is the end, there is no escape, no future.' Then both sisters turned and went out of the cathedral and the sensation vanished, leaving indignation in its wake, and rising anger. How dare those two old fools practise their mediumistic tricks on him? It was fraudulent, unhealthy; this was probably the way they lived, touring the world making everyone they met uncomfortable. Give them half a chance and they would have got money out of Laura – anything.

He felt her tugging at his sleeve again. 'Isn't she beautiful? So happy, so serene.'

'Who? What?' he asked.

'The Madonna,' she answered. 'She has a magic quality. It goes right through to one. Don't you feel it too?'

'I suppose so. I don't know. There are too many people around.'

She looked up at him, astonished. 'What's that got to do with it? How funny you are. Well, all right, let's get away from them. I want to buy some postcards anyway.'

Disappointed, she sensed his lack of interest, and began to thread her way through the crowd of tourists to the door.

'Come on,' he said abruptly, once they were outside, 'there's plenty of time for postcards, let's explore a bit,' and he struck off from the path, which would have taken them back to the centre where the little houses were, and the stalls, and the drifting crowd of people, to a narrow way amongst uncultivated ground, beyond which he could see a sort of cutting, or canal. The sight of water, limpid, pale, was a soothing contrast to the fierce sun above their heads.

'I don't think this leads anywhere much,' said Laura. 'It's a bit muddy, too, one can't sit. Besides, there are more things the guidebook says we ought to see.'

'Oh, forget the book,' he said impatiently, and, pulling her down beside him on the bank above the cutting, put his arms round her.

'It's the wrong time of day for sight-seeing. Look, there's a rat swimming there the other side.'

He picked up a stone and threw it in the water, and the animal sank, or somehow disappeared, and nothing was left but bubbles.

'Don't,' said Laura. 'It's cruel, poor thing,' and then suddenly, putting her hand on his knee, 'Do you think Christine is sitting here beside us?'

He did not answer at once. What was there to say? Would it be like this forever?

'I expect so,' he said slowly, 'if you feel she is.'

The point was, remembering Christine before the onset of the fatal meningitis, she would have been running along the bank excitedly, throwing off her shoes, wanting to paddle, giving Laura a fit of apprehension. 'Sweetheart, take care, come back . . .'

'The woman said she was looking so happy, sitting beside us, smiling,' said Laura. She got up, brushing her dress, her mood changed to restlessness. 'Come on, let's go back,' she said.

He followed her with a sinking heart. He knew she did not really want to buy postcards or see what remained to be seen; she wanted to go in search of the women again, not necessarily to talk, just to be near them. When they came to the open place by the stalls he noticed that the crowd of tourists had thinned, there were only a few stragglers left, and the sisters were not amongst them. They must have joined the main body who had come to Torcello by the ferry service. A wave of relief seized him.

'Look, there's a mass of postcards at the second stall,' he said quickly, 'and some eye-catching head scarves. Let me buy you a head scarf.'

'Darling, I've so many!' she protested. 'Don't waste your lire.'

'It isn't a waste. I'm in a buying mood. What about a basket? You know we never have enough baskets. Or some lace. How about lace?'

She allowed herself, laughing, to be dragged to the stall. While he rumpled through the goods spread out before them, and chatted up the smiling woman who was selling her wares, his ferociously bad Italian making her smile the more, he knew it would give the body of tourists more time to walk to the landing stage and catch the ferry-service, and the twin sisters would be out of sight and out of their life.

'Never,' said Laura, some twenty minutes later, 'has so much junk been piled into so small a basket,' her bubbling laugh reassuring him that all was well, he needn't worry any more, the evil hour had passed. The launch from the Cipriani that had brought them from Venice was waiting by the landing-stage. The passengers who had arrived with them, the Americans, the man with the monocle, were already assembled. Earlier, before setting out, he had thought the price for lunch and transport, there and back, decidedly steep. Now he grudged none of it, except that the outing to Torcello itself had been one of the major errors of this particular holiday in Venice. They stepped down into the launch, finding a place in the open, and the boat chugged away down the canal and into the lagoon. The ordinary ferry had gone before, steaming towards Murano, while their own craft headed past San Francesco del Deserto and so back direct to Venice.

He put his arm around her once more, holding her close, and this time she responded, smiling up at him, her head on his shoulder.

'It's been a lovely day,' she said. 'I shall never forget it, never. You know, darling, now at last I can begin to enjoy our holiday.'

He wanted to shout with relief. It's going to be all right, he decided, let her believe what she likes, it doesn't matter, it makes her happy. The beauty of Venice rose before them, sharply outlined against the glowing sky, and there was still so much to see, wandering there together, that might now be perfect because of her change of mood, the shadow having lifted, and aloud he began to discuss the evening to come, where they would dine – not the restaurant they usually went to, near the Fenice theatre, but somewhere different, somewhere new.

'Yes, but it must be cheap,' she said, falling in with his mood, 'because we've already spent so much today.'

Their hotel by the Grand Canal had a welcoming, comforting air. The clerk smiled as he handed over their key. The bedroom was familiar, like home, with Laura's things arranged neatly on the dressing-table, but with it the little festive atmosphere of strangeness, of excitement, that only a holiday bedroom brings. This is ours for the moment, but no more. While we are in it we bring it life. When we have gone it no longer exists, it fades into anonymity. He turned on both taps in the bathroom, the water gushing into the bath, the steam rising. 'Now,' he thought afterwards, 'now at last is the moment to make love,' and he went back into the bedroom, and she understood, and opened her arms and smiled. Such blessed relief after all those weeks of restraint.

'The thing is,' she said later, fixing her ear-rings before the looking-glass, 'I'm not really terribly hungry. Shall we just be dull and eat in the dining-room here?'

'God, no!' he exclaimed. 'With all those rather dreary couples at the other tables? I'm ravenous. I'm also gay. I want to get rather sloshed.'

'Not bright lights and music, surely?'

'No, no . . . some small, dark, intimate cave, rather sinister, full of lovers with other people's wives.'

'H'm,' sniffed Laura, 'we all know what *that* means. You'll spot some Italian lovely of sixteen and smirk at her through dinner, while I'm stuck high and dry with a beastly man's broad back.'

They went out laughing into the warm soft night, and the magic was about them everywhere. 'Let's walk,' he said, 'let's walk and work up an appetite for our gigantic meal,' and inevitably they found themselves by the Molo and the lapping gondolas dancing upon the water, the lights everywhere blending with the darkness. There were other couples strolling for the same sake of aimless enjoyment, backwards, forwards, purposeless, and the inevitable sailors in groups, noisy, gesticulating, and dark-eyed girls whispering, clicking on high heels.

'The trouble is,' said Laura, 'walking in Venice becomes compulsive once you start. Just over the next bridge, you say, and then the next one beckons. I'm sure there are no restaurants down here, we're almost at those public gardens where they hold the Biennale. Let's turn back. I know there's a restaurant somewhere near the church of San Zaccaria, there's a little alley-way leading to it.'

'Tell you what,' said John, 'if we go down here by the Arsenal, and cross that bridge at the end and head left, we'll come upon San Zaccaria from the other side. We did it the other morning.'

'Yes, but it was daylight then. We may lose our way, it's not very well lit.'

'Don't fuss. I have an instinct for these things.'

They turned down the Fondamenta dell'Arsenale and crossed the little bridge short of the Arsenal itself, and so on past the church of San Martino. There were two canals ahead, one bearing right, the other left, with narrow streets beside them. John hesitated. Which one was it they had walked beside the day before?

'You see,' protested Laura, 'we shall be lost, just as I said.'

'Nonsense,' replied John firmly. 'It's the left-hand one, I remember the little bridge.'

The canal was narrow, the houses on either side seemed to close in upon it, and in the daytime, with the sun's reflection on the water and the windows of the houses open, bedding upon the balconies, a canary singing in a cage, there had been an impression of warmth, of secluded shelter. Now, ill-lit, almost in darkness, the windows of the houses shuttered, the water dank, the scene appeared altogether different, neglected, poor, and the long narrow boats moored to the slippery steps of cellar entrances looked like coffins.

'I swear I don't remember this bridge,' said Laura, pausing, and holding on to the rail, 'and I don't like the look of that alley-way beyond.'

'There's a lamp halfway up,' John told her. 'I know exactly where we are, not far from the Greek quarter.'

They crossed the bridge, and were about to plunge into the alley-way when they heard the cry. It came, surely, from one of the houses on the opposite side, but which one it was impossible to say. With the shutters closed each one of them seemed dead. They turned, and stared in the direction from which the sound had come.

'What was it?' whispered Laura.

'Some drunk or other,' said John briefly. 'Come on.'

Less like a drunk than someone being strangled, and the choking cry suppressed as the grip held firm.

'We ought to call the police,' said Laura.

'Oh, for heaven's sake,' said John. Where did she think she was – Piccadilly?

'Well, I'm off, it's sinister,' she replied, and began to hurry away up the twisting alley-way. John hesitated, his eye caught by a small figure which suddenly crept from a cellar entrance below one of the opposite houses, and then jumped into a narrow boat below. It was a child, a little girl – she couldn't have been more than five or six – wearing a short coat over her minute skirt, a pixie hood covering her head. There were four boats moored, line upon line, and she proceeded to jump from one to the other with surprising agility, intent, it would seem, upon escape. Once her foot slipped and he caught his breath, for she was within a few feet of the water, losing balance; then she recovered, and hopped on to the furthest boat. Bending, she tugged at the rope, which had the effect of swinging the boat's after-end across the canal, almost touching the opposite side and another cellar entrance, about thirty feet from the spot where John stood watching her. Then the child jumped again, landing upon the cellar steps, and vanished into the house, the boat swinging back into mid-canal behind her. The whole episode could not have taken more than four minutes. Then he heard the quick patter of feet. Laura had returned. She had seen none of it, for which he felt unspeakably thankful. The sight of a child, a little girl, in what must have been near danger, her fear that the scene he had just witnessed was in some way a sequel to the alarming cry, might have had a disastrous effect on her overwrought nerves.

'What are you doing?' she called. 'I daren't go on without you. The wretched alley branches in two directions.'

'Sorry,' he told her. 'I'm coming.'

He took her arm and they walked briskly along the alley, John with an apparent confidence he did not possess.

'There were no more cries, were there?' she asked.

'No,' he said, 'no, nothing. I tell you, it was some drunk.'

The alley led to a deserted *campo* behind a church, not a church he knew, and he led the way across, along another street and over a further bridge.

'Wait a minute,' he said. 'I think we take this right-hand turning. It will lead us into the Greek quarter – the church of San Georgio is somewhere over there.'

She did not answer. She was beginning to lose faith. The place was like a maze. They might circle round and round forever, and then find themselves back again, near the bridge where they had heard the cry. Doggedly he led her on, and then surprisingly, with relief, he saw people walking in the lighted street ahead, there was a spire of a church, the surroundings became familiar.

'There, I told you,' he said. 'That's San Zaccaria, we've found it all right. Your restaurant can't be far away.'

And anyway, there would be other restaurants, some-where to eat, at least here was the cheering glitter of lights, of movement, canals beside which people walked, the atmosphere of tourism. The letters 'Ristorante', in blue lights, shone like a beacon down a left-hand alley.

'Is this your place?' he asked.

'God knows,' she said. 'Who cares? Let's feed there anyway.'

And so into the sudden blast of heated air and hum of voices, the smell of pasta, wine, waiters, jostling custom-ers, laughter. 'For two? This way, please.' Why, he thought, was one's British nationality always so obvious? A cramped little table and an enormous menu scribbled in an indecipherable mauve biro, with the waiter hovering, expecting the order forthwith.

'Two very large camparis, with soda,' John said. '*Then* we'll study the menu.'

He was not going to be rushed. He handed the bill of fare to Laura and looked about him. Mostly Italians – that meant the food would be good. Then he saw them. At the opposite side of the room. The twin sisters. They must have come into the restaurant hard upon Laura's and his own arrival, for they were only now sitting down, shed-ding their coats, the waiter hovering beside the table. John was seized with the irrational thought that this was no coincidence. The sisters had noticed them both, in the street outside, and had followed them in. Why, in the name of hell, should they have picked on this particular spot, in the whole of Venice, unless ... unless Laura herself, at Torcello, had suggested a further encounter, or the sis-ter had suggested it to her? A small restaurant near the church of San Zaccaria, we go there sometimes for dinner. It was Laura, before the walk, who had mentioned San Zaccaria ...

She was still intent upon the menu, she had not seen the sisters, but any moment now she would have chosen what she wanted to eat, and then she would raise her head and look across the room. If only the drinks would come. If only the waiter would bring the drinks, it would give Laura something to do.

'You know, I was thinking,' he said quickly, 'we really ought to go to the garage tomorrow and get the car, and do that drive to Padua. We could lunch in Padua, see the cathedral and touch St Antony's tomb and look at the Giotto frescoes, and come back by way of those various villas along the Brenta that the guidebook cracks up.'

It was no use, though. She was looking up, across the restaurant, and she gave a little gasp of surprise. It was genuine. He could swear it was genuine.

'Look,' she said. 'how extraordinary! How really amazing!'

'What?' he said sharply.

'Why, there they are. My wonderful old twins. They've seen us, what's more. They're staring this way.' She waved her hand, radiant, delighted. The sister she had spoken to at Torcello bowed and smiled. False old bitch, he thought. I know they followed us.

'Oh, darling, I must go and speak to them,' she said impulsively, 'just to tell them how happy I've been all day, thanks to them.'

'Oh, for heaven's sake!' he said. 'Look, here are the drinks. And we haven't ordered yet. Surely you can wait until later, until we've eaten?'

'I won't be a moment,' she said, 'and anyway I want scampi, nothing first. I told you I wasn't hungry.'

She got up, and, brushing past the waiter with the drinks, crossed the room. She might have been greeting the loved friends of years. He watched her bend over the table and shake them both by the hand, and because there was a vacant chair at their table she drew it up and sat down, talking, smiling. Nor did the sisters seemed surprised, at least not the one she knew, who nodded and talked back, while the blind sister remained impassive.

'All right,' thought John savagely, 'then I *will* get sloshed,' and he proceeded to down his campari and soda and order another, while he pointed out something quite unintelligible on the menu as his own choice, but remembered scampi for Laura. 'And a bottle of Soave,' he added, 'with ice.'

The evening was ruined anyway. What was to have been an intimate, happy celebration would now be heavy-laden with spiritualistic visions, poor little dead Christine sharing the table with them, which was so damned stupid when in earthly life she would have been tucked up hours ago in bed. The bitter taste of the campari suited his mood of sudden self-pity, and all the while he watched the group at the table in the opposite corner, Laura apparently listening while the more active sister held forth and the blind one sat silent, her formidable sightless eyes turned in his direction.

'She's phoney,' he thought, 'she's not blind at all. They're both of them frauds, and they could be males in drag after all, just as we pretended at Torcello, and they're after Laura.'

He began on his second campari and soda. The two drinks, taken on an empty stomach, had an instant effect. Vision became blurred. And still Laura went on sitting at the other table, putting in a question now and again, while the active sister talked. The waiter appeared with the scampi, and a companion beside him to serve John's own order, which was totally unrecognisable, heaped with a livid sauce.

'The signora does not come?' enquired the first waiter, and John shook his head grimly, pointing an unsteady finger across the room.

'Tell the signora,' he said carefully, 'her scampi will get cold.'

He stared down at the offering placed before him, and prodded it delicately with a fork. The pallid sauce dissolved, revealing two enormous slices, rounds, of what appeared to be boiled pork, bedecked with garlic. He forked a portion to his mouth and chewed, and yes, it was pork, steamy, rich, the spicy sauce having turned it curiously sweet. He laid down his fork, pushing the plate away, and became aware of Laura, returning across the room and sitting beside him. She did not say anything, which was just as well, he thought, because he was too near nausea to answer. It wasn't just the drink, but reaction from the whole nightmare day. She began to eat her scampi, still not uttering. She did not seem to notice he was not eating. The waiter, hovering at his elbow, anxious, seemed aware that John's choice was somehow an error, and discreetly removed the plate. 'Bring me a green salad,' murmured John, and even then Laura did not register surprise, or, as she might have done in more normal circumstances, accuse him of having had too much to drink. Finally, when she had finished her scampi and was sipping her wine, which John had waved away, to nibble at his salad in small mouthfuls like a sick rabbit, she began to speak.

'Darling,' she said, 'I know you won't believe it, and it's rather frightening in a way, but after they left the restaurant in Torcello the sisters went to the cathedral, as we did, although we didn't see them in that crowd, and the blind one had another vision. She said Christine was trying to tell her something about us, that we should be in danger if we stayed in Venice. Christine wanted us to go away as soon as possible.'

So that's it, he thought. They think they can run our lives for us. This is to be our problem from henceforth. Do we eat? Do we get up? Do we go to bed? We must get in touch with the twin sisters. They will direct us.

'Well?' she said. 'Why don't you say something?'

'Because,' he answered, 'you are perfectly right, I don't believe it. Quite frankly, I judge your old sisters as being a couple of freaks, if nothing else. They're obviously unbalanced, and I'm sorry if this hurts you, but the fact is they've found a sucker in you.'

'You're being unfair,' said Laura. 'They are genuine, I know it. I just know it. They were completely sincere in what they said.'

'All right. Granted. They're sincere. But that doesn't make them well-balanced. Honestly, darling, you meet that old girl for ten minutes in a loo, she tells you she sees Christine sitting beside us – well, anyone with a gift for telepathy could read your unconscious mind in an instant – and then, pleased with her success, as any old psychic expert would be, she flings a further mood of ecstasy and wants to boot us out of Venice. Well, I'm sorry, but to hell with it.'

The room was no longer reeling. Anger had sobered him. If it would not put Laura to shame he would get up and cross to their table, and tell the old fools where they got off.

'I knew you would take it like this,' said Laura unhappily. 'I told them you would. They said not to worry. As long as we left Venice tomorrow everything would come all right.'

'Oh, for God's sake,' said John. He changed his mind, and poured himself a glass of wine.

'After all,' Laura went on, 'we have really seen the cream of Venice. I don't mind going on somewhere else. And if we stayed – I know it sounds silly, but I should have a nasty nagging sort of feeling inside me, and I should keep thinking of darling Christine being unhappy and trying to tell us to go.'

'Right,' said John with ominous calm, 'that settles it. Go we will. I suggest we clear off to the hotel straight away and warn the reception we're leaving in the morning. Have you had enough to eat?'

'Oh dear,' sighed Laura, 'don't take it like that. Look, why not come over and meet them, and then they can explain about the vision to you? Perhaps you would take it seriously then. Especially as you are the one it most concerns. Christine is more worried over you than me. And the extraordinary thing is that the blind sister says you're psychic and don't know it. You are somehow *en rapport* with the unknown, and I'm not.'

'Well, that's final,' said John. 'I'm psychic, am I? Fine. My psychic intuition tells me to get out of this restaurant now, at once, and we can decide what we do about leaving Venice when we are back at the hotel.'

He signalled to the waiter for the bill and they waited for it, not speaking to each other, Laura unhappy, fiddling with her bag, while John, glancing furtively at the twins' table, noticed that they were tucking into plates piled high with spaghetti, in very un-psychic fashion. The bill disposed of, John pushed back his chair.

'Right. Are you ready?' he asked.

'I'm going to say goodbye to them first,' said Laura, her mouth set sulkily, reminding him instantly, with a pang, of their poor lost child.

'Just as you like,' he replied, and walked ahead of her out of the restaurant, without a backward glance.

The soft humidity of the evening, so pleasant to walk about in earlier, had turned to rain. The strolling tourists had melted away. One or two people hurried by under umbrellas. This is what the inhabitants who live here see, he thought. This is the true life. Empty streets by night, the dank stillness of a stagnant canal beneath shuttered houses. The rest is a bright façade put on for show, glittering by sunlight.

Laura joined him and they walked away together in silence, and emerging presently behind the ducal palace came out into the Piazza San Marco. The rain was heavy

now, and they sought shelter with the few remaining stragglers under the colonnades. The orchestras had packed up
for the evening. The tables were bare. Chairs had been
turned upside down.

The experts are right, he thought, Venice is sinking. The
whole city is slowly dying. One day the tourists will travel
here by boat to peer down into the waters, and they will
see pillars and columns and marble far, far beneath them,
slime and mud uncovering for brief moments a lost under-
world of stone. Their heels made a ringing sound on the
pavement and the rain splashed from the gutterings above.
A fine ending to an evening that had started with brave
hope, with innocence.

When they came to their hotel Laura made straight for
the lift, and John turned to the desk to ask the night-porter
for the key. The man handed him a telegram at the same
time. John stared at it a moment. Laura was already in the
lift. Then he opened the envelope and read the message.
It was from the headmaster of Johnnie's preparatory
school.

> Johnnie under observation suspected
> appendicitis in city hospital here.
> No cause for alarm but surgeon thought wise
> advise you.
>
> Charles Hill

He read the message twice, then walked slowly towards
the lift where Laura was waiting for him. He gave her the
telegram. 'This came when we were out,' he said. 'Not
awfully good news.' He pressed the lift button as she read
the telegram. The lift stopped at the second floor, and they
got out.

'Well, this decides it, doesn't it?' she said. 'Here is the
proof. We have to leave Venice because we're going home.

It's Johnnie who's in danger, not us. This is what Christine was trying to tell the twins.'

The first thing John did the following morning was to put a call through to the headmaster at the preparatory school. Then he gave notice of their departure to the reception manager, and they packed while they waited for the call. Neither of them referred to the events of the preceding day, it was not necessary. John knew the arrival of the telegram and the foreboding of danger from the sisters was coincidence, nothing more, but it was pointless to start an argument about it. Laura was convinced otherwise, but intuitively she knew it was best to keep her feelings to herself. During breakfast they discussed ways and means of getting home. It should be possible to get themselves, and the car, on to the special car train that ran from Milan through to Calais, since it was early in the season. In any event, the headmaster had said there was no urgency.

The call from England came while John was in the bathroom. Laura answered it. He came into the bedroom a few minutes later. She was still speaking, but he could tell from the expression in her eyes that she was anxious.

'It's Mrs Hill,' she said. 'Mr Hill is in class. She says they reported from the hospital that Johnnie had a restless night and the surgeon may have to operate, but he doesn't want to unless it's absolutely necessary. They've taken X-rays and the appendix is in a tricky position, it's not awfully straightforward.'

'Here, give it to me,' he said.

The soothing but slightly guarded voice of the headmaster's wife came down the receiver. 'I'm so sorry this may spoil your plans,' she said, 'but both Charles and I felt you ought to be told, and that you might feel rather easier if you were on the spot. Johnnie is very plucky, but of course he has some fever. That isn't unusual, the surgeon says, in

the circumstances. Sometimes an appendix can get dis-
placed, it appears, and this makes it more complicated.
He's going to decide about operating this evening.'

'Yes, of course, we quite understand,' said John.

'Please do tell your wife not to worry too much,' she
went on. 'The hospital is excellent, a very nice staff, and
we have every confidence in the surgeon.'

'Yes,' said John, 'Yes,' and then broke off because Laura
was making gestures beside him.

'If we can't get the car on the train, I can fly,' she said.
'They're sure to be able to find me a seat on a plane. Then
at least one of us would be there this evening.'

He nodded agreement. 'Thank you so much, Mrs Hill,'
he said, 'we'll manage to get back all right. Yes, I'm sure
Johnnie is in good hands. Thank your husband for us.
Goodbye.'

He replaced the receiver and looked round him at the
tumbled beds, suitcases on the floor, tissue-paper strewn.
Baskets, maps, books, coats, everything they had brought
with them in the car. 'Oh God,' he said, 'what a bloody
mess. All this junk.' The telephone rang again. It was the
hall porter to say he had succeeded in booking a sleeper for
them both, and a place for the car, on the following night.

'Look,' said Laura, who had seized the telephone, 'could
you book one seat on the midday plane from Venice to London today, for me? It's imperative one of us gets home this
evening. My husband could follow with the car tomorrow.'

'Here, hang on,' interrupted John. 'No need for panic
stations. Surely twenty-four hours wouldn't make all that
difference?'

Anxiety had drained the colour from her face. She
turned to him, distraught.

'It mightn't to you, but it does to me,' she said. 'I've lost
one child, I'm not going to lose another.'

'All right, darling, all right . . .' He put his hand out to her but she brushed it off, impatiently, and continued giving directions to the porter. He turned back to his packing. No use saying anything. Better for it to be as she wished. They could, of course, both go by air, and then when all was well, and Johnnie better, he could come back and fetch the car, driving home through France as they had come. Rather a sweat, though, and the hell of an expense. Bad enough Laura going by air and himself with the car on the train from Milan.

'We could, if you like both fly,' he began tentatively, explaining the sudden idea, but she would have none of it. 'That really *would* be absurd,' she said impatiently. 'As long as I'm there this evening, and you follow by train, it's all that matters. Besides, we shall need the car, going backwards and forwards to the hospital. And our luggage. We couldn't go off and just leave all this here.'

No, he saw her point. A silly idea. It was only – well, he was as worried about Johnnie as she was, though he wasn't going to say so.

'I'm going downstairs to stand over the porter,' said Laura. 'They always make more effort if one is actually on the spot. Everything I want tonight is packed. I shall only need my overnight case. You can bring everything else in the car.' She hadn't been out of the bedroom five minutes before the telephone rang. It was Laura. 'Darling,' she said, 'it couldn't have worked out better. The porter has got me on a charter flight that leaves Venice in less than an hour. A special motor-launch takes the party direct from San Marco in about ten minutes. Some passenger on the charter flight cancelled. I shall be at Gatwick in less than four hours.'

'I'll be down right away,' he told her.

He joined her by the reception desk. She no longer looked anxious and drawn, but full of purpose. She was on her way. He kept wishing they were going together. He couldn't bear to stay on in Venice after she had gone, but the thought of driving to Milan, spending a dreary night in a hotel there alone, the endless dragging day which would follow, and the long hours in the train the next night, filled him with intolerable depression, quite apart from the anxiety about Johnnie. They walked along to the San Marco landing-stage, the Molo bright and glittering after the rain, a little breeze blowing, the postcards and scarves and tourist souvenirs fluttering on the stalls, the tourists themselves out in force, strolling, contented, the happy day before them.

'I'll ring you tonight from Milan,' he told her. 'The Hills will give you a bed, I suppose. And if you're at the hospital they'll let me have the latest news. That must be your charter party. You're welcome to them!'

The passengers descending from the landing-stage down into the waiting launch were carrying hand-luggage with Union Jack tags upon them. They were mostly middle-aged, with what appeared to be two Methodist ministers in charge. One of them advanced towards Laura, holding out his hand, showing a gleaming row of dentures when he smiled. 'You must be the lady joining us for the homeward flight,' he said. 'Welcome aboard, and to the Union of Fellowship. We are all delighted to make your acquaintance. Sorry we hadn't a seat for hubby too.'

Laura turned swiftly and kissed John, a tremor at the corner of her mouth betraying inward laughter. 'Do you think they'll break into hymns?' she whispered. 'Take care of yourself, hubby. Call me tonight.'

The pilot sounded a curious little toot upon his horn, and in a moment Laura had climbed down the steps into the launch and was standing amongst the crowd of passengers, waving her hand, her scarlet coat a gay patch of colour amongst the more sober suiting of her companions. The launch tooted again and moved away from the landing-stage, and he stood there watching it, a sense of immense loss filling his heart. Then he turned and walked away, back to the hotel, the bright day all about him desolate, unseen.

There was nothing, he thought, as he looked about him presently in the hotel bedroom, so melancholy as a vacated room, especially when the recent signs of occupation were still visible about him. Laura's suitcases on the bed, a second coat she had left behind. Traces of powder on the dressing-table. A tissue, with a lipstick smear, thrown in the waste-paper basket. Even an old tooth-paste tube squeezed dry, lying on the glass shelf above the wash-basin. Sounds of the heedless traffic on the Grand Canal came as always from the open window, but Laura wasn't there any more to listen to it, or to watch from the small balcony. The pleasure had gone. Feeling had gone.

John finished packing, and leaving all the baggage ready to be collected he went downstairs to pay the bill. The reception clerk was welcoming new arrivals. People were sitting on the terrace overlooking the Grand Canal reading newspapers, the pleasant day waiting to be planned.

John decided to have an early lunch, here on the hotel terrace, on familiar ground, and then have the porter carry the baggage to one of the ferries that steamed direct between San Marco and the Porta Roma, where the car was garaged. The fiasco meal of the night before had left him empty, and he was ready for the trolley of hors d'œuvres when they brought it to him, around midday. Even here, though, there was change. The head-waiter, their especial friend, was off-duty, and the table where they usually sat was occupied by new arrivals, a honeymoon couple, he told himself sourly, observing the gaiety, the smiles, while he had been shown to a small single table behind a tub of flowers.

'She's airborne now,' John thought, 'she's on her way,'

and he tried to picture Laura seated between the Methodist ministers, telling them, no doubt, about Johnnie ill in
hospital, and heaven knows what else besides. Well, the
twin sisters anyway could rest in psychic peace. Their
wishes would have been fulfilled.

Lunch over, there was no point in lingering with a cup
of coffee on the terrace. His desire was to get away as soon
as possible, fetch the car, and be en route for Milan. He
made his farewells at the reception desk, and, escorted by
a porter who had piled his baggage on to a wheeled trolley,
made his way once more to the landing-stage of San
Marco. As he stepped on to the steam-ferry, his luggage
heaped beside him, a crowd of jostling people all about
him, he had one momentary pang to be leaving Venice.
When, if ever, he wondered, would they come again? Next
year . . . in three years . . . Glimpsed first on honeymoon,
nearly ten years ago, and then a second visit, *en passant*,
before a cruise, and now this last abortive ten days that
had ended so abruptly.

The water glittered in the sunshine, buildings shone,
tourists in dark glasses paraded up and down the rapidly
receding Molo, already the terrace of their hotel was out
of sight as the ferry churned its way up the Grand Canal.
So many impressions to seize and hold, familiar loved
façades, balconies, windows, water lapping the cellar steps
of decaying palaces, the little red house where d'Annunzio
lived, with its garden – our house, Laura called it, pretending it was theirs – and too soon the ferry would be turning
left on the direct route to the Piazzale Roma, so missing
the best of the Canal, the Rialto, the further palaces.

Another ferry was heading downstream to pass them,
filled with passengers, and for a brief foolish moment he
wished he could change places, be amongst the happy tourists bound for Venice and all he had left behind him. Then
he saw her. Laura, in her scarlet coat, the twin sisters by

her side, the active sister with her hand on Laura's arm, talking earnestly, and Laura herself, her hair blowing in the wind, gesticulating, on her face a look of distress. He stared, astounded, too astonished to shout, to wave, and anyway they would never have heard or seen him, for his own ferry had already passed and was heading in the opposite direction.

What the hell had happened? There must have been a holdup with the charter flight and it had never taken off, but in that case why had Laura not telephoned him at the hotel? And what were those damned sisters doing? Had she run into them at the airport? Was it coincidence? And why did she look so anxious? He could think of no explanation. Perhaps the flight had been cancelled. Laura, of course, would go straight to the hotel, expecting to find him there, intending, doubtless, to drive with him after all to Milan and take the train the following night. What a blasted mix-up. The only thing to do was to telephone the hotel immediately his ferry reached the Piazzale Roma and tell her to wait – he would return and fetch her. As for the damned interfering sisters, they could get stuffed.

The usual stampede ensued when the ferry arrived at the landing-stage. He had to find a porter to collect his baggage, and then wait while he discovered a telephone. The fiddling with change, the hunt for the number, delayed him still more. He succeeded at last in getting through, and luckily the reception clerk he knew was still at the desk.

'Look, there's been some frightful muddle,' he began, and explained how Laura was even now on her way back to the hotel – he had seen her with two friends on one of the ferry-services. Would the reception clerk explain and tell her to wait? He would be back by the next available service to collect her. 'In any event, detain her,' he said. 'I'll be as quick as I can.' The reception clerk understood perfectly, and John rang off.

Thank heaven Laura hadn't turned up before he had put through his call, or they would have told her he was on his way to Milan. The porter was still waiting with the baggage, and it seemed simplest to walk with him to the garage, hand everything over to the chap in charge of the office there and ask him to keep it for an hour, when he would be returning with his wife to pick up the car. Then he went back to the landing-station to await the next ferry to Venice. The minutes dragged, and he kept wondering all the time what had gone wrong at the airport and why in heaven's name Laura hadn't telephoned. No use conjecturing. She would tell him the whole story at the hotel. One thing was certain: he would not allow Laura and himself to be saddled with the sisters and become involved with their affairs. He could imagine Laura saying that they also had missed a flight, and could they have a lift to Milan?

Finally the ferry chugged alongside the landing-stage and he stepped aboard. What an anti-climax, thrashing back past the familiar sights to which he had bidden a nostalgic farewell such a short while ago! He didn't even look about him this time, he was so intent on reaching his destination. In San Marco there were more people than ever, the afternoon crowds walking shoulder to shoulder, every one of them on pleasure bent.

He came to the hotel and pushed his way through the swing door, expecting to see Laura, and possibly the sisters, waiting in the lounge to the left of the entrance. She was not there. He went to the desk. The reception clerk he had spoken to on the telephone was standing there, talking to the manager.

'Has my wife arrived?' John asked.

'No, sir, not yet.'

'What an extraordinary thing. Are you sure?'

'Absolutely certain, sir. I have been here ever since you telephoned me at a quarter to two. I have not left the desk.'

'I just don't understand it. She was on one of the vaporettos passing by the Accademia. She would have landed at San Marco about five minutes later and come on here.'

The clerk seemed nonplussed. 'I don't know what to say. The signora was with friends, did you say?'

'Yes. Well, acquaintances. Two ladies we had met at Torcello yesterday. I was astonished to see her with them on the vaporetto, and of course I assumed that the flight had been cancelled, and she had somehow met up with them at the airport and decided to return here with them, to catch me before I left.'

Oh hell, what was Laura doing? It was after three. A matter of moments from San Marco landing-stage to the hotel.

'Perhaps the signora went with her friends to their hotel instead. Do you know where they are staying?'

'No,' said John, 'I haven't the slightest idea. What's more, I don't even know the names of the two ladies. They were sisters, twins, in fact – looked exactly alike. But anyway, why go to their hotel and not here?'

The swing-door opened but it wasn't Laura. Two people staying in the hotel.

The manager broke into the conversation. 'I tell you what I will do,' he said. 'I will telephone the airport and check about the flight. Then at least we will get somewhere.' He smiled apologetically. It was not usual for arrangements to go wrong.

'Yes, do that,' said John. 'We may as well know what happened there.'

He lit a cigarette and began to pace up and down the entrance hall. What a bloody mix-up. And how unlike Laura, who knew he would be setting off for Milan directly after lunch – indeed, for all she knew he might have gone before. But surely, in that case, she would have telephoned at once, on arrival at the airport, had the flight been cancelled? The manager was ages telephoning, he had to be put through on some other line, and his Italian was too rapid for John to follow the conversation. Finally he replaced the receiver.

'It is more mysterious than ever, sir,' he said. 'The charter flight was not delayed, it took off on schedule with a full complement of passengers. As far as they could tell me, there was no hitch. The signora must simply have changed her mind.' His smile was more apologetic than ever.

'Changed her mind,' John repeated. 'But why on earth should she do that? She was so anxious to be home tonight.'

The manager shrugged. 'You know how ladies can be, sir,' he said. 'Your wife may have thought that after all she would prefer to take the train to Milan with you. I do assure you, though, that the charter party was most respectable, and it was a Caravelle aircraft, perfectly safe.'

'Yes, yes,' said John impatiently, 'I don't blame your arrangements in the slightest. I just can't understand what induced her to change her mind, unless it was meeting with these two ladies.'

The manager was silent. He could not think of anything to say. The reception clerk was equally concerned. 'Is it possible,' he ventured, 'that you made a mistake, and it was not the signora that you saw on the vaporetto?'

'Oh no,' replied John, 'it was my wife, I assure you. She was wearing her red coat, she was hatless, just as she left here. I saw her as plainly as I can see you. I would swear to it in a court of law.'

'It is unfortunate,' said the manager, 'that we do not know the name of the two ladies, or the hotel where they were staying. You say you met these ladies at Torcello yesterday?'

'Yes . . . but only briefly. They weren't staying there. At

least, I am certain they were not. We saw them at dinner in Venice later, as it happens.'

'Excuse me . . .' Guests were arriving with luggage to check in, the clerk was obliged to attend to them. John turned in desperation to the manager. 'Do you think it would be any good telephoning the hotel in Torcello in case the people there knew the name of the ladies, or where they were staying in Venice?'

'We can try,' replied the manager. 'It is a small hope, but we can try.'

John resumed his anxious pacing, all the while watching the swing-door, hoping, praying, that he would catch sight of the red coat and Laura would enter. Once again there followed what seemed an interminable telephone conversation between the manager and someone at the hotel in Torcello.

'Tell them two sisters,' said John, 'two elderly ladies dressed in grey, both exactly alike. One lady was blind,' he added. The manager nodded. He was obviously giving a detailed description. Yet when he hung up he shook his head. 'The manager at Torcello says he remembers the two ladies well,' he told John, 'but they were only there for lunch. He never learnt their names.'

'Well, that's that. There's nothing to do now but wait.'

John lit his third cigarette and went out on to the terrace, to resume his pacing there. He stared out across the canal, searching the heads of the people on passing steamers, motorboats, even drifting gondolas. The minutes ticked by on his watch, and there was no sign of Laura. A terrible foreboding nagged at him that somehow this was prearranged, that Laura had never intended to catch the aircraft, that last night in the restaurant she had made an assignation with the sisters. Oh God, he thought, that's impossible, I'm going paranoiac . . . Yet why, why? No, more likely the encounter at the airport was fortuitous, and for some incredible reason they had persuaded Laura not to board the aircraft, even prevented her from doing so, trotting out one of their psychic visions, that the aircraft would crash, that she must return with them to Venice. And Laura, in her sensitive state, felt they must be right, swallowed it all without question.

But granted all these possibilities, why had she not come to the hotel? What was she doing? Four o'clock, half-past four, the sun no longer dappling the water. He went back to the reception desk.

'I just can't hang around,' he said. 'Even if she does turn up, we shall never make Milan this evening. I might see her walking with these ladies, in the Piazza San Marco, anywhere. If she arrives while I'm out, will you explain?'

The clerk was full of concern. 'Indeed, yes,' he said. 'It is very worrying for you, sir. Would it perhaps be prudent if we booked you in here tonight?'

John gestured, helplessly. 'Perhaps, yes, I don't know. Maybe . . .'

He went out of the swing-door and began to walk towards the Piazza San Marco. He looked into every shop up and down the colonnades, crossed the piazza a dozen times, threaded his way between the tables in front of Florian's, in front of Quadri's, knowing that Laura's red coat and the distinctive appearance of the twin sisters could easily be spotted, even amongst this milling crowd, but there was no sign of them. He joined the crowd of shoppers in the Merceria, shoulder to shoulder with idlers, thrusters, window-gazers, knowing instinctively that it was useless, they wouldn't be here. Why should Laura have deliberately missed her flight to return to Venice for such a purpose? And even if she had done so, for some reason beyond his imagining, she would surely have come first to the hotel to find him.

The only thing left to him was to try to track down the

sisters. Their hotel could be anywhere amongst the hundreds of hotels and pensions scattered through Venice, or even across the other side at the Zattere, or further again on the Giudecca. These last possibilities seemed remote. More likely they were staying in a small hotel or pension somewhere near San Zaccaria handy to the restaurant where they had dined last night. The blind one would surely not go far afield in the evening. He had been a fool not to have thought of this before, and he turned back and walked quickly away from the brightly lighted shopping district towards the narrower, more cramped quarter where they had dined last evening. He found the restaurant without difficulty, but they were not yet open for dinner, and the waiter preparing tables was not the one who had served them. John asked to see the *padrone*, and the waiter disappeared to the back regions, returning after a moment or two with the somewhat dishevelled-looking proprietor in shirt-sleeves, caught in a slack moment, not in full tenue.

'I had dinner here last night,' John explained. 'There were two ladies sitting at that table there in the corner.' He pointed to it.

'You wish to book that table for this evening?' asked the proprietor.

'No,' said John. 'No, there were two ladies there last night, two sisters, due sorelle, twins, gemelle' – what was the right word for twins? – 'Do you remember? Two ladies, sorelle vecchie . . .'

'Ah,' said the man, 'si, si, signore, la povera signorina.' He put his hands to his eyes to feign blindness. 'Yes, I remember.'

'Do you know their names?' asked John. 'Where they were staying? I am very anxious to trace them.'

The proprietor spread out his hands in a gesture of regret. 'I am ver' sorry, signore, I do not know the names of the signorine, they have been here once, twice, perhaps

36

for dinner, they do not say where they were staying. Perhaps if you come again tonight they might be here? Would you like to book a table?'

He pointed around him, suggesting a whole choice of tables that might appeal to a prospective diner, but John shook his head.

'Thank you, no. I may be dining elsewhere. I am sorry to have troubled you. If the signorine should come . . .' he paused, 'possibly I may return later,' he added. 'I am not sure.'

The proprietor bowed, and walked with him to the entrance. 'In Venice the whole world meets,' he said smiling. 'It is possible the signore will find his friends tonight. Arrivederci, signore.'

Friends? John walked out into the street. More likely kidnappers . . . Anxiety had turned to fear, to panic. Something had gone terribly wrong. Those women had got hold of Laura, played upon her suggestibility, induced her to go with them, either to their hotel or elsewhere. Should he find the Consulate? Where was it? What would he say when he got there? He began walking without purpose, finding himself, as they had done the night before, in streets he did not know, and suddenly came upon a tall building with the word 'Questura' above it. This is it, he thought. I don't care, something has happened, I'm going inside. There were a number of police in uniform coming and going, the place at any rate was active, and, addressing himself to one of them behind a glass partition, he asked if there was anyone who spoke English. The man pointed to a flight of stairs and John went up, entering a door on the right where he saw that another couple were sitting, waiting, and with relief he recognised them as fellow-countrymen, tourists, obviously a man and his wife, in some sort of predicament.

'Come and sit down,' said the man. 'We've waited half

an hour but they can't be much longer. What a country! They wouldn't leave us like this at home.'

John took the proffered cigarette and found a chair beside them.

'What's your trouble?' he asked.

'My wife had her handbag pinched in one of those shops in the Merceria,' said the man. 'She simply put it down one moment to look at something, and you'd hardly credit it, the next moment it had gone. I say it was a sneak thief, she insists it was the girl behind the counter. But who's to say? These Ities are all alike. Anyway, I'm certain we shan't get it back. What have you lost?'

'Suitcase stolen,' John lied rapidly. 'Had some important papers in it.'

How could he say he had lost his wife? He couldn't even begin . . .'

The man nodded in sympathy. 'As I said, these Ities are all alike. Old Musso knew how to deal with them. Too many Communists around these days. The trouble is, they're not going to bother with our troubles much, not with this murderer at large. They're all out looking for him.'

'Murderer? What murderer?' asked John.

'Don't tell me you've not heard about it?' The man stared at him in surprise. 'Venice has talked of nothing else. It's been in all the papers, on the radio, and even in the English papers. A grizzly business. One woman found with her throat slit last week – a tourist too – and some old chap discovered with the same sort of knife wound this morning. They seem to think it must be a maniac, because there doesn't seem to be any motive. Nasty thing to happen in Venice in the tourist season.'

'My wife and I never bother with the newspapers when we're on holiday,' said John. 'And we're neither of us much given to gossip in the hotel.'

'Very wise of you,' laughed the man. 'It might have spoilt

your holiday, especially if your wife is nervous. Oh well, we're off tomorrow anyway. Can't say we mind, do we, dear?' He turned to his wife. 'Venice has gone downhill since we were here last. And now this loss of the handbag really is the limit.'

The door of the inner room opened, and a senior police officer asked John's companion and his wife to pass through.

'I bet we don't get any satisfaction,' murmured the tourist, winking at John, and he and his wife went into the inner room. The door closed behind them. John stubbed out his cigarette and lighted another. A strange feeling of unreality possessed him. He asked himself what he was doing here, what was the use of it? Laura was no longer in Venice but had disappeared, perhaps forever, with those diabolical sisters. She would never be traced. And just as the two of them had made up a fantastic story about the twins, when they first spotted them in Torcello, so, with nightmare logic, the fiction would have basis in fact; the women were in reality disguised crooks, men with criminal intent who lured unsuspecting persons to some appalling fate. They might even be the murderers for whom the police sought. Who would ever suspect two elderly women of respectable appearance, living quietly in some second-rate pension or hotel? He stubbed out his cigarette, unfinished.

'This,' he thought, 'is really the start of paranoia. This is the way people go off their heads.' He glanced at his watch. It was half-past six. Better pack this in, this futile quest here in police headquarters, and keep to the single link of sanity remaining. Return to the hotel, put a call through to the prep school in England, and ask about the latest news of Johnnie. He had not thought about poor Johnnie since sighting Laura on the vaporetto.

Too late, though. The inner door opened, the couple were ushered out.

'Usual clap-trap,' said the husband sotto voce to John. 'They'll do what they can. Not much hope. So many foreigners in Venice, all of 'em thieves! The locals all above reproach. Wouldn't pay 'em to steal from customers. Well, I wish you better luck.'

He nodded, his wife smiled and bowed, and they had gone. John followed the police officer into the inner room.

Formalities began. Name, address, passport. Length of stay in Venice, etc., etc. Then the questions, and John, the sweat beginning to appear on his forehead, launched into his interminable story. The first encounter with the sisters, the meeting at the restaurant, Laura's state of suggestibility because of the death of their child, the telegram about Johnnie, the decision to take the chartered flight, her departure, and her sudden inexplicable return. When he had finished he felt as exhausted as if he had driven three hundred miles non-stop after a severe bout of 'flu. His interrogator spoke excellent English with a strong Italian accent.

'You say,' he began, 'that your wife was suffering the after-effects of shock. This had been noticeable during your stay here in Venice?'

'Well, yes,' John replied, 'she had really been quite ill. The holiday didn't seem to be doing her much good. It was only when she met these two women at Torcello yesterday that her mood changed. The strain seemed to have gone. She was ready, I suppose, to snatch at every straw, and this belief that our little girl was watching over her had somehow restored her to what appeared normality.'

'It would be natural,' said the police officer, 'in the circumstances. But no doubt the telegram last night was a further shock to you both?'

'Indeed, yes. That was the reason we decided to return home.'

'No argument between you? No difference of opinion?'

'None. We were in complete agreement. My one regret was that I could not go with my wife on this charter flight.'

The police officer nodded. 'It could well be that your wife had a sudden attack of amnesia, and meeting the two ladies served as a link, she clung to them for support. You have described them with great accuracy, and I think they should not be too difficult to trace. Meanwhile, I suggest you should return to your hotel, and we will get in touch with you as soon as we have news.'

At least, John thought, they believed his story. They did not consider him a crank who had made the whole thing up and was merely wasting their time.

'You appreciate,' he said, 'I am extremely anxious. These women may have some criminal design upon my wife. One has heard of such things . . .'

The police officer smiled for the first time. 'Please don't concern yourself,' he said. 'I am sure there will be some satisfactory explanation.'

All very well, thought John, but in heaven's name, what?

'I'm sorry,' he said, 'to have taken up so much of your time. Especially as I gather the police have their hands full hunting down a murderer who is still at large.'

He spoke deliberately. No harm in letting the fellow know that for all any of them could tell there might be some connection between Laura's disappearance and this other hideous affair.

'Ah, that,' said the police officer, rising to his feet. 'We hope to have the murderer under lock and key very soon.'

His tone of confidence was reassuring. Murderers, missing wives, lost handbags were all under control. They shook hands, and John was ushered out of the door and so downstairs. Perhaps, he thought, as he walked slowly back to the hotel, the fellow was right. Laura had suffered a sudden attack of amnesia, and the sisters happened to be at the airport and had brought her back to Venice, to their own hotel, because Laura couldn't remember where she and John had been staying. Perhaps they were even now trying to track down his hotel. Anyway, he could do nothing more. The police had everything in hand, and, please God, would come up with the solution. All he wanted to do right now was to collapse upon a bed with a stiff whisky, and then put through a call to Johnnie's school.

The page took him up in the lift to a modest room on the fourth floor at the rear of the hotel. Bare, impersonal, the shutters closed, with a smell of cooking wafting up from a courtyard down below.

'Ask them to send me up a double whisky, will you?' he said to the boy. 'And a ginger-ale,' and when he was alone he plunged his face under the cold tap in the wash-basin, relieved to find that the minute portion of visitor's soap afforded some measure of comfort. He flung off his shoes, hung his coat over the back of a chair and threw himself down on the bed. Somebody's radio was blasting forth an old popular song, now several seasons out of date, that had been one of Laura's favourites a couple of years ago. 'I love you, Baby . . .' He reached for the telephone, and asked the exchange to put through the call to England. Then he closed his eyes, and all the while the insistent voice persisted, 'I love you, Baby . . . I can't get you out of my mind.'

Presently there was a tap at the door. It was the waiter with his drink. Too little ice, such meagre comfort, but what desperate need. He gulped it down without the ginger-ale, and in a few moments the ever-nagging pain was eased, numbed, bringing, if only momentarily, a sense of calm. The telephone rang, and now, he thought, bracing himself for ultimate disaster, the final shock, Johnnie probably dying, or already dead. In which case nothing remained. Let Venice be engulfed . . .

The exchange told him that the connection had been made, and in a moment he heard the voice of Mrs Hill at the other end of the line. They must have warned her that the call came from Venice, for she knew instantly who was speaking.

'Hullo?' she said. 'Oh, I am so glad you rang. All is well. Johnnie has had his operation, the surgeon decided to do it at midday rather than wait, and it was completely successful. Johnnie is going to be all right. So you don't have to worry any more, and will have a peaceful night.'

'Thank God,' he answered.

'I know,' she said, 'we are all so relieved. Now I'll get off the line and you can speak to your wife.'

John sat up on the bed, stunned. What the hell did she mean? Then he heard Laura's voice, cool and clear.

'Darling? Darling, are you there?'

He could not answer. He felt the hand holding the receiver go clammy cold with sweat. 'I'm here,' he whispered.

'It's not a very good line,' she said, 'but never mind. As Mrs Hill told you, all is well. Such a nice surgeon, and a very sweet Sister on Johnnie's floor, and I really am happy about the way it's turned out. I came straight down here after landing at Gatwick – the flight O.K., by the way, but such a funny crowd, it'll make you hysterical when I tell you about them – and I went to the hospital, and Johnnie was coming round. Very dopey, of course, but so pleased to see me. And the Hills are being wonderful, I've got their spare-room, and it's only a short taxi-drive into the town and the hospital. I shall go to bed as soon as we've had dinner, because I'm a bit fagged, what with the flight and the anxiety. How was the drive to Milan? And where are you staying?'

John did not recognise the voice that answered as his own. It was the automatic response of some computer.

'I'm not in Milan,' he said. 'I'm still in Venice.'

'Still in Venice? What on earth for? Wouldn't the car start?'

'I can't explain,' he said. 'There was a stupid sort of mix-up . . .'

He felt suddenly so exhausted that he nearly dropped the receiver, and, shame upon shame, he could feel tears pricking behind his eyes.

'What sort of mix-up?' Her voice was suspicious, almost hostile. 'You weren't in a crash?'

'No . . . no . . . nothing like that.'

A moment's silence, and then she said, 'Your voice sounds very slurred. Don't tell me you went and got pissed.'

Oh Christ . . . If she only knew! He was probably going to pass out any moment, but not from the whisky.

'I thought,' he said slowly, 'I thought I saw you, in a vaporetto, with those two sisters.'

What was the point of going on? It was hopeless trying to explain.

'How could you have seen me with the sisters?' she said. 'You knew I'd gone to the airport. Really, darling, you are an idiot. You seem to have got those two poor old dears on the brain. I hope you didn't say anything to Mrs Hill just now.'

'No.'

'Well, what are you going to do? You'll catch the train at Milan tomorrow, won't you?'

'Yes, of course,' he told her.

'I still don't understand what kept you in Venice,' she said. 'It all sounds a bit odd to me. However . . . thank God Johnnie is going to be all right and I'm here.'

'Yes,' he said, 'yes.'

He could hear the distant boom-boom sound of a gong from the headmaster's hall.

'You had better go,' he said. 'My regards to the Hills, and my love to Johnnie.'

'Well, take care of yourself, darling, and for goodness' sake don't miss the train tomorrow, and drive carefully.'

The telephone clicked and she had gone. He poured the remaining drop of whisky into his empty glass, and sousing it with ginger-ale drank it down at a gulp. He got up, and crossing the room threw open the shutters and leant out of the window. He felt light-headed. His sense of relief, enormous, overwhelming, was somehow tempered with a curious feeling of unreality, almost as though the voice speaking from England had not been Laura's after all but a fake, and she was still in Venice, hidden in some furtive pension with the two sisters.

The point was, he *had* seen all three of them on the vaporetto. It was not another woman in a red coat. The women *had* been there, with Laura. So what was the explanation? That he was going off his head? Or something more sinister? The sisters, possessing psychic powers of formidable strength, had seen him as their two ferries had passed, and in some inexplicable fashion had made him believe Laura was with them. But why, and to what end? No, it didn't make sense. The only explanation was that he had been mistaken, the whole episode an hallucination. In which case he needed psychoanalysis, just as Johnnie had needed a surgeon.

And what did he do now? Go downstairs and tell the management he had been at fault and had just spoken to his wife, who had arrived in England safe and sound from her charter flight? He put on his shoes and ran his fingers through his hair. He glanced at his watch. It was ten minutes to eight. If he nipped into the bar and had a quick drink it would be easier to face the manager and admit what had happened. Then, perhaps, they would get in touch with the police. Profuse apologies all round for putting everyone to enormous trouble.

He made his way to the ground floor and went straight to the bar, feeling self-conscious, a marked man, half-imagining everyone would look at him, thinking, 'There's the fellow with the missing wife.' Luckily the bar was full and there wasn't a face he knew. Even the chap behind the bar was an underling who hadn't served him before. He downed his whisky and glanced over his shoulder to the reception hall. The desk was momentarily empty. He could see the manager's back framed in the doorway of an inner room, talking to someone within. On impulse, coward-like, he crossed the hall and passed through the swing-door to the street outside.

'I'll have some dinner,' he decided, 'and then go back and face them. I'll feel more like it once I've some food inside me.'

He went to the restaurant nearby where he and Laura had dined once or twice. Nothing mattered any more, because she was safe. The nightmare lay behind him. He could enjoy his dinner, despite her absence, and think of her sitting down with the Hills to a dull, quiet evening, early to bed, and on the following morning going to the hospital to sit with Johnnie. Johnnie was safe, too. No more worries, only the awkward explanations and apologies to the manager at the hotel.

There was a pleasant anonymity sitting down at a corner table alone in the little restaurant, ordering vitello alla Marsala and half a bottle of Merlot. He took his time, enjoying his food but eating in a kind of haze, a sense of unreality still with him, while the conversation of his nearest neighbours had the same soothing effect as background music.

When they rose and left, he saw by the clock on the wall that it was nearly half-past nine. No use delaying matters any further. He drank his coffee, lighted a cigarette and paid his bill. After all, he thought, as he walked back to the hotel, the manager would be greatly relieved to know that all was well.

When he pushed through the swing-door, the first thing he noticed was a man in police uniform, standing talking to the manager at the desk. The reception clerk was there too. They turned as John approached, and the manager's face lighted up with relief.

'Eccolo!' he exclaimed. 'I was certain the signore would not be far away. Things are moving, signore. The two ladies have been traced, and they very kindly agreed to accompany the police to the Questura. If you will go there at once, this agente di polizia will escort you.'

John flushed. 'I have given everyone a lot of trouble,' he said. 'I meant to tell you before going out to dinner, but you were not at the desk. The fact is that I have contacted my wife. She did make the flight to London after all, and I spoke to her on the telephone. It was all a great mistake.'

The manager looked bewildered. 'The signora is in London?' he repeated. He broke off, and exchanged a rapid conversation in Italian with the policeman. 'It seems that the ladies maintain they did not go out for the day, except for a little shopping in the morning,' he said, turning back to John. 'Then who was it the signore saw on the vaporetto?'

John shook his head. 'A very extraordinary mistake on my part which I still don't understand,' he said. 'Obviously, I did not see either my wife or the two ladies. I really am extremely sorry.'

More rapid conversation in Italian. John noticed the clerk watching him with a curious expression in his eyes. The manager was obviously apologising on John's behalf to the policeman, who looked annoyed and gave tongue to this effect, his voice increasing in volume, to the manager's concern. The whole business had undoubtedly given enormous trouble to a great many people, not least the two unfortunate sisters.

'Look,' said John, interrupting the flow, 'will you tell the agente I will go with him to headquarters and apologise in person both to the police officer and to the ladies?'

The manager looked relieved. 'If the signore would take

the trouble,' he said. 'Naturally, the ladies were much distressed when a policeman interrogated them at their hotel, and they offered to accompany him to the Questura only because they were so distressed about the signora.'

John felt more and more uncomfortable. Laura must never learn any of this. She would be outraged. He wondered if there were some penalty for giving the police misleading information involving a third party. His error began, in retrospect, to take on criminal proportions.

He crossed the Piazza San Marco, now thronged with after-dinner strollers and spectators at the cafés, all three orchestras going full blast in harmonious rivalry, while his companion kept a discreet two paces to his left and never uttered a word.

They arrived at the police station and mounted the stairs to the same inner room where he had been before. He saw immediately that it was not the officer he knew but another who sat behind the desk, a sallow-faced individual with a sour expression, while the two sisters, obviously upset – the active one in particular – were seated on chairs nearby, some underling in uniform standing behind them. John's escort went at once to the police officer, speaking in rapid Italian, while John himself, after a moment's hesitation, advanced towards the sisters.

'There has been a terrible mistake,' he said. 'I don't know how to apologise to you both. It's all my fault, mine entirely, the police are not to blame.'

The active sister made as though to rise, her mouth twitching nervously, but he restrained her.

'We don't understand,' she said, the Scots inflection strong. 'We said goodnight to your wife last night at dinner, and we have not seen her since. The police came to our pension more than an hour ago and told us your wife was missing and you had filed a complaint against us. My sister is not very strong. She was considerably disturbed.'

'A mistake. A frightful mistake,' he repeated.

He turned towards the desk. The police officer was addressing him, his English very inferior to that of the previous interrogator. He had John's earlier statement on the desk in front of him, and tapped it with a pencil.

'So?' he queried. 'This document all lies? You not speaka the truth?'

'I believed it to be true at the time,' said John. 'I could have sworn in a court of law that I saw my wife with these two ladies on a vaporetto in the Grand Canal this afternoon. Now I realise I was mistaken.'

'We have not been near the Grand Canal all day,' protested the sister, 'not even on foot. We made a few purchases in the Merceria this morning, and remained indoors all afternoon. My sister was a little unwell. I have told the police officer this a dozen times, and the people at the pension would corroborate our story. He refused to listen.'

'And the signora?' rapped the police officer angrily. 'What happen to the signora?'

'The signora, my wife, is safe in England,' explained John patiently. 'I talked to her on the telephone just after seven. She did join the charter flight from the airport, and is now staying with friends.'

'Then who you see on the vaporetto in the red coat?' asked the furious police officer. 'And if not these signorine here, then what signorine?'

'My eyes deceived me,' said John, aware that his English was likewise becoming strained. 'I think I see my wife and these ladies but no, it was not so. My wife in aircraft, these ladies in pension all the time.'

It was like talking stage Chinese. In a moment he would be bowing and putting his hands in his sleeves.

The police-officer raised his eyes to heaven and thumped the table. 'So all this work for nothing,' he said. 'Hotels and pensiones searched for the signorine and a missing signora inglese, when here we have plenty, plenty other things to do. You maka a mistake. You have perhaps too much vino at mezzo giorno and you see hundred signore in red coats in hundred vaporetti.' He stood up, rumpling the papers on his desk. 'And you, signorine,' he said, 'you wish to make complaint against this person?' He was addressing the active sister.

'Oh no,' she said, 'no, indeed. I quite see it was all a mistake. Our only wish is to return at once to our pension.'

The police-officer grunted. Then he pointed at John. 'You very lucky man,' he said. 'These signorine could file complaint against you – very serious matter.'

'I'm sure,' began John, 'I'll do anything in my power . . .'

'Please don't think of it,' exclaimed the sister, horrified. 'We would not hear of such a thing.' It was her turn to apologise to the police-officer. 'I hope we need not take up any more of your valuable time,' she said.

He waved a hand of dismissal and spoke in Italian to the underling. 'This man walk with you to the pension,' he said. 'Buona sera, signorine,' and, ignoring John, he sat down again at his desk.

'I'll come with you,' said John. 'I want to explain exactly what happened.'

They trooped down the stairs and out of the building, the blind sister leaning on her twin's arm, and once outside she turned her sightless eyes to John.

'You saw us,' she said, 'and your wife too. But not today. You saw us in the future.'

Her voice was softer than her sister's, slower, she seemed to have some slight impediment in her speech.

'I don't follow,' replied John, bewildered.

He turned to the active sister and she shook her head at him, frowning, and put her finger on her lips.

'Come along, dear,' she said to her twin. 'You know

you're very tired, and I want to get you home.' Then, sotto voce to John, 'She's psychic. Your wife told you, I believe, but I don't want her to go into trance here in the street.'

God forbid, thought John, and the little procession began to move slowly along the street, away from police headquarters, a canal to the left of them. Progress was slow, because of the blind sister, and there were two bridges. John was completely lost after the first turning, but it couldn't have mattered less. Their police escort was with them, and anyway, the sisters knew where they were going.

'I must explain,' said John softly. 'My wife would never forgive me if I didn't,' and as they walked he went over the whole inexplicable story once again, beginning with the telegram received the night before and the conversation with Mrs Hill, the decision to return to England the following day, Laura by air, and John himself by car and train. It no longer sounded as dramatic as it had done when he had made his statement to the police officer, when, possibly because of his conviction of something uncanny, the description of the two vaporettos passing one another in the middle of the Grand Canal had held a sinister quality, suggesting abduction on the part of the sisters, the pair of them holding a bewildered Laura captive. Now that neither of the women had any further menace for him he spoke more naturally, yet with great sincerity, feeling for the first time that they were somehow both in sympathy with him and would understand.

'You see,' he explained, in a final endeavour to make amends for having gone to the police in the first place, 'I truly believed I had seen you with Laura, and I thought . . .' he hesitated, because this had been the police officer's suggestion and not his, 'I thought that perhaps Laura had some sudden loss of memory, had met you at the airport, and you had brought her back to Venice to wherever you were staying.'

They had crossed a large square and were approaching a house at one end of it, with a sign 'Pensione' above the door. Their escort paused at the entrance.

'Is this it?' asked John.

'Yes,' said the sister. 'I know it is nothing much from the outside, but it is clean and comfortable, and was recommended by friends.' She turned to the escort. 'Grazie,' she said to him, 'grazie tanto.'

The man nodded briefly, wished them 'Buona notte,' and disappeared across the campo.

'Will you come in?' asked the sister. 'I am sure we can find you some coffee, or perhaps you prefer tea?'

'No, really,' John thanked her, 'I must get back to the hotel. I'm making an early start in the morning. I just want to make quite sure you do understand what happened, and that you forgive me.'

'There is nothing to forgive,' she replied. 'It is one of the many examples of second sight that my sister and I have experienced time and time again, and I should very much like to record it for our files, if you will permit it.'

'Well, as to that, of course,' he told her, 'but I myself find it hard to understand. It has never happened to me before.'

'Not consciously, perhaps,' she said, 'but so many things happen to us of which we are not aware. My sister felt you had psychic understanding. She told your wife. She also told your wife, last night in the restaurant, that you were to experience trouble, danger, that you should leave Venice. Well, don't you believe now that the telegram was proof of this? Your son was ill, possibly dangerously ill, and so it was necessary for you to return home immediately. Heaven be praised your wife flew home to be by his side.'

'Yes, indeed,' said John, 'but why should I see her on the vaporetto with you and your sister when she was actually on her way to England?'

'Thought transference, perhaps,' she answered. 'Your

wife may have been thinking about us. We gave her our address, should you wish to get in touch with us. We shall be here another ten days. And she knows that we would pass on any message that my sister might have from your little one in the spirit world.'

'Yes,' said John awkwardly, 'yes, I see. It's very good of you.' He had a sudden rather unkind picture of the two sisters putting on headphones in their bedroom, listening for a coded message from poor Christine. 'Look, this is our address in London,' he said. 'I know Laura will be pleased to hear from you.'

He scribbled their address on a sheet torn from his pocket-diary, even, as a bonus thrown in, the telephone number, and handed it to her. He could imagine the outcome. Laura springing it on him one evening that the 'old dears' were passing through London on their way to Scotland, and the least they could do was to offer them hospitality, even the spare-room for the night. Then a seance in the living-room, tambourines appearing out of thin air.

'Well, I must be off,' he said. 'Goodnight, and apologies, once again, for all that has happened this evening.' He shook hands with the first sister, then turned to her blind twin. 'I hope,' he said, 'that you are not too tired.'

The sightless eyes were disconcerting. She held his hand fast and would not let it go. 'The child,' she said, speaking in an odd staccato voice, 'the child . . . I can see the child . . .' and then, to his dismay, a bead of froth appeared at the corner of her mouth, her head jerked back, and she half-collapsed in her sister's arms.

'We must get her inside,' said the sister hurriedly. 'It's all right, she's not ill, it's the beginning of a trance state.'

Between them they helped the twin, who had gone rigid, into the house, and sat her down on the nearest chair, the sister supporting her. A woman came running from some inner room. There was a strong smell of spaghetti from the back regions. 'Don't worry,' said the sister, 'the signorina and I can manage. I think you had better go. Sometimes she is sick after these turns.'

'I'm most frightfully sorry . . .' John began, but the sister had already turned her back, and with the signorina was bending over her twin, from whom peculiar choking sounds were proceeding. He was obviously in the way, and after a final gesture of courtesy, 'Is there anything I can do?', which received no reply, he turned on his heel and began walking across the square. He looked back once, and saw they had closed the door.

What a finale to the evening! And all his fault. Poor old girls, first dragged to police headquarters and put through an interrogation, and then a psychic fit on top of it all. More likely epilepsy. Not much of a life for the other sister, but she seemed to take it in her stride. An additional hazard, though, if it happened in a restaurant or in the street. And not particularly welcome under his and Laura's roof should the sisters ever find themselves beneath it, which he prayed would never happen.

Meanwhile, where the devil was he? The square, with the inevitable church at one end, was quite deserted. He could not remember which way they had come from police headquarters, there had seemed to be so many turnings.

Wait a minute, the church itself had a familiar appearance. He drew nearer to it, looking for the name which was sometimes on notices at the entrance. San Giovanni in Bragora, that rang a bell. He and Laura had gone inside one morning to look at a painting by Cima da Conegliano. Surely it was only a stone's throw from the Riva degli Schiavoni and the open wide waters of the San Marco lagoon, with all the bright lights of civilisation and the strolling tourists? He remembered taking a small turning from the Schiavoni and they had arrived at the church. Wasn't that the alley-way ahead? He plunged along it, but halfway down he hesitated. It didn't seem right, although it was familiar for some unknown reason.

Then he realised that it was not the alley they had taken the morning they visited the church, but the one they had walked along the previous evening, only he was approaching it from the opposite direction. Yes, that was it, in which case it would be quicker to go on and cross the little bridge over the narrow canal, and he would find the Arsenal on his left and the street leading down to the Riva degli Schiavoni to his right. Simpler than retracing his steps and getting lost once more in the maze of back streets.

He had almost reached the end of the alley, and the bridge was in sight, when he saw the child. It was the same little girl with the pixie-hood who had leapt between the tethered boats the preceding night and vanished up the cellar steps of one of the houses. This time she was running from the direction of the church the other side, making for the bridge. She was running as if her life depended on it, and in a moment he saw why. A man was in pursuit, who, when she glanced backwards for a moment, still running, flattened himself against a wall, believing himself unobserved. The child came on, scampering across the bridge, and John, fearful of alarming her further, backed into an open doorway that led into a small court.

He remembered the drunken yell of the night before which had come from one of the houses near where the man was hiding now. This is it, he thought, the fellow's after her again, and with a flash of intuition he connected the two events, the child's terror then and now, and the murders reported in the newspapers, supposedly the work of some madman. It could be coincidence, a child running from a drunken relative, and yet, and yet . . . His heart began thumping in his chest, instinct warning him to run himself, now, at once, back along the alley the way he had come – but what about the child? What was going to happen to the child?

Then he heard her running steps. She hurtled through the open doorway into the court in which he stood, not seeing him, making for the rear of the house that flanked it, where steps led presumably to a back entrance. She was sobbing as she ran, not the ordinary cry of a frightened child, but the panic-stricken intake of breath of a helpless being in despair. Were there parents in the house who would protect her, whom he could warn? He hesitated a moment, then followed her down the steps and through the door at the bottom, which had burst open at the touch of her hands as she hurled herself against it.

'It's all right,' he called. 'I won't let him hurt you, it's all right,' cursing his lack of Italian, but possibly an English voice might reassure her. But it was no use – she ran sobbing up another flight of stairs, which were spiral, twisting, leading to the floor above, and already it was too late for him to retreat. He could hear sounds of the pursuer in the courtyard behind, someone shouting in Italian, a dog barking. This is it, he thought, we're in it together, the child and I. Unless we can bolt some inner door above he'll get us both.

He ran up the stairs after the child, who had darted into a room leading off a small landing, and followed her inside and slammed the door, and, merciful heaven, there was a bolt which he rammed into its socket. The child was crouching by the open window. If he shouted for help someone would surely hear, someone would surely come before the man in pursuit threw himself against the door and it gave, because there was no one but themselves, no parents, the room was bare except for a mattress on an old bed, and a heap of rags in one corner.

'It's all right,' he panted, 'It's all right,' and held out his hand, trying to smile.

The child struggled to her feet and stood before him, the pixie-hood falling from her head on to the floor. He stared at her, incredulity turning to horror, to fear. It was not a child at all but a little thick-set woman dwarf, about three feet high, with a great square adult head too big for her body, grey locks hanging shoulder-length, and she wasn't sobbing any more, she was grinning at him, nodding her head up and down.

Then he heard the footsteps on the landing outside and the hammering on the door, and a barking dog, and not one voice but several voices, shouting, 'Open up! Police!' The creature fumbled in her sleeve, drawing a knife, and as she threw it at him with hideous strength, piercing his throat, he stumbled and fell, the sticky mess covering his protecting hands.

And he saw the vaporetto with Laura and the two sisters steaming down the Grand Canal, not today, not tomorrow, but the day after that, and he knew why they were together and for what sad purpose they had come. The creature was gibbering in its corner. The hammering and the voices and the barking dog grew fainter, and, 'Oh God,' he thought, 'what a bloody silly way to die . . .'

The third struggled to her feet and stood before him, the pale mouth falling open, blood on the floor. He wanted a bit of blood on the floor, but it was not a child until a little later, as written down... about three inches long, was a great source soon kept resting on...

Not After Midnight

I am a schoolmaster by profession. Or was. I handed in my resignation to the Head before the end of the summer term in order to forestall inevitable dismissal. The reason I gave was true enough – ill-health, caused by a wretched bug picked up on holiday in Crete, which might necessitate a stay in hospital of several weeks, various injections, etc. I did not specify the nature of the bug. He knew, though, and so did the rest of the staff. And the boys. My complaint is universal, and has been so through the ages, an excuse for jest and hilarious laughter from earliest times, until one of us oversteps the mark and becomes a menace to society. Then we are given the boot. The passer-by averts his gaze, and we are left to crawl out of the ditch alone, or stay there and die.

If I am bitter, it is because the bug I caught was picked up in all innocence. Fellow-sufferers of my complaint can plead predisposition, poor heredity, family trouble, excess of the good life, and, throwing themselves on a psycho-analyst's couch, spill out the rotten beans within and so effect a cure. I can do none of this. The doctor to whom I endeavoured to explain what had happened listened with a superior smile, and then murmured something about emotionally destructive identification coupled with repressed guilt, and put me on a course of pills. They might have helped me if I had taken them. Instead I threw them down the drain and became more deeply imbued with the poison that seeped through me, made worse of course by the fatal recognition of my condition by the youngsters I had believed to be my friends, who nudged one another when I came into class, or, with stifled laughter, bent their loathsome little heads over their desks – until the moment arrived when I knew I could not continue, and took the decision to knock on the headmaster's door.

Well, that's over, done with, finished. Before I take myself to hospital or alternatively, blot out memory, which is a second possibility, I want to establish what happened in the first place. So that, whatever becomes of me, this paper will be found, and the reader can make up his mind whether, as the doctor suggested, some want of inner balance made me an easy victim of superstitious fear, or whether, as I myself believe, my downfall was caused by an age-old magic, insidious, evil, its origins lost in the dawn of history. Suffice to say that he who first made the magic deemed himself immortal, and with unholy joy infected others, sowing in his heirs, throughout the world and down the centuries, the seeds of self-destruction.

To return to the present. The time was April, the Easter holidays. I had been to Greece twice before, but never Crete. I taught classics to the boys at the preparatory school, but my reason for visiting Crete was not to explore the sites of Knossos or Phaestus but to indulge a personal hobby. I have a minor talent for painting in oils, and this I find all-absorbing, whether on free days or in the school holidays. My work has been praised by one or two friends in the art world, and my ambition was to collect enough paintings to give a small exhibition. Even if none of them sold, the holding of a private show would be a happy achievement.

Here, briefly, a word about my personal life. I am a bachelor. Age forty-nine. Parents dead. Educated at Sherborne and Brasenose, Oxford. Profession, as you already know, schoolmaster. I play cricket and golf, badminton, and rather poor bridge. Interests, apart from teaching, art, as I have already said, and occasional travel, when I can afford it. Vices, up to the present, literally none. Which is not being self-complacent, but the truth is that my life has been uneventful by any standard. Nor has this bothered me. I am probably a dull man. Emotionally I have had no complications. I was engaged to a pretty girl, a neighbour, when I was twenty-five, but she married somebody else. It hurt at the time, but the wound healed in less than a year. One fault, if fault it is, I have always had, which perhaps accounts for my hitherto monotonous life. This is an aversion to becoming involved with people. Friends I possess, but at a distance. Once involved, trouble occurs, and too often disaster follows.

I set out for Crete in the Easter holidays with no encumbrance but a fair-sized suitcase and my painting gear. A travel agent had recommended a hotel overlooking the Gulf of Mirabello on the eastern coast, after I had told him I was not interested in archaeological sights but wanted to paint. I was shown a brochure which seemed to meet my requirements. A pleasantly situated hotel close to the sea, and chalets by the water's edge where one slept and breakfasted. Clientèle well-to-do, and although I count myself no snob I cannot abide paper-bags and orange-peel. A couple of pictures painted the previous winter – a view of St Paul's Cathedral under snow, and another one of Hampstead Heath, both sold to an obliging female cousin – would pay for my journey, and I permitted myself an added indulgence, though it was really a necessity – the hiring of a small Volkswagen on arrival at the airport of Herakleion.

The flight, with an overnight stop in Athens, was pleasant and uneventful, the forty-odd miles' drive to my destination somewhat tedious, for being a cautious driver I took it slowly, and the twisting road, once I reached the hills, was decidedly hazardous. Cars passed me, or swerved towards me, hooting loudly. Also, it was very hot, and I was hungry. The sight of the blue Gulf of Mirabello and the splendid mountains to the east acted as a spur to sagging spirits, and once I arrived at the hotel, set delightfully in its own grounds, with lunch served to me on the terrace despite the fact that it was after two in the afternoon – how different from England! – I was ready to relax and inspect my quarters. Disappointment followed. The young porter led me down a garden path flagged on either side by brilliant geraniums to a small chalet bunched in by neighbours on either side, and overlooking, not the sea, but a part of the garden laid out for mini-golf. My next-door neighbours, an obviously English mother and her brood, smiled in welcome from their balcony, which was strewn with bathing-suits drying under the sun. Two middle-aged men were engaged in mini-golf. I might have been in Maidenhead.

'This won't do,' I said, turning to my escort. 'I have come here to paint. I must have a view of the sea.'

He shrugged his shoulders, murmuring something about the chalets beside the sea being fully booked. It was not his fault, of course. I made him trek back to the hotel with me, and addressed myself to the clerk at the reception desk.

'There has been some mistake,' I said. 'I asked for a chalet overlooking the sea, and privacy above all.'

The clerk smiled, apologised, began ruffling papers, and the inevitable excuses followed. My travel agent had not specifically booked a chalet overlooking the sea. These were in great demand, and were fully booked. Perhaps in a few days there might be some cancellations, one never could tell, in the meantime he was sure I should be very comfortable in the chalet that had been allotted to me. All the furnishings were the same, my breakfast would be served me, etc., etc.

I was adamant. I would not be fobbed off with the English family and the mini-golf. Not having flown all those miles at considerable expense. I was bored by the whole affair, tired, and considerably annoyed.

'I am a professor of art,' I told the clerk. 'I have been commissioned to execute several paintings while I am here, and it is essential that I should have a view of the sea, and neighbours who will not disturb me.'

(My passport states my occupation as professor. It sounds better than schoolmaster or teacher, and usually arouses respect in the attitude of reception clerks.)

The clerk seemed genuinely concerned, and repeated his apologies. He turned again to the sheaf of papers before him. Exasperated, I strode across the spacious hall and looked out of the door on to the terrace down to the sea.

'I cannot believe,' I said, 'that every chalet is taken. It's too early in the season. In summer, perhaps, but not now.' I waved my hand towards the western side of the bay. 'That group over there,' I said, 'down by the water's edge. Do you mean to say every single one of them is booked?'

He shook his head and smiled. 'We do not usually open those until mid-season. Also, they are more expensive. They have a bath as well as a shower.'

'How much more expensive?' I hedged.

He told me. I made a quick calculation. I could afford it if I cut down on all other expenses. Had my evening meal in the hotel, and went without lunch. No extras in the bar, not even mineral water.

'Then there is no problem,' I said grandly. 'I will willingly pay more for privacy. And, if you have no objection, I should like to choose the chalet which would suit me best. I'll walk down to the sea now and then come back for the key, and your porter can bring my things.'

I gave him no time to reply, but turned on my heel and went out on to the terrace. It paid to be firm. One moment's hesitation, and he would have fobbed me off with the stuffy chalet overlooking the mini-golf. I could imagine the consequences. The chattering children on the balcony next door, the possibly effusive mother, and the middle-aged golfers urging me to have a game. I could not have borne it.

I walked down through the garden to the sea, and as I did so my spirits rose. For this, of course, was what had been so highly coloured on the agent's brochure, and why I had flown so many miles. No exaggeration, either. Little white-washed dwellings, discreetly set apart from one another, the sea washing the rocks below. There was a beach, from which doubtless people swam in high season, but no one was on it now, and, even if they should intrude, the chalets themselves were well to the left, inviolate, private. I peered at each in turn, mounting the steps, standing on the balconies. The clerk must have been telling the truth about none of them being let before full season, for all had their windows shuttered. All except one. And directly I mounted the steps and stood on the balcony I knew that it must be mine. This was the view I had imagined. The sea beneath me, lapping the rocks, the bay widening into the gulf itself, and beyond the mountains. It was perfect. The chalets to the east of the hotel, which was out of sight anyway, could be ignored. One, close to a neck of land, stood on its own like a solitary outpost with a landing-stage below, but this would only enhance my picture when I came to paint it. The rest were mercifully hidden by rising ground. I turned, and looked through the open windows to the bedroom within. Plain whitewashed walls, a stone floor, a comfortable divan bed with rugs upon it. A bedside table with a lamp and telephone. But for these last it had all the simplicity of a monk's cell, and I wished for nothing more.

I wondered why this chalet, and none of its neighbours, was unshuttered, and stepping inside I heard from the bathroom beyond the sound of running water. Not further disappointment, and the place booked after all? I put my head round the open door, and saw that it was a little Greek maid swabbing the bathroom floor. She seemed startled at the sight of me. I gestured, pointed, said, 'Is this taken?' She did not understand, but answered me in Greek. Then she seized her cloth and pail and, plainly terrified, brushed past me to the entrance, leaving her work unfinished.

I went back into the bedroom and picked up the telephone, and in a moment the smooth voice of the reception clerk answered.

'This is Mr Grey,' I told him, 'Mr Timothy Grey. I was speaking to you just now about changing my chalet.'

'Yes, Mr Grey,' he replied. He sounded puzzled. 'Where are you speaking from?'

'Hold on a minute,' I said. I put down the receiver and crossed the room to the balcony. The number was above the open door. It was 62. I went back to the telephone. 'I'm speaking from the chalet I have chosen,' I said. 'It happened to be open – one of the maids was cleaning the bathroom, and I'm afraid I scared her away. This chalet is ideal for my purpose. It is No. 62.'

He did not answer immediately, and when he did he sounded doubtful. 'No. 62?' he repeated. And then, after a moment's hesitation, 'I am not sure if it is available.'

'Oh, for heaven's sake . . .' I began, exasperated, and I heard him talking in Greek to someone beside him at the desk. The conversation went back and forth between them; there was obviously some difficulty, which made me all the more determined.

'Are you there?' I said. 'What's the trouble?'

More hurried whispers, and then he spoke to me again. 'No trouble, Mr Grey. It is just that we feel you might be more comfortable in No. 57, which is a little nearer to the hotel.'

'Nonsense,' I said, 'I prefer the view from here. What's wrong with No. 62? Doesn't the plumbing work?'

'Certainly the plumbing works,' he assured me, while the whispering started again. 'There is nothing wrong with the chalet. If you have made up your mind I will send down the porter with your luggage and the key.'

He rang off, possibly to finish his discussion with the whisperer at his side. Perhaps they were going to step up the price. If they did, I would have further argument. The chalet was no different from its empty neighbours, but the position, dead centre to sea and mountains, was all I had dreamed and more. I stood on the balcony, looking out across the sea and smiling. What a prospect, what a place! I would unpack and have a swim, then put up my easel and do a preliminary sketch before starting serious work in the morning.

I heard voices, and saw the little maid staring at me from halfway up the garden path, cloth and pail still in hand. Then, as the young porter advanced downhill bearing my suitcase and painting gear, she must have realised that I was to be the occupant of No. 62, for she stopped him midway, and another whispered conversation began. I had evidently caused a break in the smooth routine of the hotel. A few moments later they climbed the steps to the chalet together, the porter to set down my luggage, the maid doubtless to finish her swabbing of the bathroom floor. I had no desire to be on awkward terms with either of them, and, smiling cheerfully, placed coins in both their hands.

'Lovely view,' I said loudly, pointing to the sea. 'Must go for a swim,' and made breast-stroke gestures to show my intent, hoping for the ready smile of the native Greek, usually so responsive to goodwill.

The porter evaded my eyes and bowed gravely, accepting my tip nevertheless. As for the little maid, distress was evident in her face, and forgetting about the bathroom floor she hurried after him. I could hear them talking as they walked up the garden path together to the hotel.

Well, it was not my problem. Staff and management must sort out their troubles between them. I had got what

I wanted, and that was all that concerned me. I unpacked and made myself at home. Then, slipping on bathing trunks, I stepped down to the ledge of rock beneath the balcony, and ventured a toe into the water. It was surprisingly chill, despite the hot sun that had been upon it all day. Never mind. I must prove my mettle, if only to myself. I took the plunge and gasped, and being a cautious swimmer at the best of times, especially in strange waters, swam round and round in circles rather like a sea-lion pup in a zoological pool.

Refreshing, undoubtedly, but a few minutes were enough, and as I climbed out again on to the rocks I saw that the porter and the little maid had been watching me all the time from behind a flowering bush up the garden path. I hoped I had not lost face. And anyway, why the interest? People must be swimming every day from the other chalets. The bathing-suits on the various balconies proved it. I dried myself on the balcony, observing how the sun, now in the western sky behind my chalet, made dappled patterns on the water. Fishing-boats were returning to the little harbour port a few miles distant, the chug-chug engines making a pleasing sound.

I dressed, taking the precaution of having a hot bath, for the first swim of the year is always numbing, and then set up my easel and instantly became absorbed. This was why I was here, and nothing else mattered. I worked for a couple of hours, and as the light failed, and the colour of the sea deepened and the mountains turned a softer purple blue, I rejoiced to think that tomorrow I should be able to seize this after-glow in paint instead of charcoal, and the picture would begin to come alive.

It was time to stop. I stacked away my gear, and before changing for dinner and drawing the shutters – doubtless there were mosquitoes, and I had no wish to be bitten – watched a motor-boat with gently purring engine draw in

softly to the eastward point with the landing-stage away
to my right. Three people aboard, fishing enthusiasts no
doubt, a woman amongst them. One man, a local, probably, made the boat fast, and stepped on the landing-stage
to help the woman ashore. Then all three stared in my
direction, and the second man, who had been standing in
the stern, put up a pair of binoculars and fixed them on
me. He held them steady for several minutes, focusing, no
doubt, on every detail of my personal appearance, which
is unremarkable enough, heaven knows, and would have
continued had I not suddenly become annoyed and with-
drawn into the bedroom, slamming the shutters to. How
rude can you get, I asked myself. Then I remembered that
these western chalets were all unoccuppied, and mine was
the first to open for the season. Possibly this was the reason
for the intense interest I appeared to cause, beginning with
members of the hotel staff and now embracing guests as
well. Interest would soon fade. I was neither pop star nor
millionaire. And my painting efforts, however pleasing to
myself, were hardly likely to draw a fascinated crowd.

Punctually at eight o'clock I walked up the garden path
to the hotel and presented myself in the dining-room for
dinner. It was moderately full and I was allotted a table in
the corner, suitable to my single status, close to the screen
dividing the service entrance from the kitchens. Never
mind. I preferred this position to the centre of the room,
where I could tell immediately that the hotel clientèle were
on what my mother used to describe as an 'all fellows to
football' basis.

I enjoyed my dinner, treated myself – despite my de luxe
chalet – to half a bottle of domestica wine, and was peeling
an orange when an almighty crash from the far end of the
room disturbed us all. Waiters hurried to the scene. Heads
turned, mine amongst them. A hoarse American voice,
hailing from the deep South, called loudly, 'For God's sake

clear up this God-darn mess!' It came from a square-shouldered man of middle age, whose face was so swollen and blistered by exposure to the sun that he looked as if he had been stung by a million bees. His eyes were sunk into his head, which was bald on top, with a grizzled thatch on either side, and the pink crown had the appearance of being tightly stretched, like the skin of a sausage about to burst. A pair of enormous ears the size of clams gave further distortion to his appearance, while a drooping wisp of moustache did nothing to hide the protruding underlip, thick as blubber and about as moist. I have seldom set eyes on a more unattractive individual. A woman, I suppose his wife, sat beside him, stiff and bolt upright, apparently unmoved by the debris on the floor, which appeared to consist chiefly of bottles. She was likewise middle-aged, with a mop of tow-coloured hair turning white, and a face as sunburnt as her husband's, but mahogany brown instead of red.

'Let's get the hell out of here and go to the bar!' The hoarse strains echoed across the room. The guests at the other tables turned discreetly back to their own dinner, and I must have been the only one to watch the unsteady exit of the bee-stung spouse and his wife – I could see the deaf-aid in her ear, hence possibly her husband's rasping tones – as he literally rolled past me to the bar, a lurching vessel in the wake of his steady partner. I silently commended the efficiency of the hotel staff, who made short work of clearing the wreckage.

The dining-room emptied. 'Coffee in the bar, sir,' murmured my waiter. Fearing a crush and loud chatter I hesitated before entering, for the camaraderie of hotel bars has always bored me, but I hate going without my after-dinner coffee. I need not have worried. The bar was empty, apart from the white-coated server behind the bar, and the American sitting at a table with his wife. Neither of them was speaking. There were three empty beer bottles already on the table before him. Greek music played softly from some lair behind the bar. I sat myself on a stool and ordered coffee.

The bar-tender, who spoke excellent English, asked if I had spent a pleasant day. I told him yes. I had had a good flight, found the road from Herakleion hazardous, and my first swim rather cold. He explained that it was still early in the year. 'In any case,' I told him, 'I have come to paint, and swimming will take second place. I have a chalet right on the water-front, No. 62, and the view from the balcony is perfect.'

Rather odd. He was polishing a glass, and his expression changed. He seemed about to say something, then evidently thought better of it, and continued with his work.

'Turn that God-damn record off!'

The hoarse, imperious summons filled the empty room. The bar-man made at once for the gramophone in the corner and adjusted the switch. A moment later the summons rang forth again.

'Bring me another bottle of beer!'

Now, had I been the bar-tender I should have turned to the man and, like a parent to a child, insisted that he said please. Instead, the brute was promptly served, and I was just downing my coffee when the voice from the table echoed through the room once more.

'Hi, you there, chalet No. 62. You're not superstitious?'

I turned on my stool. He was staring at me, glass in hand. His wife looked straight in front of her. Perhaps she had removed her deaf-aid. Remembering the maxim that one must humour madmen and drunks, I replied courteously enough.

'No,' I said, 'I'm not superstitious. Should I be?'

He began to laugh, his scarlet face creasing into a hundred lines.

'Well, God darn it, I would be,' he answered. 'The fellow from that chalet was drowned only two weeks ago. Missing for two days, and then his body brought up in a net by a local fisherman, half-eaten by octopuses.'

He began to shake with laughter, slapping his hand on his knee. I turned away in disgust, and raised my eyebrows in inquiry to the bar-tender.

'An unfortunate accident,' he murmured. 'Mr Gordon such a nice gentleman. Interested in archaeology. It was very warm the night he disappeared, and he must have gone swimming after dinner. Of course the police were called. We were all most distressed here at the hotel. You understand, sir, we don't talk about it much. It would be bad for business. But I do assure you that bathing is perfectly safe. This is the first accident we have ever had.'

'Oh, quite,' I said.

Nevertheless . . . It was rather off-putting, the fact that the poor chap had been the last to use my chalet. However, it was not as though he had died in the bed. And I was not superstitious. I understood now why the staff had been reluctant to let the chalet again so soon, and why the little maid had been upset.

'I tell you one thing,' boomed the revolting voice. 'Don't go swimming after midnight, or the octopuses will get you too.' This statement was followed by another outburst of laughter. Then he said, 'Come on, Maud. We're for bed,' and he noisily shoved the table aside.

I breathed more easily when the room was clear and we were alone.

'What an impossible man,' I said. 'Can't the management get rid of him?'

The bar-tender shrugged. 'Business is business. What can they do? The Stolls have plenty of money. This is their second season here, and they arrived when we opened in March. They seem to be crazy about the place. It's only this year, though, that Mr Stoll has become such a heavy drinker. He'll kill himself if he goes on at this rate. It's always like this, night after night. Yet his day must be healthy enough. Out at sea fishing from early morning until sundown.'

'I dare say more bottles go over the side than he catches fish,' I observed.

'Could be,' the bar-tender agreed. 'He never brings his fish to the hotel. The boatman takes them home, I dare say.'

'I feel sorry for the wife.'

The bar-tender shrugged. 'She's the one with the money,' he replied sotto voce, for a couple of guests had just entered the bar, 'and I don't think Mr Stoll has it all his own way. Being deaf may be convenient to her at times. But she never leaves his side, I'll grant her that. Goes fishing with him every day. Yes, gentlemen, what can I get for you?'

He turned to his new customers, and I made my escape. The cliché that it takes all sorts to make a world passed through my head. Thank heaven it was not my world, and Mr Stoll and his deaf wife could burn themselves black under the sun all day at sea as far as I was concerned, and break beer bottles every evening into the bargain. In any event, they were not neighbours. No. 62 may have had the unfortunate victim of a drowning accident for its last occupant, but at least this had insured privacy for its present tenant.

I walked down the garden path to my abode. It was a clear starlit night. The air was balmy, and sweet with the scent of the flowering shrubs planted thickly in the red earth. Standing on my balcony I looked out across the sea towards the distant shrouded mountains and the harbour lights from the little fishing port. To my right winked the lights of the other chalets, giving a pleasing, almost fairy impression, like a clever backcloth on a stage. Truly a wonderful spot, and I blessed the travel agent who had recommended it.

I let myself in through my shuttered doorway and turned on the bedside lamp. The room looked welcoming and snug; I could not have been better housed. I undressed, and before getting into bed remembered I had left a book I wanted to glance at on the balcony. I opened the shutters and picked it up from the deck-chair where I had thrown it, and once more, before turning in, glanced out at the open sea. Most of the fairy lights had been extinguished, but the chalet that stood on its own on the extreme point still had its light burning on the balcony. The boat, tied to the landing-stage, bore a riding-light. Seconds later I saw something moving close to my rocks. It was the snorkel of an under-water swimmer. I could see the narrow pipe, like a minute periscope, move steadily across the still, dark surface of the sea. Then it disappeared to the far left out of sight. I drew my shutters and went inside.

I don't know why it was, but the sight of that moving object was somehow disconcerting. It made me think of the unfortunate man who had been drowned during a midnight swim. My predecessor. He too, perhaps, had sallied forth one balmy evening such as this, intent on under-water exploration, and by so doing lost his life. One would imagine the unhappy accident would scare off other hotel visitors from swimming alone at night. I made a firm decision never to bathe except in broad daylight, and – chicken-hearted, maybe – well within my depth.

I read a few pages of my book, then, feeling ready for sleep, turned to switch out my light. In doing so I clumsily bumped the telephone, which fell to the floor. I bent over, picked it up, luckily no damage done, and saw that the small drawer that was part of the fixture had fallen open. It contained a scrap of paper, or rather card, with the name Charles Gordon upon it, and an address in Bloomsbury. Surely Gordon had been the name of my predecessor? The little maid, when she cleaned the room, had not thought to open the drawer. I turned the card over. There was something scrawled on the other side, the words 'Not after midnight'. And then, maybe as an afterthought, the figure 38. I replaced the card in the drawer and switched off the light. Perhaps I was overtired after the journey, but it was well past two before I finally got off to sleep. I lay awake for no rhyme or reason, listening to the water lapping against the rocks beneath my balcony.

I painted solidly for three days, never quitting my chalet except for the morning swim and my evening meal at the hotel. Nobody bothered me. An obliging waiter brought my breakfast, from which I saved rolls for midday lunch, the little maid made my bed and did her chores without disturbing me, and when I had finished my impressionistic scene on the afternoon of the third day I felt quite certain it was one of the best things I had ever done. It would take pride of place in the planned exhibition of my work. Well satisfied, I could now relax, and I determined to explore along the coast the following day, and discover another view to whip up inspiration. The weather was glorious. Warm as a good English June. And the best thing about the whole site was the total absence of neighbours. The other guests kept to their side of the domain, and, apart from bows and nods from adjoining tables as one entered the dining-room for dinner, no one attempted to strike up acquaintance. I took good care to drink my coffee in the bar before the obnoxious Mr Stoll had left his table.

I realised now that it was his boat which lay anchored off the point. They were away too early in the morning for me to watch their departure, but I used to spot them returning in the late afternoon; his square, hunched form was easily recognisable, and the occasional hoarse shout to the man in charge of the boat as they came to the landing-stage. Theirs, too, was the isolated chalet on the point, and I wondered if he had picked it purposely in order to soak himself into oblivion out of sight and earshot of his nearest neighbours. Well, good luck to him, as long as he did not obtrude his offensive presence upon me.

Feeling the need of gentle exercise, I decided to spend the rest of the afternoon taking a stroll to the eastern side of the hotel grounds. Once again I congratulated myself on having escaped the cluster of chalets in this populated quarter. Mini-golf and tennis were in full swing, and the little beach was crowded with sprawling bodies on every available patch of sand. But soon the murmur of the world was behind me, and screened and safe behind the flowering shrubs I found myself on the point near to the landing-stage. The boat was not yet at its mooring, nor even in sight out in the gulf.

A sudden temptation to peep at the unpleasant Mr Stoll's chalet swept upon me. I crept up the little path, feeling as furtive as a burglar on the prowl, and stared up at the shuttered windows. It was no different from its fellows, or mine for that matter, except for a tell-tale heap of bottles lying in a corner of the balcony. Brute . . . Then something else caught my eye. A pair of frog-feet, and a snorkel. Surely, with all that liquor inside him, he did not venture his carcass under water? Perhaps he sent the local Greek whom he employed as crew to seek for crabs. I remembered the snorkel on my first evening, close to the rocks, and the riding-light in the boat.

I moved away, for I thought I could hear someone coming down the path and did not want to be caught prying, but before doing so I glanced up at the number of the chalet. It was 38. The figure had no particular significance for me then, but later on, changing for dinner, I picked up the tie-pin I had placed on my bedside table, and on sudden impulse opened the drawer beneath the telephone to look at my predecessor's card again. Yes, I thought so. The scrawled figure *was* 38. Pure coincidence, of course, and yet ... 'Not after midnight'. The words suddenly had meaning. Stoll had warned me about swimming late on my first evening. Had he warned Gordon too? And Gordon had jotted down the warning on his card with Stoll's chalet-number underneath? It made sense, but obviously poor Gordon had disregarded the advice. And so, apparently, did one of the occupants of Chalet 38.

I finished changing, and instead of replacing the card in the telephone drawer put it in my wallet. I had an uneasy feeling that it was my duty to hand it in to the reception desk in case it threw any light on my unfortunate predecessor's demise. I toyed with the thought through dinner, but came to no decision. The point was, I might become involved, questioned by the police. And as far as I knew the case was closed. There was little point in my suddenly coming forward with a calling-card lying forgotten in a drawer that probably had no significance at all.

It so happened that the people seated to the right of me in the dining-room appeared to have gone, and the Stolls' table in the corner now came into view without my being obliged to turn my head. I could watch them without making it too obvious, and I was struck by the fact that he never once addressed a word to her. They made an odd contrast. She stiff as a ramrod, prim-looking, austere, forking her food to her mouth like a Sunday school teacher on an outing, and he, more scarlet than ever, like a great swollen sausage, pushing aside most of what the waiter placed before him after the first mouthful, and reaching out a pudgy, hairy hand to an ever-emptying glass.

I finished my dinner and went through to the bar to drink my coffee. I was early, and had the place to myself. The bartender and I exchanged the usual pleasantries and then, after an allusion to the weather, I jerked my head in the direction of the dining-room.

'I noticed our friend Mr Stoll and his lady spent the whole day at sea as usual,' I said.

The bar-tender shrugged. 'Day after day, it never varies,' he replied, 'and mostly in the same direction, westward out of the bay into the gulf. It can be squally, too, at times, but they don't seem to care.'

'I don't know how she puts up with him,' I said. 'I watched them at dinner – he didn't speak to her at all. I wonder what the other guests make of him.'

'They keep well clear, sir. You saw how it was for yourself. If he ever does open his mouth it's only to be rude. And the same goes for the staff. The girls dare not go in to clean the chalet until he's out of the way. And the smell!' He grimaced, and leant forward confidentially. 'The girls say he brews his own beer. He lights the fire in the chimney, and has a pot standing, filled with rotting grain, like some sort of pig swill! Oh, yes, he drinks it right enough. Imagine the state of his liver, after what he consumes at dinner and afterwards here in the bar!'

'I suppose,' I said, 'that's why he keeps his balcony light on so late at night. Drinking pig-swill until the small hours. Tell me, which of the hotel visitors is it who goes under-water swimming?'

The bar-tender looked surprised. 'No one, to my knowledge. Not since the accident, anyway. Poor Mr Gordon liked a night swim, at least so we supposed. He was one of the few visitors who ever talked to Mr Stoll, now I think of it. They had quite a conversation here one evening in the bar.'

'Indeed?'

'Not about swimming, though, or fishing either. They were discussing antiquities. There's a fine little museum here in the village, you know, but it's closed at present for repairs. Mr Gordon had some connection with the British Museum in London.'

'I wouldn't have thought,' I said, 'that would interest friend Stoll.'

'Ah,' said the bar-tender, 'you'd be surprised. Mr Stoll is no fool. Last year he and Mrs Stoll used to take the car and visit all the famous sites, Knossos, Mallia, and other places not so well known. This year it's quite different. It's the boat and fishing every day.'

'And Mr Gordon,' I pursued, 'did he ever go fishing with them?'

'No, sir. Not to my knowledge. He hired a car, like you, and explored the district. He was writing a book, he told me, on archaeological finds in eastern Crete, and their connection with Greek mythology.'

'Mythology?'

'Yes, I understood him to tell Mr Stoll it was mythology, but it was all above my head, you can imagine, nor did I hear much of the conversation – we were busy that evening in the bar. Mr Gordon was a quiet sort of gentleman, rather after your own style, if you'll excuse me, sir, seeming very interested in what they were discussing, all to do with the old gods. They were at it for over an hour.'

H'm . . . I thought of the card in my wallet. Should I, or should I not, hand it over to the reception clerk at the desk? I said goodnight to the bar-tender and went back through the dining-room to the hall. The Stolls had just left their table and were walking ahead of me. I hung back until the way was clear, surprised that they had turned their backs upon the bar and were making for the hall. I stood by the rack of postcards, to give myself an excuse for loitering, but out of their range of vision, and watched Mrs Stoll take her coat from a hook in the lobby near the entrance, while her unpleasant husband visited the cloakroom, and then the pair of them walked out of the front door which led direct to the car park. They must be going for a drive. With Stoll at the wheel in his condition?

I hesitated. The reception clerk was on the telephone. It wasn't the moment to hand over the card. Some impulse, like that of a small boy playing detective, made me walk to my own car, and when Stoll's tail-light was out of sight – he was driving a Mercedes – I followed in his wake. There was only the one road, and he was heading east towards the village and the harbour lights. I lost him, inevitably, on reaching the little port, for, instinctively making for the quayside opposite what appeared to be a main café, I thought he must have done the same. I parked the Volkswagen, and looked around me. No sign of the Mercedes. Just a sprinkling of other tourists like myself, and local inhabitants, strolling, or drinking in front of the café.

Oh well, forget it, I'd sit and enjoy the scene, have a lemonade. I must have sat there for over half an hour, savouring what is known as 'local colour', amused by the passing crowd, Greek families taking the air, pretty, self-conscious girls eyeing the youths, who appeared to stick together, practising a form of segregation, a bearded Orthodox priest who smoked incessantly at the table next to me, playing some game of dice with a couple of very old men, and of course the familiar bunch of hippies from my own country, considerably longer-haired than anybody else, dirtier, and making far more noise. When they switched on a transistor and squatted on the cobbled stones behind me, I felt it was time to move.

I paid for my lemonade, and strolled to the end of the quay and back – the line upon line of fishing-boats would be colourful by day, and possibly the scene worth painting – and then I crossed the street, my eye caught by a glint of water inland, where a side-road appeared to end in a cul-de-sac. This must be the feature mentioned in the guidebook as the Bottomless Pool, much frequented and photographed by tourists in the high season. It was larger than I had expected, quite a sizeable lake, the water full of scum and floating debris, and I did not envy those who had the temerity to use the diving-board at the further end of it by day.

Then I saw the Mercedes. It was drawn up opposite a dimly-lit café, and there was no mistaking the hunched figure at the table, beer-bottles before him, the upright lady at his side, but to my surprise, and I may add disgust, he was not imbibing alone but appeared to be sharing his after-dinner carousal with a crowd of raucous fishermen at the adjoining table.

Clamour and laughter filled the air. They were evidently mocking him, Greek courtesy forgotten in their cups, while strains of song burst forth from some younger member of the clan, and suddenly he put out his hand and swept the empty bottles from his table on to the pavement, with the inevitable crash of broken glass and the accompanying cheers of his companions. I expected the local police to appear at any moment and break up the party, but there was no sign of authority. I did not care what happened to Stoll – a night in gaol might sober him up – but it was a wretched business for his wife. However, it wasn't my affair, and I was turning to go back to the quay when he staggered to his feet, applauded by the fishermen, and, lifting the remaining bottle from his table, swung it over his head. Then, with amazing dexterity for one in his condition, he pitched it like a discus-thrower into the lake. It must have missed me by a couple of feet, and he saw me duck. This was too much. I advanced towards him, livid with rage.

'What the hell are you playing at?' I shouted.

He stood before me, swaying on his feet. The laughter from the café ceased as his cronies watched with interest. I expected a flood of abuse, but Stoll's swollen face creased into a grin, and he lurched forward and patted me on the arm.

'Know something?' he said. 'If you hadn't been in the way I could have lobbed it into the centre of the God-damn pool. Which is more than any of those fellows could. Not a pureblooded Cretan amongst them. They're all of them God-damn Turks.'

I tried to shake him off, but he clung on to me with the effusive affection of the habitual drunkard who has suddenly found, or imagines he has found, a life-long friend.

'You're from the hotel, aren't you?' he hiccoughed. 'Don't deny it, buddy boy, I've got a good eye for faces. You're the fellow who paints all day on his God-damn porch. Well, I admire you for it. Know a bit about art myself. I might even buy your picture.'

His bonhomie was offensive, his attempt at patronage intolerable.

'I'm sorry,' I said stiffly, 'the picture is not for sale.'

'Oh, come off it,' he retorted. 'You artists are all the same. Play hard to get until someone offers 'em a darn good price. Take Charlie Gordon now . . .' He broke off, peering slyly into my face. 'Hang on, you didn't meet Charlie Gordon, did you?'

'No,' I said shortly, 'he was before my time.'

'That's right, that's right,' he agreed, 'poor fellow's dead. Drowned in the bay there, right under your rocks. At least, that's where they found him.'

His slit eyes were practically closed in his swollen face, but I knew he was watching for my reaction.

'Yes,' I said, 'so I understand. He wasn't an artist.'

'An artist?' Stoll repeated the word after me, then burst into a guffaw of laughter. 'No, he was a connoisseur, and I guess that means the same God-damn thing to a chap like me. Charlie Gordon, connoisseur. Well, it didn't do him much good in the end, did it?'

'No,' I said, 'obviously not.'

He was making an effort to pull himself together, and

still rocking on his feet he fumbled for a packet of cigarettes and a lighter. He lit one for himself, then offered me the packet. I shook my head, telling him I did not smoke. Then, greatly daring, I observed, 'I don't drink either.'

'Good for you,' he answered astonishingly, 'neither do I. The beer they sell you here is all piss anyway, and the wine is poison.' He looked over his shoulder to the group at the café and with a conspiratorial wink dragged me to the wall beside the pool.

'I told you all those bastards are Turks, and so they are,' he said, 'wine-drinking, coffee-drinking Turks. They haven't brewed the right stuff here for over five thousand years. They knew how to do it then.'

I remembered what the bar-tender had told me about the pigswill in his chalet. 'Is that so?' I enquired.

He winked again, and then his slit eyes widened, and I noticed that they were naturally bulbous and protuberant, a discoloured muddy brown with the whites red-flecked. 'Know something?' he whispered hoarsely. 'The scholars have got it all wrong. It was beer the Cretans drank here in the mountains, brewed from spruce and ivy, long before wine. Wine was discovered centuries later by the God-damn Greeks.'

He steadied himself, one hand on the wall, the other on my arm. Then he leant forward and was sick into the pool. I was very nearly sick myself.

'That's better,' he said, 'gets rid of the poison. Doesn't do to have poison in the system. Tell you what, we'll go back to the hotel and you shall come along and have a night-cap at our chalet. I've taken a fancy to you, Mr What's-your-Name. You've got the right ideas. Don't drink, don't smoke, and you paint pictures. What's your job?'

It was impossible to shake myself clear, and I was forced to let him tow me across the road. Luckily the group at the café had now dispersed, disappointed, no doubt, because we had not come to blows, and Mrs Stoll had climbed into the Mercedes and was sitting in the passenger seat in front.

'Don't take any notice of her,' he said. 'She's stone-deaf unless you bawl at her. Plenty of room at the back.'

'Thank you,' I said, 'I've got my own car on the quay.'

'Suit yourself,' he answered. 'Well, come on, tell me, Mr Artist, what's your job? An academician?'

I could have left it at that, but some pompous strain in me made me tell the truth, in the foolish hope that he would then consider me too dull to cultivate.

'I'm a teacher,' I said, 'in a boys' preparatory school.'

He stopped in his tracks, his wet mouth open wide in a delighted grin. 'Oh my God,' he shouted, 'that's rich, that's really rich. A God-damn tutor, a nurse to babes and sucklings. You're one of us, my buddy, you're one of us. And you've the nerve to tell me you've never brewed spruce and ivy!'

He was raving mad, of course, but at least this sudden burst of hilarity had made him free my arm, and he went on ahead of me to his car, shaking his head from side to side, his legs bearing his cumbersome body in a curious jog-trot, one-two . . . one-two . . . like a clumsy horse.

I watched him climb into the car beside his wife, and then I moved swiftly away to make for the safety of the quayside, but he had turned his car with surprising agility, and had caught up with me before I reached the corner of the street. He thrust his head out of the window, smiling still.

'Come and call on us, Mr Tutor, any time you like. You'll always find a welcome. Tell him so, Maud. Can't you see the fellow's shy?'

His bawling word of command echoed through the street. Strolling passers-by looked in our direction. The stiff, impassive face of Mrs Stoll peered over her husband's shoulder. She seemed quite unperturbed, as if nothing was wrong, as if driving in a foreign village beside a drunken husband was the most usual pastime in the world.

'Good evening,' she said in a voice without any expression. 'Pleased to meet you, Mr Tutor. Do call on us. Not after midnight. Chalet 38 . . .'

Stoll waved his hand, and the car went roaring up the street to cover the few kilometres to the hotel, while I followed behind, telling myself that this was one invitation I should never accept if my life depended on it.

It would not be true to say the encounter cast a blight on my holiday and put me off the place. A half-truth, perhaps. I was angry and disgusted, but only with the Stolls. I awoke refreshed after a good night's sleep to another brilliant day, and nothing seems so bad in the morning. I had only the one problem, which was to avoid Stoll and his equally half-witted wife. They were out in their boat all day, so this was easy. By dining early I could escape them in the dining-room. They never walked about the grounds, and meeting them face to face in the garden was not likely. If I happened to be on my balcony when they returned in the evening from fishing, and he turned his field-glasses in my direction, I would promptly disappear inside my chalet. In any event, with luck, he might have forgotten my existence, or, if that was too much to hope for, the memory of our evening's conversation might have passed from his mind. The episode had been unpleasant, even, in a curious sense, alarming, but I was not going to let it spoil the days that remained to me.

The boat had left its landing-stage by the time I came on to my balcony to have breakfast, and I intended to carry out my plan of exploring the coast with my painting gear, and, once absorbed in my hobby, could forget all about them. And I would not pass on to the management poor Gordon's scribbled card. I guessed now what had happened. The poor devil, without realising where his conversation in the bar would lead him, had been intrigued by Stoll's smattering of mythology and nonsense about ancient Crete, and, as an archaeologist, had thought further conversation might prove fruitful. He had accepted an invitation to visit Chalet 38 – the uncanny similarity of the words on the card and those spoken by Mrs Stoll still haunted me – though why he had chosen to swim across the bay instead of walking the slightly longer way by the rock path was a mystery. A touch of bravado, perhaps? Who knows? Once in Stoll's chalet he had been induced, poor victim, to drink some of the hell-brew offered by his host, which must have knocked all sense and judgement out of him, and when he took to the water once again, the carousal over, what followed was bound to happen. I only hoped he had been too far gone to panic, and sank instantly. Stoll had never come forward to give the facts, and that was that. Indeed, my theory of what had happened was based on intuition alone, coincidental scraps that appeared to fit, and prejudice. It was time to dismiss the whole thing from my mind and concentrate on the day ahead.

Or rather, days. My exploration along the coast westward, in the opposite direction from the harbour, proved even more successful than I had anticipated. I followed the winding road to the left of the hotel, and having climbed for several kilometres descended again from the hills to sea level, where the land on my right suddenly flattened out to what seemed to be a great stretch of dried marsh, sun-baked, putty-coloured, the dazzling blue sea affording a splendid contrast as it lapped the stretch of land on either side. Driving closer I saw that it was not marsh at all but salt flats, with narrow causeways running between them, the flats themselves contained by walls intersected by dykes to allow the sea-water to drain, leaving the salt behind. Here and there were the ruins of abandoned wind-mills, their rounded walls like castle keeps, and in a rough patch of ground a few hundred yards distant, and close to the sea, was a small church – I could see the minute cross on the roof shining in the sun. Then the salt flats ended abruptly, and the land rose once more to form the long, narrow isthmus of Spinalongha beyond.

I bumped the Volkswagen down to the track leading to the flats. The place was quite deserted. This, I decided, after viewing the scene from every angle, would be my pitch for the next few days. The ruined church in the fore-ground, the abandoned windmills beyond, the salt-flats on the left, and blue water rippling to the shore of the isth-mus on my right.

I set up my easel, planted my battered felt hat on my head, and forgot everything but the scene before me. Those three days on the salt-flats – for I repeated the expe-dition on successive days – were the high-spot of my holiday. Solitude and peace were absolute. I never saw a single soul. The occasional car wound its way along the coast road in the distance and then vanished. I broke off for sandwiches and lemonade, which I'd brought with me, and then, when the sun was hottest, rested by the ruined windmill. I returned to the hotel in the cool of the evening, had an early dinner, and then retired to my chalet to read until bedtime. A hermit at his prayers could not have wished for greater seclusion.

The fourth day, having completed two separate paint-ings from different angles, yet loath to leave my chosen territory, which had now become a personal stamping ground, I stacked my gear in the car and struck off on foot to the rising terrain of the isthmus, with the idea of choos-ing a new site for the following day. Height might give an added advantage. I toiled up the hill, fanning myself with my hat, for it was extremely hot, and was surprised when

I reached the summit to find how narrow was the isthmus, no more than a long neck of land with the sea immediately below me. Not the calm water that washed the salt-flats I had left behind, but the curling crests of the outer gulf itself, whipped by a northerly wind that nearly blew my hat out of my hand. A genius might have caught those varying shades on canvas – turquoise blending into Aegean blue with wine-deep shadows beneath – but not an amateur like myself. Besides, I could hardly stand upright. Canvas and easel would have instantly blown away.

I climbed downwards towards a clump of broom affording shelter, where I could rest for a few minutes and watch that curling sea, and it was then that I saw the boat. It was moored close to a small inlet where the land curved and the water was comparatively smooth. There was no mistaking the craft: it was theirs all right. The Greek they employed as crew was seated in the bows, with a fishing-line over the side, but from his lounging attitude the fishing did not seem to be serious, and I judged he was taking his siesta. He was the only occupant of the boat. I glanced directly beneath me to the spit of sand along the shore, and saw there was a rough stone building, more or less ruined, built against the cliff-face, possibly used at one time as a shelter for sheep or goats. There was a haversack and a picnic-basket lying by the entrance, and a coat. The Stolls must have landed earlier from the boat, although nosing the bows of the craft on to the shore must have been hazardous in the running sea, and were now taking their ease out of the wind. Perhaps Stoll was even brewing his peculiar mixture of spruce and ivy, with some goat-dung added for good measure, and this lonely spot on the isthmus of Spinalonga was his 'still'.

Suddenly the fellow in the boat sat up, and winding in his line he moved to the stern and stood there, watching the water. I saw something move, a form beneath the surface, and then the form itself emerged, head-piece, goggles, rubber suiting, aqualung and all. Then it was hidden from me by the Greek bending to assist the swimmer to remove his top-gear, and my attention was diverted to the ruined shelter on the shore. Something was standing in the entrance. I say 'something' because, doubtless owing to a trick of light, it had at first the shaggy appearance of a colt standing on its hind legs. Legs and even rump were covered with hair, and then I realised that it was Stoll himself, naked, his arms and chest as hairy as the rest of him. Only his swollen scarlet face proclaimed him for the man he was, with the enormous ears like saucers standing out from either side of his bald head. I had never in all my life seen a more revolting sight. He came out into the sunlight and looked towards the boat, and then, as if well pleased with himself and his world, strutted forward, pacing up and down the spit of sand before the ruined shelter with that curious movement I had noticed earlier in the village, not the rolling gait of a drunken man but a stumping jog-trot, arms akimbo, his chest thrust forward, his backside prominent behind him.

The swimmer, having discarded goggles and aqualung, was now coming into the beach with long leisurely strokes, still wearing flippers – I could see them thrash the surface like a giant fish. Then, flippers cast aside on the sand, the swimmer stood up, and despite the disguise of the rubber suiting I saw, with astonishment, that it was Mrs Stoll. She was carrying some sort of bag around her neck, and advancing up the sand to meet her strutting husband she lifted it over her head and gave it to him. I did not hear them exchange a word, and they went together to the hut and disappeared inside. As for the Greek, he had gone once more to the bows of the boat to resume his idle fishing.

I lay down under cover of the broom and waited. I would give them twenty minutes, half an hour, perhaps, then make my way back to the salt-flats and my car. As it happened, I did not have to wait so long. It was barely ten minutes before I heard a shout below me on the beach, and peering through the broom I saw that they were both standing on the spit of sand, haversack, picnic-basket, and flippers in hand. The Greek was already starting the engine, and immediately afterwards he began to pull up the anchor. Then he steered the boat slowly inshore, touching it beside a ledge of rock where the Stolls had installed themselves. They climbed aboard, and in another moment the Greek had turned the boat, and it was heading out to sea away from the sheltered inlet and into the gulf. Then it rounded the point and was out of my sight.

Curiosity was too much for me. I scrambled down the cliff on to the sand and made straight for the ruined shelter. As I thought, it had been a haven for goats; the muddied floor reeked, and their droppings were everywhere. In a corner, though, a clearing had been made, and there were planks of wood, forming a sort of shelf. The inevitable beer bottles were stacked beneath this, but whether they had contained the local brew or Stoll's own poison I could not tell. The shelf itself held odds and ends of pottery, as though someone had been digging in a rubbish dump and had turned up broken pieces of discarded household junk. There was no earth upon them, though; they were scaled with barnacles, and some of them were damp, and it suddenly occurred to me that these were what archaeologists call 'sherds', and came from the sea-bed. Mrs Stoll had been exploring, and exploring under-water, whether for shells or for something of greater interest I did not know, and these pieces scattered here were throwouts, of no use, and so neither she nor her husband had botherd to remove them. I am no judge of these things, and after looking around me, and finding nothing of further interest, I left the ruin.

The move was a fatal one. As I turned to climb the cliff I heard the throb of an engine, and the boat had returned once more, to cruise along the shore, so I judged from its position. All three heads were turned in my direction, and inevitably the squat figure in the stern had field-glasses poised. He would have no difficulty, I feared, in distinguishing who it was that had just left the ruined shelter and was struggling up the cliff to the hill above.

I did not look back but went on climbing, my hat pulled down well over my brows in the vain hope that it might afford some sort of concealment. After all, I might have been any tourist who had happened to be at that particular spot at that particular time. Nevertheless, I feared recognition was inevitable. I tramped back to the car on the salt-flats, tired, breathless and thoroughly irritated. I wished I had never decided to explore the further side of the peninsula. The Stolls would think I had been spying upon them, which indeed was true. My pleasure in the day was spoilt. I decided to pack it in and go back to the hotel. Luck was against me, though, for I had hardly turned on to the track leading from the marsh to the road when I noticed that one of my tyres was flat. By the time I had put on the spare wheel – for I am ham-fisted at all mechanical jobs – forty minutes had gone by.

My disgruntled mood did not improve, when at last I reached the hotel, to see that the Stolls had beaten me to it. Their boat was already at its moorings beside the landing-stage, and Stoll himself was sitting on his balcony with field-glasses trained upon my chalet. I stumped up the steps feeling as self-conscious as someone under a television camera and went into my quarters, closing the shutters behind me. I was taking a bath when the telephone rang.

'Yes?' Towel round the middle, dripping hands, it could not have rung at a more inconvenient moment.

'That you, Mr Tutor-boy?'

The rasping, wheezing voice was unmistakable. He did not sound drunk though.

'This is Timothy Grey,' I replied stiffly.

'Grey or Black, it's all the same to me,' he said. His tone was unpleasant, hostile. 'You were out on Spinalongha this afternoon. Correct?'

'I was walking on the peninsula,' I told him. 'I don't know why you should be interested.'

'Oh, stuff it up,' he answered, 'you can't fool me. You're just like the other fellow. You're nothing but a God-damn spy. Well, let me tell you this. The wreck was clean-picked centuries ago.'

'I don't know what you're talking about,' I said. 'What wreck?'

There was a moment's pause. He muttered something under his breath, whether to himself or to his wife I could not tell, but when he resumed speaking his tone had moderated, something of pseudo-bonhomie had returned.

'O.K . . . O.K. Tutor-boy,' he said. 'We won't argue the point. Let us say you and I share an interest. Schoolmasters, university professors, college lecturers, we're all alike under the skin, and above it too sometimes.' His low chuckle was offensive. 'Don't panic, I won't give you away,' he continued. 'I've taken a fancy to you, as I told you the other night. You want something for your God-darn school museum, correct? Something you can show the pretty lads and your colleagues, too? Fine. Agreed. I've got just the thing. You call round here later this evening, and I'll make you a present of it. I don't want your God-damn money . . .' He broke off, chuckling again, and Mrs Stoll must have made some remark, for he added, 'That's right, that's right. We'll have a cosy little party, just the three of us. My wife's taken quite a fancy to you too.'

The towel round my middle slipped to the floor, leaving

me naked. I felt vulnerable for no reason at all. And the patronising, insinuating voice infuriated me.

'Mr Stoll,' I said, 'I'm not a collector for schools, colleges, or museums. I'm not interested in antiquities. I am here on holiday to paint, for my own pleasure, and quite frankly I have no intention of calling upon you or any other visitor at the hotel. Good evening.'

I slammed down the receiver and went back to the bathroom. Infernal impudence. Loathsome man. The question was, would he now leave me alone, or would he keep his glasses trained on my balcony until he saw me go up to the hotel for dinner, and then follow me, wife in tow, to the dining-room? Surely he would not dare to resume the conversation in front of waiters and guests? If I guessed his intentions aright, he wanted to buy my silence by fobbing me off with some gift. Those day-long fishing expeditions of his were a mask for under-water exploration – hence his allusion to a wreck – during which he hoped to find, possibly had found already, objects of value that he intended to smuggle out of Crete. Doubtless he had succeeded in doing this the preceding year, and the Greek boatman would be well paid for holding his tongue.

This season, however, it had not worked to plan. My unfortunate predecessor at Chalet 62, Charles Gordon, himself an expert in antiquities, had grown suspicious. Stoll's allusion, 'You're like the other fellow. Nothing but a God-damn spy', made this plain. What if Gordon had received an invitation to Chalet 38, not to drink the spurious beer but to inspect Stoll's collection and be offered a bribe for keeping silent? Had he refused, threatening to expose Stoll? Did he really drown accidentally, or had Stoll's wife followed him down into the water in her rubber-suit and mask and flippers, and then, once beneath the surface . . . ?

My imagination was running away with me. I had no proof of anything. All I knew was that nothing in the world would get me to Stoll's chalet, and indeed, if he attempted to pester me again, I should have to tell the whole story to the management.

I changed for dinner, then opened my shutters a fraction and stood behind them, looking out towards his chalet. The light shone on his balcony, for it was already dusk, but he himself had disappeared. I stepped outside, locking the shutters behind me, and walked up the garden to the hotel.

I was just about to go through to the reception hall from the terrace when I saw Stoll and his wife sitting on a couple of chairs inside, guarding, as it were, the passage-way to lounge and dining-room. If I wanted to eat I had to pass them. Right, I thought. You can sit there all evening waiting. I went back along the terrace, and circling the hotel by the kitchens went round to the car park and got into the Volkswagen. I would have dinner down in the village, and damn the extra expense. I drove off in a fury, found an obscure taverna well away from the harbour itself, and instead of the three-course hotel meal I had been looking forward to on my en pension terms – for I was hungry after my day in the open and meagre sandwiches on the salt-flats – I was obliged to content myself with an omelette, an orange and a cup of coffee.

It was after ten when I arrived back in the hotel. I parked the car, and skirting the kitchen quarters once again made my way furtively down the garden path to my chalet, letting myself in through the shutters like a thief. The light was still shining on Stoll's balcony, and by this time he was doubtless deep in his cups. If there was any trouble with him the next day I would definitely go to the management.

I undressed and lay reading in bed until after midnight, then, feeling sleepy, switched out my light and went across the room to open the shutters, for the air felt stuffy and close. I stood for a moment looking out across the bay. The chalet lights were all extinguished except for one. Stoll's, of course. His balcony light cast a yellow streak on the water beside his landing-stage. The water rippled, yet there was no wind. Then I saw it. I mean, the snorkel. The little pipe was caught an instant in the yellow gleam, but before I lost it I knew that it was heading in a direct course for the rocks beneath my chalet. I waited. Nothing happened, there was no sound, no further ripple on the water. Perhaps she did this every evening. Perhaps it was routine, and while I was lying on my bed reading, oblivious of the world outside, she had been treading water close to the rocks. The thought was discomforting, to say the least of it, that regularly after midnight she left her besotted husband asleep over his hell-brew of spruce and ivy and came herself, his under-water-partner, in her black-seal rubber suit, her mask, her flippers, to spy upon Chalet 62. And on this night in particular, after the telephone conversation and my refusal to visit them, coupled with my new theory as to the fate of my predecessor, her presence in my immediate vicinity was more than ominous, it was threatening.

Suddenly, out of the dark stillness to my right, the snorkel-pipe was caught in a finger-thread of light from my own balcony. Now it was almost immediately below me. I panicked, turned, and fled inside my room, closing the shutters fast. I switched off the balcony light and stood against the wall between my bedroom and bathroom, listening. The soft air filtered through the shutters beside me. It seemed an eternity before the sound I expected, dreaded, came to my ears. A kind of swishing movement from the balcony, a fumbling of hands, and heavy breathing. I could see nothing from where I stood against the wall, but the sounds came through the chinks in the shutters, and I knew she was there. I knew she was holding on to the hasp, and the water was dripping from the skin-tight rubber suit, and that even if I shouted, 'What do you want?' she would not hear. No deaf-aids under water, no mechanical device for soundless ears. Whatever she did by night must be done by sight, by touch.

She began to rattle on the shutters. I took no notice. She rattled again. Then she found the bell, and the shrill summons pierced the air above my head with all the intensity of a dentist's drill upon a nerve. She rang three times. Then silence. No more rattling of the shutters. No more breathing. She might yet be crouching on the balcony, the water dripping from the black rubber suit, waiting for me to lose patience, to emerge.

I crept away from the wall and sat down on the bed. There was not a sound from the balcony. Boldly I switched on my bedside light, half expecting the rattling of the shutters to begin again, or the sharp ping of the bell. Nothing happened, though. I looked at my watch. It was half-past twelve. I sat there hunched on my bed, my mind that had been so heavy with sleep now horribly awake, full of foreboding, my dread of that sleek black figure increasing minute by minute so that all sense and reason seemed to desert me, and my dread was the more intense and irrational because the figure in the rubber suit was female. What did she want?

I sat there for an hour or more until reason took possession once again. She must have gone. I got up from the bed and went to the shutters and listened. There wasn't a sound. Only the lapping of water beneath the rocks. Gently, very gently, I opened the hasp and peered through the shutters. Nobody was there. I opened them wider and stepped on to the balcony. I looked out across the bay, and there was no longer any light shining from the balcony of No. 38. The little pool of water beneath my shutters was evidence enough of the figure that had stood there an hour ago, and the wet footmarks leading down the steps towards the rocks suggested she had gone the way she came. I breathed a sigh of relief. Now I could sleep in peace.

It was only then that I saw the object at my feet, lying close to the shutter's base. I bent and picked it up. It was a small package, wrapped in some sort of waterproof cloth. I took it inside and examined it, sitting on the bed. Foolish suspicions of plastic bombs came to my mind, but surely a journey underwater would neutralise the lethal effect? The package was sewn about with twine, criss-crossed. It felt quite light. I remembered the old classical proverb, 'Beware of the Greeks when they bear gifts'. But the Stolls were not Greeks, and, whatever lost Atlantis they might have plundered, explosives did not form part of the treasure-trove of that vanished continent.

I cut the twine with a pair of nail-scissors, then unthreaded it piece by piece and unfolded the waterproof wrapping. A layer of finely-meshed net concealed the object within, and, this unravelled, the final token itself lay in my open hand. It was a small jug, reddish in colour, with a handle on either side for safe holding. I had seen this sort of object before – the correct name, I believe, is rhyton – displayed behind glass cases in museums. The body of the jug had been shaped cunningly and brilliantly into a man's face, with upstanding ears like scallop-shells, while protruding eyes and bulbous nose stood out above the leering, open mouth, the moustache drooping to the rounded beard that formed the base. At the top, between the handles, were the upright figures of three strutting men, their faces similar to that upon the jug, but here human resemblance ended, for they had neither hands nor feet but hooves, and from each of their hairy rumps extended a horse's tail.

I turned the object over. The same face leered at me from the other side. The same three figures strutted at the top. There was no crack, no blemish that I could see, except a faint mark on the lip. I looked inside the jug and saw a note lying on the bottom. The opening was too small for my hand, so I shook it out. The note was a plain white card, with words typed upon it. It read: 'Silenos, earth-born satyr, half-horse, half-man, who, unable to distinguish truth from falsehood, reared Dionysus, god of intoxication, as a girl in a Cretan cave, then became his drunken tutor and companion.'

That was all. Nothing more. I put the note back inside the jug, and the jug on the table at the far end of the room. Even then the lewd mocking face leered back at me, and the three strutting figures of the horsemen stood out in bold relief across the top. I was too weary to wrap it up again. I covered it with my jacket and climbed back into bed. In the morning I would cope with the laborious task of packing it up and getting my waiter to take it across to Chalet 38. Stoll could keep his rhyton – heaven knew what the value might be – and good luck to him. I wanted no part of it.

Exhausted, I fell asleep, but, oh God, to no oblivion. The dreams which came, and from which I struggled to awaken, but in vain, belonged to some other unknown world horribly intermingled with my own. Term had started, but the school in which I taught was on a mountain top hemmed in by forest, though the school buildings were the same and the classroom was my own. My boys, all of them familiar faces, lads I knew, wore vine-leaves in their hair, and had a strange, unearthly beauty both endearing and corrupt. They ran towards me, smiling, and I put my arms about them, and the pleasure they gave me was insidious and sweet, never before experienced, never before imagined, the man who pranced in their midst and played with them was not myself, not the self I knew, but a demon shadow emerging from a jug, strutting in his conceit as Stoll had done upon the spit of sand at Spinalongha.

I awoke after what seemed like centuries of time, and

indeed broad daylight seeped through the shutters, and it was a quarter to ten. My head was throbbing. I felt sick, exhausted. I rang for coffee, and looked out across the bay. The boat was at its moorings. The Stolls had not gone fishing. Usually they were away by nine. I took the jug from under my coat, and with fumbling hands began to wrap it up in the net and waterproof packing. I had made a botched job of it when the waiter came on to the balcony with my breakfast tray. He wished me good morning with his usual smile.

'I wonder,' I said, 'if you would do me a favour.'

'You are welcome, sir,' he replied.

'It concerns Mr Stoll,' I went on. 'I believe he has Chalet 38 across the bay. He usually goes fishing every day, but I see his boat is still at the landing-stage.'

'That is not surprising,' the waiter smiled. 'Mr and Mrs Stoll left this morning by car.'

'I see. Do you know when they will be back?'

'They will not be back, sir. They have left for good. They are driving to the airport en route for Athens. The boat is probably vacant now if you wish to hire it.'

He went down the steps into the garden, and the jar in its waterproof packing was still lying beside the breakfast tray.

The sun was already fierce upon my balcony. It was going to be a scorching day, too hot to paint. And anyway, I wasn't in the mood. The events of the night before had left me tired, jaded, with a curious sapped feeling due not so much to the intruder beyond my shutters as to those interminable dreams. I might be free of the Stolls themselves, but not of their legacy.

I unwrapped it once again and turned it over in my hands. The leering, mocking face repelled me; its resemblance to the human Stoll was not pure fancy but compelling, sinister, doubtless his very reason for palming it off on me – I remembered the chuckle down the telephone – and if he possessed treasures of equal value to this rhyton, or even greater, then one object the less would not bother him. He would have a problem getting them through Customs, especially in Athens. The penalties were enormous for this sort of thing. Doubtless he had his contacts, knew what to do.

I stared at the dancing figures near the top of the jar, and once more I was struck by their likeness to the strutting Stoll on the shore of Spinalongha, his naked, hairy form, his protruding rump. Part man, part horse, a satyr . . . 'Silenos, drunken tutor to the god Dionysus.'

The jar was horrible, evil. Small wonder that my dreams had been distorted, utterly foreign to my nature. But not perhaps to Stoll's? Could it be that he too had realised its bestiality, but not until too late? The bar-tender had told me that it was only this year he had gone to pieces, taken to drink. There must be some link between his alcoholism and the finding of the jar. One thing was very evident, I must get rid of it – but how? If I took it to the management questions would be asked. They might not believe my story about its being dumped on my balcony the night before; they might suspect that I had taken it from some archaeological site, and then had second thoughts about trying to smuggle it out of the country or dispose of it somewhere on the island. So what? Drive along the coast and chuck it away, a rhyton centuries old and possibly priceless?

I wrapped it carefully in my jacket pocket and walked up the garden to the hotel. The bar was empty, the bar-tender behind his counter polishing glasses. I sat down on a stool in front of him and ordered a mineral water.

'No expedition today, sir?' he enquired.

'Not yet,' I said. 'I may go out later.'

'A cool dip in the sea and a siesta on the balcony,' he suggested, 'and by the way, sir, I have something for you.'

He bent down and brought out a small screw-topped bottle filled with what appeared to be bitter lemon.

'Left here last evening with Mr Stoll's compliments,' he said. 'He waited for you in the bar until nearly midnight, but you never came. So I promised to hand it over when you did.'

I looked at it suspiciously. 'What is it?' I asked.

The bar-tender smiled. 'Some of his chalet home-brew,' he said. 'It's quite harmless, he gave me a bottle for myself and my wife. She says it's nothing but lemonade. The real smelling stuff must have been thrown away. Try it.' He had poured some into my mineral water before I could stop him.

Hesitant, wary, I dipped my finger into the glass and tasted it. It was like the barley-water my mother used to make when I was a child. And equally tasteless. And yet . . . it left a sort of aftermath on the palate and the tongue. Not as sweet as honey nor as sharp as grapes, but pleasant, like the smell of raisins under the sun, curiously blended with the ears of ripening corn.

'Oh well,' I said, 'here's to the improved health of Mr Stoll,' and I drank my medicine like a man.

'I know one thing,' said the bar-tender, 'I've lost my best customer. They went away early this morning.'

'Yes,' I said, 'so my waiter informed me.'

'The best thing Mrs Stoll could do would be to get him into hospital,' the bar-tender continued. 'Her husband's a sick man, and it's not just the drink.'

'What do you mean?'

He tapped his forehead. 'Something wrong up here,' he said. 'You could see for yourself how he acted. Something on his mind. Some sort of obsession. I rather doubt we shall see them again next year.'

I sipped my mineral water, which was undoubtedly improved by the barley taste.

'What was his profession?' I asked.

'Mr Stoll? Well, he told me he had been professor of classics in some American university, but you never could tell if he was speaking the truth or not. Mrs Stoll paid the bills here, hired the boatman, arranged everything. Though he swore at her in public he seemed to depend on her. I sometimes wondered, though . . .'

He broke off.

'Wondered what?' I enquired.

'Well . . . She had a lot to put up with. I've seen her look at him sometimes, and it wasn't with love. Women of her age must seek some sort of satisfaction out of life. Perhaps she found it on the side while he indulged his passion for liquor and antiques. He had picked up quite a few items in Greece, and around the islands and here in Crete. It's not too difficult if you know the ropes.'

He winked. I nodded, and ordered another mineral water. The warm atmosphere in the bar had given me a thirst.

'Are there any lesser known sites along the coast?' I asked. 'I mean, places they might have gone ashore to from the boat?'

It may have been my fancy, but I thought he avoided my eye.

'I hardly know, sir,' he said. 'I dare say there are, but they would have custodians of some sort. I doubt if there are any places the authorities don't know about.'

'What about wrecks?' I pursued. 'Vessels that might have been sunk centuries ago, and are now lying on the sea bottom?'

He shrugged his shoulders. 'There are always local rumours,' he said casually, 'stories that get handed down through generations. But it's mostly superstition. I've never believed in them myself, and I don't know anybody with education who does.'

He was silent for a moment, polishing a glass. I wondered

if I had said too much. 'We all know small objects are discovered from time to time,' he murmured, 'and they can
be of great value. They get smuggled out of the country,
or if too much risk is involved they can be disposed of
locally to experts and a good price paid. I have a cousin in
the village connected with the local museum. He owns the
café opposite the Bottomless Pool. Mr Stoll used to patro-
nise him. Papitos is the name. As a matter of fact, the boat
hired by Mr Stoll belongs to my cousin; he lets it out on
hire to the visitors here at the hotel.'

'I see.'

'But there . . . You are not a collector, sir, and you're not
interested in antiques.'

'No,' I said, 'I am not a collector.'

I got up from the stool and bade him good morning. I
wondered if the small package in my pocket made a bulge.

I went out of the bar and strolled on to the terrace. Nagging curiosity made me wander down to the landing-stage
below the Stolls' chalet. The chalet itself had evidently been
swept and tidied, the balcony cleared, the shutters closed.
No trace remained of the last occupants. Before the day was
over, in all probability, it would be opened for some English
family who would strew the place with bathing-suits.

The boat was at its moorings, and the Greek hand was
swabbing down the sides. I looked out across the bay to
my own chalet on the opposite side and saw it, for the first
time, from Stoll's viewpoint. As he stood there, peering
through his field-glasses, it seemed clearer to me than ever
before that he must have taken me for an interloper, a spy –
possibly, even, someone sent out from England to enquire
into the true circumstances of Charles Gordon's death.
Was the gift of the jar, the night before departure, a gesture
of defiance? A bribe? Or a curse?

Then the Greek fellow on the boat stood up and faced
towards me. It was not the regular boatman, but another

one. I had not realised this before when his back was turned. The man who used to accompany the Stolls had been younger, dark, and this was an older chap altogether. I remembered what the bar-tender had told me about the boat belonging to his cousin, Papitos, who owned the café in the village by the Bottomless Pool.

'Excuse me,' I called, 'are you the owner of the boat?'

The man climbed on to the landing-stage and stood before me.

'Nicolai Papitos is my brother,' he said. 'You want to go for trip round the bay? Plenty good fish outside. No wind today. Sea very calm.'

'I don't want to fish,' I told him. 'I wouldn't mind an outing for an hour or so. How much does it cost?'

He gave me the sum in drachmae, and I did a quick reckoning and made it out to be not more than two pound for the hour, though it would doubtless be double that sum to round the point and go along the coast as far as that spit of sand on the isthmus of Spinalongha. I took out my wallet to see if I had the necessary notes or whether I should have to return to the reception desk and cash a traveller's cheque.

'You charge to hotel,' he said quickly, evidently reading my thoughts. 'The cost go on your bill.'

This decided me. Damn it all, my extras had been moderate to date.

'Very well,' I said, 'I'll hire the boat for a couple of hours.'

It was a curious sensation to be chug-chugging across the bay as the Stolls had done so many times, the line of chalets in my wake, the harbour astern on my right and the blue waters of the open gulf ahead. I had no clear plan in mind. It was just that, for some inexplicable reason, I felt myself drawn towards that inlet near the shore where the boat had been anchored on the previous day. 'The wreck was picked clean centuries ago . . .' Those had been

Stoll's words. Was he lying? Or could it be that day after day, through the past weeks, that particular spot had been his hunting-ground, and his wife, diving, had brought the dripping treasure from its sea-bed to his grasping hands? We rounded the point, and inevitably, away from the sheltering arm that had hitherto encompassed us, the breeze appeared to freshen, the boat became more lively as the bows struck the short curling seas.

The long isthmus of Spinalongha lay ahead of us to the left, and I had some difficulty in explaining to my helmsman that I did not want him to steer into the comparative tranquillity of the waters bordering the salt-flats, but to continue along the more exposed outward shores of the isthmus bordering the open sea.

'You want to fish?' he shouted above the roar of the engine. 'You find very good fish in there,' pointing to my flats of yesterday.

'No, no,' I shouted back, 'further on along the coast.'

He shrugged. He couldn't believe I had no desire to fish, and I wondered, when we reached our destination, what possible excuse I could make for heading the boat inshore and anchoring, unless – and this seemed plausible enough – I pleaded that the motion of the boat was proving too much for me.

The hills I had climbed yesterday swung into sight above the bows, and then, rounding a neck of land, the inlet itself, the ruined shepherd's hut close to the shore.

'In there,' I pointed. 'Anchor close to the shore.'

He stared at me, puzzled, and shook his head. 'No good,' he shouted, 'too many rocks.'

'Nonsense,' I yelled. 'I saw some people from the hotel anchored here yesterday.'

Suddenly he slowed the engine, so that my voice rang out foolishly on the air. The boat danced up and down in the troughs of the short seas.

'Not a good place to anchor,' he repeated doggedly. 'Wreck there, fouling the ground.'

So there was a wreck . . . I felt a mounting excitement, and I was not to be put off.

'I don't know anything about that,' I replied, with equal determination, 'but this boat did anchor here, just by the inlet, I saw it myself.'

He muttered something to himself, and made the sign of the cross.

'And if I lose the anchor?' he said. 'What do I say to my brother Nicolai?'

He was nosing the boat gently, very gently, towards the inlet, and then, cursing under his breath, he went forward to the bows and threw the anchor overboard. He waited until it held, then returned and switched off the engine.

'If you want to go in close, you must take the dinghy,' he said sulkily. 'I blow it up for you, yes?'

He went forward once again, and dragged out one of those inflatable rubber affairs they use on air-sea rescue craft.

'Very well,' I said, 'I'll take the dinghy.'

In point of fact, it suited my purpose better. I could paddle close inshore, and would not have him breathing over my shoulder. At the same time, I couldn't forbear a slight prick to his pride.

'The man in charge of the boat yesterday anchored further in without mishap,' I told him.

My helmsman paused in the act of inflating the dinghy.

'If he like to risk my brother's boat that is his affair,' he said shortly. 'I have charge of it today. Other fellow not turn up for work this morning, so he lose his job. I do not want to lose mine.'

I made no reply. If the other fellow had lost his job it was probably because he had pocketed too many tips from Stoll.

The dinghy inflated and in the water, I climbed into it gingerly and began to paddle myself towards the shore. Luckily there was no run upon the spit of sand, and I was able to land successfully and pull the dinghy after me. I noticed that my helmsman was watching me with some interest from his safe anchorage, then, once he perceived that the dinghy was unlikely to come to harm, he turned his back and squatted in the bows of the boat, shoulders humped in protest, meditating, no doubt, upon the folly of English visitors.

My reason for landing was that I wanted to judge, from the shore, the exact spot where the boat had anchored yesterday. It was as I thought. Perhaps a hundred yards to the left of where we had anchored today, and closer inshore. The sea was smooth enough, I could navigate it perfectly in the rubber dinghy. I glanced towards the shepherd's hut, and saw my footprints of the day before. There were other footprints too. Fresh ones. The sand in front of the hut had been disturbed. It was as though something had lain there, and then been dragged to the water's edge where I stood now. The goatherd himself, perhaps, had visited the place with his flock earlier that morning.

I crossed over to the hut and looked inside. Curious . . . The little pile of rubble, odds and ends of pottery, had gone. The empty bottles still stood in the far corner, and three more had been added to their number, one of them half-full. It was warm inside the hut, and I was sweating. The sun had been beating down on my bare head for nearly an hour – like a fool I had left my hat back in the chalet, not having prepared myself for this expedition – and I was seized with an intolerable thirst. I had acted on impulse, and was paying for it now. It was, in retrospect, an idiotic thing to have done. I might become completely dehydrated, pass out with heat-stroke. The half-bottle of beer would be better than nothing.

I did not fancy drinking from it after the goatherd, if it was indeed he who had brought it here; these fellows were none too clean. Then I remembered the jar in my pocket. Well, it would at least serve a purpose. I pulled the package out of its wrappings and poured the beer into it. It was only after I had swallowed the first draught that I realised it wasn't beer at all. It was barley-water. It was the same home-brewed stuff that Stoll had left for me in the bar. Did the locals, then, drink it too? It was innocuous enough. I knew that; the bar-tender had tasted it himself, and so had his wife.

When I had finished the bottle I examined the jar once again. I don't know how it was, but somehow the leering face no longer seemed so lewd. It had a certain dignity that had escaped me before. The beard, for instance. The beard was shaped to perfection around the base – whoever had fashioned it was a master of his craft. I wondered whether Socrates had looked thus when he strolled in the Athenian agora with his pupils and discoursed on life. He could have done. And his pupils may not necessarily have been the young men whom Plato said they were, but of a tenderer age, like my lads at school, like those youngsters of eleven and twelve who had smiled upon me in my dreams last night.

I felt the scalloped ears, the rounded nose, the full soft lips of the tutor Silenos upon the jar, the eyes no longer protruding but questioning, appealing, and even the naked horsemen on the top had grown in grace. It seemed to me now they were not strutting in conceit but dancing with linked hands, filled with a gay abandon, a pleasing, wanton joy. It must have been my fear of the midnight intruder that had made me look upon the jar with such distaste.

I put it back in my pocket, and walked out of the hut and down the spit of beach to the rubber dinghy. Supposing I went to the fellow Papitos who had connections with the local museum, and asked him to value the jar? Supposing it was worth hundreds, thousands, and he could dispose of it for me, or tell me of a contact in London? Stoll must be doing this all the time, and getting away with it. Or so the bar-tender had hinted . . . I climbed into the dinghy and began to paddle away from the shore, thinking of the difference between a man like Stoll, with all his wealth, and myself. There he was, a brute with a skin so thick you couldn't pierce it with a spear, and his shelves back at home in the States loaded with loot. Whereas I . . . Teaching small boys on an inadequate salary, and all for what? Moralists said that money made no difference to happiness, but they were wrong. If I had a quarter of the Stolls' wealth I could retire, live abroad, on a Greek island, perhaps, and winter in some studio in Athens or Rome. A whole new way of life would open up, and just at the right moment too, before I touched middle-age.

I pulled out from the shore and made for the spot where I judged the boat to have anchored the day before. Then I let the dinghy rest, pulled in my paddles and stared down into the water. The colour was pale green, translucent, yet surely fathoms deep, for, as I looked down to the golden sands beneath, the sea-bed had all the tranquillity of another world, remote from the one I knew. A shoal of fish, silver-bright and gleaming, wriggled their way towards a tress of coral hair that might have graced Aphrodite, but was seaweed moving gently in whatever currents lapped the shore. Pebbles that on land would have been no more than rounded stones were brilliant here as jewels. The breeze that rippled the gulf beyond the anchored boat would never touch these depths, but only the surface of the water, and as the dinghy floated on, circling slowly without pull of wind or tide, I wondered whether it was the motion in itself that had drawn the unhearing Mrs Stoll to under-water swimming. Treasure was the excuse, to satisfy her husband's greed, but down there, in the depths, she would escape from a way of life that must have been unbearable.

Then I looked up at the hills above the retreating spit of sand, and I saw something flash. It was a ray of sunlight upon glass, and the glass moved. Someone was watching me through field-glasses. I rested upon my paddles and stared. Two figures moved stealthily away over the brow of the hill, but I recognised them instantly. One was Mrs Stoll, the other the Greek fellow who had acted as their crew. I glanced over my shoulder to the anchored boat. My helmsman was still staring out to sea. He had seen nothing.

The footsteps outside the hut were now explained. Mrs Stoll, the boatman in tow, had paid a final visit to the hut to clear the rubble, and now, their mission accomplished, they would drive on to the airport to catch the afternoon plane to Athens, their journey made several miles longer by the detour along the coast road. And Stoll himself? Asleep, no doubt, at the back of the car upon the salt-flats, awaiting their return.

The sight of that woman once again gave me a profound distaste for my expedition. I wished I had not come. And my helmsman had spoken the truth; the dinghy was now floating above rock. A ridge must run out here from the shore in a single reef. The sand had darkened, changed in texture, become grey. I peered closer into the water, cupping my eyes with my hands, and suddenly I saw the vast encrusted anchor, the shells and barnacles of centuries upon its spokes, and as the dinghy drifted on the bones of the long-buried craft itself appeared, broken, sparless, her decks, if decks there had been, long since dismembered or destroyed.

Stoll had been right: her bones had been picked clean. Nothing of any value could now remain upon that skeleton. No pitchers, no jars, no gleaming coins. A momentary breeze rippled the water, and when it became clear again and all was still I saw the second anchor by the skeleton bows, and a body, arms outstretched, legs imprisoned in the anchor's jaws. The motion of the water gave the body life, as though, in some desperate fashion, it still struggled for release, but, trapped as it was, escape would never come. The days and nights would follow, months and years, and slowly the flesh would dissolve, leaving the frame impaled upon the spikes.

The body was Stoll's, head, trunk, limbs grotesque, inhuman, as they swayed backwards and forwards at the bidding of the current.

I looked up once more to the crest of the hill, but the two figures had long since vanished, and in an appalling flash of intuition a picture of what had happened became vivid: Stoll strutting on the spit of sand, the half-bottle raised to his lips, and then they struck him down and dragged him to the water's edge, and it was his wife who towed him, drowning, to his final resting-place beneath the surface, there below me, impaled on the crusted anchor. I was sole witness to his fate, and no matter what lies she told to account for his disappearance I would remain silent; it was not my responsibility; guilt might increasingly haunt me, but I must never become involved.

I heard the sound of something choking beside me – I realise now it was myself, in horror and in fear – and I struck at the water with my paddles and started pulling away from the wreck back to the boat. As I did so my arm brushed against the jar in my pocket, and in sudden panic I dragged it forth and flung it overboard. Even as I did so, I knew the gesture was in vain. It did not sink immediately but remained bobbing on the surface, then slowly filled with that green translucent sea, pale as the barley liquid laced with spruce and ivy. Not innocuous but evil, stifling conscience, dulling intellect, the hell-brew of the smiling god Dionysus, which turned his followers into drunken sots, would claim another victim before long. The eyes in the swollen face stared up at me, and they were not only those of Silenos the satyr tutor, and of the drowned Stoll, but my own as well, as I should see them soon reflected in a mirror. They seemed to hold all knowledge in their depths, and all despair.

A Border-Line Case

He had been asleep for about ten minutes. Certainly no longer. Shelagh had brought up some of the old photograph albums from the study to amuse her father, and they had been laughing and going through them together. He seemed so much better. The nurse had felt free to go off duty for the afternoon and take a walk, leaving her patient in the care of his daughter, while Mrs Money herself had slipped off in the car to the village to have her hair done. The doctor had reassured them all that the crisis was past; it was just a matter of rest and quiet, and taking things easy.

Shelagh was standing by the window looking down into the garden. She would remain at home, of course, as long as her father wanted her – indeed, she could not bear to leave him if there was any doubt about his condition. It was only that, if she turned down the offer the Theatre Group had made to her of playing the lead in their forthcoming series of Shakespeare plays, the chance might not come her way again. Rosalind . . . Portia . . . Viola – Viola surely the greatest fun of all. The yearning heart concealed beneath a cloak of dissimulation, the whole business of deception whetting appetite.

Unconsciously she smiled, pushing her hair behind her ears, tilting her head, one hand on her hip, apeing Cesario, and she heard a sudden movement from the bed and saw her father struggling to sit upright. He was staring at her, an expression of horror and disbelief upon his face, and he cried out, 'Oh, no . . . Oh, Jinnie . . . Oh, my God!' and as she ran to his side, saying to him, 'What is it, darling, what's wrong?' he tried to wave her aside, shaking his head, and then he collapsed backwards on his pillows, and she knew that he was dead.

She ran out of the room, calling for the nurse, then remembered that she had gone for a walk. She could have gone across the fields, anywhere. Shelagh rushed downstairs to find her mother, but the house was empty, and the garage doors were wide open – her mother must have gone somewhere in the car. Why? What for? She had never said she was going out. Shelagh seized the telephone in the hall with shaking hands and dialled the doctor's number, but when the answering click came it was not the doctor himself but his recorded voice, toneless, automatic, saying, 'This is Doctor Dray speaking. I shall not be available until five o'clock. Your message will be recorded. Please start now . . .', and there was a ticking sound, just as when one rang to know the time and the voice said, 'At the third stroke it will be two, forty-two, and twenty seconds . . .'

Shelagh flung down the receiver and began to search the telephone directory feverishly for the number of Doctor Dray's partner, a young man lately joined the practice – she did not even know him – and this time a live voice answered, a woman. There was the sound of a child crying in the distance and a radio blaring, and she heard the woman shout impatiently at the child to be quiet.

'This is Shelagh Money speaking, of Whitegates, Great Marsden. Please ask the doctor to come at once, I think my father has just died. The nurse is out and I'm alone in the house. I can't get Doctor Dray.'

She heard her own voice break, and the woman's reply, swift, sympathetic, 'I'll contact my husband immediately', made further explanation impossible. She couldn't speak, but turned away blindly from the telephone and ran up the stairs again into the bedroom. He was lying as she had left him, the expression of horror still on his face, and she went and knelt beside him and kissed his hand, the tears pouring down her cheeks. 'Why?' she asked herself. 'What happened? What did I do?' Because when he cried out, using her pet name Jinnie, it was not as if he had been seized with sudden pain on waking from sleep. It did not seem like that at all, but more as though his cry was one of accusation, that she had done something so appalling that it suspended all belief. 'Oh, no . . . Oh, Jinnie . . . Oh, my God . . . !' Then trying to ward her off as she ran to his side, and dying instantly.

I can't bear it, I can't bear it, she thought, what did I do? She got up, still blinded by tears, and went and stood by the open window and looked back over her shoulder to the bed, but it was no longer the same. He was not staring at her any more. He was still. He had gone. The moment of truth had vanished for ever, and she would never know. What had happened was. Then, was already past, in some other dimension of time, and the present was Now, part of a future he could not share. This present, this future, was all blank to him, like the empty spaces in the photograph album beside the bed, waiting to be filled. Even, she thought, if he had read my mind, which he often did, he would not have cared. He knew I wanted to play those parts with the Theatre Group, he encouraged me, he was delighted. It was not as though I were planning to go off at any moment and leave him . . . Why the expression of horror, of disbelief? Why? Why?

She stared out of the window, and the carpet of autumn leaves scattered here and there on the lawn was suddenly blown in a gust of wind up into the air like birds and tossed in all directions, only to drift apart, and tumble, and fall. The leaves that had once budded tight and close upon the parent tree, to glisten thick and green throughout the summer, had no more life. The tree disowned them, and they had become the sport of any idle wind that chanced to blow. Even the burnished gold was reflected sunlight, lost when the sun had set, so that in shadow they became crinkled, barren, dry.

Shelagh heard the sound of a car coming down the drive, and she went out of the room and stood at the top of the stairs. It was not the doctor, though, it was her mother. She came through the front door to the hall, peeling off her gloves, her hair bunched high on her head, gleaming and crisp from the drier. Unconscious of her daughter's eyes she hovered a moment before the mirror, patting a stray curl into place. Then she took her lipstick from her bag and made up her mouth. A door banging in the direction of the kitchen made her turn her head.

'That you, Nurse?' she called. 'How about tea? We can all have it upstairs.'

She looked back into the mirror, cocking her head, then dabbed off the surplus lipstick with a tissue.

The nurse appeared from the kitchen. She looked different out of uniform. She had borrowed Shelagh's dufflecoat for her walk, and her hair, usually so trim, was dishevelled.

'Such a lovely afternoon,' she said. 'I've been for quite a tramp across the fields. It was so refreshing. Blown all the cobwebs away. Yes, let's have tea, by all means. How's my patient?'

They are living in the past, Shelagh thought, in a moment of time that does not exist any more. The nurse would never eat the buttered scones she had anticipated, glowing from her walk, and her mother, when she glanced into the mirror later, would see an older, more haggard face beneath the piled-up coiffure. It was as if grief, coming so unexpectedly, had sharpened intuition, and she could see the nurse already installed by the bedside of her next patient, some querulous invalid, unlike her father, who teased and made jokes, while her mother, dressed suitably in black and white (black alone she would consider too severe), replied to the letters of condolence, those from the more important people first.

Then they both became aware of her, standing at the top of the stairs.

'He's dead,' Shelagh said.

Their upturned faces stared at her in disbelief, as his had done, but without the horror, without the accusation, and as the nurse, recovering first, brushed past her up the stairs, she saw her mother's carefully preserved and still lovely face disintegrate, crumple, like a plastic mask.

You must not blame yourself. There was nothing you could have done. It was bound to happen, sooner or later . . . Yes, thought Shelagh, but why not later rather than sooner, because when one's father dies there is so much that has been left unsaid. Had I known, that last hour sitting there, talking and laughing about trivial things, that there was a clot forming like a time-bomb close to his heart, ready to explode, I would surely have behaved differently, held on to him, at least thanked him for all my nineteen years of happiness and love. Not flipped over the photographs in the album, mocking bygone fashions, nor yawned halfway through, so that, sensing boredom, he let the album drop to the floor and murmured, 'Don't bother about me, pet, I'll have a kip.'

It's always the same when you come face to face with death, the nurse told her, you feel you could have done more. It used to worry me a lot when I was training. And of course with a close relative it's worse. You've had a great shock, you must try and pull yourself together for your mother's sake . . . My mother's sake? My mother would not mind if I walked out of the house this moment, Shelagh was on the point of saying, because then she would have all the attention, all the sympathy, people would say how wonderfully she was bearing up, whereas with me in the house sympathy will be divided. Even Doctor Dray, when he finally arrived in the wake of his partner, patted her on the shoulder before her mother and said, 'He was very proud of you, my dear, he was always telling me so.' So death, Shelagh decided, was a moment for compliments, for everyone saying polite things about everybody else which they would not dream of saying at another time. Let me run upstairs for you . . . Let me answer the telephone . . . Shall I put on the kettle? An excess of courtesy, like mandarins in kimonos bowing, and at the same time an attempt at self-justification for not having been there when the explosion happened.

The nurse (to the doctor's partner): 'I would never have gone for a walk if I hadn't been quite sure he was comfortable. And I believed that both Mrs Money and her daughter were in the house. Yes, I had given him the tablets . . .', etc., etc.

She is in the witness-box, on trial, thought Shelagh, but so are we all.

Her mother (also to the doctor's partner): 'It had entirely slipped my memory that Nurse was going out. There has been so much to think of, so much anxiety, and I thought it would relax me to pay a quick visit to the hairdresser, and he had seemed so much better, really his old self. I would never have dreamt of leaving the house, leaving his room, if I had thought for one moment . . .'

'Isn't that the trouble?' Shelagh burst in. 'We never *do* think, any of us. You didn't, Nurse didn't, Doctor Dray didn't, and above all I didn't, because I'm the only one who saw what happened, and I shall never forget the look on his face as long as I live.'

She stormed along the passage to her own room, sobbing hysterically in a way she had not done for years – the last time was when the post-van smashed into her first car when it was parked in the entrance drive, all that twisted metal, the lovely plaything ruined. *That* will teach them a lesson, she told herself, that will shake them out of this business of trying to behave so well, of being noble in the face of death, of making out that it's a merciful release and everything is really for the best. None of them really minding, caring, that someone has gone forever. But *forever* . . .

Later that evening, everyone gone to bed, death being so exhausting to all but the departed, Shelagh crept along the landing to her father's room and found the photograph album, tactfully tidied away on a corner table by the nurse, and carried it back with her to her own bedroom. Earlier, during the afternoon, the photographs had been without significance, familiar as old Christmas cards hoarded in a drawer, but now they were a kind of obituary, like stills flashed in tribute on a television screen.

The befrilled baby on a rug, mouth agape, his parents playing croquet. An uncle, killed in the first world war. Her father again, no longer a baby on a rug but in breeches, holding a cricket-bat too big for him. Homes of grandparents long dead. Children on beaches. Picnics on moors. Then Dartmouth, photographs of ships. Rows of lined-up boys, youths, men. As a child it had been her pride to point to him at once. 'There you are, that's you', the smallest boy at the end of the line, then in the next photograph slimmer and standing in the second row, then growing quite tall and suddenly handsome, a child no longer, and she would turn the pages rapidly because the photographs would be of places, not of people – Malta, Alexandria, Portsmouth, Greenwich. Dogs that had been his which she had not known. 'There's dear old Punch . . .' (Punch, he used to tell her, always knew when his ship was due home, and waited at an upstairs window.) Naval officers riding donkeys . . . playing tennis . . . running races, all this before the war, and it had made her think, 'unconscious of their doom, the little victims play', because on the next page it became suddenly sad, the ship he had loved blown up, and so many of those laughing young men lost. 'Poor old Monkey White, he would have been an admiral had he lived.' She tried to imagine the grinning face of Monkey White in the photo turned into an admiral, bald-headed, perhaps, stout, and something inside her was glad that he had died, although her father said he was a loss to the Service. More officers, more ships, and the great day when Mountbatten visited the ship, her father in command, meeting him as he was piped aboard. The courtyard at Buckingham Palace. Standing rather self-consciously before the press photographer, displaying medals.

'Not long now before we come to you,' her father used to say as he turned the page to the full-blown and never-to-him-admitted rather silly photograph of her mother in evening dress which he so much admired, wearing her soulful look that Shelagh knew well. It embarrassed her, as a child, to think that her father had fallen in love, or, if men must love, then it should have been someone else, someone dark, mysterious and profoundly clever, not an ordinary person who was impatient for no reason and cross when one was late for lunch.

The naval wedding, her mother smiling in triumph – Shelagh knew that look too, she wore it when she got her way about anything, which she generally did – and her father's smile, so different, not triumphant, merely happy. The frumpish bridesmaids wearing dresses that made them fatter than they were – she must have chosen them on purpose not to be outdone – and the best man, her father's friend Nick, not nearly so good-looking as her father. He was better in one of the earlier groups on the ship, but here he looked supercilious, bored.

The honeymoon, the first house, and then her own appearance, the childhood photographs that were part of her life; on her father's knee, on his shoulders, and right through childhood and adolescence until last Christmas. It could be my obituary too, she thought, we've shared this book together, and it ends with his snapshot of me standing in the snow and mine of him, smiling at me through the study window.

In a moment she would cry again, which was self-pity; if she cried it must not be for herself but for him. When was it, that afternoon, that he had sensed her boredom and pushed the album aside? It was while they were discussing hobbies. He had told her she was physically lazy, didn't take enough exercise.

'I get all the exercise I need in the theatre,' she said, 'pretending to be other people.'

'It's not the same,' he said. 'You should get away from people sometimes, imaginary and real. I tell you what. When I'm up and about again and in the clear we'll go over to Ireland and fish, the three of us. It would do your Mum a power of good, and I haven't fished for years.'

Ireland? Fish? Her instinct was selfish, one of dismay. It would interfere with her Theatre Group plans. She must joke him out of it.

'Mum would hate every minute,' she said. 'She would much rather go to the south of France to stay with Aunt Bella.' (Bella was her mother's sister. Had a villa at Cap d'Ail.)

'I dare say,' he smiled, 'but that wouldn't be my idea of convalescence. Have you forgotten I'm half-Irish? Your grandfather came from County Antrim.'

'I've not forgotten,' she said, 'but grandfather's been dead for years, and lies buried in a Suffolk churchyard. So much for your Irish blood. You haven't any friends over there, have you?'

He did not answer immediately, and then he said, 'There's poor old Nick.'

Poor old Nick . . . Poor old Monkey White . . . Poor old Punch . . . She was momentarily confused between friends and dogs she had never known.

'Do you mean your best man at the wedding?' she frowned. 'Somehow I thought he was dead.'

'Dead to the world,' he said shortly. 'He was badly smashed up in a car crash some years ago, and lost an eye. Lived like a recluse ever since.'

'How sad. Is that why he never sends you a Christmas card?'

'Partly . . . Poor old Nick. Gallant as they come, but mad as a hatter. A border-line case. I couldn't recommend him for promotion, and I'm afraid he bore me a grudge ever afterwards.'

'That's hardly surprising, then. I'd feel the same if I'd been somebody's close friend and they turned me down.'

He shook his head. 'Friendship and duty are two separate things,' he said, 'and I put duty first. You are another generation, you wouldn't understand. I was right in what I did, I'm sure of that, but it wasn't very pleasant at the time. A chip on the shoulder can turn a man sour. I'd hate to think myself responsible for what he may have got mixed up in.'

'What do you mean?' she asked.

'Never mind,' he said, 'none of your business. Anyway, it's over and done with long ago. But I sometimes wish . . .'

'What do you wish, darling?'

'That I could shake the old boy by the hand once more and wish him luck.'

They turned over a few more pages of the album, and it was soon afterwards that she yawned, glancing idly about the room, and he sensed her boredom and said he would have a kip. No one could die of a heart attack because his daughter was bored . . . But supposing he had had a nightmare in which she had figured? Supposing he had thought himself back in that sinking ship during the war, with poor old Monkey White, and Nick, and all those drowning men, and somehow she had been with him in the water? Everything became jumbled up in dreams, it was a known thing. And all the time that clot getting bigger, like an excess of oil in the workings of a clock. At any moment the hands would falter, the clock stop ticking.

Somebody tapped at her bedroom door. 'Yes?' she called.

It was the nurse. Still professional, despite her dressing-gown.

'Just wondered if you were all right,' she whispered. 'I saw your light under the door.'

'Thanks. I'm O.K.'

'Your mother's fast asleep. I gave her a sedative. She was fussing about tomorrow being Saturday, and the difficulty of getting an announcement in *The Times* and *Telegraph* before Monday. She's being so plucky.'

Was there hidden reproach in her voice because Shelagh had not thought of taking charge of these things herself? Surely tomorrow would have done? Aloud she said, 'Can nightmares kill?'

'What do you mean, dear?'

'Could my father have had a terrible nightmare and died of shock?'

The nurse advanced to the bed and straightened the eiderdown. 'Now, I told you earlier, and the doctors said the same, it would have happened anyway. You really must not keep on going over it in your mind. It doesn't help. Let me get you a sedative too.'

'I don't want a sedative.'

'You know, dear, forgive me, but you're being just a little bit childish. Grief is natural, but to worry about him in this way is the last thing your father would have wanted. It's all over now. He's at peace.'

'How do you know he's at peace?' Shelagh exploded. 'How do you know he's not hovering beside us at this minute in an astral body absolutely furious that he's dead, and saying to me, "That bloody nurse gave me too many pills"?'

Oh no, she thought, I didn't mean that, people are too vulnerable, too naked. The poor woman, shaken out of professional calm, sagged in her dressing-gown, drooped before her eyes, and in a tremulous voice said, 'What a terribly unkind thing to say! You know I did no such thing.'

Impulsively Shelagh leapt out of bed and put her arms round the nurse's shoulders.

'Forgive me,' she pleaded, 'of course you didn't. And he liked you very much. You were a wonderful nurse to him. What I meant was' – she searched in her mind for some explanation –'what I meant was that we don't know what happens when a person dies. They might be waiting in some queue at St Peter's gate with all the other people who have died that day, or else pushing into some awful purgatorial night-club with the ones who were destined for hell, or just drifting in a kind of fog until the fog clears and everything becomes clear. All right, I will have a sedative, you have one too, then we'll both be fresh for the morning. And please don't think any more about what I said.'

The trouble is, she thought, after she had taken her sedative and gone back to bed, words leave a wound, the wound leaves a scar. The nurse will never give out pills to patients again without a doubt somewhere at the back of her mind as to whether she is doing the right thing. Like the question-mark in her father's conscience about not passing poor old Nick for promotion and so giving him his chip on the shoulder. It was bad to die with something on your conscience. One ought to have some warning, so that one could send a telegram to anyone who might have been wronged, saying, 'Forgive me', and then the wrong would be cancelled, blotted out. This was why, in the old days, people flocked round a dying person's bed, hoping, not to be left something in the will, but for mutual forgiveness, a cessation of ill-feeling, a smoothing out of right and wrong. In fact, a sort of love.

Shelagh had acted on impulse. She knew she always would. It was part of her character, and had to be accepted by family and friends. It was not until she was on her way, though, driving north from Dublin in the hired car, that her journey, hastily improvised, took on its real meaning. She was here on a mission, a sacred trust. She was carrying a message from beyond the grave. It was absolutely secret, though, and no one must know about it, for she was sure that if she had told anyone questions would have been asked, arguments raised. So, after the funeral, complete silence about her plans. Her mother, as Shelagh guessed she would, had decided to fly to Aunt Bella at Cap d'Ail.

'I feel I must get right away,' she had said to her daughter. 'You may not realise it, but Dad's illness was a fearful strain. I've lost half a stone. I feel that all I want to do is to close my eyes and lie on Bella's sun-drenched balcony, and try to forget the misery of the past weeks.'

It was like an advertisement for some luxury soap. Pamper yourself. A naked woman deep in a bath of bubbling foam. In point of fact, the first shock over, her mother looked better already, and Shelagh knew that the sun-drenched balcony would soon fill up with Aunt Bella's very mixed bunch of friends – socialites, bogus artists, boring old homos, what her father used to call 'phoney riff-raff', but they amused her mother. 'What about you? Why don't you come too?' – the suggestion half-hearted but nevertheless made.

Shelagh shook her head. 'Rehearsals start next week. I thought, before going to London, I'd push off alone in the car somewhere. No sort of plan. Just drive.'

'Why not take a friend?'

'Anyone would get on my nerves at the moment. I'm better alone.'

No further contact between them on anything more than the practical level. Neither said to the other, 'How unhappy are you really? Is this the end of the road for me, for you? What does the future hold?' Instead there were discussions about the gardener and his wife coming to live in, visits from lawyers left until after her mother returned from Cap d'Ail, letters to be forwarded, etc., etc . . . Without emotion, like two secretaries, they sat side by side reading and replying to the letters of condolence. You take A to K. I'll take L to Z. And more or less the same message to each: 'Deeply touched . . . Your sympathy so helpful . . .' It was like sending out the Christmas cards every December, but the wording was different.

Looking through her father's old address book, she came across the name Barry. Commander Nicolas Barry, D.S.O., R.N. (Retd.), Ballyfane, Lough Torrah, Eire. Both name and address had a line through them, which generally meant that the person had died. She glanced at her mother.

'I wonder why that old friend of Dad's, Commander Barry, hasn't written?' she asked casually. 'He isn't dead, is he?'

'Who?' Her mother looked vague. 'Oh, you mean Nick? I don't think he's dead. He was in some frightful car crash years ago. But they were out of touch before that. He hasn't written to us for years.'

'I wonder why.'

'I don't know. They had some row, I never heard what about. Did you see this very sweet letter from Admiral Arbuthnot? We were all together in Alexandria.'

'Yes, I saw it. What was he like? Not the Admiral – Nick.'

Her mother leant back in her chair, considering the matter.

'Frankly, I never could quite make him out,' she said. 'He'd either be all over one and the greatest fun, especially at parties, or ignoring everybody and making sarcastic remarks. He had a wild streak in him. I remember him coming to stay soon after Dad and I were married – he was best man, you know, at the wedding – and he turned all the furniture upside down in the drawing-room and got very tight. Such a silly thing to do. I was livid.'

'Did Dad mind?'

'I don't think so, I can't remember. They knew each other so well, served together, been at Dartmouth as boys. Then Nick left the Navy and went back to live in Ireland, and they somehow drifted apart. I had the impression actually that he had the sack, but I never liked to ask. You know what an oyster Dad was about Service matters.'

'Yes . . .'

(Poor old Nick. A chip on the shoulder. I'd like to shake him by the hand again and wish him luck . . .)

She saw her mother off at the airport a few days afterwards, and made her own plans for departure to Dublin. The night before she left, searching amongst her father's papers, she found a scrap of paper with a list of dates and the name Nick alongside with a question-mark, but no word of explanation as to what the dates referred to. June 5, 1951. June 25, 1953. June 12, 1954. October 17, 1954. April 24, 1955. August 13, 1955. The list bore no relevance to the rest of the papers in the file, and must have been slipped in there by accident. She copied them down, and put them in an envelope inside her tourist guide.

Well, that was that, and here she was, on the road to . . . to do what? To apologise, in her deceased father's name, to a retired naval commander passed over for promotion?

Wild in his youth? The greatest fun at parties? The image conjured up was not one to whip the appetite, and she began to picture a middle-aged buffer with a hyena laugh who put booby-traps on the top of every door. Perhaps he had tried it on the First Sea Lord and received the boot for his pains. A car accident turned him into a recluse, an embittered one-time clown (but gallant, her father said, which meant what – plunging into oil-infested waters to rescue drowning sailors in the war?) who sat gnawing his finger-nails in some old Georgian mansion or mock castle, drinking Irish whisky and regretting all those apple-pie beds.

Some seventy-odd miles from Dublin on a balmy October afternoon, though, with the countryside becoming greener, lusher, yet somehow sparsely inhabited, the glint of water more frequent away to the west, and suddenly a myriad pools and lakes with tongues of land thrusting between them, the prospect of ringing the bell of a Georgian mansion faded. Here were no high walls encircling stately demesnes, only wet fields beyond the road, and surely no means of access to the silver-splintered lakes beyond.

The description of Ballyfane in the official guide had been laconic. 'Situated west of Lough Torrah with numerous smaller loughs close to the village.' The Kilmore Arms had six bedrooms, but there was no mention of mod. cons. If the worst came to the worst she could telephone Nick – his old friend's daughter stranded in the neighbourhood, could he suggest a comfortable hotel within ten miles, and she hoped to call upon him in the morning. A butler would answer, an old retainer. 'The Commander would be pleased if you would accept his hospitality here at Ballyfane Castle.' Irish wolfhounds baying, and her host himself appearing on the steps, leaning on a stick . . .

A church tower appeared over the crest of the road, and

here was Ballyfane itself, a village street straggling up a rise flanked by a few sombre houses and shops, names like Driscoll and Murphy painted on boards above doors. The Kilmore Arms could have done with a coat of whitewash, but marigolds in a window-box making a valiant attempt at a second flowering suggested someone with an eye for colour.

Shelagh parked her Austin Mini and surveyed the scene. The door of the Kilmore Arms was open. The entrance hall that also served as a lounge was bare and neat. Nobody was in sight, but a handbell standing on the counter to the left of the entrance seemed there for a purpose. She rang it briskly, and as a sad-faced man emerged from an inner room, limping and wearing spectacles, she had a fearful feeling that it was Nick himself, having fallen on hard times.

'Good afternoon,' she said. 'I was wondering if I could have tea?'

'You can,' he told her. 'A full tea or just the pot?'

'Well, full, I think,' she replied, with a vision of hot scones and cherry jam, flashing him the smile she generally reserved for the stage-doorkeeper.

'It will take about ten minutes,' he said. 'The dining-room is to the right, just three steps down. Have you come far?'

'From Dublin,' she said.

'It's a pleasant drive. I was in Dublin myself a week ago,' he told her. 'My wife, Mrs Doherty, has relatives there. She's away sick at present.'

She wondered whether she should apologise for giving trouble, but he had already disappeared to get the tea, and she went down the steps into the dining-room. Six tables laid ready, but she had the impression nobody had eaten there for days. A clock on the wall ticked loudly, breaking the silence. Presently a little maid emerged from the back regions, breathing heavily, bearing a tray that had upon it a large pot of tea and, not the scones and cherry jam she had anticipated, but a plate with two fried eggs and three fat slices of bacon, as well as a heap of fried potatoes. A full tea . . . She would have to eat it, or Mr Doherty would be offended. The maid vanished, and a black and white cat that had made its appearance with the tea arched itself against her legs, purring loudly. Furtively she fed it the bacon and one of the eggs, then tackled the remainder. The tea was piping hot and strong, and she could feel it searing her inside as she swallowed it.

The little maid emerged once more. 'Is the tea to your liking?' she asked anxiously. 'I could fry you another egg if you're still hungry.'

'No,' said Shelagh, 'I've done very well, thank you. Could I see your telephone directory? I want to look up the number of a friend.'

The directory was produced and she thumbed the pages. Barrys galore, but none in this district. No Commander. No Nicolas Barry, R.N. (Retd.). The journey had been in vain. Her mood of high expectancy, of daring, turned to despondency.

'How much do I owe for the tea?' she asked.

The little maid murmured a modest sum. Shelagh thanked her, paid, and went out into the hall and through the open doorway to the street. The post office was on the opposite side. One last enquiry and then, if that was unlucky too, she would turn the car round again and make for some hotel back on the road to Dublin, where she could at least relax in a steaming bath and spend the night in comfort. She waited patiently while an old woman bought stamps and a man enquired about parcels to America. Then she turned to the postmaster behind the grille.

'Excuse me,' she asked, 'I wonder if you can help me? Do you happen to know if Commander Barry lives anywhere in the district?'

The man stared. 'He does,' he said. 'He's lived here these twenty years.'

Oh joy! Oh, the relief! The mission was on again. All was not lost.

'The thing is,' Shelagh explained, 'I couldn't find his name in the telephone directory.'

'That isn't surprising,' the man said. 'There is no telephone on Lamb Island.'

'Lamb Island?' repeated Shelagh. 'You mean he lives on an island?'

The man stared as if she had asked a stupid question. 'It's on the southern side of Lough Torrah,' he said, 'about four miles from here as the crow flies. You can't reach it except by boat. If you want to get in touch with Commander Barry you'd best write for an appointment. He doesn't see many people.'

The chip on the shoulder . . . The recluse . . . 'I see,' said Shelagh. 'I hadn't realised. Can one get a glimpse of the island from the road?'

The man shrugged. 'There's a turning down to the lough a mile or so out of Ballyfane,' he told her, 'but it's no more than a rough track. You can't take a car there. If you have stout shoes it's an easy enough walk. Best done in daylight. You would miss your way if it came on for dusk, and the mist rises too over the lake.'

'Thank you,' said Shelagh, 'thank you very much.'

She went out of the post office with the feeling that the postmaster was staring after her. What now? Better not risk it this evening. Better endure the doubtful comforts of the Kilmore Arms and indigestion. She returned to the hotel and came face to face with Mr Doherty on the doorstep.

'I suppose,' she said, 'you couldn't let me have a room for the night?'

'I could indeed, you'd be very welcome,' he told her. 'It's

quiet now, but in the tourist season you'd be surprised – we've seldom an empty bed. I'll bring in your baggage. Your car will come to no harm there in the street.'

Anxious to please he limped to the boot of the car, brought out her suitcase, conducted her inside the Kilmore Arms and led the way upstairs, showing her into a small double room overlooking the street.

'I'll only charge you for the one bed,' he said. 'Twenty-two shillings and your breakfast. There's a bathroom across the passage.'

Oh well, it was rather fun – and mod. cons. after all. Later on the locals would come into the bar and break into song. She would drink Guinness out of an enormous tankard and watch them, join in herself, perhaps.

She inspected the bathroom. It reminded her of digs on tour. One tap dripping, leaving a brown stain, and when she turned it on the water gushed forth like the Niagara Falls. Still, it was hot. She unpacked her night things, bathed, dressed again and went downstairs. Voices drifted down the passage. She followed the sound and came to the bar. Mr Doherty himself stood behind the counter. The voices ceased as she entered, and everyone stared. Everyone being about half a dozen men, and amongst them she recognised the postmaster.

'Good evening,' she said brightly.

A mumbled response from all, but uninterested. They went on talking amongst themselves. She ordered whisky from Mr Doherty and felt suddenly self-conscious, perched there on the stool, which was perfectly ridiculous, because she was used to going into every sort of bar on tour, and there was nothing very singular about this one anyway.

'Is it your first visit to Ireland?' asked Mr Doherty, still anxious to please, pouring out the whisky.

'Yes, it is,' she told him. 'I'm rather ashamed I've never

been over before. My grandfather was Irish. I'm sure the scenery is lovely around here. I must do some exploring tomorrow, down by the lake.'

She glanced across the bar, and was aware of the post-master's eye upon her.

'You'll be with us for a few days, then?' asked Mr Doherty. 'I could arrange some fishing for you, if that's what you like.'

'Oh well . . . I'm not sure. It rather depends.'

How loud and English her voice sounded on the air, reminding her of her mother. Like a socialite out of a glossy magazine. And the local chatter had momentarily ceased. The Irish bonhomie she had visualised was absent. Nobody here was going to seize a fiddle and dance a jig and burst into song. Perhaps girls who stayed the night in pubs on their own were suspect.

'Your dinner is ready when you are,' said Mr Doherty.

She took the cue and slipped from the bar-stool and so on into the dining-room, feeling about ten years old. Soup, fish, roast beef – the trouble they had taken, when all she needed was a wafer slice of ham, but impossible to leave anything on her plate. Trifle to finish with, doused in sherry.

Shelagh looked at her watch. It was only half-past eight.

'Will you take your coffee in the lounge?'

'Thank you, yes.'

'There's a television set. I'll switch it on for you.'

The little maid drew up an armchair close to the television, and Shelagh sat down to the coffee she did not want while an American comedy, vintage 1950, flickered from the box. The murmur of voices droned on from the direction of the bar. Shelagh poured the coffee back into the pot and crept upstairs to fetch her coat. Then, leaving the television blaring in the empty lounge, she went out into the street. There was nobody about. All Ballyfane was already in bed or safe within doors. She got into the car and drove away through the empty village, back along the road she had travelled earlier that afternoon. A turning, the postmaster had said, a mile or so out of Ballyfane.

This must be it, here on the left. A crooked signpost with the lettering 'Footpath to Lough Torrah' showed up in the glare of her head-lights. The footpath, narrow and twisting, led downhill. Silly to attempt it without a torch, and the moon, three-quarters full, giving only a fitful gleam behind banks of racing cloud. Still . . . She could go part of the way, if only for the benefit of the exercise.

She left the car close to the signpost and began to walk. Her shoes, luckily flat, squelched in the mud. As soon as I catch a glimpse of the lake, she thought, I'll turn back, and then be up early tomorrow and come here again, bring a packed lunch, decide upon my plan of attack. The footpath was opening out between the banks, and suddenly before her was the great sheet of water, encircled by jutting lips of land, and in the centre was the island itself, shrouded in trees. It had an eerie, sombre quality, and the moon, breaking through the clouds, turned the water silver, while the island remained black, humped like the back of a whale.

Lamb Island . . . Inconsequentially it made her think of legends, not of Irish chiefs long dead or tribal feuds, but of sacrifices to ancient gods before the dawn of history. Stone altars in a glade. A lamb with its throat cut lying amidst the ashes of a fire. She wondered how far it was from the shore. Distances were hard to judge by night. A stream on her left ran down into the lake, fringed by reeds. She advanced towards it, picking her way carefully amongst the pebbles and the mud, and then she saw the boat, tied to a stump, and the figure of a man standing beside it. He was staring in her direction. Foolish panic seized her, and she backed away. It was no good, though. He walked swiftly up the mud and stood beside her.

'Were you looking for someone?' he said.

He was a young man, strongly built, wearing a fisherman's jersey and dungarees. He spoke with the local accent.

'No,' Shelagh answered, 'no, I'm a visitor to the district. It was a lovely evening and I thought I'd take a walk.'

'A lonely spot for a walk. Have you come far?'

'Only from Ballyfane,' she told him. 'I'm staying at the Kilmore Arms.'

'I see,' he said. 'You're here for the fishing, maybe. The fishing is better the other side of Ballyfane.'

'Thank you. I'll remember that.'

There was a pause. Shelagh wondered if she should say any more or whether she should turn and go, bidding him a cheerful goodnight. He was looking beyond her shoulder towards the footpath, and she heard the sound of somebody else's footsteps squelching through the mud. Another figure loomed out of the shadow and advanced towards them. Shelagh saw that it was the postmaster from Ballyfane. She was not sure whether to be sorry or relieved.

'Good evening again,' she said, her voice a shade too hearty. 'You see I didn't wait until morning after all, I found my way successfully, thanks to your advice.'

'So,' replied the postmaster. 'I noticed your car up there on the road parked by the turning, and thought it best to follow in case you came to harm.'

'That was kind of you,' said Shelagh. 'You shouldn't have bothered.'

'No bother at all. Better be sure than sorry.' He turned to the young man in the fisherman's jersey. 'It's a fine night, Michael.'

'It is, Mr O'Reilly. This young lady tells me she's here for the fishing. I've explained she'll have better sport the other side of Ballyfane.'

'That's true, if it's fishing she's after,' said the postmaster, and he smiled for the first time, but unpleasantly, too

knowing. 'The young lady was in the post office this evening asking for Commander Barry. She was surprised he
was not on the telephone.'

'Fancy that, now,' said the young man, and disconcert-
ingly he produced a torch from his pocket and flashed it
in her face. 'Excuse the liberty, miss, but I haven't had the
pleasure of meeting you before. If you'd care to tell me
your business with the Commander I will pass on the
message.'

'Michael here lives on Lamb Island,' said the postmaster.
'He's by way of being a watch-dog to the Commander, and
keeps unwelcome visitors at bay, you might say.'

He said this with the same knowing smile which she
found so unpleasant, and she wished she could be away
and out of it, back in the neat little bedroom at the Kilmore
Arms, not here beside the sinister lake with these two
strange men.

'I'm afraid I can't give a message,' she said. 'It's a private
matter. Perhaps it would be better if I wrote to Commander Barry from the hotel. He isn't expecting me, you
see. It's all rather difficult.'

Her loss of composure was evident to the two men. She
saw them exchange glances. Then the young man jerked
his head at the postmaster and drew him aside, and they
spoke together out of earshot. Her uneasiness increased.

The young man turned back to her. 'I tell you what I'll
do,' and he was smiling now, but a shade too broadly. 'I'll
run you over to the island in the boat, and the Commander
shall decide for himself whether he wants to see you
or not.'

'Oh no . . .' said Shelagh, backing away, 'not tonight. It's
much too late. I'll come back in the morning, and you can
run me across then.'

'It would be better to get it over with tonight,' said
Michael.

Get it over with? What did he mean? A few months ago she had boasted to some friends after a first-night party that she had never been frightened of anything in her life, except drying-up. She was frightened now.

'They'll be waiting up for me at the hotel,' she said quickly. 'If I don't return soon Mr Doherty will get in touch with the police.'

'Don't fret yourself,' said the postmaster. 'I have a friend standing by up the road. He'll drive your car back to the Kilmore Arms and we'll make it all right between us with Tim Doherty.'

Before she could protest further they had seized her arms and were marching her between them down to the boat. It can't be true, she thought, it can't be happening, and a strangled sob escaped her, like that of a terrified child.

'Ah, sshh now,' said Michael, 'no one's going to touch a hair of your head. You said yourself it's a fine night. It's finer still on the water. You may see the fish jumping.'

He helped her into the boat and pushed her firmly on the stern seat. The postmaster remained on shore. That's better, she thought, at least there's only one of them.

'So long, Mr O'Reilly,' Michael called softly, starting the engine, then loosening the painter from the mooring-post.

'So long, Michael my boy,' called the postmaster.

The boat glided away from the reeds on to the open lough, the chug-chug of the little engine quiet, subdued. The postmaster waved his hand, then turned back and started walking up the shore towards the footpath.

The journey from mainland to island took barely five minutes, but seen from the lake the mainland appeared dark, remote, the hills in the distance an ominous smudge. The comforting lights of Ballyfane were out of sight. She had never felt so vulnerable, so alone. Michael said nothing until the boat drew in alongside a small landing-stage built out from the narrow shore. The trees clustered thickly to the water's edge. He tied up the boat, then held out his hand to her.

'Now then,' he said when he had helped her on to the landing-stage, 'the truth is that the Commander is away at a meeting the other side of the lough, but he should be back by midnight or thereabouts. I'll take you up to the house and the steward will look after you.'

The steward . . . The Ballyfane castle and the Georgian mansion had returned to the land of fantasy whence they had sprung, but steward had a medieval ring to it, Malvolio with a tapering staff, stone steps leading to an audience chamber. Wolfhounds guarding doors. A faint measure of confidence returned to her. Michael was not going to strangle her under the trees.

Surprisingly, the house was revealed after little more than a hundred yards, set in a clearing amidst the trees. A long, low, one-storied building, built surely of timber put up in sections, like pictures of relief hospitals erected by missionaries in jungles for sick natives. A verandah ran the whole length of it, and as Michael led her up the steps and paused before a door marked Galley Entrance a dog barked from within, not the deep-throated baying of a wolfhound but shriller, sharper, and Michael laughed, turned to her and said, 'They don't need me as watchdog when Skip's around. She'd smell strangers twenty miles away.'

The door opened. A short, stocky, middle-aged man stood before them, dressed in the uniform of a naval steward.

'A small problem for you, Bob,' said Michael. 'The young lady here was wandering down by the lough just now in the darkness and all, and it appears she was enquiring off Mr O'Reilly for the Commander.'

The steward's face remained impassive, but his eyes

travelled down from Shelagh's face to her clothes, and her jacket pockets in particular.

'There's nothing on her,' said Michael, 'and she must have left her handbag in the car beside the road. The young lady is staying up at the Arms, but we thought it best to bring her straight here. You never can tell.'

'Please come inside, miss,' said the steward to Shelagh, his voice courteous but firm. 'You're from England, I take it.'

'Yes,' she replied. 'I flew over to Dublin today, and drove straight here. My business with Commander Barry is a personal matter, and I don't want to discuss it with anyone else.'

'I see,' said the steward.

The little dog, a schipperke, with pricked ears and bright, intelligent eyes, was sniffing daintily at Shelagh's ankles.

'Would you give me your coat?' asked the steward.

A strange request. She was wearing a short tweed jacket and matching skirt. She handed over the jacket, and he examined the pockets and placed it over the back of the chair. Then – and this was disconcerting – he ran his hands in a brisk professional way over her body, while Michael watched with interest.

'I don't know why you're doing this,' she said. 'You've hijacked me, not the other way round.'

'It's a way we have with visitors we don't know,' said the steward. 'It saves argument in the long run.' He jerked his head at Michael. 'You did right to bring the young lady along. I'll explain matters to the Commander when he returns.'

Michael grinned, winked at Shelagh, raised his hand in a mock salute and went out, shutting the door behind him.

'Will you come with me, please?' said the steward.

Reluctant to see the last of Michael, who seemed

suddenly an ally, not a prospective rapist, Shelagh followed Bob the steward (not Malvolio after all) along a corridor to a room at the further end. The steward threw open the door and ushered her in.

'Cigarettes on the table by the fire,' he said. 'Ring the bell if there is anything you require. Would you care for coffee?'

'Please,' said Shelagh. If she was going to sit up all night coffee would help.

The room was spacious, comfortable, a blue carpet fitted wall-to-wall. A settee, a couple of deep armchairs, a large flat-topped desk near the window. Pictures of ships on the wall. A log-fire burning brightly in the hearth. The setting reminded her of something. She had seen some place like it in the past, reminding her of childhood days. Then she remembered. It was a duplicate of the captain's cabin in *Excalibur,* her father's cabin. Lay-out, furnishings, were identical. The familiar surroundings were uncanny, it was like stepping back into the past.

She wandered round the room, trying to take it in. She crossed to the window and drew aside the curtains, half-expecting to see the deck outside, and beyond, in the distance, other ships at anchor in Portsmouth harbour. There was no deck, though, no ships. Only the long verandah, the shrouded trees and the pathway to the lough, the silver water shining beneath the moon. The door opened once again, and the steward brought in coffee on a silver tray.

'The Commander won't be long now,' he said. 'I've just had word his launch left fifteen minutes ago.'

Launch . . . They had more than one boat, then. And just had word. There had been no sound of a telephone ringing, and anyway the house wasn't on the phone. He went out and closed the door. She began to panic once again, realised she was lost without her bag, left in the car. No comb, no lipstick. She hadn't touched her face since before going down to the bar at the Kilmore Arms. She peered into the mirror hanging on the wall beyond the desk. Hair dank, face white and pinched, she looked frantic. She wondered whether it would be best for him to find her sitting in one of the armchairs, drinking her coffee, seemingly relaxed, or standing rather boyishly before the fireplace, hands in her jacket pockets. She needed direction, she needed someone like Adam Vane to tell her what to do, how to place herself before the curtain rose.

She turned round from the mirror, facing the desk, and saw the photograph in the blue leather frame. The photograph of her mother as a bride, her veil thrown back, the irritating smile of triumph on her face. There was something wrong, though. The groom standing beside her was not Shelagh's father. It was Nick, the best man, hair *en brosse*, supercilious, bored. She looked closer, baffled, and realised that the photograph had been cleverly faked. Nick's head and shoulders had been transposed on to her father's figure, while her father's head, sleek-haired, smiling happily, had been shifted to the lanky figure behind, standing between the bridesmaids. It was only because she knew the original photograph on her father's desk at home, and had a copy herself somewhere, stuck away in a drawer, that she recognised the transposition instantly. A stranger would think the photograph genuine. But why on earth? Whom did Nick want to deceive, unless it was himself?

Shelagh moved away from the desk, uneasy. People who were mentally sick deceived themselves. What was it her father had said? Nick had always been a border-line case . . . She had been frightened before, standing on the shore by the lake questioned by the two men, but that had been physical fear, a natural reaction in the face of possible brutality. This was different – a feeling of revulsion, a strange apprehension. The room that had seemed warm and familiar become kinky, queer. She wanted to get out of it.

She went to the French window and pulled aside the curtains. The window was locked. No key, no way of escape. Then she heard the sound of voices in the hall, and this is it, she thought, I've got to face it. I must lie, make up my lines, improvise. I'm alone here, but for the steward, with someone who is sick, who is mad. The door opened, and he came into the room.

Surprise was mutual. He had caught her, literally, on the wrong foot, hovering between armchair and coffee-table, semi-bent, an awkward position, no sort of poise. She straightened herself and stared. So did he. He was not in the least like the best man in the authentic wedding group, except for the figure, lanky and tall. The hair was no longer *en brosse* because there was little of it, and the small black patch over the left eye suggested Moshe Dayan. The right eye was very bright and blue. The mouth thin. As he stood there, staring, the little dog pranced in behind him. He called over his shoulder to the steward. 'See that Operation B goes forward as of now, Bob,' he said, without taking his eye off Shelagh, and 'Aye, aye, sir,' replied the steward from the corridor.

The door closed, and Nick came into the room and said, 'I see Bob brought you some coffee. Is it cold?'

'I don't know,' Shelagh replied. 'I haven't drunk any yet.'

'Add some whisky to it, you'll feel better.'

He opened a wall-cupboard and brought out a tray with decanter, soda syphon, and glasses upon it. He put it on the table between the two chairs, then flung himself down on the one opposite her, the dog on his lap. Shelagh poured some whisky into her cup of coffee, aware that her hand trembled. She was sweating, too. His voice was clear, rather clipped, authoritative, reminding her of a director who used to teach at drama school and had half his students in tears. All except her. She had walked out of class one morning, and he had had to apologise.

'Come on, relax,' said her host. 'You're as taut as a bowstring. I apologise for the abduction, but it was your own fault for wandering down by the lake late in the evening.'

'The signpost said footpath to Lough Torrah,' she replied. 'I didn't see a notice forbidding trespassers, or warning people away. They ought to advise visitors at the airport never to wander after sundown, but I suppose they can't, it would hit the tourist trade for six.'

Stuff that up, she thought, and tossed down her whisky-laced coffee. He smiled, but not with her, at her, and began to stroke the smooth, sleek coat of the little dog. The one eye was disconcerting. She had the impression that the left eye was still there behind the patch.

'What's your name?'

Her reply was instinctive. 'Jinnie,' she told him, and added, 'Blair.'

Jennifer Blair was her stage-name. Shelagh Money had never sounded right. But nobody except her father had ever called her Jinnie. It must have been nerves that had made her blurt it out now.

'M'm,' he said. 'Jinnie. Rather nice. Why did you want to see me, Jinnie?'

Improvisation. Play it by ear, Adam Vane always said. This is the situation, take it from here. Starting now . . .

There was a cigarette box on the table, and a lighter. She leant forward and took a cigarette from the box. He did not attempt to light it for her.

'I'm a journalist. My editors want to run a new series in the spring about the effects of retirement on Service men. Whether they like it, whether they're bored. Their hobbies, and so on. You know the kind of thing. Well, four of us were given the assignment. You were on my list, and here I am.'

'I see.'

She wished he would take that eye off her for one moment. The little dog, in ecstasy at the stroking hand, was now lying on its back, paws in the air.

'What made you think I should be of any interest to your readers?'

'That wasn't really my problem,' she told him. 'Other people do the check-ups in the office. I was merely given brief particulars. Service career, good war record, retired, lives at Ballyfane, and told to take it from there. Bring back a story. Human interest, and all that . . .'

'Curious,' he said, 'that your bosses should have picked on me when there are many far more distinguished persons living over here in retirement. Generals, rear-admirals, scores of 'em.'

She shrugged her shoulders. 'If you ask me,' she said, 'they pick the names out of a hat. And someone, I forget who, said you were a recluse. They love that sort of thing. Find out what makes him tick, they told me.'

He poured himself a drink, then leant back again in his chair.

'What's the name of your paper?' he asked.

'It isn't a newspaper, it's a magazine. One of the new glossies, very up and coming, published every fortnight. *Searchlight*. You may have seen it.'

Searchlight was, in point of fact, a recent publication. She had skimmed through it in the aircraft coming over.

'No, I've not seen it,' he told her, 'but then, living as a recluse, that's hardly surprising, is it?'

'No. No, I suppose not.'

The eye was watchful. She blew a cloud of smoke into the air.

'So it was professional curiosity that took you wandering to the lake by night, rather than wait until daylight to approach me?'

'Naturally. And the fact that you live on an island. Islands are always mysterious. Especially by night.'

'You're not easily scared?'

'I was scared when your henchman Michael and the rather unpleasant postmaster seized me by the arms and forced me into the boat.'

'What did you think they were going to do?'

'Assault, rape, murder, in that order.'

'Ah, that's what comes of reading the English newspapers and writing for glossy magazines. We're a peaceable lot in Ireland, you'd be surprised. We shoot each other up, but that's traditional. Rape is uncommon. We seldom seduce our women. They seduce us.'

Now it was Shelagh who smiled, in spite of herself. Confidence was returning. Parry and thrust. She could keep this sort of thing going for hours.

'May I quote you on that?' she asked.

'I'd rather you didn't. Bad for the national image. We like to think of ourselves as devils. We get more respect that way. Have some more whisky.'

'Thank you, I will.'

If this was rehearsal, she thought, the director would tell me to change position. Pour myself another drink from the decanter and stand up, look about the room. No, on second thoughts better stay put.

'Now it's your turn to answer questions,' she said. 'Does your boatman make a habit of hi-jacking tourists?'

'No, You are the first. You should be flattered.'

'I told him,' she went on, 'and the postmaster as well, that it was too late for an evening call, and I'd come back in the morning. They wouldn't listen. And when I got here your steward searched me – frisked me, I believe they call it.'

'Bob's very thorough. It's an old naval custom. We used to frisk the local girls when they came aboard. It was part of the fun.'

'Liar,' she said.

'No, I assure you. They've put a stop to it now, I'm told. Like the daily tots of rum. Another reason why youngsters won't join the Navy any more. You can quote me on that, if you like.'

She watched him over the rim of her glass. 'Do you regret leaving the Service?'

'Not in the slightest. I had all I wanted from it.'

'Except promotion?'

'Oh, to hell with promotion. Who wants to command a ship in peacetime when a vessel is obsolete before she's even launched? Nor did I fancy sitting on my backside in the Admiralty or some establishment ashore. Besides, I had more worthwhile things to do here at home.'

'Such as?'

'Finding out about my own country. Reading history. Oh, not Cromwell and all that – the ancient stuff, which is much more fascinating. I've written thousands of words on the subject which will never get printed. Articles appear sometimes in scholarly journals, but that's about all. I don't get paid for them. Not like you, writing for magazines.'

He smiled again. It was rather a good smile. Not good in the accepted sense of the word, but in hers. Whipping-up, in fact, challenging. ('He used to be such fun at parties.') Had the moment come? Did she dare?

'Tell me,' she asked, 'I know it's personal, but my readers will want to know. I couldn't help noticing that photograph on your desk. You've been married, then?'

'Yes,' he said, 'the one tragedy of my life. She was killed in a car crash a few months after we were married. Unluckily I survived. That's when I lost my eye.'

Her mind went blank. Improvise . . . improvise.

'How terrible for you,' she murmured. 'I'm very sorry.'

'That's all right. It happened years ago. I took a long time to get over it, of course, but I learnt to live with the situation, to adapt. There was nothing else I could do. I'd retired from the Navy by then, which admittedly didn't help matters. However, there it was, and, as I told you, it happened a long time ago.'

Then he really believed it? He really believed he had been married to her mother, and she had been killed in a car crash? Something must have happened to his brain when he lost the eye, something had gone wrong. And when had he tampered with the photograph? Before the accident or afterwards? And why? Doubt and mistrust returned. She was just beginning to like him, to feel at ease with him, and now her confidence was shattered. If he was insane, how must she handle him, what must she do? She got up and stood by the fireplace, and how odd, she thought, the movement is natural, it's not acting, not a stage direction, the play is becoming real.

'Look,' she said, 'I don't think I want to write this article after all. It isn't fair to you. You've been through too much. I hadn't realised. And I'm sure my editor would agree. It's not our policy to probe into a person's suffering. *Searchlight* isn't that sort of magazine.'

'Oh really?' he replied. 'How disappointing. I was looking forward to reading all about myself. I'm rather conceited, you know.'

He began stroking the dog again, but his eye never left her face.

'Well,' she said, searching for words, 'I could say a bit about your living here alone on the island, fond of your dog, keen on ancient history . . . and so on.'

'Wouldn't that be rather dull and hardly worth printing?'

'No, not at all.'

Suddenly he laughed, put the dog on the floor and stood up on the hearth-rug beside her. 'You'd have to do rather better than this to get away with it,' he said. 'Let's discuss it in the morning. You can tell me then, if you like, who you really are. If you're a journalist, which I doubt, you weren't sent here to write about my hobbies and my pet dog. Funny, you remind me of someone, but I can't for the life of me think who it is.'

He smiled down at her, very confident of himself, not at all mad, reminding her . . . of what? Being in her father's cabin on board *Excalibur*? Being swept up in the air by her father, screaming with delight and fear? Oh, the smell of eau-de-cologne that he used, and this man too, not like the stinking after-shave they all swamped themselves with today . . .

'I'm always reminding people of somebody else,' she said. 'No personality of my own. You remind me of Moshe Dayan.'

He touched his eye-shade. 'Just a gimmick. If he and I sported them pink, we'd be ignored. The fact that it's black transforms it. Has the same effect on women that black stockings have on men.'

He walked across the room and threw open the door. 'Bob?' he called.

'Sir,' came the reply from the kitchen.

'Operation B under way?'

'Sir. Michael coming alongside now.'

'Right!' He turned to Shelagh. 'Let me show you the rest of the house.'

She inferred, from the nautical language, that Michael was standing by to escort her by boat to the mainland. Time enough when she got back to the Kilmore Arms to decide whether to return in the morning and brazen it out, or forget all about the mission and beat it for home. He escorted her down the corridor, throwing open one door after the other, with names upon them. Control Room . . . Signals . . . Sick Bay . . . Crew's Quarters . . . This must be it, she told herself. He has a fantasy of living on board ship.

This is how he has come to terms with life, with disappointment, with injury.

'We're highly organised,' he told her. 'I've no use for the telephone – communication with the mainland is by short-wave radio. If you live on an island you've got to be self-sufficient. Like a ship at sea. I've built all this up from scratch. There wasn't even a log house when I came to Lamb Island, and now it's a complete flagship. I could control a fleet from here.'

He smiled at her in triumph, and he *is* mad, she thought, raving mad, but for all that attractive – very, in fact. It would be easy to be taken in, to believe everything he said.

'How many of you live here?'

'Ten, including myself. These are my quarters.'

They had reached a door at the end of the corridor. He led the way through it to a separate wing. There were three rooms and a bathroom. One door had Commander Barry written upon it.

'I'm in here,' he said, throwing open the door, revealing a typical captain's cabin, with a bed, though, not a bunk. The layout was familiar, giving her a sudden poignant nostalgia.

'Guest-rooms next door,' he said. 'Numbers One and Two. Number One has a better view of the lake.'

He advanced into the room and drew aside the curtains. The moon had risen high, and shone down upon the sheet of water beyond the trees. It was very peaceful, very still. There was nothing sinister about Lamb Island now. The situation was reversed, and it was the distant mainland that seemed shrouded, drear.

'Even I should become a recluse if I lived here,' she said, and then, turning from the window, added, 'I mustn't keep you up. Perhaps Michael is waiting to take me back.'

He had switched on the bedside lamp. 'You're not going back. Operation B has been put into effect.'

'What do you mean?'

The single eye was upon her, discomfiting, amused. 'When I was told that a young woman wanted to see me, I decided upon a plan of action. Operation A meant that whoever it was signified nobody of interest, and could be returned to Ballyfane. Operation B meant that the visitor would be my guest, and her luggage fetched from the Kilmore Arms and matters explained to Tim Doherty. He's very discreet.'

She stared at him, her sense of unease returning. 'You didn't give yourself much time to consider. I heard you give orders about Operation B as soon as you came into the room down there.'

'That's right. I'm in the habit of coming to quick decisions. Here is Bob with your things now.'

There was a cough, a quiet knock on the door. The steward came in bearing her luggage. Everything had evidently been put back into her suitcase, all the small litter from her bedroom at the hotel. He also had her maps and her handbag from the car. Nothing had been forgotten.

'Thank you, Bob,' Nick said. 'Miss Blair will ring down for breakfast when she wants it.'

The steward placed her things on a chair, murmured, 'Goodnight, miss,' and withdrew. So that is that, thought Shelagh, and where do we go from here? He was still watching her, the smile of amusement on his face. When in doubt, she told herself, yawn. Be casual. Pretend this sort of thing happens every night of your life. She picked up her bag and found her comb, ran it through her hair, humming a tune under her breath.

'You should never have retired,' she said. 'Such a waste of your organising powers. You ought to be commanding the Mediterranean Fleet. Planning an exercise, or something.'

'That's exactly what I am doing. You'll get your orders

when this ship is at action stations. Now I've got some work to do, so I'll leave you. By the way . . .' he paused, his hand on the door, 'you don't have to lock this, you're perfectly safe.'

'I wouldn't dream of locking it,' she replied. 'As a journalist I'm used to shake-downs in the most unlikely places, and prowling about unknown corridors in the middle of the night.'

Punch-line, she thought. That will teach you. Now disappear and turn all your furniture upside down . . .

'Ah,' he said, 'so that's your form. It's not a case of you locking your door but of me locking mine. Thanks for the warning.'

She heard him laughing as he went down the corridor. Curtain. Damn. He had had the last word.

She went to her suitcase and threw it open. The few clothes, night-things, make-up, neatly packed. Her handbag untouched. A lucky thing the papers for the hired Austin were all in her stage name. Nothing to connect her with Shelagh Money. The only thing that had been shaken and folded differently was the map and the tourist guide. Well, that didn't matter. She had marked Ballyfane and Lough Torrah with blue pencil, but a journalist would have done that anyway. Something was missing, though – the copper-coloured paper-clip had gone. She shook the tourist guide, but nothing fell out. The envelope was no longer there. The envelope containing the slip of paper with the dates upon it, which she had copied from the file in her father's study.

When Shelagh awoke the sun was streaming into the room. She glanced at her travelling-clock beside the bed. A quarter past nine. She had slept soundly for nearly ten hours. She got out of bed and went to the window, drawing the curtains aside. Her room appeared to be at the extreme end of the building, and immediately beyond her window a grass bank sloped towards the trees, and through the trees themselves a narrow clearing led down to the lake. The glimpse she could catch of the lake showed the water to be sparkling blue, the surface that had been so still last evening now turned to wavelets, whipped by a scudding breeze. Nick had told the steward she would ring down for her breakfast, and she picked up the telephone by the bed. Bob's voice came at once.

'Yes, miss. Orange-juice? Coffee? Rolls? Honey?'

'Please . . .'

Service, she thought. I shouldn't be getting this at the Kilmore Arms. Bob brought the tray to her bedside within four minutes. The morning paper was also upon it, neatly folded.

'The Commander's compliments, miss,' he said. 'He hopes you slept well. If there is anything else you require you have only to tell me.'

I'd like to know if it was Mr Doherty at the Kilmore Arms or Mr O'Reilly from the post office who took the envelope from the tourist guide, she was thinking. Or could it be you, Malvolio? Nobody would have bothered about it if I hadn't scribbled on the envelope, 'N. Barry. Dates possibly significant.'

'I have everything I need, thank you, Bob,' she said.

When she had breakfasted, dressed herself in sweater and jeans, and made up her eyes with rather greater care than she had done the day before, she was ready to face whatever surprises Nick had in store for her. She walked down the corridor, passed through the swing-door and came to the living-room. The door was open, but he was not there. Somehow she had expected to see him at his desk. She went across to it, glancing furtively over her shoulder, and stared at the photograph once again. Nick was much better now than then, she thought. As a young man he must have been irritating, over-pleased with himself, and she had a feeling that his hair had been red. The whole truth was, she supposed, that they had both been in love with her mother, and when her father won this had helped to turn Nick sour. Started the chip. Odd that her mother had not mentioned the fact. She generally preened her feathers about old admirers. Disloyal, Shelagh knew, but what had both men seen in her except that very obvious pretty-pretty face? Far too much lipstick, like they wore in those days. And a bit of a snob, always name-dropping. She and her father used to wink at each other if she did it in front of other people.

A discreet cough warned her that the steward was watching her from the corridor beyond.

'The Commander is in one of the wood clearings, miss, if you were looking for him. I can point you the way.'

'Oh, thank you, Bob.'

They went out together, and he said, 'You'll find the Commander working down on the site about ten minutes' walk away.'

The site . . . Felling trees, perhaps. She set off through the woods, the foliage thick and green on either side of the path, dense as a miniature forest, without a glimpse of the lake to be seen. If one strayed from the path, she thought, and wandered amongst the trees, one would be lost instantly, striking for the lake and not finding it, moving round and round in circles. The wind sighed in the branches above her head. No birds, no movement, no lapping water near at hand. A person could be buried here in all the undergrowth and never found. Perhaps she should turn back, retrace her steps to the house, tell the steward she preferred to wait indoors for Commander Barry. She hesitated, but it was too late. Michael was advancing through the trees towards her. He carried a spade in his hand.

'The Commander is waiting for you, miss. He wants to show you the grave. We've just uncovered it.'

Oh God, what grave, for whom? She felt the colour drain from her face. Michael was not smiling. He jerked his head towards a clearing just ahead. Then she saw the others. There were two other men besides Nick. They were stripped to the waist, bending over something in the ground. She felt her legs weaken under her, and her heart began thumping in her breast.

'Miss Blair is here, sir,' said Michael.

Nick turned and straightened. He was dressed like the others, in singlet and jeans. He did not carry a spade, but had a small axe in his hand.

'So,' he said, 'the moment has arrived. Come over here and kneel down.'

He placed his hand on her shoulder, and drew her towards the crater that opened wide before her. She could not speak. She could only see the brown earth piled on either side of the crater, the tumbled leaves, the branches tossed aside. Instinctively, as she knelt, she buried her face in her hands.

'What *are* you doing?' He sounded surprised. 'You can't see with your eyes covered. This is a great occasion, you know. You're probably the first Englishwoman to be present at the uncovering of a megalithic tomb in Ireland. Court cairns, we call them. The boys and I have been working on this one for weeks.'

The next thing she knew was that she was sitting humped against a tree with her head between her legs. The world stopped spinning, gradually became clear. She was sweating all over.

'I think I'm going to be sick,' she said.

'Go ahead,' he replied. 'Don't mind me.'

She opened her eyes. The men had all disappeared and Nick was crouching beside her.

'That's what comes of only having coffee for breakfast,' he told her. 'Quite fatal starting the day on an empty stomach.'

He rose to his feet and wandered back to the crater.

'I've tremendous hopes of this find. It's in a better state of preservation than many others I've seen. We only stumbled upon it by chance a few weeks ago. We've uncovered the forecourt and part of what I think is a gallery for the burial place itself. It's not been disturbed since about 1500 years B.C. Can't have the outside world getting wind of it, or we shall have all the archaeological chaps over here wanting to take photographs, and that would put the fat in the fire all right. Feeling better?'

'I don't know,' she said weakly. 'I think so.'

'Come and have a look, then.'

She dragged herself to the crater and peered into the depths. A lot of stones, a sort of rounded arch affair, a kind of wall. Impossible to show enthusiasm, her misunderstanding and fear had been too great.

'Very interesting,' she said, and then to her shame, far worse than being sick, she burst into tears. He stared at her, momentarily nonplussed, then taking her by the hand began walking briskly through the wood without speaking, whistling between his teeth, until within a few minutes the trees had cleared and they were standing by the side of the lake.

'Ballyfane is over to the west. You can't see it from here. The lake broadens to the north on this side, and winds in and out against the mainland like a patchwork quilt. In winter the duck fly in and settle amongst the reeds. I never shoot them, though. In summer I come and swim here before breakfast.'

Shelagh had recovered. He had given her time to pull herself together, which was all that mattered, and she was grateful to him.

'I'm sorry,' she said, 'but frankly, when I saw Michael with the spade and he said something about a grave, I thought my last moment had come.'

He stared at her, astonished. Then he smiled. 'You're not so hard-bitten as you like to pretend. That swagger of yours is all bluff.'

'Partly,' she admitted, 'but it's a new situation to me, being dumped on an island with a recluse. I see now why I was hijacked. You don't want anyone leaking about your megalithic find to the press. O.K., I won't. That's a promise.'

He did not answer immediately. He stood there, stroking his chin.

'H'm,' he said after a moment. 'Well, that's very sporting of you. Now, I'll tell you what we'll do. We'll go back to the house, get Bob to make up a packed lunch, and I'll take you for a tour of the lake. And I promise not to push you overboard.'

He's only mad, she thought, nor-nor-west. He's sane in every respect save for the photograph. But for that . . . but for the photograph she would come clean at once and tell him the truth about herself, about her reason for coming to Ballyfane. Not yet, though.

Nothing could be more different, Shelagh decided several hours later, than the Nick described by her father, with a chip on the shoulder, a grudge against the world, soured by disappointment, than this man who put himself out to entertain her, to see that she enjoyed every moment of the hours spent in his company. The twin-engined launch, with a small cabin for'ard – not the little chug-chug craft in which Michael had brought her to the island the day before – glided smoothly across the lake, dodging in and out amongst the tongues of land, while he pointed out to her, from the helmsman's seat, the various points of interest on the mainland. The distant hills to the west, a ruined

castle, the tower of an ancient abbey. Never once did he
allude to the reason for her visit, nor press her for information about her own life. They ate hard-boiled eggs and cold
chicken seated side by side in the small cabin, and she kept
thinking how her father would have loved it, how this
would have been just his way of spending a day had he lived
to take that holiday. She could picture him and Nick
together, chaffing, slanging away at each other, showing
off, in a curious sort of way, because she was there. Not her
mother, though. She would have wrecked the whole thing.

'You know,' she said in a burst of confidence, the effect
of a tot of whisky before the Guinness, 'the Commander
Barry I imagined wasn't a scrap like you.'

'What did you imagine?' he asked.

'Well, because of your being this recluse they told me
about, I pictured someone living in a castle filled with old
retainers and baying wolfhounds. Rather a buffer. Either
grim and very rude, shouting at the retainers, or terribly
hearty, playing practical jokes.'

He smiled. 'I can be very rude when I choose, and I often
shout at Bob. As to practical jokes . . . I've played them in
my time. Still do. Have another Guinness?' She shook her
head and leant back against the bulkhead. 'The trouble
was,' he said, 'the sort of jokes I played were mostly to
amuse myself. They've gone out of fashion, anyway. I don't
suppose you, for instance, ever put white mice in your editor's desk?'

For editor's desk substitute star's dressing-room, she
thought.

'Not white mice,' she replied, 'but I once put a stink-
bomb under my boss's bed. He hopped out of it pretty
quick, I don't mind telling you.'

Manchester it was, and Bruce never forgave her, either.
What he thought was boiling up to be a discreet affair
between them vanished in smoke.

'That's what I meant,' he said. 'The best of jokes are only fun for oneself. A bit of a gamble, though, to pick on your boss.'

'Self-protection,' she told him. 'I was bored at the thought of getting into bed with him.'

He started to laugh, then checked himself. 'Forgive me, I'm being hearty. Do you have a lot of trouble with your editors?'

She pretended to reflect. 'It all depends. They can be rather demanding. And if you're ambitious, which I am, it earns you promotion. The whole thing's a chore, though. I'm not really permissive.'

'Meaning what?'

'Well, I don't strip down at the flick of a hat. It has to be someone I like. Am I shocking you?'

'Not in the least. A buffer like myself likes to know how the young live.'

She reached for a cigarette. This time he lighted it for her.

'The thing is,' she said, and she might have been talking to her father after Sunday supper, with her mother safe in the other room, only actually this was more fun, 'the thing is, I find sex over-rated. Men make such a fuss, put one off, all that groaning. Some even cry. The only reason one does it is to claim a scalp, like playing Red Indians. The whole thing's a dead loss, in my opinion. But there, I'm only nine-teen. Plenty of time to ripen up.'

'I wouldn't count on it. Nineteen is getting on a bit. It's later than you think.' He rose from the locker, strolled over to his helmsman's seat and switched on the engine. 'It gives me enormous satisfaction,' he added, 'to think of all those heads you've scalped, and the groaning that goes on in Fleet Street. I must warn my friends amongst the press that they had better watch out.'

She looked up at him, startled. 'What friends?'

He smiled. 'I have my contacts.' He turned the launch back in the direction of Lamb Island, and it's only a matter of time, she told herself, before he checks my press credentials, discovers they don't exist. As for Jennifer Blair, he'd have to contact a fair number of theatre managers before one of them said, 'You mean that brilliant young actress the Stratford people have been trying to get hold of for next season?'

Too soon by far he was bringing the launch alongside the landing-stage-cum-boathouse of his domain, cunningly masked by the thickly planted trees, Michael there to receive them, and she remembered her fright of the morning, the partly uncovered megalithic cairn in the heart of the wooded island.

'I've spoilt your day,' she said to Nick. 'You were all of you working on that site, and would have gone on with it but for me.'

'Not necessarily. Relaxation takes varying forms. The digging can wait. Any news, Michael?'

'Some signals received, sir, up at the house. Everything in order.'

Metamorphosis was complete by the time they reached the house. The companion had become brusque, alert, intent upon matters other than herself. Even the little dog who leapt into his arms as soon as she heard her master's voice was swiftly put down again.

'Everyone in the control-room for briefing in five minutes, Bob,' he said.

'Sir.'

Nick turned to Shelagh. 'You must amuse yourself, if you don't mind. Books, radio, T.V., records, all in the room we were in last night. I shall be busy for several hours.'

Several hours ... It was only just after six. Would his business, whatever it was, take him until nine or ten? She had hoped for something different, a long intimate

evening stretched out in front of the fire when anything
might happen.

'O.K.,' she said with a shrug. 'I'm in your hands. I'd like
to know, by the way, how long you intend to keep me here.
I have certain commitments back in London.'

'I bet you have. But the scalping will have to wait. Bob,
see that Miss Blair has some tea.'

He disappeared along the corridor, the dog at his heels.
She flung herself down on the settee, sulking. What a bore!
Especially when the day had gone so well. She had no
desire to read or listen to records. His taste would be like
her father's, old Peter Cheyneys and John Buchans, he used
to read them over and over again. And music of the lighter
sort, probably *South Pacific*.

The steward brought in her tea, and this time there were
cherry jam and scones, freshly baked, what's more. She
wolfed the lot. Then she pottered around the room, inspect-
ing the shelves. No Peter Cheyney, no John Buchan, endless
books on Ireland, which she expected anyway, Yeats forever, Synge, A.E., a volume on the Abbey Theatre. That
might be interesting, but, 'I'm not in the vein,' she thought,
'I'm not in the vein.' The records were mostly classical,
Mozart, Haydn, Bach, stacks of the damn things. All right
if he'd been in the room and they could have listened
together. The photograph on the desk she ignored. Even
to glance at it produced intense irritation. How could he?
What had he seen in her? Indeed, what had her father seen,
for that matter? But for Nick, obviously more intellectual
than her father had ever been, to go round the bend about
somebody like her mother, granting she had been pretty
in her day, passed all comprehension.

'I know what I'll do,' thought Shelagh, 'I'll go and wash
my hair.'

It was frequently a remedy when all else failed. She
walked along the corridor, passing the door with the words

Control Room upon it. She could hear the murmur of
voices from within. Then Nick laughed, and she hurried
past in case the door opened and she was caught trying to
eavesdrop. The door did open, when she was safely on her
way, and glancing back over her shoulder she saw a boy
come out, one of those who had been helping to uncover
the cairn that morning. She remembered his mop of light
hair. He couldn't be more than eighteen. They were all
young, now she came to think of it. All except Nick himself, and Bob. She passed through the swing-door to her
own room and sat down on her bed, stunned by a new idea
that had suddenly come to her.

Nick was a homo. They were all homos. That was why
Nick had been sacked from the Navy. Her father had found
out, couldn't pass him for promotion, and Nick had borne
a grudge ever afterwards. Perhaps, even, the dates she had
copied from the list referred to times when Nick had got
into trouble. The photograph was a blind – homos often
tried to cover themselves by pretending they were married.
Oh, not Nick . . . It was the end. She couldn't bear it. Why
must the only attractive man she had ever met in her life
have to be like it? God damn and blast them all, stripped
to the waist there down by that megalithic tomb. They
were probably doing the same in the Control Room now.
There was no point in anything any more. No sense in her
mission. The sooner she left the island and flew back home
the better.

She turned the taps in her wash-basin, and plunged her
head into the water furiously. Even the soap – Aegean
Blue – was far too exotic for a normal man to have under
his roof. She dried her hair, twisting the towel round it
turban fashion, tore off her jeans and put on another pair.
They didn't look right. She dragged on her travelling skirt
instead. 'That will show him I've no desire to go around
apeing boys.'

There was a tap at her door.

'Come in,' she said savagely.

It was Bob. 'Excuse me, miss, the Commander would like to see you in the Control Room.'

'I'm sorry, he'll have to wait. I've just washed my hair.'

The steward coughed. 'I wouldn't advise you, miss, to keep the Commander waiting.'

He could not have been more courteous, and yet . . . There was something implacable about his square, stocky frame.

'Very well,' said Shelagh. 'The Commander must put up with my appearance, that's all.'

She stalked along the corridor after him, the twisted turban giving her the appearance of a Bedouin sheik.

'Beg pardon,' murmured the steward, and tapped on the door of the Control Room. 'Miss Blair to see you, sir,' he announced.

She was ready for anything. Young men sprawling in the nude on bunks. Joss sticks burning. Nick, as Master of Ceremonies, directing unspeakable operations. Instead, she saw the seven young men seated round a table, Nick at the head of it. An eighth man was sitting in the corner with headphones over his ears. The seven at the table stared at her, then averted their gaze. Nick raised his eyebrows briefly, then picked up a piece of paper. She recognised it as the list with the dates upon it that had been missing from her tourist guide.

'I apologise for interrupting the *haute coiffure*,' he said, 'but these gentlemen and I would like to know the significance of these dates that you were carrying in your tourist guide.'

Obey the well-tried maxim. Attack is the best form of defence.

'That is exactly what I would have asked you, Commander Barry, had you granted me an interview. But I dare say you would have avoided the question. They obviously have great significance for you, otherwise your gentlemen friends would never have pinched them in the first place.'

'Fair enough,' he said. 'Who gave you the list?'

'It was with the other papers which the office gave me when I was put on to this job. They were just part of the briefing.'

'You mean the editorial office of *Searchlight*?'

'Yes.'

'Your assignment was to write an article about a retired naval officer – myself – and describe how he filled his time, hobbies, etc?'

'That's right.'

'And other members of the staff were to write similar articles about other ex-Service officers?'

'Yes. It sounded a bright idea. Something new.'

'Well, I'm sorry to spoil your story, but we've checked with the editor of *Searchlight,* and not only have they no intention of publishing such a series of articles, but they don't possess a Miss Jennifer Blair even amongst the most junior members of their staff.'

She might have known it. His contacts amongst the press. Pity she wasn't a journalist. Whatever it was he was trying to hide would win her a fortune if it was published in one of the Sunday newspapers.

'Look,' she said, 'this is a delicate matter. Could I possibly speak to you alone?'

'Very well,' Nick said, 'if you prefer it.'

The seven rose to their feet. They were a tough-looking bunch. She supposed that was the way he liked it.

'If you don't mind,' Nick added, 'the wireless operator has to stay at his post. Messages are continually coming through. He won't hear anything you say.'

'That's all right,' she said.

The seven young men shuffled from the room, and Nick

leant back in his chair. The bright blue eye never wavered from her face.

'Take a seat and fire away,' he said.

Shelagh sat down in one of the vacant seats, conscious suddenly of the twisted towel round her head. It could hardly add to her dignity. Never mind. It was his dignity she hoped to shatter now. She would tell the truth up to a certain point, them improvise, wait for his reaction.

'The *Searchlight* editor was perfectly right,' she began, drawing a deep breath. 'I've never worked for them, or for any other magazine. I'm not a journalist, I'm an actress, and few people on the stage have heard of me either, as yet. I'm a member of a young theatre group. We travel a lot, and we've just succeeded in getting our own theatre in London. If you want to check up on that you can. It's the New World Theatre, Victoria, and everybody there knows Jennifer Blair. I'm booked to play the lead in their forthcoming series of Shakespearean comedies.'

Nick smiled. 'That's more like it. Congratulations.'

'You can keep them for the opening night,' she replied, 'which will be in about three weeks' time. The director and the rest of the group know nothing about this business, they don't even know I'm here in Ireland. I'm here as the result of a bet.'

She paused. This was the tricky part.

'A boy-friend of mine, nothing to do with the theatre, has naval connections. That list of dates came into his hands, with your name scribbled beside it. He knew it must signify something, but didn't know what. We got slightly lit up one evening after dinner, and he bet me twenty-five quid, plus expenses, that I wasn't a good enough actress to pose as a journalist and bounce you into an interview just for the hell of it. Done, I told him. And that's why I'm here. I must admit I hadn't expected to be hi-jacked on to an island as part of the experience. I was slightly shaken last night to find the list had been pinched from my tourist guide. So, I told myself, then the dates *did* stand for something which wouldn't bear reporting. They were all in the fifties, around the time you retired from the Navy, according to the naval list which I ran to earth in a public library. Now, candidly, I don't give a damn what those dates signify, but, as I said before, they obviously mean a lot to you, and I wouldn't mind betting something pretty shady too, not to say illegal.'

Nick tilted his chair, rocking it gently to and fro. The eye shifted, examined the ceiling. He was evidently at a loss for an answer, which suggested her arrow had scored a bull's eye.

'It depends,' he said softly, 'what you call shady. And illegal. Opinions differ. You might be considerably shocked by actions for which my young friends and I find perfect justification.'

'I'm not easily shocked,' said Shelagh.

'No, I gathered that. The trouble is, I have to convince my associates that such is indeed the case. What happened in the fifties does not concern them – they were children at the time – but what we do jointly today concerns all of us very much indeed. If any leak of our actions reached the outside world we should, as you rightly surmise, find ourselves up against the law.'

He got up and began to straighten the papers on his table. So, Shelagh thought, whatever illegal practices her father had suspected Nick of, he was still engaged in them, here in Ireland. Smuggling archaeological finds to the U.S.A.? Or had her hunch this evening been correct? Could Nick and his bunch of friends be homosexual? Eire made so much fuss about morality that anything of the kind might well be against the law. It was obvious he wouldn't let on about it to her.

Nick went and stood beside the man with the headphones, who was writing something on a pad. Some message, she supposed. Nick read it, and scribbled something himself in answer. Then he turned back to Shelagh.

'Would you like to see us in action?' he asked.

She was startled. She had been prepared for anything when she came into the Control Room, but to be asked point blank . . . 'What do you mean?' she asked defensively.

Her turban had slipped on to the floor. He picked it up and handed it to her.

'It would be an experience,' he said, 'you are never likely to have again. You won't have to take part in it. The display will be at a distance. Very stimulating. Very discreet.'

He was smiling, but there was something disconcerting in the smile. She backed away from him towards the door. She had a sudden vision of herself seated somewhere in the woods, by that prehistoric grave, perhaps, unable to escape, while Nick and the young men performed some ancient and unspeakable rite.

'Quite honestly . . .' she began, but he interrupted her, still smiling.

'Quite honestly, I insist. The display will be an education in itself. We shall proceed part of the way by boat, and then take to the road.'

He threw open the door. The men were lined up in the corridor, Bob amongst them.

'No problem,' he said. 'Miss Blair will give no trouble. Action stations.'

They began to file away down the corridor. Nick took Shelagh by the arm and propelled her towards the swing-door leading to his own quarters.

'Get your coat, and a scarf, if you have one. It may be cold. Look sharp.'

He disappeared into his own room. When she came out again into the corridor he was waiting for her, wearing a high-necked jersey and a windcheater. He was looking at his watch.

'Come on,' he said.

The men had all vanished, except the steward. He was standing at the entrance to the galley door, the little dog in his arms.

'Good luck, sir,' he said.

'Thank you, Bob. Two lumps of sugar for Skip, no more.'

He led the way down the narrow path through the woods to the boathouse. The engine of the launch was humming gently. There were only two men on board, Michael and the young man with the mop of hair. 'Sit in the cabin and stay there,' Nick told Shelagh. He himself moved to the controls. The launch began to slip away across the lake, the island disappearing astern. Shelagh soon lost direction, seated as she was inside the cabin. The mainland was a distant blur, coming close at times and then receding, but none of it taking shape under the dark sky. Sometimes, as she peered through the small porthole, they passed so near to a bank that the launch almost brushed the reeds, and then a moment afterwards there was nothing but water, black and still, save for the white foam caused by the bow's thrust. The engine was barely audible. Nobody spoke. Presently the gentle throbbing ceased – Nick must have nosed his craft into shallow water beside a bank. He lowered his head into the cabin and held out his hand to her.

'This way. You'll get your feet wet, but it can't be helped.'

She could see nothing around her but water and reeds and sky. She stumbled after him on the soggy ground, clinging to his hand, the fair boy just ahead, the mud oozing through her shoes. They were leading her on to some sort of track. A shape loomed out of the shadows. It looked like a van, and a man she did not recognise was standing beside it. He opened the van door. Nick got in first, dragging Shelagh after him. The fair boy went round to the front beside the driver, and the van lurched and lumbered up the track until, topping what seemed to be a rise, it came to a smooth surface that must be road. She tried to sit upright, and banged her head against a shelf above her. Something rattled and shook.

'Keep still,' said Nick. 'We don't want all the bread down on top of us.'

'Bread?'

It was the first word she had spoken since leaving the island. He flicked on a lighter, and she saw that the partition between themselves and the driver was shut. All around them were loaves of bread, neatly stacked upon shelves, and cakes, pastries, confectionery, and tinned goods as well.

'Help yourself,' he told her. 'It's the last meal you'll get tonight.'

He put out his arm and seized a loaf, then broke it in two. He flicked off the lighter, leaving them in darkness again. I couldn't be more helpless, she thought, if I were riding in a hearse.

'Have you stolen the van?' she asked.

'Stolen it? Why the hell should I steal a van? It's on loan from the grocer in Mulldonagh. He's driving it himself. Have some cheese. And a spot of this.' He put a flask to her lips. The neat spirit nearly choked her, but gave warmth and courage at the same time. 'Your feet must be wet. Take your shoes off. And fold up your jacket under your head. Then we can really get down to it.'

'Down to what?'

'Well, we've a drive of some thirty-six miles before we reach the border. A smooth road all the way. I propose to scalp you.'

She was travelling by sleeper back to boarding-school in the north of England. Her father was waving goodbye to her from the platform. 'Don't go,' she called out, 'don't ever leave me.' The sleeper dissolved, became a dressing room in a theatre, and she was standing before the looking-glass dressed as Cesario in *Twelfth Night*. Sleeper and dressing-room exploded . . .

She sat up, bumped her head on the rack of loaves. Nick was no longer with her. The van was stationary. Something had awakened her, though, from total blackout – they must have burst a tyre. She could see nothing in the darkness of the van, not even the face of her watch. Time did not exist. It's body chemistry, she told herself, that's what does it. People's skins. They either blend or they don't. They either merge and melt into the same texture, dissolve and become renewed, or nothing happens, like faulty plugs, blown fuses, switchboard jams. When the thing goes right, as it has for me tonight, then it's arrows splintering the sky, it's forest fires, it's Agincourt. I shall live till I'm ninety-five, marry some nice man, have fifteen children, win stage awards and Oscars, but never again will the world break into fragments, burn before my eyes: I've bloody had it . . .

The van door opened and a rush of cold air blew in upon her. The boy with the mop of hair was grinning at her.

'The Commander says if you're fond of fireworks come and take a look. It's a lovely sight.'

She stumbled out of the van after him, rubbing her eyes. They had parked beside a ditch, and beyond the ditch was a field, a river surely running through it, but the foreground was dark. She could distinguish little except what seemed to be farm buildings around a bend in the road. The sky in the distance had an orange glow as if the sun, instead of setting hours ago, had risen in the north, putting all time to odds, while tongues of flame shot upwards, merging with pillars of black smoke. Nick was standing by the driver's seat, the driver himself alongside, both of them staring at the sky. A muffled voice was speaking from a radio fixed near to the dashboard.

'What is it?' she asked. 'What's happening?'

The driver, a middle-aged man with a furrowed face, turned to her, smiling.

'It's Armagh burning, or the best part of it. But there'll be no damage done to the cathedral. St Patrick's will stand when the rest of the town is black.'

The young man with the mop of hair had bent his ear to the radio. He straightened himself, touched Nick on the arm.

'First explosion has gone off at Omagh, sir,' he said. 'We should have the report on Strabane in three minutes' time. Enniskillen in five.'

'Fair enough,' replied Nick. 'Let's go.'

He bundled Shelagh back into the van and climbed in beside her. The van sprang into action, did a U-turn, and sped along the road once more.

'I might have known it,' she said. 'I should have guessed. But you had me fooled with your cairns in the wood and all that cover-up.'

'It isn't a cover-up. I've a passion for digging. But I love explosions too.'

He offered her a nip from the flask but she shook her head.

'You're a murderer. Helpless people away there burning in their beds, women and children dying perhaps in hundreds.'

'Dying nothing,' he replied. 'They'll be out in the streets applauding. You mustn't believe Murphy. He lives in a dream world. The town of Armagh will hardly feel it. A warehouse or two may smoulder, with luck the barracks.'

'And the other places the boy mentioned?'

'A firework display. Very effective.'

It was all so obvious now, thinking back to that last conversation with her father. He had been on to it all right. Duty before friendship. Loyalty to his country first. No wonder the pair of them had stopped exchanging Christmas cards.

Nick took an apple from the shelf above and began to munch it.

'So . . .' he said, 'you're a budding actress.'

'Budding is the operative word.'

'Oh come, don't be modest. You'll go far. You tricked me almost as neatly as I tricked you. All the same, I'm not sure I quite swallow the one about the friend with naval connections. Tell me his name.'

'I won't. You can kill me first.'

Thank heaven for Jennifer Blair. She would not have stood a chance as Shelagh Money.

'Oh well,' he said, 'it doesn't matter. It's all past history now.'

'Then the dates did make sense to you?'

'Very good sense, but we were amateurs in those days. June 5, 1951, a raid on Ebrington Barracks, Derry. Quite a success. June 25, 1953, Felstead School Officers' Training Corps, Essex. Bit of a mix-up. June 12, 1954, Gough Barracks, Armagh. Nothing much gained, but good for morale. October 17, 1954, Omagh Barracks. Brought us some recruits. April 24, 1955, Eglington Naval Air Base at Derry. H'm . . . No comment. August 13, 1955, Arborfield Depot, Berkshire. Initial success, but a proper cock-up later. After that, everyone had to do a lot of homework.'

There was an Italian opera by Puccini with a song in it, 'O! my beloved father'. It always made her cry. Anyway, she thought, wherever you are, darling, in your astral body, don't blame me for what I've done, and may very well do again before the night is over. It was one way to settle your last request, though you wouldn't have approved of the method. But then, you had high ideals and I have none. And what happened in those days was not my problem. My problem is much more basic, much more direct. I've fallen hook, line and sinker for your one-time friend.

'Politics leave me cold,' she said. 'What's the point of banging off bombs and upsetting everyone's lives? You hope for a united Ireland?'

'Yes,' he replied, 'so do we all. It will come eventually, though it may be dull for some of us when it does. Take Murphy, now. No excitement in driving a grocer's van around the countryside and being in bed by nine. This sort of thing keeps him young. If that's to be his future in a united Ireland he'll die before his seventieth birthday. I said to him last week when he came to the island for briefing, 'Johnnie's too young' – Johnnie's his son, the boy sitting beside him in front now – 'Johnnie's too young,' I told him. 'Maybe we shouldn't let him risk his life yet awhile.' 'Risk be damned,' says Murphy. 'It's the only way to keep a lad out of trouble, with the world in the state it is today.'

'You're all of you raving mad,' said Shelagh. 'I'll feel safer when we're back across your side of the border.'

'My side of the border?' he repeated. 'We never crossed it. What do you take me for? I've done some damnfool things in my time, but I wouldn't bounce about in a grocer's van in hostile territory. I wanted you to see the fun, that's all. Actually, I'm only a consultant these days. "Ask Commander Barry," somebody says, "he may have a suggestion or two to make", and I come, in from clearing cairns or writing history, and get cracking on the short wave. It keeps me young in heart, like Murphy.' He began pulling down some of the loaves from the rack and settling them under his head. 'That's better. Gives me support for my neck. I once made love to a girl with my backside against a heap of hand-grenades, but I was younger then. Girl never fluffed. Thought they were turnips.'

Oh no, she thought. Not again. I can't take any more just

yet. The battle's over, won, I'll sue for peace. All I want to do now is to lie like this, with my legs thrown across his knees and my head on his shoulder. This is safety.

'Don't,' she said.

'Oh really? No stamina?'

'Stamina nothing, I'm suffering from shock. I shall smoulder for days, like your barracks in Armagh. By the way, I belong by rights to the Protestant north. My grandfather was born there.'

'Was he, indeed? That explains everything. You and I have a love-hate relationship. It's always the same with people who share a common border. Attraction and antagonism mixed. Very peculiar.'

'I dare say you're right.'

'Of course I'm right. When I lost my eye in the car crash I had letters of sympathy from dozens of people across the border who would gladly have seen me dead.'

'How long were you in hospital?'

'Six weeks. Plenty of time to think. And plan.'

Now, she thought. This is the moment. Go carefully, watch your step.

'That photograph,' she said, 'that photograph on your desk. It's a phoney, isn't it?'

He laughed. 'Oh well, it takes an actress to spot deception. A throwback to the days of practical jokes. It makes me smile whenever I look at it, that's why I keep it on my desk. I've never been married, I invented that tale on the spur of the moment for your benefit.'

'Tell me about it.'

He shifted position to ensure greater comfort for both of them.

'The real bridegroom was Jack Money, a very close friend. I saw he died the other day, I was sorry for it. We'd been out of touch for years. Anyway, I was his best man. When they sent me a print of the wedding-group I switched the heads round and sent a copy to Jack. He laughed his head off, but Pam, his wife, was not amused. Outraged, in fact. He told me she tore the thing up and threw the pieces in the waste-paper basket.'

She would, thought Shelagh, she would. I bet she didn't even smile.

'I got my own back, though,' he said, moving one of the loaves from under his head. 'I dropped in on them one evening unexpectedly. Jack was out at some official dinner. Pam received me rather ungraciously, so I mixed the martinis extra strong, and had a rough-and-tumble with her on the sofa. She giggled a bit, then passed out cold. I upset all the furniture to look as if a cyclone had hit the house, and carried her up to her bed and dumped her there. On her own, I may add. She'd forgotten all about it by the morning.'

Shelagh lay back against his shoulder and stared at the roof of the van.

'I knew it,' she said.

'Knew what?'

'That your generation did perfectly revolting things. Far worse than us. Under your best friend's roof. It makes me sick to think of it.'

'What an extraordinary statement,' he said, astonished. 'No one was ever the wiser, so what the hell? I was devoted to Jack Money, although he did bog my chances of promotion shortly afterwards, but for a different reason. He only acted according to his lights. Thought I might put a spoke in the slowly-grinding wheels of naval intelligence, I presume, and he was bloody right.'

Now I can't tell him. It's just not on. Either I go back to England battered and defeated, or I don't go at all. He's deceived my father, deceived my mother (serve her right), deceived the England he fought for for so many years, tarnished the uniform he wore, degraded his rank, spends his time now, and has done for the past twenty years, trying to split this country wider apart than ever, and I just don't care. Let them wrangle. Let them blow themselves to pieces. Let the whole world go up in smoke. I'll write him a bread-and-butter letter from London saying, 'Thanks for the ride,' and sign it Shelagh Money. Or else . . . or else I'll go down on all fours like the little dog who follows him and leaps on his lap, and beg to stay with him forever.

'I start rehearsing Viola in a few days' time,' she said. ' "My father had a daughter loved a man . . ." '

'You'll do it very well. Especially Cesario. Concealment like a worm in the bud will feed on your damask cheek. You may pine in thought, but I doubt with a green and yellow melancholy.'

Murphy did another U-turn and the loaves rattled. How many miles to Lough Torrah? Don't let it end.

'The trouble is,' she said, 'I don't want to go home. It's not home to me any more. Nor do I care two straws for the Theatre Group, *Twelfth Night,* or anything else. You can have Cesario.'

'I can indeed.'

'No . . . What I mean is, I'm willing to chuck the stage, give up my English status, burn all my bloody boats, and come and throw bombs with you.'

'What, become a recluse?'

'Yes, please.'

'Absurd. You'd be yawning your head off after five days.'

'I would not . . . I would not . . .'

'Think of all that applause you'll be getting soon. Viola-Cesario is a cinch. I tell you what. I won't send you flowers for your opening night, I'll send you my eye-shade. You can hang it up in your dressing-room to bring you luck.'

I want too much, she thought. I want everything. I want day and night, arrows and Agincourt, sleeping and waking, world without end, amen. Someone warned her once that it was fatal to tell a man you loved him. They kicked you out of bed forthwith. Perhaps Nick would kick her out of Murphy's van.

'What I really want,' she said, 'deep down, is stillness, safety. The feeling you'd always be there. I love you. I think I must have loved you without knowing it all my life.'

'Ah!' he said. 'Who's groaning now?'

The van drew up, stopped. Nick crawled forward, threw open the doors. Murphy appeared at the entrance, his furrowed face wreathed in smiles.

'I hope I didn't shake you about too much,' he said. 'The side roads are not all they should be, as the Commander knows. The main thing is that the young lady should have enjoyed her outing.'

Nick jumped down on to the road. Murphy put out his hand and helped Shelagh to alight.

'You're welcome to come again, my dear, any time you like. It's what I tell the English tourists when they visit us. Things are more lively here than what they are across the water.'

Shelagh looked around her, expecting to see the lake, and the bumpy track near the reeds where they had left Michael with the boat. Instead, they were standing in the main street of Ballyfane. The van was parked outside the Kilmore Arms. She turned to Nick, her face a question-mark. Murphy was knocking on the hotel door.

'Twenty minutes' more driving time, but worth it,' said Nick. 'At least for me, and I hope for you as well. Farewells should be sharp and sweet, don't you agree? There's Doherty at the door, so cut along in. I have to get back to base.'

Desolation struck. He could not mean it. He surely did not expect her to say goodbye on the side of the street, with Murphy and his son hovering, and the landlord at the entrance of the hotel?

'My things,' she said, 'my case. They're on the island, in the bedroom there.'

'Not so,' he told her. 'Operation C brought them back to the Kilmore Arms while we were junketing about on the border.'

Desperately she fought for time, pride non-existent.

'Why?' she asked. 'Why?'

'Because that's the way it is, Cesario. I sacrifice the lamb that I do love to spite my own raven heart, which alters the text a bit.'

He pushed her in front of him towards the door of the hotel.

'Look after Miss Blair, Tim. The exercise went well, by all accounts. Miss Blair is the only casualty.'

He had gone, and the door had closed behind him. Mr Doherty looked at her with sympathy.

'The Commander is a great one for hustle. It's always the same. I know what it is to be in his company, he seldom lets up. I've put a thermos of hot milk beside your bed.'

He limped up the stairs before her, and threw open the door of the bedroom she had quitted two nights earlier. Her suitcase was on the chair. Bag and maps on the dressing-table. She might never have left it.

'Your car has been washed and filled up with petrol,' he continued. 'A friend of mine has it in his garage. He'll bring it round for you in the morning. And there's no charge for your stay. The Commander will settle for everything. Just you get to bed now and have a good night's rest.'

A good night's rest . . . A long night's melancholy. Come away, come away, death, and in sad cypress let me be laid. She threw open the window and looked out upon the street. Drawn curtains and blinds, shuttered windows. The black-and-white cat mewing from the gutter opposite. No lake, no moonlight.

'The trouble with you is, Jinnie, you won't grow up. You

live in a dream world that doesn't exist. That's why you opted for the stage.' Her father's voice, indulgent but firm. 'One of these days,' he added, 'you'll come to with a shock.'

It was raining in the morning, misty, grey. Better, perhaps, like this, she thought, than golden bright like yesterday. Better to go off in the hired Austin with windscreen wipers slashing from side to side, and then with luck I might skid and crash in a ditch, be carried to hospital, become delirious, clamour for him to come. Nick kneeling at the bedside, holding her hand and saying, 'All my fault, I should never have sent you away.'

The little maid was waiting for her in the dining-room. Fried egg-and-bacon. A pot of tea. The cat, come in from the gutter, purred at her feet. Perhaps the telephone would ring, and a message would flash from the island before she left. 'Operation D put into effect. The boat is waiting for you.' Possibly, if she hovered about in the hall, something would happen. Murphy would appear in his van, or even the postmaster O'Reilly with a few words scribbled on a piece of paper. Her luggage was down, though, and the Austin was in the street outside. Mr Doherty was waiting to say goodbye.

'I hope I shall have the pleasure,' he said, 'of welcoming you to Ballyfane again. You'd enjoy the fishing.'

When she came to the signpost pointing to Lake Torrah she stopped the car and walked down the muddied track in the pouring rain. One never knew, the boat might be there. She came to the end of the track and stood there a moment, looking out across the lake. It was shrouded deep in mist. She could barely see the outline of the island. A heron rose from the reeds and flapped its way over the water. I could take off all my things and swim, she thought. I could just about make it, exhausted, almost drowned, and stagger through the woods to the house and fall at his feet on the verandah. 'Bob, come quick! It's Miss Blair. I think she's dying . . .'

She turned, walked back up the track and got into the car. Started the engine, and the windscreen wipers began thrashing to and fro.

> When that I was and a little tiny boy,
> With hey, ho, the wind and the rain,
> A foolish thing was but a toy,
> For the rain it raineth every day.

It was still raining when she arrived at Dublin airport. First she had to get rid of the car, then book a seat on the first available plane to London. She did not have long to wait – there was a flight taking off within the next half-hour. She sat in the departure lounge with her eyes fixed on the door leading back to the reception hall, for even now a miracle might take place, the door swing open, a lanky figure stand there, hatless, black patch over his left eye. He would brush past officials, come straight towards her. 'No more practical jokes. That was the last. Come back with me to Lamb Island right away.'

Her flight was called, and Shelagh shuffled through with the rest, her eyes searching her fellow-travellers. Walking across the tarmac she turned to stare at the spectators waving goodbye. Someone tall in a mackintosh held a handkerchief in his hand. Not him – he stooped to pick up a child ... Men in overcoats taking off hats, putting dispatch-cases on the rack overhead, any one of them could have been, was not, Nick. Supposing, as she fastened her safety-belt, a hand came out from the seat in front of her, on the aisle, and she recognised the signet-ring on the little finger? What if the man humped there in the very front seat – she could just see the top of his slightly balding head – should suddenly turn, black patch foremost, and stare in her direction, then break into a smile?

'Pardon.'

A latecomer squeezed in beside her, treading on her toes. She flashed him a look. Black squash hat, spotty faced, pale, the fag end of a cigar between his lips. Some woman, somewhere, had loved, would love, this unhealthy brute. Her stomach turned. He opened a newspaper wide, jerking her elbow. Headlines glared.

'Explosions Across the Border. Are There More to Come?'

A secret glow of satisfaction warmed her. Plenty more, she thought, and good luck to them. I saw it, I was there, I was part of the show. This idiot sitting beside me doesn't know.

London Airport. Customs check. 'Have you been on holiday, and for how long?' Was it her imagination, or did the Customs Officer give her a particularly searching glance? He chalked her case and turned to the next in line.

Cars shot past the bus as it lumbered through the traffic to the terminal. Aircraft roared overhead, taking other people away and out of it. Men and women with drab, tired expressions waited on pavements for red to change to green. Shelagh was going back to school with a vengeance. Not to peer at the notice board in the draughty assembly-hall, shoulder to shoulder with giggling companions, but to examine another board, very similar, hanging on the wall beside the stage door. Not, 'Have I *really* got to share a room with Katie Matthews this term? It's too frantic for words', and smiling falsely, 'Hullo, Katie, yes, wonderful hols, super', but wandering instead into that rather poky cubby-hole they called the dressing-room at the bottom of the stairs, and finding that infuriating Olga Brett hogging the mirror, using Shelagh's or one of the other girls' lipstick instead of her own, and drawling, 'Hullo, darling, you're late for rehearsal, Adam is tearing his hair out in hand-fuls. But literally . . .'

Useless to ring up home from the air terminal and ask

Mrs Warren the gardener's wife to make up her bed. Home was barren, empty, without her father. Haunted, too, his things untouched, his books on the bedside table. A memory, a shadow, not the living presence. Better go straight to the flat, like a dog to a familiar kennel smelling only of its own straw, untouched by its master's hands.

Shelagh was not late at the first rehearsal on the Monday morning, she was early.

'Any letters for me?'

'Yes, Miss Blair, a postcard.'

Only a postcard? She snatched it up. It was from her mother at Cap d'Ail. 'Weather wonderful. Feeling so much better, really rested. Hope you are too, darling, and that you had a nice little trip in your car wherever it was. Don't exhaust yourself rehearsing. Aunt Bella sends her love and so do Reggie and May Hillsborough, who are here on their yacht at Monte Carlo. Your loving Mum.' (Reggie was the fifth Viscount Hillsborough.)

Shelagh dropped the postcard into a waste-paper basket and went down on to the stage to meet the group. A week, ten days, a fortnight, nothing came. She had given up hope. She would never hear from him. The theatre must take over, become meat and drink, love and sustenance. She was neither Shelagh nor Jinnie, she was Viola-Cesario, and must move, think, dream in character. Here was her only cure, stamp out all else. She tried to get Radio Eire on her transistor but it did not succeed. The voice of the announcer might have sounded like Michael's, like Murphy's, and roused some sort of feeling other than a total void. So on with the damned motley, and drown despair.

Olivia. Where goes Cesario?

Viola. After him I love,

  More than I love these eyes, more than my life . . .

Adam Vane, crouching like a black cat at the side of the stage, his horn-rimmed glasses balanced on his straggling hair, 'Don't pause, dear, that's very good, very good indeed.'

On the day of the dress rehearsal she left the flat in good time, picking up a taxi en route for the theatre. There was a jam at the corner of Belgrave Square, cars hooting, people hanging about on the pavement, mounted policemen. Shelagh opened the glass panel between herself and the driver.

'What's going on?' she asked. 'I'm in a hurry, I can't afford to be late.'

He grinned back at her over his shoulder. 'Demonstration,' he said, 'outside the Irish Embassy. Didn't you hear the one o'clock news? More explosions on the border. It looks as if it's brought the London–Ulster crowd out in force. They must have been throwing stones at the embassy windows.'

Fools, she thought. Wasting their time. Good job if the mounted police ride them down. She never listened to the one o'clock news, and she hadn't even glanced at the morning paper. Explosions on the border, Nick in the Control Room, the young man with the headphones over his ears, Murphy in the van, and I'm here in a taxi driving to my own show, my own fireworks, and after it's over my friends will crowd round me saying, 'Wonderful, darling, wonderful!'

The hold-up had put her timing out. She arrived at the theatre to find the atmosphere a mixture of excitement, confusion, last-minute panic. Never mind, she could cope. Her first scene as Viola over, she tore back to the dressing-room to change to Cesario. 'Oh, get out, can't you? I want the place to myself.' That's better, she thought, now I'm in control. I'm the boss around this place, or very soon will be. Off with Viola's wig, a brush to her own short hair. On with the breeches, on with the hose. Cape set on my shoulders. Dagger in my belt. Then a tap at the door. What the hell now?

'Who is it?' she called.

'A packet for you, Miss Blair. It's come express.'

'Oh, throw it down.'

Last minute touch to eyes, then stand back, take a last look, you'll do, you'll do. They'll all be shouting their heads off tomorrow night. She glanced away from the mirror, down to the packet on the table. A square-shaped envelope. It bore the post-mark Eire. Her heart turned over. She stood there a moment holding it in her hands, then tore the envelope open. A letter fell out, and something hard, between cardboard. She seized the letter first.

Dear Jinnie,

I'm off to the U.S. in the morning to see a publisher who has finally shown interest in my scholarly works, stone circles, ring forts, Early Bronze Age in Ireland, etc., etc., but I spare you . . . I shall probably be away for some months, and you can read in your glossy magazines about a one-time recluse spouting his head off in universities to the American young. In point of fact it suits me well to be out of the country for a while, what with one thing and another, as they say.

I have been burning some of my papers before leaving, and came across the enclosed photograph amongst a pile of junk in the bottom drawer of my desk. I thought it might amuse you. You may remember I told you that first evening you reminded me of someone. I see now that it was myself! *Twelfth Night* was the bond. Good luck, Cesario, and happy scalping.

Love, Nick.

America . . . From her viewpoint it might just as well be Mars. She took the photograph out of its cardboard covers and looked at it, frowning. Another practical joke? But she had never had a photograph taken of herself as Viola-Cesario, so how could he have possibly faked this? Had he snapped her when she wasn't aware of it, then placed the head on other shoulders? Impossible. She turned it over. He had written across the back, 'Nick Barry as Cesario in *Twelfth Night*. Dartmouth. 1929.'

She looked at the photograph again. Her nose, her chin, the cocky expression, head tip-tilted in the air. Even the stance, hand on hip. The thick cropped hair. Suddenly she was not standing in the dressing-room at all but in her father's bedroom, beside the window, and she heard him move, and she turned to look at him. He was staring at her, an expression of horror and disbelief upon his face. It was not accusation she had read in his eyes, but recognition. He had awakened from no nightmare, but from a dream that had lasted twenty years. Dying, he discovered truth.

They were knocking at the door again. 'Curtain coming down on Scene Three in four minutes' time, Miss Blair.'

She was lying in the van, his arms around her. 'Pam giggled a bit, then passed out cold. She'd forgotten all about it by the morning.'

Shelagh raised her eyes from the photograph she was holding in her hand and stared at herself in the mirror.

'Oh no . . .' she said. 'Oh, Nick . . . Oh my God!'

Then she took the dagger from her belt and stabbed it through the face of the boy in the photograph, ripping it apart, throwing the pieces into the waste-paper basket. And when she went back on to the stage it was not from the Duke's palace in Illyria that she saw herself moving henceforth, with painted backcloth behind her and painted boards beneath her feet, but out into a street, any street, where there were windows to be smashed and houses to burn, and stones and bricks and petrol to hand, where there were causes to despise and men to hate, for only by hating can you purge away love, only by sword, by fire.

The Way of the Cross

The Rev. Edward Babcock stood beside one of the lounge windows of the hotel on the Mount of Olives looking across the Kedron Valley to the city of Jerusalem on the opposite hill. Darkness had come so suddenly, between the time of arrival with his small party, the allotting of rooms, unpacking, a quick wash; and now, with hardly a moment to get his bearings and study his notes and guide-book, the little group would be on him, primed with questions, each requiring some measure of individual attention.

He had not chosen this particular assignment: he was deputising for the vicar of Little Bletford, who had succumbed to an attack of influenza and had been obliged to stay on board the S.S. *Ventura* in Haifa, leaving his small party of seven parishioners without a shepherd. It had been felt that, in the absence of their own vicar, another clergyman would be the most suitable person to lead them on the planned twenty-four-hour excursion to Jerusalem, and so the choice had fallen on Edward Babcock. He wished it had been otherwise. It was one thing to visit Jerusalem for the first time as a pilgrim amongst other pilgrims, even as an ordinary tourist, and quite another to find himself in charge of a group of strangers who would be regretting the unavoidable absence of their own vicar, and would in addition expect him to show qualities of leadership or, worse, the social bonhomie that was so evident a characteristic of the sick man. Edward Babcock knew the type only too well. He had observed the vicar on board, forever moving amongst the more affluent of the passengers, hob-nobbing with the titled, invariably at his ease. One or two even called him by his Christian name, notably Lady Althea Mason, the most prominent of the group from Little Bletford, and the *doyenne*, apparently, of Bletford Hall. Babcock, used to his own slum parish on the outskirts of Huddersfield, had no objection to Christian names – the members of his own youth club referred to him as Cocky often enough over a game of darts, or during one of the informal chats which the lads appeared to enjoy as much as he did himself – but snobbery was something he could not abide; and if the ailing vicar of Little Bletford thought that he, Babcock, was going to abase himself before a titled lady and her family, he was very much mistaken. Babcock had instantly summed up Lady Althea's husband, Colonel Mason, a retired army officer, as one of the old school tie brigade, and considered that their spoilt grandson Robin, instead of attending some private preparatory school, would have done better rubbing shoulders with the kids on a local council estate.

Mr and Mrs Foster were of a different calibre, but equally suspect in Babcock's eyes. Foster was managing director of an up-and-coming plastics firm, and from his conversation on the bus journey from Haifa to Jerusalem he seemed to think more of the possibilities of doing business with the Israelis than he did of visiting the Holy Places. His wife had countered the business chat by holding forth about the distress and starvation amongst Arab refugees, which, she insisted, was the responsibility of the whole world. She might have contributed towards this, thought Babcock, by wearing a less expensive fur coat, and giving the money saved to the refugees.

Mr and Mrs Smith were a young honeymoon couple. This had made them a special object of attention, giving rise to the usual indulgent glances and smiles – and even a few ill-judged jokes from Mr Foster. They would have done better, Babcock couldn't help telling himself, to have stayed in the hotel on the shores of Galilee and got to know each other properly, rather than trail around Jerusalem, the historical and religious importance of which they couldn't possibly grasp in their present mood.

The eighth, and oldest, member of the party was a spinster, Miss Dean. She was nearing seventy, she had informed them all, and it had been her life's dream to come to Jerusalem under the auspices of the vicar of Little Bletford. The substitution of the Rev. Edward Babcock for her beloved vicar, whom she alluded to as Father, had evidently spoilt her idyll.

So, thought the shepherd of the flock, glancing at his watch, the position is not an enviable one, but it is a challenge, and one that I must face. It is also a privilege.

The lounge was filling up, and the clamour of the many tourists and pilgrims who were already taking their places in the dining-room beyond rose in the air with discordant sound. Edward Babcock looked out once more towards the lights of Jerusalem on the opposite hill. He felt alien, alone, and curiously nostalgic for Huddersfield. He wished his crowd of friendly, though often rowdy, lads from the youth club could have been standing at his side.

Althea Mason was sitting on the stool before the dressing-table arranging a piece of blue organza round her shoulders. She had chosen the blue to match her eyes. It was her favourite colour, and she always managed to wear it somewhere on her person, no matter the circumstances, but this evening it looked particularly well against the darker shade of her dress. With the string of pearls, and the small pearl ear-rings, the effect was just right. Kate Foster would be overdressed as usual, of course – all that costume jewellery was in such bad taste, and the blue rinse to the hair added to her years, if she only realised it. It was a fact of life that however much money a woman had – or a man either, for that matter – it could never make up for lack of breeding. The Fosters were amiable enough, and everyone said Jim Foster would stand for Parliament one of these days, which one did not begrudge him – after all, it was a known thing that his firm gave large sums to the Conservative Party – but there was just that little touch of ostentation, of vulgarity, which betrayed his origins. Althea smiled. Her friends always told her she was shrewd, a keen judge of human nature.

'Phil?' she called over her shoulder to her husband. 'Are you ready?'

Colonel Mason was in the bathroom filing his nails. A minute speck of grime had wedged itself beneath his thumbnail and was almost impossible to extract. He resembled his wife in one particular only. A man must be well-groomed. A lack of polish to the shoes, an unbrushed shoulder, a dingy finger-nail, these things were taboo. Besides, if he and Althea were well turned out it set an example to the rest of the party, and above all to their grandson Robin. True, he was only nine years old, but a boy was never too young to learn, and heaven knows he was quick enough in the uptake. He would make a fine soldier one of these days – that is, if his scruffy scientist of a father ever allowed him to join the army. Seeing that the grandparents were paying for the boy's education, they should be allowed a say in his future. Curious thing that the younger men of today were glib enough when they talked of ideals and how everyone must progress in a changing world, but when the crunch came they were very ready to let the older generation pay the piper. Take this cruise, for instance. Robin was with them because it suited the parents' plans. Whether it suited himself and Althea was another matter. It so happened that it did, for he and Althea were devoted to the child, but that was not the point; it occurred too often during school holidays to be a coincidence.

'Coming,' he called, and straightening his tie went

through to the bedroom. 'All very comfortable, I must say,' he observed. 'I wonder if the rest of our party have it as good. Of course, none of this existed when I was here twenty years ago.'

Oh dear, thought Althea, are we going to have non-stop comparison with his time in the army and during the British occupation? Phil was not above demonstrating strategic positions with salt-cellars to Jim Foster during dinner.

'I did stipulate a view over Jerusalem for all of us,' she said, 'but whether the others realise that they have me to thank for the whole idea I can't make out. They've taken it very much for granted. Such a pity dear Arthur can't be with us; it really is a tragedy that he had to stay on board. He would have brought such life into it all. I don't think I take very much to young Babcock.'

'Oh, I don't know,' replied her husband. 'Seems a nice enough chap. Bit of an ordeal for him, coping at a moment's notice. We must make allowances.'

'He should have refused, if he wasn't equal to it,' said Althea. 'I must say I am continually amazed at the type of young man entering the Church today. Certainly not out of the top drawer. Have you noticed his accent? Still, one never knows what to expect in this day and age.'

She stood up for a final glance in the mirror. Colonel Mason cleared his throat and glanced at his watch. He hoped Althea would not put on her superior manner in front of the luckless parson.

'Where's Robin?' he asked. 'We ought to be getting on down.'

'I'm here, Grandfather.'

The boy had been standing behind the drawn curtains all the time, looking at the view of the city. Funny little chap. Always appearing out of nowhere. Pity he had to wear those spectacles. Made him the spit image of his father.

'Well, my boy,' said Colonel Mason, 'what do you make

of it all? I don't mind telling you Jerusalem wasn't lighted up like that twenty years ago.'

'No,' replied his grandson, 'I don't suppose it was. Nor two thousand years ago either. Electricity has made an enormous difference to the world. I was saying to Miss Dean as we came along in the bus that Jesus would be very surprised.'

H'm . . . No answer to that one. Extraordinary things children said. He exchanged looks with his wife. She smiled indulgently, and patted Robin's shoulder. She liked to think that nobody but herself understood what she was fond of calling his little ways.

'I hope Miss Dean wasn't shocked.'

'Shocked?' Robin put his head on one side and considered the matter. 'I'm sure she wasn't,' he replied, 'but I was rather shocked myself when we saw that car that had broken down by the side of the road, and we drove past it without stopping.'

Colonel Mason closed the bedroom door behind them, and all three walked along the corridor.

'Car?' he asked. 'What car? I don't remember seeing one.'

'You were looking the other way, Grandfather,' said Robin. 'You were pointing out to Mr Foster a place where there had been machine-guns in your day. Perhaps nobody saw the broken-down car but myself. The guide was busy showing us the site of the Good Samaritan Inn. The car was a few yards further along the road.'

'The driver had probably run out of petrol,' said Althea. 'I dare say somebody came along shortly. It seemed a busy road.'

She caught sight of her reflection in the long mirror at the end of the corridor, and adjusted the piece of blue organza.

Jim Foster was having a quick one in the bar. Or two, to be exact. Then when the others appeared he would stand

everybody drinks, and Kate would have to lump it. She
would scarcely have the nerve to tick him off in front of
everyone with threats of a coronary and the number of
calories contained in a double gin. He looked round at the
chattering throng. God, what a mob! The Chosen Race in
full possession, and good luck to them, especially the
women, although the young ones were better looking in
Haifa. Nobody worth crossing the room for here. This lot
were probably from New York's East Side anyway, and not
indigenous. The hotel was lousy with tourists, and it would
be worse tomorrow in Jerusalem proper. He had a good
mind to cry off the sight-seeing and hire a car to take himself and Kate down to the Dead Sea, where there was this
talk of installing a plant for making plastics. The Israelis
had hit on a new method of processing, and you could bet
your life that if they were on to something they believed
in it would prosper. Bloody silly to come all this way and
not be able to talk with authority about the site when he
got home. Sheer waste of expense account. Hullo, here
came the honeymooners. No need to ask what they had
been doing since decanting from the bus! Though on
second thoughts you never could be sure. Bob Smith
looked a bit strained. Perhaps the bride, like all red-heads,
was insatiable. A drink would put new strength into both
of them.

'Come on, the bridal pair,' he called. 'The choice of
drinks is yours, the damage mine. Let's all relax.'

Gallantly he slid off his stool and offered it to Jill Smith,
taking care to allow his hand to remain just one instant
beneath her small posterior as she mounted his vacated
seat.

'Thanks ever so, Mr Foster,' said the bride, and to prove
that she had not lost her self-possession, and was aware
that his lingering hand was intended for a compliment, she
added, 'I don't know about Bob, but I'd like champagne.'

The remark was made with such defiance that the bride-groom flushed scarlet. Oh hell, he thought. Mr Foster will fluff. He can't help fluffing from Jill's tone that . . . that it's not working out, that I just can't somehow get going. It's a nightmare, I don't know what's wrong, I shall have to ask a doctor, I . . .

'Whisky, please, sir,' he said.

'Whisky it shall be,' smiled Jim Foster, 'and for heaven's sake don't either of you call me anything but Jim.'

He commanded a champagne cocktail for Jill, a double whisky for Bob, and a large gin-and-tonic for himself, and as he did so his wife Kate pushed through the crowd hovering at the bar and heard him give the order.

I knew it, thought Kate. I knew that was the reason he came downstairs before I had finished dressing, so that he could get to the bar before me. And he's got his eye on that chit of a girl, what's more. Hasn't the decency to leave anything young and female alone, even on her honeymoon. Thank heaven she had put a stop to his idea of meeting up with business friends in Tel Aviv and letting her come to Jerusalem alone. She was not going to let him get away with that one, thank you very much. If only Colonel Mason wasn't such an old bore and Lady Althea such a colossal snob the visit to Jerusalem could be so rewarding, especially to anyone with a spark of intelligence and an interest in world affairs. But what did they care? They hadn't even bothered to come to the talk she had given in Little Bletford on the world refugee problem a few weeks ago, making the excuse that they never went out in the evenings, which was quite untrue. If Lady Althea thought more about other people and less about the fact that she was the only surviving daughter of a peer who had never even risen to his feet in the House of Lords, and was said to be dotty anyway, Kate would have more respect for her.

As it was . . . She looked about her, indignation rising. All these tourists drinking and enjoying themselves, and spending the money that might have gone to Oxfam or some other worthwhile charity, it made her feel quite ashamed to be amongst them. Well, if there was nothing active she could do to help world causes at the moment, she could at least break up Jim's little party and put him in his place. She advanced towards the bar, her high colour clashing with her magenta blouse.

'Now, Mr Smith,' she said, 'don't encourage my husband. He's been told by his doctor to cut down on his drinking and smoking, or he'll have a coronary. It's no use making that face at me, Jim, you know it's true. As a matter of fact, we'd all of us be better without alcohol. Statistics prove that the damage to the liver through even quite a modest intake is incalculable.'

Bob Smith replaced his glass on the bar counter. He was just beginning to feel more sure of himself. Now Mrs Foster had gone and spoilt it all.

'Oh, don't mind me,' she said, 'nobody ever listens to a word I say, but one of these days the world will wake up to the fact that by drinking only pure fruit juices the human being can stand ten times the stress and strain of modern life. We should all live longer, look younger, achieve greater things. Yes, I'd like a grape-fruit juice, please. Plenty of ice.'

Pheugh! It was stuffy. She could feel the flush rising from her neck right up to her temples, and then descending in a slow-moving wave. What a fool she was . . . She had forgotten to take her hormones.

Jill Smith watched Kate Foster over the rim of her champagne glass. She must be older than he was. Looked it, anyway. You never could tell with middle-aged people, and men were most deceptive. She had read somewhere that men went on doing it until they were nearly ninety, but women lost interest after the change of life. Perhaps Mrs

Foster was right about fruit-juice being good for you. Oh, why did Bob have to wear that spotted tie? It made him look so pasty. And he had such a schoolboy appearance beside Mr Foster. Fancy telling them to call him Jim! He was touching her arm again. Honestly! The fact that she was on her honeymoon didn't seem to put men off but rather egged them on, if he was anything to go by. She nodded when he suggested another glass of champagne.

'Don't let Mrs Foster hear you,' she whispered. 'She would say it would damage my liver.'

'My dear girl,' he murmured, 'a liver as young as yours will stand years of punishment. Mine is already pickled.'

Jill giggled. The things he said! And drinking down her second champagne cocktail she forgot about the unhappy scene in the bedroom upstairs, with Bob, white and tense, telling her she wasn't responding properly and it was not his fault. Staring defiantly at Bob, who was agreeing politely with Mrs Foster about starvation in the Middle East and Asia and India, she leant pointedly against Jim Foster's arm and said, 'I don't know why Lady Althea picked on this hotel. The one the purser recommended was right in Jerusalem, and it runs a tour of the city by night, ending up in a night club, drinks included.'

Miss Dean peered about her short-sightedly. How was she going to find the rest of the party amongst such a crowd of strangers? If only dear Father Garfield had been with them, he would never have left her to fend for herself. That young clergyman who was replacing him had barely said two words to her, and she felt sure he wasn't an Anglican. Probably disapproved of vestments, and had never intoned in his life. If she could catch sight of Lady Althea or the Colonel it would be something, although Lady Althea, bless her, was inclined to be just a little snubby sometimes, but then she must have a lot on her mind. It was so good of her to take all the trouble she had done with the tour.

Jerusalem . . . Jerusalem . . . Well, the daughters of Jerusalem would certainly weep if they could see this big agnostic crowd on the Mount of Olives. It really did not seem right to have a modern hotel on such a hallowed spot, where Our Lord had wandered so frequently with his disciples on his way to Jerusalem from Bethany. How she had missed Father when the bus paused for a few minutes in the village and the guide had pointed out the ruined church beneath which, so he said, the home of Mary and Martha and Lazarus had stood two thousand years ago! Father would have brought it so vividly to life. She could have pictured the modest but comfortable home, the well-swept kitchen, Martha in charge and Mary not too helpful, probably, with clearing the dishes, reminding her, when she read the passage in the Gospel, of her own younger sister Dora, who never did a hand's turn if there was a good programme on television. Not that one could compare Mary at Bethany listening to Our Lord's wonderful sermons with someone like Malcolm Muggeridge asking the question why, but after all, as Father always said, one should try and relate the past to the present, and then one would come to a better understanding of what everything meant.

Ah, there was Lady Althea coming along the corridor now. How distinguished she looked, so English, so refined amongst the rest of the people here in the hotel, who seemed mostly foreigners, and the Colonel at her side every inch the soldier and gentleman. Little Robin was such an original child. Fancy him making that remark about Our Lord being surprised if he could see electric light. 'But He invented it, dear,' she had told him. 'Everything that has ever been invented or discovered was Our

Lord's doing.' She was afraid it had not sunk into his little mind. No matter. There would be other opportunities to make the right impression upon him.

'Well, Miss Dean,' said the Colonel, advancing towards her, 'I hope you feel rested after the long bus ride, and have a good appetite for dinner?'

'Thank you, Colonel, yes, I am quite refreshed, but a little bewildered. Do you think we shall have English food, or will it be that greasy foreign stuff? I have to be careful with my inside.'

'Well, if my experience in the Near East is anything to go by, avoid fresh fruit and melon. Likewise salad. They never wash them properly. Had more tummy trouble amongst the troops in the old days with fruit and salad than anything else.'

'Oh, Phil, what nonsense,' smiled Lady Althea. 'You're living in the past. Of course everything is washed in an up-to-date place like this. Don't take any notice of him, Miss Dean. We shall be served a five-course dinner, and you must do justice to everything they put on your plate. Just picture your sister Dora sitting down to a boiled egg at home, and think how she would envy you.'

Now that, thought Miss Dean, was kindly meant but uncalled for. Why should Lady Althea imagine that she and Dora never had more than a boiled egg for supper? It was true they ate sparsely in the evening, but that was because they both had small appetites. It was nothing to do with the way they lived or what they could afford. Now, if Father had been here he would have known just how to answer Lady Althea. He would have told her – laughingly, of course, for he was so courteous – that he had been better fed by the two Miss Deans in Syringa Cottage than anywhere else in Little Bletford.

'Thank you, Colonel,' she said, addressing herself pointedly to him, 'I shall follow your advice about the fruit and salad. As to the five-course menu, I shall reserve judgement until I see what they have to offer.'

She hoped she would be sitting next to the Colonel at dinner. He was so considerate. And he knew Jerusalem of old – he was quite an authority.

'Your grandson,' she said to him, 'makes friends very easily. He is not at all shy.'

'Oh, yes,' replied Colonel Mason, 'Robin's an excellent mixer. Part of my training, I like to think. He reads a lot too. Most children never open a book.'

'Your son-in-law is a scientist, is he not?' said Miss Dean. 'Scientists are such clever men. Perhaps the little boy takes after his father.'

'H'm, I don't know about that,' said the Colonel.

Silly old fool, he thought. Doesn't know what she's talking about. Robin was a Mason all right. Reminded him of himself at the same age. He used to be a great reader too. And imaginative.

'Come on, Robin,' he called, 'your grandmother wants her dinner.'

'Really, Phil,' said Lady Althea, half-amused but not entirely so, 'you make me sound like the wolf in Red Riding Hood.'

She walked leisurely through the lounge, aware of the many heads that were turned in her direction, not because of her husband's remark, which few people had heard, but because she knew that, despite her sixty-odd years, she was the best-looking and most distinguished woman present. She looked around for the party from Little Bletford, deciding as she did so how she would seat them at dinner. Oh, there they were in the bar – all, that is to say, except Babcock. She dispatched her husband in search of him, and moving into the restaurant summoned the head waiter with an imperious finger.

Her seating plan worked out very well, and everyone

appeared satisfied. Miss Dean did justice to the five-course dinner and the wine, though possibly it was a little tactless to lift her glass as soon as it was filled and say to her left-hand neighbour, the Rev. Babcock, 'Let us wish dear Father a speedy recovery, and I am sure he knows how sorely we all miss him here this evening.'

It was not until they were embarking upon the third course that she realised the full import of her words, and remembered that the young man talking to her was not a social worker in the midlands at all but a clergyman himself, acting as deputy for her own beloved vicar. The glass of sherry in the bar had made her light-headed, and the fact that the Rev. Babcock did not wear a clergyman's collar had somehow confused the whole situation.

'Be very careful what you eat,' she said to him, hoping to make amends for any small hurt her words had caused. 'The Colonel says that fruit and salad are not advisable. The native people do not rinse them thoroughly. I think roast lamb would be a wise choice.'

Edward Babcock stared at her use of the word native. Did Miss Dean imagine herself in the wilds of Africa? Just how out of touch with the world of today could you get, he wondered, living in a village in southern England?

'In my rough-and-ready fashion,' he told her, helping himself to ragout of chicken, 'I believe we do more good in the world by seeing how the other half lives than by just sticking to our own routine. We have quite a number of Pakistanis and Jamaicans in our club, amongst our own local lads, and they take it in turn to prepare a meal in the canteen. We get some surprises, I don't mind telling you! But it's a case of share and share alike, and the boys enjoy it.'

'Quite right, padre, quite right,' said the Colonel, who had heard the tail-end of this remark. 'It's absolutely essential to promote a spirit of goodwill in the Mess. Morale goes to pieces if you don't.'

Jim Foster pushed Jill Smith's foot under the table. The old boy was off again. Where did he think he was – Poona? Jill Smith retaliated by bumping her knee against his. They had reached the stage of mutual for-want-of-anything-better-attraction when bodily contact brings warmth, and the most harmless remark made by others suggests a double meaning.

'Depends what you share and who you share it with, don't you agree?' he murmured.

'Once married a girl has no choice,' she murmured back. 'She has to take what her husband gives her.'

Then, noticing Mrs Foster staring at her across the table, she opened her eyes, wide and innocent, and bumped Jim Foster's knee once more to cement duplicity.

Lady Althea, glancing round the restaurant at the occupants of the other tables, wondered if Jerusalem had been such a good choice after all. Nobody of much interest here. Perhaps there would be a better class of people in the Lebanon. Still, it was only for twenty-four hours, and then they would rejoin the boat and go on to Cyprus. She would be content that Phil and darling Robin were enjoying themselves. She must tell Robin not to sit with his mouth open. He was such a good-looking child, and it made him appear half-witted. Kate Foster was surely feeling the heat, she had become very flushed.

'But you *should* have signed the petition against the manufacture of nerve gas,' Kate was saying to Bob Smith. 'I got more than a thousand names on my appeal list, and it's up to every one of us to see that this frightful business is stopped. How will you like it,' she demanded, banging on the table, 'when your children are born deaf, maimed and blind, because of this terrible chemical that will pollute succeeding generations unless we all unite to prevent its manufacture?'

'Oh, come,' protested the Colonel, 'the authorities have

everything under control. And the stuff isn't lethal. We must have a certain amount in stock in case of riots. Somebody has to deal with the scallywags of the world. Now, in my humble opinion . . .'

'Never mind your humble opinion, Phil dear,' interrupted his wife. 'I think we are all getting a little too serious, and we haven't come to Jerusalem to discuss nerve gas, or riots, or anything of the sort. We are here to take back pleasant memories of one of the most famous cities in the world.'

Silence was instant. She smiled upon them all. A good hostess knew when to change a party's mood. Even Jim Foster, momentarily quelled, removed his hand from Jill Smith's knee. The question was, who would be the first to speak and set the ball rolling in a new direction? Robin knew that his moment had arrived. He had been awaiting his opportunity all through dinner. His scientist father had told him never to introduce a subject or speak about it unless he were sure of his facts, and he had taken good care to be well-primed. He had consulted the courier-guide in the foyer before dinner, and he knew that his facts were correct. The grown-ups would be obliged to listen. The very thought of this was delicious, giving him a tremendous sense of power. He leant forward across the table, his spectacles slightly out of balance, his head on one side.

'I wonder if any of you know,' he said, 'that today is the 13th day of Nisan?' Then he leant back in his chair for his words to take effect.

The adults at the table stared back at him, nonplussed. What on earth was the child talking about? His grandfather, trained to be prepared for the unexpected, was the first to reply.

'The 13th day of Nisan?' he repeated. 'Now, my lively lad, stop trying to be clever and tell us what you mean.'

'I'm not trying to be clever, Grandfather,' replied Robin,

'I'm just stating a fact. I'm going by the Hebrew calendar. Tomorrow, the 14th day of Nisan, at sunset, is the start of Pesach, the Feast of Unleavened Bread. The guide told me. That's why there are so many people staying here. They've come on pilgrimage from all over the world. Well, everybody knows – at least Mr Babcock does, I'm sure – that according to St John and many other authorities Jesus and his disciples ate the Last Supper on the 13th day of Nisan, the day before the Feast of Unleavened Bread, so it seemed to me rather appropriate that we should all just have finished our supper here this evening. Jesus was doing precisely the same thing two thousand years ago.'

He pushed his spectacles back on his forehead and smiled. The effect of his words was not so stunning as he had hoped. No burst of applause. No exclamations of wonder at his general knowledge. Everyone looked rather cross.

'H'm,' said Colonel Mason, 'this is your province, padre.'

Babcock did a rapid calculation. He was used to problems being fired at him on the Any Questions programme he gave quarterly at the youth club, but he wasn't prepared for this one.

'You have evidently read your gospels thoroughly, Robin,' he said. 'Matthew, Mark and Luke appear to disagree with John as to the exact date. However, I must admit I had not checked up on the fact that tomorrow is the 14th day of Nisan, and so the Jewish holiday begins at sunset. It was rather remiss of me not to have talked to the guide myself.'

His statement did not do much to clear the air. Miss Dean was frankly bewildered.

'But how can this be the day of the Last Supper?' she asked. 'We all celebrated Easter early this year. Surely Easter Day was the 29th of March?'

'The Jewish calendar is different from ours,' said

Babcock. 'Pesach, or Passover, as we term it, does not necessarily coincide with Easter.'

Surely he was not expected to enter into a theological discussion because a small boy enjoyed showing off?

Jim Foster clicked his fingers in the air. 'That explains why I couldn't get Rubin on the telephone, Kate,' he said. 'They told me the office in Tel Aviv would be shut until the 21st. A public holiday.'

'I hope the shops and bazaars will be open,' Jill exclaimed. 'I want to buy souvenirs for the family and friends back home.'

After a moment's thought Robin nodded his head. 'I think they will,' he said, 'at least until sunset. You could give your friends some unleavened bread.' An idea suddenly struck him, and he turned delightedly to the Rev. Babcock. 'Seeing that it's the evening of the 13th day of Nisan,' he said, 'oughtn't we all to walk down the hill to the Garden of Gethsemane? It's not very far away. I asked the guide. Jesus and the disciples crossed the valley, but we needn't do that. We could just imagine we had gone back two thousand years and they were going to be there.'

Even his grandmother, who generally applauded his every action, looked a little uncomfortable.

'Really, Robin,' she said, 'I don't think any of us are quite prepared to set forth after dinner and stumble about in the dark. We aren't taking part in your end of term play, remember.' She turned to Babcock. 'They put on a very sweet little nativity play last Christmas,' she said. 'Robin was one of the Three Wise Men.'

'Oh yes,' he countered, 'my Huddersfield lads staged a nativity play at the club. Set the scene in Vietnam. I was very impressed.' Robin was gazing at him with more than usual intensity, and he made a supreme effort to meet the challenge. 'Look,' he said, 'if you really want to walk down the hill to Gethsemane I'm willing to go with you.'

'Splendid!' said the Colonel. 'I'm game. A breath of fresh air would do us all good. I know the terrain – you won't be lost with me in charge.'

'How about it?' murmured Jim Foster to his neighbour Jill. 'If you hold on tight I won't let you go.'

A delighted smile spread over Robin's face. Things were going his way after all. No risk now of being packed off early to bed.

'You know,' he said, touching the Rev. Babcock's arm, his voice sounding very loud and clear, 'if we were really the disciples and you were Jesus, you would have to line us all up in a row against the wall there and start to wash our feet. But my grandmother would probably say that was going a bit too far.'

He stood aside, bowing politely, to let the grown-up people pass. He was destined for Winchester, and he remembered the motto, Manners Makyth Man.

The air was sharp and clean, like a sword's blade. No wind – the air alone made the cutting edge. The stony path led downwards, steep and narrow, bound on either side by walls. On the right the sombre cluster of cypress trees and pines masked the seven spires of the Russian cathedral and the smaller humped dome of the Dominus Flevit church. In the daytime the onion spires of St Mary Magdalene would gleam golden under the sun, and across the valley of Kidron the city walls which encompassed Jerusalem, with the Dome of the Rock prominent in the foreground and the city itself spreading ever further west and north, would not fail to awaken some response in every pilgrim heart, as it had done through the centuries, but tonight . . . Tonight thought Edward Babcock, with the pale yellow moon coming up behind us and the dark sky above our heads, even the low hum of the traffic beneath us on the main road to Jericho seems to blend and merge into the silence. As the steep path descended so the city rose, and the valley separating it from the Mount of Olives down which they walked became sombre, black, like a winding river-bed. Mosques, domes, spires, towers, the roof-tops of a myriad human dwellings fused together, blotted against the sky, and only the walls of the city remained, steadfast on the opposite hill, a threat, a challenge.

'I'm not ready for this,' he thought. 'It's too big, I can't take it, I shan't be able to explain what it means, not even to this small handful of people who are with me. I ought to have stayed in the hotel reading up my notes and studying the map so as to be able to speak with some sort of authority tomorrow. Or, better still, have come here on my own.'

It was wrong of him, uncharitable, but the perpetual chatter of the Colonel at his side got on his nerves, made him edgy, irritable. Who cared what his regiment had been doing in '48? It was out of keeping with the scene spread out before them.

'And so,' the Colonel was saying, 'the Mandate was handed over to the U.N. in May, and we were all out of the country by July 1st. To my mind we should have stayed. The whole thing has been a bloody nonsense ever since. No one will ever settle down in this part of the world, and they'll still be fighting over Jerusalem when you and I have been in our graves for years. Beautiful spot, you know, from this distance. Used to be pretty scruffy inside the Old City.'

The pine trees to their right were motionless. Everything was still. To their left the hillside appeared bare, uncultivated, but Babcock could be mistaken: moonlight was deceptive, those white shapes that seemed to be rocks and boulders could be tombs. Once there would have been no sombre pines, no cypresses, no Russian cathedral, only the olive trees with silver branches sweeping the stony ground, and the sound of the brook trickling through the valley below.

'Funny thing,' said the Colonel, 'I never did any proper soldiering once I left this place behind me. Served for a time back home, at Aldershot, but what with reorganisation in the army, and one thing and another, and my wife wasn't too fit at the time, I decided to pack it in and quit. I should have been given command of my regiment if I had stayed, and gone to Germany, but Althea was all against it, and it didn't seem fair to her. Her father left her the Hall, you know, in Little Bletford. She had been brought up there, and her life was centred in it. Still is, in fact. She does a great deal locally.'

Edward Babcock made an effort to attend, to show some sign of interest. 'You regret leaving the army?'

The Colonel did not answer immediately, but when he did the usual tone of brisk self-confidence had gone; he sounded puzzled, strained.

'It was my whole life,' he said. 'And that's another funny thing, padre – I don't think I've ever realised it before tonight. Just standing here, looking at that city across the valley, makes me remember.'

Something moved in the shadows below. It was Robin. He had been crouching against the wall. He had a map in his hand and a small torch.

'Look, Mr Babcock,' he said, 'that's where they must have come, from the gate in the wall over to the left. We can't see it from here, but it's marked on the map. Jesus and his disciples, I mean, after they had had their supper. And the gardens and trees were probably all up this hill then, not just down at the bottom where the church stands today. In fact, if we go on a bit further and sit down by that wall, we can picture the whole thing. The soldiers and the high priests' attendants coming down with flares from the other gate, perhaps where that car is showing now. Come on!'

He began running down the hill in front of them, flicking his small torch to and fro, until he disappeared round a turn of the wall.

'Watch your step, Robin,' called his grandfather. 'You might fall. It's jolly steep down there.' Then he turned to his companion. 'He can read a map as well as I can myself. Only nine years old.'

'I'll go after him,' said Babcock. 'See he doesn't get into trouble. You wait here for Lady Althea.'

'You needn't worry, padre,' replied the Colonel. 'The boy knows what he's doing.'

Babcock pretended not to hear. It was an excuse to be alone, if only for a few minutes, otherwise the scene beneath him would never make the deep impression he desired, so that he could describe it later to all the lads, when he returned to Huddersfield.

Colonel Mason remained motionless beside the wall. The slow, careful footsteps of his wife and Miss Dean descending the path behind him were only a short distance away, and Althea's voice carried on the still cold air.

'If we don't see them we'll turn back,' she was saying, 'but I know what Phil can be like when he's in charge of an expedition. He always thinks he knows the way, and only too often he doesn't at all.'

'I can hardly credit that,' said Miss Dean, 'as a military man.'

Lady Althea laughed. 'Dear Phil,' she said. 'He likes everyone to think he might have become a general. But the truth is, Miss Dean, he would never have made the grade. I had it on the highest authority from one of his brother officers. Oh, they were all fond of him, but the dear old boy would never have gone any further, not in the army as it is today. That's why we all persuaded him to retire when he did. I sometimes wish he would be just a little more active where local affairs are concerned, but there it is, I have to act for us both. And he has done wonders in the garden.'

'That lovely herbaceous border!' said Miss Dean.

'Yes, and the rock plants too. They make quite a show the whole year through.'

The slow footsteps passed without stopping, neither woman looking to right or left, so intent were they upon the rough path under their feet. For one moment their two figures were sharply outlined against the trees beyond, then they turned the corner as Robin had done, and Babcock, and disappeared.

Colonel Mason let them go without calling them back. Then he turned up the collar of his coat, for it seemed suddenly colder, and began to retrace his steps slowly towards the hotel above. He had nearly made the ascent when he bumped into two other members of the party coming down.

'Hullo,' said Jim Foster, 'you crying off already? I thought you'd be in Jerusalem by now!'

'Turned very cold,' said the Colonel shortly. 'Not much sense in stumping on down to the bottom. You'll find the others scattered about the hillside.'

He climbed on past them towards the hotel with a hasty goodnight.

'Now, if he runs into my wife up there and tells her you and I are together we shall be in trouble,' said Jim Foster. 'Willing to risk it?'

'Risk what?' asked Jill Smith. 'We're not doing anything.'

'Now that, my girl, is what I call a direct invitation. Never mind, Kate can console your husband in the bar. Watch your step, this path is steep. The slippery slope to ruin for the pair of us. Don't leave go of my arm.'

Jill threw off her head-scarf and drew a deep breath, clinging tightly to her companion.

'Look at all the city lights,' she said. 'I bet there's plenty going on up there. Makes me feel envious. We seem to be stuck at the back of beyond up here.'

'Don't worry. You'll see it all tomorrow, led by his

reverence. But I doubt if he'll take you into a discotheque, if that's what you're after.'

'Well, naturally we must see the historical part first – that's why we're here, isn't it? But I want to go to the shopping centre too.'

'Suks, my girl, suks. Lot of little trinket-booths in back alleys with dark-eyed young salesmen trying to pinch your bottom.'

'Oh, you think I'd let them, do you?'

'I don't know. But I wouldn't blame them for trying.'

He glanced back over his shoulder. No sign of Kate. Perhaps she had decided against joining the expedition after all. The last he had seen of her was the back of her figure making for the lift en route for their room. As for Bob Smith, if he couldn't keep an eye on his bride that was his lookout. The clump of trees on the other side of the wall further down the path looked enticing. Just the right spot for a little harmless fun.

'What do you make of marriage, Jill?' he asked.

'It's too early to say,' she answered, instantly on the defensive.

'Of course it is. Silly question. But most honeymoons are a flop. I know mine was. It took Kate and me months to get adjusted. That Bob of yours is a great fellow, but he's still very young. All bridegrooms suffer from nerves, you know, even in these enlightened days. Think they know it all, but they damn well don't, and the poor girls suffer for it in consequence.' She did not answer, and he steered her towards the trees. 'It's not until a man has been married for some time that he knows how to make his wife respond. It's technique, like everything else in life – not a question of letting nature take its course. And all women vary. Their moods, their likes and dislikes. Am I shocking you?'

'Oh no,' she said, 'not at all.'

'Good. I wouldn't want to shock you. You're far too

sweet and precious for that. I don't see any sign of the others, do you?'

'No.'

'Let's go and lean against the wall down there, and look at the city lights. Wonderful spot. Wonderful evening. Does Bob ever tell you how lovely you are? Because it's true, you know . . .'

Kate Foster, who had been upstairs to take her hormone pills, came down to the lounge to look for her husband. When she couldn't find him she went into the bar, and saw Bob Smith all alone, drinking a double whisky.

'Where is everybody?' she asked. 'Our lot, I mean,' for the room was still crowded.

'Gone out, I think,' he answered.

'What about your wife?'

'Oh yes, she went. She followed Lady Althea and Miss Dean. Your husband was with her.'

'I see.'

She did see, too. Only too well. Jim had deliberately given her the slip when she went upstairs.

'Well, it won't do you any good sitting there drinking that poison,' she said. 'I suggest you get your coat and come with me and join the rest of the party. No sense in mooning here on your own.'

Perhaps she was right. Perhaps it *was* wet and ineffectual to sit drinking all alone when by rights Jill should have been with him. But the way she had smiled at Foster was more than he could stand, and he had thought, by staying here, that it would be a sort of lesson to her. In fact, he had only been punishing himself. Jill probably couldn't care less.

'All right,' he said, sliding off the stool, 'we'll go after them. They can't have gone far.'

They set off together down the path that led to the valley, a strangely ill-assorted couple, Bob Smith long and lanky, a mop of dark hair nearly touching his shoulders, hands thrust deep in the pockets of his coat, and Kate Foster in her mink jacket, gold ear-rings dangling beneath blue-rinsed hair.

'If you ask me,' she said, as she stumped down the path in her unsuitable shoes, 'this whole outing to Jerusalem has been a mistake. Nobody is really interested in the place. Except perhaps Miss Dean. But you know what Lady Althea is, she had everything arranged with the vicar, and has to play lady of the manor whether she's in England, on board ship or in the Middle East. As for Babcock, he's worse than useless. We'd have been better without him. And as for you two . . . Well, it's hardly the best start for married life to let your wife do just as she pleases all the time. You want to show a little authority.'

'Jill's very young,' he said, 'barely twenty.'

'Oh, youth . . . Don't talk to me about youth. You all have it too good these days. In our country, anyway. Very different for some of the youngsters in this part of the world – I'm thinking of the Arab countries in particular – where husbands keep a tight watch on their brides to make sure they don't get into trouble.'

I don't know why I'm saying all this, she thought, it won't sink in. They none of them think of anyone but themselves. If only I didn't feel things so acutely, it does no good, I make myself ill with worry about everything – the state of the world, the future, Jim . . . Where on earth has he got to with that girl? My heart keeps missing a beat. I wonder if those pills suit me . . . ?

'Don't walk so fast,' she said. 'I can't keep up with you.'

'I'm sorry, Mrs Foster. I thought I saw two figures in the distance over by those trees.'

And if it is them, he wondered, what of it? I mean, what can I do? I can't make a scene just because Jill chose to wander out of the hotel with another member of the party. I shall have to hang about and say nothing, and then wait until we're back at the hotel and give her hell. If only this bloody woman would stop talking for one moment . . .

The two figures turned out to be Lady Althea and Miss Dean.

'Have you seen Jim?' Kate Foster called.

'No,' replied Lady Althea. 'I was just wondering what's happened to Phil. I wish our menfolk wouldn't tear off in this way. It's so inconsiderate. I do think Babcock at least should have waited for us.'

'So different from dear Father,' murmured Miss Dean. 'He would have had it all so well organised, and known just what to show us. As it is, we don't know whether the Garden of Gethsemane is further on along this path or all around us as we stand here.'

The trees beyond the wall were so very dark, and the path seemed to get stonier and stonier. If Father had been with them she could have leant on his arm. Lady Althea was being very kind, but it wasn't the same.

'I'll go on,' said Bob. 'You three stay here.'

He strode ahead of them down the path. If the rest of the party were all together, they couldn't be far away. The Colonel would be in charge, he would keep an eye on Jill.

There was a break in the trees about a hundred yards ahead, and open ground, with clumps of small olives and rough unbroken soil, nothing looking like a garden, what a bloody silly expedition anyway, and all to do over again tomorrow. Then he saw a figure, only one, though, humped against a piece of rock. It was Babcock. For one embarrassed moment Bob thought he was praying, and then he saw that he was bent over a notebook, scribbling with the aid of a torch. He lifted his head at the sound of Bob's footsteps and waved the torch.

'Where are the others?' called Bob.

'The Colonel's up behind you on the road,' returned Babcock, 'and the boy's down there, where he can get a better view of Gethsemane. But the garden itself is shut. It doesn't really matter, though. You can get the atmosphere from here.' He smiled in a rather shamefaced fashion as Bob approached him. 'If I don't write down what I see, I shan't remember it. Robin lent me his torch. I want to lecture about this when I get home. Well, not a straight lecture. Just my impressions to the lads.'

'Have you seen Jill?' asked Bob.

Babcock stared. Jill . . . Oh yes, his young wife.

'No,' he said. 'Isn't she with you?'

'You can see she isn't with me,' Bob almost shouted in exasperation. 'And there are only Mrs Foster and Lady Althea and Miss Dean up the road.'

'Oh,' said Babcock. 'Well, I'm afraid I can't help you. The Colonel is around somewhere. I came on alone with the boy.'

Bob could feel the anger mounting within him. 'Look here,' he said, 'I don't mean to be rude, but just who is in charge of this outfit?'

The Rev. Babcock flushed. There was no call for Bob Smith to get so excited.

'There's no question of anybody being in charge,' he said. 'The Colonel and Robin and I left the hotel on our own. If the rest of you chose to follow on and got lost, I'm afraid it's your own affair.'

He was used to rough talk from the lads, but this was different. Anyone would think he was a paid courier.

'I'm sorry,' said Bob. 'The fact is . . .' The fact was he had never felt more helpless, more alone. Weren't parsons supposed to help one in trouble? 'The fact is, I'm worried stiff. Everything's gone wrong. I had one hell of a row with Jill before dinner, and I can't think straight.'

Babcock put down his notebook and extinguished his torch. No more impressions of Gethsemane tonight. Well, it couldn't be helped.

'I'm sorry to hear that,' he said, 'but it happens all the time, you know. Young married couples have arguments, and they feel it's the end of the world. You'll both look at it differently in the morning.'

'No,' said Bob, 'that's just it. I don't think we shall. I keep wondering if we haven't made a terrible mistake in getting married.'

His companion was silent. The poor chap was overtired, probably. He had let things get on top of him. It was difficult to give advice when one didn't know either of them. If things hadn't been going too well, the vicar of Little Bletford should have spotted it and had a word with them both. He probably would have, if he had been here, and not on the boat in Haifa.

'Well,' he said, 'marriage is give and take, you know. It's not just ... how shall I put it? It's not just a physical relationship.'

'It's the physical side of it that's gone wrong,' said Bob Smith.

'I see.'

Babcock wondered if he should advise the lad to see a doctor when he got home. There was nothing much that could be done about it here tonight.

'Look,' he said, 'don't worry too much. Take it easy. Be as gentle as you can with your wife, and perhaps . . .'

But he couldn't continue, for at that moment a small figure darted up from the trees below. It was Robin.

'The actual Garden of Gethsemane looks very small,' he called. 'I feel sure Jesus and the disciples wouldn't have sat down there. They would more likely have climbed up here, amongst all the olive trees that were growing in those days. What puzzles me, Mr Babcock, is why the disciples kept falling asleep, if it was as cold as it is tonight. Do you suppose the climate has changed in two thousand years? Or could the disciples have had too much wine at supper?'

Babcock handed Robin back his torch and pushed him gently along the homeward path. 'We don't know, Robin, but we have to remember they had all had a long and very exhausting day.'

That's not the right answer, he thought, but it's the best I can do. And I haven't helped Bob Smith either. Nor was I particularly sympathetic to the Colonel. The trouble is, I don't know any of these people. Their own vicar would have known how to deal with them. Even if he had given them quite the wrong answers they would have been satisfied.

'There they are,' said Robin, 'standing in a huddle up the road and stamping their feet. That's the most sensible way to try and keep awake.'

It was Lady Althea who was stamping her feet. She had wisely changed into sensible shoes before setting forth. Kate Foster was not so well shod, but she scored over Lady Althea by being well wrapped-up in her mink jacket. Miss Dean was a little apart from them both. She had found a break in the wall, and was sitting on a pile of crumbling stones. She had become rather weary of listening to her two companions, who could discuss nothing except the whereabouts of their respective husbands.

I'm glad I never married, she thought. There always seems to be such endless argument going on between husband and wife. I dare say some marriages are ideal, but very few. It was very sad for dear Father losing his wife all those years ago, but he has never tried to replace her. She smiled tenderly, thinking of the manly smell in the vicar's study. He smoked a pipe, and whenever Miss Dean called, which she generally did twice a week to bring flowers to brighten up his bachelor solitude, or with a special cake she had baked, or a jar of homemade jam or marmalade, she would give a quick look through the open door of the study to see if his housekeeper had tidied it properly, brought some sort of order to the chaos of books and papers. Men were such boys, they needed looking after. That was why Mary and Martha invited Our Lord so often to Bethany. They probably fed Him well after those long walks across the hills, mended His clothes – darned His socks, she was about to say, but of course men didn't wear socks in those days, only sandals. What a blessed honour it must have been to soak the travel-stained garments in the wash-tub . . .

Miss Dean became aware of some sort of scuffle in the trees behind her. Could the menfolk have climbed over the stones and wandered into what seemed like private property? Then she heard a man laugh, and a woman whisper 'Shshsh . . . !'

'It's all right,' murmured the man, 'it's only Miss Dean. Sitting all on her own lamenting the absence of her beloved vicar.'

'If she only knew,' came the answering murmur, 'that he hides whenever he sees her walking up the vicarage drive. She's the thorn in his flesh, he told Mum once. Pursued him for years, despite her age.'

There was a sound of stifled laughter, and then suddenly Jim Foster coughed loudly and emerged from the cluster of dark trees, Jill Smith at his heels.

'Well, well, Miss Dean,' he said, 'what a surprise. We've been looking for the rest of the party. Ah, isn't that Kate standing up the road with Lady Althea? And some more of them coming from the opposite direction? Rendezvous all round.' He held out his hand to Jill and helped her over the stones. 'Now, Miss Dean, what about you? Will you take my arm?'

'Thank you, Mr Foster,' she said quietly, 'I can manage on my own.'

Jill Smith threw a quick look down the path. Bob was there, and the Rev. Babcock and young Robin. Robin was chattering and waving a torch. It would look better if she stayed with Miss Dean. She nudged Jim Foster with her elbow, and immediately he understood and began walking alone up the path to where Kate and Lady Althea were standing.

'Hullo, hullo there,' he called, 'we all seem to have been going round in circles. I can't think how I came to miss you.'

The tight-lipped expression on his wife's face made him hesitate a moment, then he smiled, and strolled up to her casually, self-confident.

'Sorry, old girl,' he said. 'Been here long?'

He put his arm round her shoulders and kissed her lightly on the cheek.

'Twenty minutes at least,' she replied. 'More like half an hour.'

The three of them turned their heads as Robin came running towards them flicking the light of his torch in all their faces.

'Oh, Mr Foster,' he called delightedly, 'that looked so sinister as you kissed Mrs Foster. You could have been Judas. Mr Babcock and I have had a tremendous time. We've been right down to Gethsemane and back on our own.'

'In that case, where were you?' Kate turned to her husband.

'Oh, Mr Foster and Mrs Smith were under the trees through the gap in that wall,' said Robin, 'and I'm afraid they can't have had a very good view of Jerusalem. I flashed my torch on you once, Mr Foster, but your back was turned.'

Thank God for that, thought Jim Foster. Because if it hadn't been turned . . .'What I want to know is what in the world has become of Phil?' asked Lady Althea.

'Oh, he returned to the hotel,' said Jim Foster, relieved that attention had switched from him. 'I passed him as I was coming down. Said he was cold and had had enough of it.'

'*Cold?*' queried Lady Althea. 'Phil's never cold. What an extraordinary thing for him to say.'

Slowly the little party began to wind their way back up the path towards the hotel on the summit. They walked in couples, Lady Althea and Robin in the lead, the Fosters following closely behind in silence, and some distance in the rear the young Smiths, hotly arguing.

'Naturally I preferred to go out rather than sit with you soaking in the bar,' Jill was saying. 'I felt thoroughly ashamed of you.'

'Ashamed?' Bob answered. 'That's fine, coming from you. How do you think I felt when Mrs Foster asked me to help find her husband? I knew very well where he was. And so do you.'

The Rev. Babcock held back with Miss Dean. It would only distress her to hear the young couple quarrelling. They must really work things out between them. There was nothing in the world he could do. Miss Dean herself, generally such a chatterbox, was strangely silent.

'I'm so sorry,' he began awkwardly, 'that things haven't turned out quite as you had hoped. I know I make a poor substitute for your vicar. Never mind, you'll be able to describe everything to him when we return on board. It's been a wonderful experience for all of us to have walked above the Garden of Gethsemane by night.'

Miss Dean did not hear him. She was many hundreds of miles away. She was walking up the vicarage drive, a basket over her arm, and suddenly she saw a figure dart from behind the curtain in the study window and efface itself against the wall. When she rang the bell nobody answered.

'Are you feeling all right, Miss Dean?' asked the Rev. Babcock.

'Thank you,' she said, 'I'm perfectly well. It's just that I'm very tired.'

Her voice faltered. She must not disgrace herself. She must not cry. It was just that she felt an overwhelming sense of loss, of betrayal . . .

'I can't imagine,' said Lady Althea to Robin, 'why your grandfather went back to the hotel. Did he tell you he felt cold?'

'No,' replied Robin. 'He was talking to Mr Babcock about old days, and how he would have been given command of his regiment, but he had to leave the army because you weren't very well at the time, and your life was centred on Little Bletford. He didn't say anything about being cold, though. He just sounded rather sad.'

Left the army because of her? How could he have said such a thing, and to a stranger like Babcock? It wasn't true. It was very unjust. Phil had never for one moment hinted, all that time ago, that . . . Or had he? Were things said and she hadn't listened, had brushed them away? But Phil had always appeared so content, so busy with the garden, and arranging his military papers and books in the library . . . Doubt, guilt, bewilderment swept over her in turn. It had all happened so long ago. Why should Phil have suddenly felt resentful tonight? Have gone back on his own, not looked for her, even? Babcock must have said something to put Phil out, made some tactless remark.

One by one they climbed the hill, went into the hotel, hovered for a moment in the entrance to bid one another goodnight. Each member of the little party looked tired, strained. Robin could not understand it. He had enjoyed himself immensely, despite the cold. Why did everyone seem to be in such a bad mood? He kissed his grandmother goodnight, promised not to read late, and waited by the door of his bedroom for Mr Babcock to enter the room next door.

'Thank you for a splendid evening,' he said. 'I hope you liked it as much as I did.'

The Rev. Babcock summoned a smile. The boy was not so bad really. He couldn't help his precocity, spending most of his time with adults.

'Thank you, Robin,' he said. 'It was your idea, you know. I would never have thought of it on my own.' And then, quite spontaneously, he heard himself adding, 'I blame myself for not having made the walk more interesting for the rest of the party. They're all a bit lost without your vicar.'

Robin considered the matter, head cocked on one side. He liked being treated as an adult, it gave him status. He must say something to put poor Mr Babcock at his ease, and his mind harked back to the conversation between his grandparents earlier that evening before dinner.

'It must be difficult to be a clergyman in this day and age,' he said. 'Quite an ordeal, in fact.'

The Rev. Babcock looked surprised. 'Yes, it is. At least sometimes.'

Robin nodded gravely. 'My grandfather was saying people must make allowances, and my grandmother remarked that so many clergymen were not out of the top drawer nowadays. I'm not sure what that means exactly, but I suppose it's to do with passing exams. I hope you sleep well, Mr Babcock.'

He clicked his heels and bowed, as his grandmother had taught him to do, and went into his bedroom, shutting the door behind him. He crossed the floor and drew aside the curtains. The lights were still burning bright in the city of Jerusalem.

'On that other 13th day of Nisan the disciples would all be scattered by now,' he thought, 'and only Peter left, stamping about to keep warm by the charcoal fire in the courtyard. That shows it was a cold night.'

He undressed and got into bed, then switched on his

bedside light and spread the map of Jerusalem over his knees. He compared it with a second map that his father had borrowed for him, showing the city as it was around AD30. He studied both maps for about half an hour, then, remembering the promise to his grandmother, switched off the light.

The priests and scholars have got it all wrong, he thought. They've made Jesus go out of the wrong gate. Tomorrow I shall discover Golgotha for myself.

'Visitors to the Holy City of Jerusalem, this way please.' 'You wish for a guide? English-speaking? German? American?' 'The church of St Anne on your right, birthplace of the Virgin Mary.' 'Walk to your left and enter the superb Haram Esh Sharif, see the Dome of the Rock, the Dome of the Chain, the Al Aqsa Mosque.' 'This way, please, to the Jewish Quarter, the site of the Temple, the Wailing Wall.' 'Pilgrims to the Holy Sepulchre proceed by the Via Dolorosa straight ahead. Straight ahead for the Via Dolorosa, the Way of the Cross . . .'

Edward Babcock, standing just inside St Stephen's Gate with his small party, was besieged on all sides by guides of every nationality. He waved them aside. He carried a street map of his own, and a sheaf of scribbled instructions handed him at the last moment by the courier at the hotel.

'Let us all try and keep together,' he said, turning this way and that in search of his own little group amongst the pushing crowd. 'If we don't keep together we shan't see anything. The first thing to remember is that the Jerusalem we are going to visit has been built upon the foundations of the one that was known to Our Lord. We shall be walking, and standing, many feet above where He walked and stood. That is to say . . .'

He consulted his notes again, and the Colonel seized him by the arm.

'First things first,' he said briskly. 'Deploy your troops where they can take advantage of the ground. I suggest we lead off with the church of St Anne. Follow me.'

The signal was obeyed. The little flock trailed after the temporary shepherd to find themselves within a large courtyard, the church of St Anne on their right.

'Built by the Crusaders,' declaimed the Colonel. 'Finished in the twelfth century. They knew what they were doing in those days. One of the finest examples of Crusader architecture you'll ever see.' He turned to the Rev. Babcock. 'I know it of old, padre,' he added.

'Yes, Colonel.'

Babcock heaved a sigh of relief, and stuffed his notes in his pocket. He needn't refer to them for the moment anyway, and the Colonel, who had seemed below his usual form when they had met at breakfast, had now regained something of his old zest and confidence. The group followed their leader dutifully around the almost empty church. They had seen one already, the Franciscan Church of All Nations in the Garden of Gethsemane, and, although this second one was very different, the compulsion to silence was the same, the shuffling footsteps, the wandering eyes, the inability to distinguish one feature from another, the sensation of relief when the inspection was over and it was possible to go out once more into the bright sunlight.

'If you've seen one, you've seen the lot,' Jim Foster whispered to Jill Smith, but she avoided his eye and he turned away, shrugging his shoulders. Guilty conscience? Oh well, if that was to be the mood she must get on with it. She had sung a very different tune last night . . .

Lady Althea, adjusting a blue chiffon scarf around her head so that it fell loosely about her shoulders, observed her husband closely. He seemed to be himself again. She had been relieved to find him in bed and asleep when she had entered their bedroom the night before. Nor had she questioned him. Better to let things alone . . . She had caught sight of friends driving away from the Church of All Nations, Lord and Lady Chase-borough, who were apparently staying at the King David Hotel, and they had agreed to meet by the Dome of the Rock at eleven o'clock. Such a surprise. If only she had known they were coming to Jerusalem she would have arranged to stay at the King David Hotel too. Never mind. At least she would get a glimpse of them, be able to exchange news of mutual friends.

'There's something going on at the far end of this courtyard,' said Robin. 'Look, Grandfather, quite a big queue. Shall we join them? It looks like some sort of excavation.'

'Pool of Bethesda,' replied the Colonel. 'They've done a lot of work there since my day. I doubt if there's much to see. Part of the city drain.'

But Robin was already running ahead to join the queue. His attention had been drawn to a screaming child, carried in the arms of her father, who was pushing his way to the head of the queue.

'What on earth are they doing with that child?' asked Kate Foster.

Babcock had been glancing at his notes again. 'The site of the old sheep market. You remember Chapter 5 of St John's Gospel, Mrs Foster, and the Pool of Bethesda, where the infirm waited to be healed, and how the angel came at certain times to trouble the water? Our Lord healed the man who had been lame for thirty-eight years.' He turned to the Colonel. 'I think we should just take a look at it.'

'Come along, then, follow me,' said the Colonel, 'but I warn you, it's only part of the old sewer system. We had trouble with it in '48.'

Miss Dean was still standing outside the church of St Anne. She felt confused by all the chatter and bustle. What did the Rev. Babcock mean by saying they would be walking several feet above where Our Lord had trodden? The church here was very beautiful, no doubt, but the Colonel said even this had been built on the foundations of an earlier one, which in its turn had been erected over the simple dwelling of St Joachim and St Anne. Was she to understand that the parents of Our Lady had lived underground? In that curious sort of grotto they had visited before coming out of the church? She had hoped to be inspired by it, but instead she was disenchanted. She had always had such a happy picture of St Joachim and St Anne living in a pleasant whitewashed house with flowers growing in a small garden, and their blessed daughter learning to sew by her mother's side. There had been a calendar once with just such a painting upon it; she had treasured it for years until Dora took it off the wall and threw it away.

She looked around her, trying to conjure up the garden that no longer existed, but there were too many people present, none of them behaving with the slightest reverence, and one young woman was actually sucking an orange and giving pieces to the small child trailing at her skirt, then scattering the peel on the ground. Oh dear, sighed Miss Dean, how Our Lady would have hated litter . . .

The pressure was intense around the steps descending to the Pool of Bethesda, and an official was standing with his hand on the rail, directing the people to go down one by one. The little girl in her father's arms was screaming louder than ever.

'Why is she making such a fuss?' asked Robin.

'I don't think she wants to go to the Pool,' replied Babcock in some hesitation. He averted his eyes. The child was obviously spastic, and the father, with his anxious wife by his side, was apparently intent upon dipping her in the Pool, hoping for a miracle.

'I think,' said the Colonel, sizing up the situation, 'we'd

be well advised to push on to the Praetorium before the crowds get worse.'

'No, wait a minute,' said Robin. 'I want to see what happens to the little girl.'

He leant over the rail and stared down into the Pool with interest. It was certainly not much of a place, the water dark and rather slimy, the steps slippery-looking too. Grandfather must be right, and it formed part of the city drain. The man who had been lame for thirty-eight years was lucky when Jesus came along and healed him instantly, rather than waiting for someone to lift him into the Pool. Perhaps Jesus realised the water was bad. There they go, he said to himself, as the father, ignoring the child's terrified screams, slowly descended the steps. Freeing one hand, he dipped it in the pool and sloshed the water three times over his daughter, wetting her face, her neck, her arms. Then, smiling in triumph at the curious watchers above, he ascended the steps to safety, his wife smiling with him, mopping the child's face with a towel. The child herself, bewildered, distraught, rolled her frightened eyes over the heads of the crowd. Robin waited to see if the father would put her down, cured. Nothing happened, though. She began screaming again, and the father, making soothing sounds, bore her away from the top of the steps and was lost in the crowd.

Robin turned to the Rev. Babcock. 'No luck, I'm afraid. There wasn't a miracle. I didn't really think there would be, but of course you never know.'

The rest of the little party had moved away, embarrassed, distressed, unwilling witnesses of what appeared to be an excess of faith. All but Miss Dean, who, still standing before the church of St Anne, had seen nothing of the incident. Robin ran towards her.

'Miss Dean,' he called, 'you haven't seen the Pool of Bethesda.'

'The Pool of Bethesda?'

'Yes, you know. It comes in St John. The pool where the Angel troubled the water and the lame man was healed. Except that Jesus healed him, not the pool.'

'Yes, of course,' said Miss Dean. 'I remember well. The poor fellow had no one to carry him down, and he used to wait day after day.'

'Well,' said Robin proudly, 'it's over there. I've just seen a little girl carried down to it. But she wasn't cured.'

The Pool of Bethesda . . . What a strange and curious coincidence. She had turned to that very chapter in the Gospel the night before on returning to the hotel, and the whole scene was vivid in her recollection. It had made her think of Lourdes, of all the poor sick people who travelled there every year, and some of them indeed were cured, doctors and priests were quite confounded, there was never a medical explanation. Of course some came back without being cured, but then it could be that they did not have sufficient faith.

'Oh, Robin,' she said, 'I would like to see it. Will you show it me?'

'Well,' he replied, 'actually it's a bit disappointing. Grandfather says it's a drain. He remembers it in '48. And the rest of us are going on to the Praetorium where Jesus was scourged by the soldiers.'

'I don't think I could bear to go there,' said Miss Dean, 'especially if it's underground, like everything else.'

Robin, intent upon the next adventure, was not going to waste time showing the Pool of Bethesda to Miss Dean.

'The pool is over there,' he said. 'There's a man who stands at the top of the steps. See you later.'

His grandmother was waving to him in the distance. Lady Althea was impatient to meet her friends at the Dome of the Rock.

'Do go back and tell Miss Dean to hurry up, Robin,' she called.

'She doesn't want to see the Praetorium,' he replied.

'Neither do I,' said his grandmother. 'I'm meeting the Chaseboroughs instead. Miss Dean will really have to take care of herself. Darling, you had better run ahead and join Grandfather. He's just passing under the archway now.'

Everything was so disorganised owing to Babcock's lack of experience that it was a case of each one for himself, she decided. If Miss Dean failed to join up with the rest of the party, she could always go and sit in the hotel bus that was parked just round the corner outside St Stephen's Gate. If the crowds were too impossible, the Chaseboroughs might invite herself and Phil and Robin back to lunch at the King David Hotel. She watched Robin until he had caught up with his grandfather, and the pair of them were lost in the throng of sightseers and pilgrims, then she followed the sign pointing towards the Dome of the Rock.

'Via Dolorosa . . . the Way of the Cross . . .'

The Colonel pushed ahead, ignoring the eager guides. The street was very narrow, flanked by high walls, the walls themselves spanned by archways covered in vine-leaves. Walking was difficult, indeed impossible. Some of the pilgrims were already on their knees.

'What's everybody kneeling for?' asked Robin.

'First Station of the Cross,' said the Colonel. 'In point of fact, we're on the site of the Praetorium, padre, this was all part of the old Antonia fortress. We can get a better idea of it inside the Convent of the Ecce Homo.'

He was not sure, though. Things seemed to have altered since '48. Men were seated at a table taking tickets. He had a murmured consultation with Babcock.

'How many of us are there?' he asked, searching the eyes of strangers.

He could see none of his party except himself, Robin and the padre. The place seemed to be full of nuns. The pilgrims were being divided into groups.

'Better do what they tell us,' he muttered to Babcock. 'Call themselves the Soeurs de Sion, can't understand a word they say.'

They were descending to a lower level, and this, thought Robin, must be what Miss Dean didn't want to do. It's not particularly frightening, though. Not nearly as bad as the Ghost Train at a fair.

The nun in charge of their party was explaining that they were descending to the lithostratus or, as the Hebrew had it, the Gabbatha, the stone-paved judgement-place of Pilate. The pavement had only recently been discovered, she told them, and perhaps the most striking proof that it was indeed the site of the place where the Seigneur had been held by Pilate, and scourged and mocked, was furnished by the curious markings on the flagstones themselves, the criss-cross lines and pits which, the experts told them, the Roman soldiers used for games of chance. Here in this corner they would have sat, dicing, guarding their prisoner, and we now know too, she said, that it was a Roman custom to play a game called The King, when a condemned prisoner was crowned king during his last few hours, and treated with mock ceremony.

The gaping pilgrims stared about them. The place was low, vaulted, like an immense cellar, the flagstones hard and rugged beneath their feet. The whispering voices died away. The nun herself was silent.

'Perhaps,' thought Robin, 'the soldiers didn't actually mock Jesus at all. It was just a game, which they let him join in. He might even have thrown dice with them. The crown and the purple robe were just dressing-up. It was the Romans' idea of fun. I don't believe when a prisoner is condemned to death the people guarding him are beastly. They try and make the time go quickly, because they feel sorry for him.'

He could imagine the soldiers squatting on the flagstones, and with them, chained to a fellow-prisoner, a thief, was a young man, smiling, who threw his dice with greater skill than his gaolers, and so won the prize and was elected king. The laughter that greeted his skill was not mockery, it was applause.

'That's it,' thought Robin. 'People have been teaching it all wrong through the years. I must tell Mr Babcock.'

He looked about him, but he could see none of his party except his grandfather, who was standing very still, staring towards the far end of the vaulted room. People began to drift away but the Colonel did not move, and Robin, content to squat on the flagstones and trace the curious lines and markings with his finger, waited until his grandfather was ready.

We only acted under instructions, the Colonel told himself. They came direct from High Command. Terrorism was rife at the time, the Palestine Police Force couldn't deal with it, we had to take control. The Jews were laying mines at street corners, the situation was deteriorating daily. They had blown up the King David Hotel in July. We had to arm the troops, and protect them and the civilian population against terrorist attack. The trouble was, there was no political policy back at home, with a Labour government in power. They told us to go soft, but how can you go soft when people on the spot are being killed? The Jewish Agency insisted that they were against terrorism, but it was all talk and no action. Well, then we picked up this Jewish boy and flogged him. He was a terrorist, right enough. Caught him in the act. Nobody likes inflicting pain . . . There were reprisals afterwards, of course. One of our officers and three N.C.O.'s kidnapped and flogged. Hell of a row about it at home. I don't know why standing here should bring the whole scene back so vividly. I haven't thought of it since. Suddenly he remembered the expression on the boy's face. The look of panic. And his mouth twisting as the lashes fell. He was very young. The boy was standing there in front of him once again, and his eyes were Robin's eyes. They did not accuse him. They simply stared at him in dumb appeal. Oh God, he thought, oh God, forgive me. And his years of service fell away, became as nothing, were wasted, useless.

'Come on, let's go,' he said abruptly, but even as he turned on his heel and walked across the flagged stones he could hear the sound of the blows, could see the Jewish boy writhe and fall. He pushed his way through the crowd up into the open air, Robin at his heels, and so out into the street, looking neither to right nor to left.

'Hold on, Grandfather,' called Robin. 'I want to know exactly where Pilate stood.'

'I don't know,' said the Colonel. 'It doesn't matter.'

Another queue was already forming to descend to the paved Gabbatha, and here outside the pilgrims were thicker than ever. A new guide was standing at his elbow, who plucked at his sleeve and said, 'This way, the Via Dolorosa. Straight on for the Way of the Cross.'

Lady Althea, wandering within the Temple area, was doing her best to shake off Kate Foster before they met the Chaseboroughs.

'Yes, yes, very impressive,' she said vaguely as Kate pointed out the various domes, and began reading something out of a guidebook about Mameluke Sultan Quait Bai who had built a fountain over the Holy of Holies. They wandered from one edifice to another, mounted row upon row of steps, descended them again, saw the rock where Isaac was sacrificed by Abraham and Mohammed rose to Heaven, and still no sign of her friends. The sun, directly overhead, blazed down upon them.

'I think I've had enough,' she said. 'I really don't think I want to fag right over there and see the inside of that mosque.'

'You'll be missing the finest sight in the whole of Jerusalem,' retorted Kate. 'The stained-glass windows of the

Al Aqsa mosque are world-famous. I'm only hoping they weren't damaged in the bomb explosions one read about.'

Lady Althea sighed. Middle East politics bored her, except when they were being discussed in an authoritative manner by a member of Parliament over dinner. There was so little to distinguish between Jews and Arabs anyway. They all threw bombs.

'Go and look at your mosque,' she said. 'I'll wait for you here.'

She watched her companion disappear and then, loosening her chiffon scarf, strolled back again towards the flight of steps leading to the Dome of the Rock. The one great advantage in being in this Temple area was that there were fewer crowds than in that narrow, stifling Via Dolorosa. So much more space in which to move about. She wondered what Betty Chaseborough would be wearing – she had only caught sight of her white hat in the car. Pity she had let her figure go these last few years.

Lady Althea installed herself against one of the triple pillars above the flight of steps. They surely would not miss her here. She felt rather empty; coffee and breakfast seemed a long time ago. She opened her bag, remembering the piece of ring-shaped bread that Robin had pressed her into buying from some vendor who had been standing with a donkey outside the Church of All Nations. 'It's not unleavened bread,' he had told her, 'but the next best thing to it.' She smiled. His little ways were so amusing.

She bit into the bread – it was a lot harder than it looked – and as she did so she saw Eric Chaseborough and his wife emerging with a group of sightseers from some building Kate had said was Solomon's Stables. She waved her hand to attract their attention, and Eric Chaseborough waved his hat in reply. Lady Althea dropped the piece of bread back into her bag, and was instantly aware, from the odd sensation in her mouth, that something was terribly wrong. She thrust her tongue upwards. It pricked against two sharp points. She looked down again at the piece of bread, and there, impaled in the ring, were her two front teeth, capped by her dentist just before she left London. She seized her hand-mirror in horror. The face that was hers belonged to her no longer. The woman who stared back at her had two small filed pegs stuck in her upper gums where the teeth should have been. They looked like broken matchsticks, discoloured, black. All trace of beauty had gone. She might have been some peasant who, old before her time, stood begging at a street corner.

'Oh no . . .' she thought, 'oh no, not here, not now!' And in an agony of shame and humiliation she tried to cover her mouth with her blue chiffon scarf as the Chaseboroughs, smiling, advanced towards her.

'Run you to earth at last,' called Eric Chaseborough, but she could only shake her head, gesticulating, trying to wave them off.

'What's the matter with Althea? Is she feeling ill?' asked his wife.

The tall, elegant figure backed away from them, groping with her scarf, and as they hurried to her side the chiffon fell back, revealing the tragedy, and the owner of the scarf, endeavouring to mumble between closed lips, pointed to the impaled teeth on the piece of bread within her bag.

'Oh, I say,' murmured Eric Chaseborough, 'bad luck. What a wretched thing to happen.'

He looked about him helplessly, as if, amongst the people mounting the steps, there might be someone who could give them the address of a dentist in Jerusalem.

His wife, sensing the humiliation of her friend, held on to her arm.

'Don't worry,' she said. 'It doesn't show. Not if you keep your scarf over your mouth. You're not in pain?'

Lady Althea shook her head. Pain she could have borne,

but not this loss of pride, this misery of shame, the knowledge that in that one moment of biting the bread she had thrown away all grace, all dignity.

'The Israelis are very up to date,' said Eric Chaseborough. 'There's sure to be a first-rate man who can fix you up. The reception clerk at the King David will be able to tell us.'

Lady Althea shook her head again, thinking of the endless appointments in Harley Street, the careful probing, the highspeed drill, the hours of patience to keep beauty intact. She thought of the lunch ahead, herself eating nothing, while her friends tried to behave as if all was quite usual. The vain search for a dentist who could at best patch up the ravages that had taken place. Phil's gasp of astonishment. Robin's curious gaze. The averted eyes of the rest of the party. The remainder of the tour a nightmare.

'There's someone coming up the steps who seems to know you,' murmured Eric Chaseborough.

Kate Foster, having inspected the Al Aqsa Mosque, had resolutely turned her back on the entrance to the Wailing Wall – too many Orthodox Jews pressing forward over the enormous space where their government had had the ruthless audacity to bulldoze Jordanian dwellings and condemn more Jordanians to desert tents – and returned towards the Dome of the Rock. There she caught sight of Lady Althea being supported between strangers. She hurried to her rescue.

'What on earth's wrong?' she enquired.

Lord Chaseborough introduced himself and explained the situation.

'Poor Althea is very distressed,' he murmured. 'I'm not quite sure what's the best thing to do.'

'Lost her front teeth?' said Kate Foster. 'Well, it's not the end of the world, is it?' She stared in some curiosity at the stricken woman who, proud and confident, had strolled by her side such a short while ago. 'Let's have a look.'

Lady Althea, her hand trembling, lowered the chiffon scarf, and with a tremendous effort tried to smile. To her consternation, and that of her sympathetic friends, Kate Foster burst out laughing.

'Well, I must say,' she exclaimed, 'you couldn't have made a cleaner job of it if you'd been in a prize-fight.'

It seemed to Lady Althea, as she stood there above the steps, that all the people pressing forward were staring, not at the Dome of the Rock, but at her alone, and were nudging one another, whispering, smiling; for she knew, from her own experience of mocking others, that there is nothing more likely to unite a crowd of strangers in a wave of laughter than the sight of someone who, with dignity shattered, becomes suddenly grotesque.

'Straight on for the Via Dolorosa . . . Straight on for the Way of the Cross.'

Jim Foster, dragging Jill Smith by the hand, was held up at every turn by kneeling pilgrims. Jill had expressed a wish to visit the markets, or the suks, or whatever they called themselves, and to the suks she should go. Besides, he could buy something for Kate, and make his peace with her.

'I think I ought to wait for Bob,' said Jill, hanging back.

But Bob was nowhere to be seen. He had followed Babcock to the Praetorium.

'You didn't want to wait for him last night,' replied Jim Foster.

Amazing how a girl could change gear between midnight and noon. She might have been a different creature altogether. Last night under the trees, at first protesting, then moaning with pleasure at his touch, and now prickly, off-hand, it was almost as if she wanted nothing more to do with him. Well, fine, O.K., let it be so. But it was a bit of a slap in the face all the same. A guilty conscience was one thing, a brush-off another. He wouldn't put it past her to have run bleating to her fool of a husband last night, telling him she had been the victim of assault. Though Bob Smith would never have the nerve to do anything about it. Well, it was probably the last thrill she would ever get out of sex, poor girl. Something to remember all her life.

'Come on,' he urged, 'if you want that brass bangle.'

'We can't,' she whispered. 'That clergyman there is praying.'

'*We adore thee, O Christ, and we bless thee.*'

The priest, just ahead of them, was on his knees, his head bowed.

'*Because by the Holy Cross thou hast redeemed the world.*'

The response came from the group of pilgrims kneeling behind him.

I shouldn't have let him, thought Jill Smith. I shouldn't have let Jim Foster do what he did last night. It wasn't right. I feel terrible when I think of it. And we came here to see the Holy Places, and all these people praying around us, and Jesus Christ dying for our sins. I feel awful, I feel really bad. On my honeymoon, too. What would everyone say if they knew? They'd say I was nothing but a scrubber, a slut, and it's not as if I were in love with him, I'm not, I love Bob. I just don't know what came over me to let Jim Foster do what he did.

The pilgrims rose to their feet and passed on up the Via Dolorosa, and thank goodness it didn't seem so holy once they had gone. The street was full of ordinary people, women with baskets on their heads, and they were coming to stalls full of vegetables, butchers' shops with carcasses of lambs hanging up on hooks, and traders shouting and calling their wares, but it was all so close and huddled together you could hardly move, you could hardly breathe.

The street was dividing, and there were booths and

shops on either side, and flights of steps to the right flanked by stalls piled with oranges, grapefruit, enormous cabbages, onions, and beans.

'We're in the wrong suk,' said Jim Foster impatiently. 'Nothing but blasted foodstuffs here.'

Through an archway he espied a row of booths hung with belts and scarves, and next to it a stall where an old man was displaying cheap jewellery. 'Here, this is more like it,' he said, but a donkey loaded with melons barred his path, and a woman with a basket on her head tripped over his foot.

'Let's go back,' said Jill. 'We're getting hopelessly lost.'

A young man sidled up to her, a sheaf of pamphlets in his hand.

'You wish to visit Holyland Hill for superb panoramic view?' he inquired. 'Also see the Artist Colony and Night Club?'

'Oh, please go away,' said Jill. 'I don't want to see any of them.'

She had let go of Foster's hand, and now he was the other side of the street, beckoning to her. This might be the moment to give him the slip and try to retrace her steps and find Bob, yet she was scared at the thought of being on her own in these narrow, bewildering streets.

Jim Foster, standing by the booth selling jewellery, picked up one object after another and threw it down again. Complete junk. Nothing worth buying. Medallions with the Dome of the Rock, and head-scarves printed all over with donkeys. Hardly do to buy one of those for Kate – she might think it was a joke in bad taste. He turned round to look for Jill, forgetting that he still held one of the despised medallions in his hand. He could just see her disappearing down the street. Bloody girl, what was the matter with her? He started to cross the road, when an angry voice shouted after him from the stall.

'Three dollars for the medallion. You owe me three dollars!'

He looked back over his shoulder. The vendor behind the stall was red with anger.

'Here, take it, I don't want the damn thing,' said Jim, and threw the medallion back on to the stall.

'You pick it up, you buy,' shouted the man, and he began jabbering to his neighbour, and the pair of them started shaking their fists, attracting the attention of other vendors in the market, and other purchasers. Jim hesitated a moment, then panicked. You never knew what might happen with a Middle East crowd. He walked quickly away, and as the uproar rose behind him, and heads turned, he quickened his pace and began to run, elbowing people aside, head down, and the crowds intent upon their shopping, or merely strolling, stepped back upon one another, causing more upheaval. 'What is it? Is he a thief? Has he planted a bomb?'

Murmurs were all behind him, and as Jim mounted a flight of steps he saw two Israeli policemen coming down, and he turned again, and tried to carve his way through the crowd below in the narrow street. His breath came quickly, there was a pain under his left rib like a knife, and the sensation of panic increased, for perhaps the Israeli policemen had questioned someone in the crowd and even now were pursuing him, believing him to be a thief, an anarchist, anything . . . How could he clear himself? How could he explain?

He fought his way through the crowd, losing all control, all sense of direction, and came out into a broader street, and now there was no escape because the way was barred by a throng of pilgrims walking with linked arms, and he had to fall back against a wall. They seemed to be all men, wearing dark trousers and white shirts. They didn't look like pilgrims, for they were laughing and singing. He was borne along with them, like a piece of flotsam on the crest of a wave, unable to turn back, and he found himself in the centre of a great open space, in the midst of which young men similarly dressed were dancing, hand in hand, shoulder to shoulder.

The pain under his left rib was intense. He could move no further. If he could only sit down for one moment, but there was no space. If he could only lean against something . . . against that enormous, lemon-coloured wall. He couldn't reach it, though, he could only stand and stare, for the way to it was barred by a line of black-hatted men with curling hair, who were bowing and praying and beating their breasts. They are all Jews, he thought, I am alien, I'm not one of them, and his sense of panic returned, of fear, of desolation, for what if the two Israeli policemen were even now close to him on the fringe of the crowd, and forced their way to his side, and instead of bowing and praying before the Wailing Wall the line of men turned and looked upon him in accusation, and a cry arose from the whole lot of them calling, 'Thief . . . Thief . . .'?

Jill Smith had only one thought in mind, and that was to put as great a distance as possible between herself and Jim Foster. She didn't want to have anything more to do with him. She would have to be polite, of course, as long as they were all together, but they were due to leave Jerusalem later in the day, and once they were on board ship again none of them need have any close contact. Thank heaven she and Bob were going to live several miles from Little Bletford.

She walked quickly back along the narrow crowded street, away from the market quarter and the shops, passing tourists, sightseers, pilgrims, priests, but still no sign of Bob, nor of any of their party. There were signposts everywhere to the Holy Sepulchre, but she ignored them. She didn't want to go inside the Holy Sepulchre. It didn't seem right. It didn't seem, well, clean. It would be hypocritical and false to go amongst all those people praying. She wanted to find some place where she could sit and think and be alone. The walls of the Old City seemed to be closing in upon her, and perhaps if she continued walking she would be free of them, find more air, and there would be less noise, less hustle.

Then she saw a gate in the distance, at the far end, but it was not St Stephen's Gate, by which they had entered earlier. The letters said 'Shechem', and another sign read 'Damascus'. It did not matter to her what it was called, as long as it led her out of the city.

She passed under the great archway, and there were cars and buses parked in rows outside, just as there had been at St Stephen's Gate, and more tourists than ever coming down across the broad thoroughfare into the city. And there, standing in the midst of them, looking as lost and bewildered as she probably did herself, was Kate Foster. Too late to turn back – Kate had seen her. Reluctantly Jill went towards her.

'Have you seen Jim?' asked Kate.

'No,' she replied. 'I lost him in all those narrow streets. I'm looking for Bob.'

'Well, you'll never find him,' said Kate. 'I've never met with such total disorganisation. The crowds are absolute murder. None of our party has kept together. Lady Althea has gone back to the hotel practically having a nervous breakdown. She's lost her teeth.'

'She's *what*?' asked Jill.

'Lost her front teeth. They came out on a piece of bread. She looks an absolute fright.'

'Oh dear, how dreadful for her, I am sorry,' said Jill.

A car was hooting at them and they moved to the side of the street, walking out of the stream of traffic but in no particular direction.

'The friends who were with her kept talking about finding a dentist, but how do you know where to get hold of one in such a place of turmoil? Then luckily we ran into the Colonel near St Stephen's Gate, and he took over.'

'What did he do?'

'Found a taxi at once and bundled her into it. She was nearly in tears, but he sent her friends packing and got in beside her, and if you ask me, though she usually spends her time snubbing him, she was never more relieved to see anyone in her life. I wish I could find Jim. What was he doing when you saw him last?'

'I'm not sure,' faltered Jill. 'I think he wanted to buy you a present.'

'I know Jim's presents,' said Kate. 'I always get one when he has a guilty conscience. God! I could do with a cup of tea. Or at least somewhere to sit where I could take the weight off my feet.'

They went on walking, looking aimlessly about them, and came to a sign with the words 'Garden of the Resurrection' upon it.

'I don't suppose,' said Jill, 'we could get a cup of tea there?'

'You never know,' replied Kate. 'All these tourist centres carry ridiculous names. It's like Stratford-on-Avon. Everything is either Shakespeare or Ann Hathaway. Here it's Jesus Christ.'

They found themselves descending into an enclosure surrounded by rock, with paved ways all about it, and an official in the centre handed them a pamphlet. It said something about the Garden of Joseph of Arimathea.

'No tea here,' said Kate. 'No, thank you, we don't want a guide.'

'We can at least,' murmured Jill, 'sit down on that little wall. They surely won't make us pay for that.'

The official moved away, shrugging his shoulders. The

garden would soon be full of pilgrims showing greater interest. Kate was studying the pamphlet.

'It's a rival site to the Holy Sepulchre,' she said. 'I suppose they like to spread the tourists around. That curious little tumble-down place built against the rock must be the tomb.'

They walked across and peered into the opening in the wall.

'It's empty,' said Jill.

'Well, it would be, wouldn't it?' answered Kate.

It was peaceful, anyway. They could sit down beside it and rest. The garden was practically empty, and Kate supposed it was still too early in the day for the usual hordes to stamp all over it. She glanced sideways at her companion, who looked tired and strained. Perhaps she had misjudged her after all. It was probably Jim who had made the running the night before.

'If you take my advice,' she said shortly, 'you'll start your family right away. We waited, with the result we've had no children. Oh yes, I tried everything. Opening the fallopian tubes, the lot. It didn't work. The doctors told me they thought Jim was probably sterile, but he wouldn't take a test. Now, of course, it's all too late. I'm plumb in the middle of change of life.'

Jill did not know what to say. Everything Kate Foster told her made her feel more guilty.

'I'm so sorry,' she said.

'No use being sorry. I've got to put up with it. Be thankful you're young, and have all your life before you. Sometimes I feel there's absolutely nothing left, and that Jim wouldn't give a damn if I died tomorrow.'

To Kate's dismay, Jill Smith suddenly burst into tears.

'What on earth's wrong?' Kate asked.

Jill shook her head. She couldn't speak. How could she

explain the wave of guilt, of remorse, that was sweeping over her?

'Please forgive me,' she said. 'The thing is, I don't feel very well. I've been tired and out of sorts all day.'

'Got the curse?'

'No . . . No . . . It's just that sometimes I wonder if Bob really loves me, if we're suited. Nothing seems to go right with us.'

Oh, what was she saying, and as if Kate Foster could possibly care anyway?

'You probably married too young,' said her companion. 'I did too. Everyone marries too young. I often think single women have a far better time.'

What was the use, though? She had been married to Jim for over twenty years, and despite all the anxiety and stress he caused her she could never consider parting from him. She loved him, he depended upon her. If he became ill he would look to her before anyone else.

'I hope he's all right,' she said suddenly.

Jill looked up from blowing her nose. Did she mean Bob, or Jim?

'What do you mean?' she asked.

'Jim hates crowds, always has done, that's why as soon as I saw the mob of pilgrims in that narrow street I wanted him to come with me to the Mosque area, where I knew it would be quieter, but he would go tearing off with you in the opposite direction. Jim panics in crowds. Gets claustrophobia.'

'I didn't realise,' said Jill, 'he never said . . .'

Perhaps Bob also panicked in crowds. Perhaps Bob, and Jim too, were at this moment trying to fight their way out of that terrible mass of people, those clamouring street-vendors, those chanting pilgrims.

She looked around her at the silent garden, at the

scattered shrubs somebody had planted, at the dreary little empty tomb. Even the official had moved out of sight, leaving them alone.

'It's no use staying here,' she said. 'They'll never come.'

'I know,' said Kate, 'but what are we to do? Where can we go?'

The thought of plunging back into the hated city was appalling, but there was no alternative. On, on, searching the faces of the passers-by for their husbands and never finding them, always coming upon strangers, people who did not know, did not care.

Miss Dean waited until the stream of visitors to the church of St Anne and to the Pool of Bethesda had cleared, and then she walked very slowly towards the entrance to the pool and the flight of steps descending to it. A strange and rather wonderful idea had come into her head. She had been hurt, deeply hurt, by what she had overheard the night before. A thorn in the flesh. Jill Smith had told Mr Foster that Father had said to her mother that she, Mary Dean, was a thorn in his flesh. Had pursued him for years. It was a lie, of course. Father would never say such a thing. Mrs Smith had told a deliberate lie. Nevertheless, the fact that such a thing could be said, that possibly stories were told about her all over Little Bletford, had given her so much pain and distress that she had hardly slept. And to have overheard this above the Garden of Gethsemane of all places . . .

Then that dear little Robin, who seemed to be the only one in the party who ever read his Gospel, had explained to her that she was standing close to the Pool of Bethesda itself, and that a child had already been carried down to the pool to be cured of some disease. Well, perhaps the cure was not instantaneous, perhaps it would take some hours, or even days, for the miracle to show. Miss Dean had no disease, she was perfectly healthy, and strong. But if she could fill her small eau-de-cologne bottle with some of the water from the pool, and take it back with her to Little Bletford, and give it to Father to put in the holy water stoup in the entrance of the church, he would be overcome by her thought, by her gesture of faith. She could picture his expression when she handed the bottle to him. 'Father, I have brought you water from the Pool of Bethesda.' 'Oh, Miss Dean, what a tender, wonderful thing to have done!'

The trouble was, it might be forbidden by the authorities to take water from the pool, whoever the authorities were, but the man standing near the entrance doubtless repre-sented them. Therefore – and it was in a good cause, a holy cause – she would wait until he had moved away, and would then descend the steps and fill the little bottle with water. Deceitful, perhaps, but deceitful in the name of the Lord.

Miss Dean bided her time, and presently – and the Lord must have been on her side – the man moved a short dis-tance away towards a group of people who were obviously questioning him about some excavations further on. This must be her chance.

She moved gingerly towards the steps, placed her hand carefully on the handrail and began to descend. Robin was right in a sense. It did look rather like a drain, but there was plenty of water, and it was in a deep sort of chasm, and after what the Rev. Babcock had told them about everything being underground then there was no doubt about this being the genuine place. She felt truly inspired. Nobody descending to the pool but herself. She reached the slab at the bottom of the steps, and glancing above her, to make quite sure nobody had followed and she was not observed, she took out her handkerchief, knelt upon it, and emptied the eau-de-cologne on to the stone beside her. It seemed rather a waste, but in a way it was a kind of offering.

She leant over the pool and allowed the water to flow

into the bottle. Then she stood up and replaced the cork, but as she did so her foot slipped on the damp stone slab, and the bottle fell out of her hand into the water. She gave a little cry of dismay and tried to retrieve it, but already it was out of reach, and she herself was falling, falling, into the dank, deep waters of the pool.

'Oh, dear Lord,' she called. 'Oh, dear Lord, help me!'

Thrusting outwards with her arms she tried to reach the slippery wet slab on which she had stood, but the water was entering her open mouth, was choking her, and there was nothing and no one around her but the stagnant water, and the great high walls, and the patch of blue sky above her head.

The Rev. Babcock had been almost as moved by the pavement floor below the Ecce Homo convent as the Colonel, although his reason was less personal. He too saw a man being scourged, guarded by soldiers, but it was happening two thousand years ago, and the man who was suffering was God. It made him feel utterly unworthy, and at the same time privileged, to have stood on hallowed ground. He wished he could in some way prove himself, and leaving the Praetorium, and watching the stream of pilgrims proceed slowly up the Via Dolorosa, halting at successive Stations of the Cross, he knew that no gesture of his, now or in the future, could atone for what had happened in that First Century A D He could only bow his head and follow, with equal humility, those pilgrims who went before.

'Oh Lord,' he prayed, 'let me drink the cup that you have drunk, let me share your suffering.'

He felt someone pluck him by the arm. It was the Colonel. 'Will you carry on?' he asked. 'I'm going to take my wife back to the hotel. She's had a slight accident.'

Babcock expressed concern.

'No, it's nothing really,' the Colonel reassured him. 'An

unfortunate mishap to her front teeth. She's rather upset, and I want to get her away from the crowds.'

'Of course. Please express my sympathy. Where are the others?'

The Colonel looked over his shoulder. 'I can only see two of them, our Robin and young Bob Smith. I've told them not to lose sight of you.'

He turned back towards St Stephen's Gate and disappeared.

Babcock resumed his slow progress towards Calvary, hemmed in on either side by the devout. We're really a cross-section of the Christian world, he thought, every nationality, men, women, children, all walking where our Master walked before. And in His day, too, the curious stared, pausing about their daily business to watch the condemned pass by. In His day, too, the traders and shopkeepers sold their wares, women brushed past, or halted in doorways with baskets on their heads, youths shouted from stalls, dogs chased cats under benches, old men argued, children cried.

Via Dolorosa . . . The Way of the Cross.

Left, then right again, and now, on the turn, the band of pilgrims beside whom he walked mingled with another group in front, and yet a second and third dovetailed into them. Babcock, turning for one backward glance, could see no sign of Robin or Bob Smith, no sign of any of his flock. His pilgrim partners were now, immediately in front of him, a company of nuns, and behind him, bearded and black-robed, a group of Greek Orthodox priests. To move either to right or left was out of the question. He hoped he was not too conspicuous as the one lone figure bunched between them, the singing nuns ahead, the chanting priests in the rear.

The nuns were saying the Hail Mary in Dutch. At least, he thought it was Dutch, but it could have been German.

They went down on their knees when they came to the Fifth and Sixth Stations, and Babcock, fumbling for his little pilgrim's handbook, reminded himself that the Fifth was the spot where the Cross had been laid upon Simon of Cyrene, and the Sixth where the face of Our Lord had been wiped by Veronica. He wondered whether he should kneel with the nuns, or stand with the Greek Orthodox priests. He decided to kneel with the nuns. It showed greater reverence, greater humility.

On, on, ever upwards, ever climbing, the dome of the Church of the Holy Sepulchre rearing above him, and now a final pause because they had arrived in the paved court before the great basilica itself, and in a moment the nuns, he himself and the priests would be passing through the imposing door to the final Stations, within the church itself.

It was then that Babcock became aware, though not for the first time – he had known a momentary queasiness within the Ecce Homo convent – that all was far from well with his own inside. A sharp pain gripped him, passed, then gripped him again. He began to sweat. He looked to right and left, but there was no means of extricating himself from the pilgrims who surrounded him. The chanting continued, the door of the church was before him, and despite his efforts to turn and go back the priests barred his way. He *must* go on and into the church, there was no other way.

The church of the Holy Sepulchre enveloped him. He was aware of darkness, scaffolding, steps, the smell of many bodies and much incense. What can I do, he asked himself in agony, where can I go, the lingering taste of last night's chicken ragout rising from his belly to confound him, and as he stumbled up the steps to the Chapel of Golgotha in the wake of the nuns, with altars to right and left of him, candles, lights, crosses, votive offerings in profusion all about him, he saw nothing, heard nothing, he could only feel the pressure within his body, the compelling summons of his bowels, which no prayer, no will-power, no Divine Mercy from on high could overcome.

Bob Smith, bunched in behind the Greek Orthodox priests some distance in the rear, with Robin at his side, had been the first to observe the signs of distress on Babcock's face. He had noticed that when Babcock knelt for the final time, before being swept through the door of the church, he was looking very white, and was wiping his forehead with his handkerchief.

'I wonder,' he thought, 'if he's feeling ill. Faint, or something.' He turned to Robin. 'Look,' he said, 'I'm a bit worried about the parson. I don't think we ought to let him out of our sight.'

'All right,' said Robin. 'Why don't you follow him? Perhaps he feels awkward walking with all those nuns.'

'I don't think it's that,' replied Bob. 'I think he may be feeling ill.'

'Perhaps,' said Robin, 'he wants to go to the toilet. I wouldn't mind going myself, as a matter of fact.'

He looked about him for a practical solution. Bob Smith hesitated.

'Why don't you stay here,' he suggested, 'and wait for us to come out? That is, unless you're terribly keen to see inside the Holy Sepulchre.'

'I'm not at all keen,' said Robin. 'I don't believe it's the correct site anyway.'

'Right, then. I'll see if I can find him inside.'

Bob pushed through the door, and like Babcock before him was met with darkness, scaffolding, chanting pilgrims, priests, a flight of steps and chapels on either side. Most of the pilgrims were descending, the nuns amongst them, closely followed by the priests. The figure of Babcock, so conspicuous in their midst winding his way up the Via Dolorosa, was no longer to be seen.

Then Bob Smith spied him, huddled against the base of the wall in the second chapel, his face buried in his hands, a sacristan – Greek, Coptic, Armenian, Bob didn't know which – crouching by his side. The sacristan raised his head as Bob approached.

'An English pilgrim,' he whispered, 'taken very unwell. I will go to find help.'

'That's O.K.,' said Bob. 'I know him. He belongs to our party. I'll manage.' He bent down and touched Babcock on the arm. 'Don't worry,' he said. 'I'm here.'

Babcock motioned with his hand. 'Ask him to go away,' he whispered. 'The most frightful thing has happened.'

'Yes,' said Bob, 'it's all right. I understand.'

He gestured to the sacristan, who nodded, and crossed the chapel to prevent the incoming batch of pilgrims from approaching, and Bob helped Babcock to his feet.

'It could happen to any one of us,' he said. 'It must be happening all the time. I remember once at the Cup Final . . .'

He didn't finish his sentence. His unfortunate companion was too distressed, too doubled up with weakness, with shame. Bob took his elbow and helped him down the steps, and out of the church to the court beyond.

'You'll be better in a moment,' he said, 'in the fresh air.'

Babcock clung to him. 'It was the chicken,' he said, 'that chicken I had last night for dinner. I particularly didn't touch any fruit or salad, Miss Dean warned me against them. I thought chicken would be safe.'

'Don't worry,' said Bob. 'You just couldn't help it. Do you think . . . do you think the worst is over?'

'Yes, yes, it's over.'

Bob looked about him, but there was no sign of Robin. He must have gone into the church after all. What the hell should he do? The child ought not to be left to himself, but then no more should Babcock. He might be taken ill again. Bob should escort him back to the bus at St Stephen's Gate. He would return for Robin.

'Look,' he said, 'I feel you should get back to the hotel as soon as possible, to change and lie down. I'll come with you as far as the bus.'

'I'm so grateful,' murmured his companion, 'so terribly grateful.'

He no longer cared if he had become conspicuous. It no longer mattered whether people turned and stared. As they retraced their steps downhill, back along the Via Dolorosa, past more chanting pilgrims, more tourists, more crying vendors of vegetables, onions, and the carcasses of lambs, he knew that he had indeed descended to the depths of humiliation, that by his final act of human weakness he had suffered a shame that only a man could suffer, and to which perhaps his Master had also succumbed, in his loneliness, in his fear, before being nailed to his criminal's cross.

When they came to St Stephen's Gate the first thing they saw was an ambulance drawn up alongside their bus, and a crowd of people, strangers, grouped round it. An official, white in the face, was directing them to move away. Bob's first thought was for Jill. Something had happened to Jill ... Then Jim Foster, limping, his hair dishevelled, appeared from the midst of them.

'There's been an accident,' he said.

'Are you hurt?' asked Bob.

'No ... no, nothing wrong with me, I got caught up in some sort of demonstration and managed to get away ... It's Miss Dean. She fell into that drain they call the Pool of Bethesda.'

'Oh, God in heaven ...' exclaimed Babcock, and he looked despairingly from Jim Foster back to Bob. 'This is all my fault, I should have been taking care of her. I didn't know. I thought she was with the rest of you.' He moved forward to the ambulance, then remembered his own plight and spread out his hands in a gesture of despair. 'I don't think I can go to her,' he said. 'I'm not in a fit state to see anyone . . .'

Jim Foster was staring at him, then glanced enquiringly at Bob Smith.

'He's not in good shape,' murmured Bob. 'He was taken ill a short while ago, up at the church. A bad tummy upset. He ought to get back to the hotel as soon as possible.'

'Poor devil,' replied Jim Foster under his breath, 'what an awful thing. Look . . .' he turned to Babcock, 'get up into the bus right away. I'll tell the driver to take you straight to the hotel. I'll go with Miss Dean in the ambulance.'

'How bad is she?' asked Babcock.

'They don't seem to know,' said Jim Foster. 'It's shock chiefly, I imagine. She was practically unconscious when the guide fellow pulled her out of the water. Luckily he was only at the top of the steps. Meanwhile, I can't think what has happened to either Bob's wife or mine. They're somewhere back in that infernal city.'

He took hold of Babcock by the arm and steered him towards the bus. Funny thing how other people's misfortunes made you forget your own. The panic he himself had experienced had vanished at his first sight of the ambulance as he stumbled down through St Stephen's Gate, giving way to a deeper anxiety that Kate might be the victim the stretcher-bearers were carrying to it. But it was only Miss Dean. Poor wretched Miss Dean. Thank heaven, not Kate.

The bus rumbled off with the pale, unhappy Babcock staring at them from one of the windows.

'Well, he's on his way, that's one thing,' said Jim Foster. 'What a calamity, what a situation. I wish the Colonel was here to handle it.'

'I'm worried now about Robin,' said Bob Smith. 'I told

him to wait for us outside the church of the Holy Sepulchre, and he was missing when we came out.'

'Missing? In that mob?' Jim Foster stared, aghast.

Then, with unspeakable relief, he saw his wife, with Jill beside her, coming through St Stephen's Gate. He ran across to her.

'Thank heaven you've come,' he said. 'We've got to get Miss Dean to hospital. She's in the ambulance already. I'll explain everything on the way. There's been a series of mishaps all round. Babcock ill, Robin missing, it's been a disastrous day.'

Kate seized his arm. 'But you?' she said. 'Are you all right?'

'Yes, yes . . . Of course I'm all right.'

He dragged her towards the ambulance. He did not even look at Jill. Bob hesitated, wondering what he ought to do. Then he turned, and saw Jill standing beside him.

'Where have you been?' he asked.

'I don't know,' she said wearily. 'In a sort of garden. I was looking for you but I couldn't find you. Kate was with me. She was worried about her husband. He can't stand crowds.'

'Nor can any of us,' he said, 'but we'll have to face them again. Young Robin is lost, and I must go and find him. There's nobody else left.'

'I'll come with you.'

'Are you sure? You look absolutely done in.'

The Fosters were climbing into the ambulance. The siren wailed, and the spectators moved away. Jill thought of that endless winding street they called the Via Dolorosa, the chanting pilgrims, the chattering vendors, the repetition of a scene she never wanted to see again, the clatter, the noise.

'I can face it,' she sighed. 'It won't seem so long if we're together.'

Robin was enjoying himself. Being on his own always gave him a sense of freedom, of power. And he had become very bored trailing along in the path of the pilgrims, with people going down on their knees every other moment. It wasn't even as if they were walking the right way. The city had been pulled down and rebuilt so many times that it was altogether different from what it had been two thousand years ago. The only way to reconstruct it would be to pull it down again, and then dig and dig and reveal all the foundations. He might well become an archaeologist when he grew up, if he didn't become a scientist like his father. The two professions were rather similar, he decided. He certainly would not become a clergyman like Mr Babcock. Not in this day and age.

He wondered how long they would stay inside the church. Hours, probably. It was full to the brim with priests and pilgrims wanting to pray, and they would all bump into each other. This made him laugh, and laughing made him want to go to the toilet – his grandmother hated the word toilet, but everyone used it at school – and so, as there wasn't a real one handy, he went and relieved himself against the wall of the church. Nobody saw. Then he sat down on a step, opened his two maps and spread them across his knees. The thing was, Jesus had either been held in the Antonia Fortress or in the Citadel. Probably both. But which one had he been held in last, before he had to carry his Cross with the two other prisoners, and set out for Golgotha? The description in the Gospels did not make it clear. He was brought before Pilate, but Pilate could just as well have been in the one place as in the other. Pilate delivered Jesus to the high priests to be crucified, but where were the high priests waiting for him? That was the point. It could have been at Herod's Palace, where the Citadel stood now, and in that case Jesus and the two thieves would all have left the city by the Genath Gate. He looked from one map to the other: the Genath Gate was now called Jaffa Gate, or in Hebrew Yafo – it depended which language you spoke.

Robin looked at the church door. They would be ages yet. He decided to walk to the Jaffa Gate and see how it was for himself. It wasn't very far, and with the help of the modern map he wouldn't lose the way. It took him less than ten minutes to reach the gate, and here he paused to take stock of his surroundings. People were passing in and out, and there were cars drawn up outside, as there had been by St Stephen's Gate at the opposite end of the walled city. The trouble was, of course, that instead of the bare hillside and gardens, which was how it would have been two thousand years ago, there was now a main road, and the modern city spreading itself everywhere. He consulted his old map once again. There used to be a fortress tower called Psephinus, standing proud and mighty by the north-west corner of the city, and this was the tower that the Emperor Titus rode to inspect, when he camped with his Roman legions before capturing and sacking Jerusalem in AD70. There was something built on the present site called the Collège des Frères. Wait a moment, though. Was it the Collège des Frères or a hotel called the Knight's Palace? Either way it was still inside the walls of the city, and somehow that was not right, even with the walls having been rebuilt.

'I'll imagine,' he told himself, 'that I'm Jesus, and I've just come out of the Genath Gate, and all this is bare hillside and sloping gardens, and they don't crucify a person in a garden, but a decent distance away, especially before the Feast of the Passover, otherwise the people would make a disturbance, and there had been enough riots already. So Jesus and the two other condemned prisoners were made to walk a fair way, that's why they made Simon the farm-labourer – and Cyrene means farm-labourer in Aramaic, the Headmaster told me so – carry the cross. He was just coming in from work in the fields. Jesus couldn't manage it, being weak from all that scourging. And they took him and the others out to some rough scrubby ground overlooked by the Psephinus tower, where the soldiers would have had a guard posted, so that if there should have been an attempt at rescue the attempt would fail.'

Pleased with his deduction, Robin turned to the right out of the Jaffa Gate and walked along the main road until he judged that he was the right distance from the long-vanished tower of Psephinus. He found that he had reached a junction, with main roads going in all directions and traffic roaring by, and the great building across the other side of the central square was the town hall, according to his modern map.

'So this is it,' he thought. 'This is scrubby ground, with fields where the town hall stands, and the farm-labourer is sweating, and so are Jesus and the others. And the sun is overhead in a blazing sky, as it is now, and when the crosses are set up the men nailed on them won't see the fields behind them, they'll be looking at the city.'

He shut his eyes a moment, and turned, and looked back at the city and the walls, and they were a golden colour, very fine and splendid. For Jesus, who had spent most of his life wandering about the hills and lakes and villages, it would have seemed the finest and most splendid city in the world. But after staring at it for three hours, in pain, it would not seem so splendid – in fact, it would be a relief to die.

A horn blared, and he stepped out of the way of the incoming traffic. If he didn't watch out he would die too, and there wouldn't be much sense in that.

He decided to walk back to the city through the New Gate, which was just along to the right. Some men were repairing a place in the road, and they looked up as Robin approached. They shouted, pointing to the traffic, and although Robin got the message, and skipped to safety beside them, he couldn't understand what they were saying. It could be Yiddish, or possibly Hebrew, but he wished it could have been Aramaic. He waited until the man with the drill ceased his ear-splitting probe, and then he called to them.

'Does anyone speak English?' he asked.

The man with the drill smiled and shook his head, then called out to one of his companions, who was bending over a piece of piping. The man looked up. He was young, like the rest, and had very white teeth and black curly hair.

'I speak English, yes,' he said.

Robin peered down into the pit beneath. 'Can you tell me, then,' he asked, 'if you have found anything interesting down there?'

The young man laughed, and picked up a small animal by its tail. It looked like a dead rat.

'Tourist souvenir?' he suggested.

'No skulls? No bones?' Robin asked hopefully.

'No,' smiled the labourer. 'For that we have to drill very deep, below the rock. Here, you can catch?' He threw a small piece of rock up to Robin from the pit in which he stood. 'Keep it,' he said. 'The rock of Jerusalem. It will bring you luck.'

'Thank you very much,' said Robin.

He wondered whether he should tell them that they were standing within a hundred yards or so, perhaps, of a place where three men had been crucified two thousand years ago, and then he decided they would not believe him; or, if they did, it would not impress them very much. For Jesus was not important to them, not like Abraham or David, and, anyway, so many men had been tortured and killed around Jerusalem since then that the young man might very well say, with justice, so what? It would be more tactful to wish them a happy holiday instead. It was the 14th day of Nisan, and at sundown all work would cease. He put the small piece of rock in his pocket.

'I hope you have a very pleasant Pesach,' he said.

The young man stared. 'You Jewish?'

'No,' answered Robin, uncertain whether the question related to his nationality or to his religion. If the latter, he would have to reply that his father was an atheist, and his mother went to church once a year on Christmas Day. 'No, I come from Little Bletford in England, but I do know that today is the 14th day of Nisan and that you have a public holiday tomorrow.'

This, in fact, was the reason for so much traffic, he supposed, and the reason why the city itself had been so crowded. He hoped the young man was suitably impressed by his knowledge.

'It's your Feast of Unleavened Bread,' he told him.

The young man smiled again, showing his row of white teeth, and, laughing, he called something over his shoulder to his companion with the drill, who shouted in reply, before applying his drill to the surface of the road again. The earsplitting sound began once more, and the young man cupped his hands to his mouth and called up to Robin, 'It is also the Festival of our Freedom,' he shouted. 'You are young, like us. Enjoy it too.'

Robin waved his hand and began walking towards the New Gate, his hand clenched tightly round the piece of rock in his pocket. The Festival of our Freedom ... It sounded better than the Passover. More modern, more up to date. More suitable for, as his grandmother would say, this day and age. And whether it meant freedom from bondage, as it did in the Old Testament, or freedom from the rule of the Roman Empire, which the Jews hoped for at the time of the crucifixion, or freedom from hunger and poverty and homelessness, which the young men digging in the road had won for themselves today, it was all one and the same thing. Everyone, everywhere, wanted freedom from something, and Robin decided that it would be a good idea if Pesach and Easter could be combined throughout the world, and then all of us, he thought, could join in celebrating the Festival of our Freedom.

The bus took the road north from the Mount of Olives before sundown. There had been no further drama. Bob and Jill Smith, having searched the precincts of the Holy Sepulchre in vain, had turned their steps in the direction of the New Gate and had come across Robin, perfectly composed, entering the city behind a group of singing pilgrims from the coast. The bus had been late departing because of Miss Dean. The ambulance had taken her to hospital, where she had been detained for a number of hours suffering from shock, but luckily with no external or internal injuries. She had been given an injection and a sedative, and then the doctor had pronounced her fit to travel, with strict injunctions that she should be put straight to bed directly they were back in Haifa. Kate Foster had become nurse in charge of the patient.

'It is so kind of you,' Miss Dean had murmured, 'so very kind.'

It was decided by all not to mention her unfortunate accident. Nor did Miss Dean allude to it herself. She sat silently, with a rug over her knees, between the Fosters. Lady Althea was silent too. Her blue chiffon scarf masked the lower part of her face, giving her the appearance of a Moslem woman who had not relinquished the veil. If anything, it added to her dignity and grace. She too had a rug over her knees, and the Colonel held her hand beneath it.

The young Smiths held hands more openly, Jill sporting a new bangle, an inexpensive one that Bob had bought for her as they passed near one of the suks on their return earlier in the day after finding Robin.

Babcock sat beside Robin. Like Miss Dean, he also wore a change of clothing – a pair of trousers borrowed from

Jim Foster which were a shade too large for him. No one passed any remarks, and for this he was unspeakably thankful. No one looked back at the city of Jerusalem as the bus skirted Mount Scopus – that is to say, no one but Robin. The ninth hour of the 14th day of Nisan had come and gone, and the thieves, or the insurrectionists, whichever they were, had been taken down from their crosses. Jesus too, his body perhaps in a grave deep in the rock below where the young labourers had been drilling. Now the young men could go home, and wash, and meet their families, and look forward to the public holiday. Robin turned to the Rev. Babcock at his side.

'It's rather a shame,' he said, 'that we couldn't have stayed two more days.'

Babcock, who wished for nothing more than to be safely back on board ship so that he could shut himself in his cabin and try to forget his shame in the church of the Holy Sepulchre, marvelled at the resilience of the young. The boy had been dragging round the city all day, and had nearly lost himself into the bargain.

'Why, Robin?' he asked.

'Well, you never know,' Robin replied. 'Of course it's not very probable in this day and age, but we might have seen the Resurrection.'

The Breakthrough

My part in the affair started on September 18th, when my chief sent for me and told me he was transferring me to Saxmere on the east coast. He was sorry about it, he said, but I was the only one with the necessary technical qualifications for the particular work they had on hand. No, he couldn't give me any details; they were an odd lot down there, and shut themselves up behind barbed wire at the slightest provocation. The place had been a radar experimental station a few years back, but this was finished, and any experiments that were going on now were of an entirely different nature, something to do with vibrations and the pitch of sound.

'I'll be perfectly frank with you,' said my chief, removing his horn-rimmed spectacles and waving them in the air apologetically. 'The fact is that James MacLean is a very old friend of mine. We were at Cambridge together and I saw a lot of him then and afterwards, but our paths diverged, and he tied himself up in experimental work of rather a dubious nature. Lost the government a lot of money, and didn't do his own reputation much good either. I gather that's forgotten, and he's been reinstated down at Saxmere with his own handpicked team of experts and a government grant. They're stuck for an electronics engineer – which is where you come in. MacLean has sent me an S.O.S. for someone I can vouch for personally – in other words, he wants a chap who won't talk. You'd do me a personal favour if you went.'

Put like this, there was little I could do but accept. It was a damned nuisance, all the same. The last thing in the world I wanted to do was to leave Associated Electronics

257

Ltd., and its unique facilities for research, and drift off to the east coast to work for someone who had blotted his copybook once and might do so again.

'When do you want me to go?' I asked.

The chief looked more apologetic than ever.

'As soon as you can make it. The day after tomorrow? I'm really very sorry, Saunders. With any luck you'll be back by Christmas. I've told MacLean I'm lending you to him for this particular project only. No question of a long-term transfer. You're too valuable here.'

This was the sop. The pat on the back. A.E.L. would forget about me for the next three months. I had another question, though.

'What sort of a chap is he?'

'MacLean?' My chief paused before replacing his horn-rims, always a signal of dismissal. 'He's what I'd call an enthusiast, the kind that don't let go. A fanatic in his way. Oh, he won't bore you. I remember at Cambridge he spent most of his time bird-watching. He had some peculiar theory then about migration, but he didn't inflict it on us. He nearly chucked physics for neurology, but thought better of it – the girl he later married persuaded him. Then came the tragedy. She died after they'd only been married a year.'

My chief replaced his spectacles. He had no more to say or, if he had, it was beside the point. As I was leaving the room he called after me, 'You can keep that last piece of information to yourself. About his wife, I mean. His staff down there may not know anything about it.'

It was not until I had actually packed up at A.E.L. and left my comfortable digs, and the train was drawing out of Liverpool Street station, that the full force of my situation hit me. Here I was, lumbered with a job I didn't want in an outfit I knew nothing about, and all as a personal favour to my chief, who obviously had some private reason for obliging his onetime colleague. As I stared moodily out of the carriage window, feeling more bloody-minded every minute, I kept seeing the expression on my successor's face when I told him I was going to Saxmere.

'That dump?' he said. 'Why, it's a joke – they haven't done any serious research there for years. The Ministry have given it over to the crackpots, hoping they'll blow themselves to pieces.'

A few discreet off-hand inquiries in other quarters had brought the same answer. A friend of mine with a sense of humour advised me over the telephone to take golf-clubs and plenty of paperbacks. 'There's no sort of organisation,' he said. 'MacLean works with a handful of chaps who think he's the Messiah. If you don't fall into line he ignores you, and you'll find yourself doing sweet f.a.'

'Fine. That suits me. I need a holiday,' I lied, hanging up with feelings of intense irritation against the world in general.

It was typical, I suppose, of my approach to the whole business that I hadn't checked thoroughly on timetables, and therefore an added annoyance to find that I had to get out at Ipswich, wait forty minutes, and board a slow train to Thirlwall, which was the station for Saxmere. It was raining when I finally descended upon the empty wind-swept platform, and the porter who took my ticket told me that the taxi which usually waited for this particular train had been snapped up five minutes before.

'There's a garage opposite the Three Cocks,' he added. 'They might still be open and could run you over to Saxmere.'

I walked past the booking office carrying my bags and blaming myself for my bad staff-work. As I stood outside the station wondering whether to brave the doubtful hospitality of the Three Cocks – it was close on seven, and even if a car was not available I could do with a drink – a very ancient Morris came swerving into the station-yard and pulled up in front of me. The driver got out and made a dive for my bags.

'You are Saunders, I take it?' he asked, smiling. He was young, not more than about nineteen, with a shock of fair hair.

'That's right,' I said. 'I was just wondering where the hell I'd raise a taxi.'

'You wouldn't,' he answered. 'On a wet night the Yanks swipe the lot. Anything on wheels that will take 'em out of Thirlwall. Hop in, will you?'

I'd forgotten about Thirlwall being a U.S. air-base, and made a mental note to avoid the Three Cocks in my leisure hours. American personnel on the loose are not among my favourite companions.

'Sorry about the rattle,' apologised the driver as we swerved through the town to the accompaniment of what sounded like a couple of petrol cans rolling under the back seat. 'I keep meaning to fix it, but never find time. My name's Ryan, by the way, Ken Ryan, always known as Ken. We don't go in for surnames at Saxmere.'

I said nothing. My Christian name is Stephen, nor had anyone ever shortened it to Steve. My gloom increased and I lit a cigarette. Already the houses of Thirlwall lay behind us and our road, having traversed a mile or two of flat countryside consisting of turnip fields, suddenly shot up on to a sandy track across a heath, over which we proceeded in a series of bumps until my head nearly hit the roof.

My companion apologised once more.

'I could have taken you in by the main entrance,' he said, 'but this way is so much shorter. Don't worry, the springs are used to it.'

The sandy track topped a rise and there below us, stretching into infinity, lay acre upon acre of waste land, marsh and reed, bounded on the left by sand-dunes with the open sea beyond. The marshes were intersected here and there by dykes, beside which stood clumps of forlorn rushes bending to the wind and rain, the dykes in their turn forming themselves into dank pools, one or two of them miniature lakes, ringed about with reeds.

Our road, the surface of which was now built up with clinkers and small stones, descended abruptly to this scene of desolation, winding like a narrow ribbon with the marsh on either side. In the far distance a square tower, grey and squat, stood out against the skyline, and as we drew nearer I could see beyond the tower itself the curving spiral of the one-time radar installation, brooding over the waste land like a giant oyster-shell. This, then, was Saxmere. My worst forebodings could not have conjured up a more forbidding place.

My companion, sensing probably from my silence that I lacked enthusiasm, gave me a half-glance.

'It looks a bit grim in this light,' he said, 'but that's the rain. The weather's pretty good on the whole, though the wind is keen. We get some stunning sunsets.'

The laugh with which I greeted his remark was intended to be ironic, but it missed its mark, or was taken as encouragement, for he added, 'If you're keen on birds you've come to the right spot. Avocets breed here in the spring, and last March I heard the bittern boom.'

I choked back the expletive that rose to my lips – his phraseology struck me as naïve – and while admitting indifference to all objects furred or feathered I expressed surprise that anything in such a dreary locality should have a desire to breed at all. My sarcasm was lost, for he said, quite seriously, 'Oh, you'd be surprised,' and ground the Morris to a halt before a gate set in a high wired fence.

'Have to unlock this,' he told me, jumping out of the car, and I saw that now we had come to Saxmere itself. The area ahead was bounded on all sides by this same fence, some ten feet in height, giving the place the look of a concentration camp. This agreeable vista was enhanced by the sudden appearance of an Alsatian dog, who loped out of the marshes to the left, and stood wagging its tail at young Ken as he unlocked the gate.

'Where are the tommy-guns?' I asked, when he climbed back into the driving-seat. 'Or does the dog's handler watch us unseen from some concrete dug-out in the marsh?'

This time he had the grace to laugh as we passed through the barricade. 'No guns, no handlers,' he said. 'Cerberus is as gentle as a lamb. Not that I expected to find him here, but Mac will have him under control.'

He got out once more and locked the gate, while the dog, his head pointing across the marsh, took no more notice of us. Then all at once, pricking his ears, he dived into the reeds, and I watched him running along a narrow muddy track in the direction of the tower.

'He'll be home before we are,' said Ken, letting in the clutch, and the car swerved to the right along a broad asphalt road, the marsh giving place now to scrub and shingle.

The rain had stopped, the clouds had broken into splintered fragments, and the squat tower of Saxmere stood out bold and black against a copper sky. Did this, I wondered, herald one of the famous sunsets? If so, no member of the staff appeared to be taking advantage of it. Road and marsh alike were deserted. We passed the fork to the main entrance and turned left towards the disused radar installation and the tower itself, grouped about with sheds and concrete buildings. The place looked more like a deserted Dachau than ever.

Ken drove past the tower and the main buildings, taking a side road running seaward, at the end of which was a row of prefabricated huts.

'Here we are,' he said, 'and what did I tell you? Cerberus has beaten us to it.'

The dog emerged from a track on the left and ran off behind the huts.

'How is he trained?' I asked. 'A hi-fi whistle?'

'Not exactly,' answered my companion.

I got out of the car and he heaved my bags from the rear seat.

'These are the sleeping-quarters, I suppose?'

I glanced about me. The pre-fabs at least looked wind- and water-tight.

'It's the whole works,' replied Ken. 'We sleep, feed, and do everything here.'

He ignored my stare and led the way ahead. There was a small entrance hall, and a corridor beyond running right and left. Nobody was about. The walls of both hall and corridor were a dull grey, the floor covered with linoleum. The impression was that of a small-town country surgery after hours.

'We feed at eight, but there's loads of time,' said Ken. 'You'd like to see your room and have a bath, perhaps.'

I had no particular desire for a bath, but I badly needed a drink. I followed him down the left-hand corridor, and he opened a door and switched on the light, then crossed the floor and pulled aside the curtains.

'Sorry about that,' he said. 'Janus likes to bed us down early before going through to the kitchen. Winter or summer, these curtains are drawn at six-thirty, and the covers removed from the beds. He's a stickler for routine.'

I looked around. Whoever designed the room must have had a hospital training all right. It had the bare essentials. Bed, wash-basin, chest-of-drawers, wardrobe, one chair. The window gave on to the entrance front. The blankets on the bed were folded hospital fashion, and a military hospital at that.

'O.K.?' asked Ken. He looked puzzled. Possibly my expression surprised him.

'Fine,' I answered. 'Now what about a drink?'

I followed him up the corridor once more, across the entrance hall, and on through a swing-door at the far end. I heard the light clack-clack of ping-pong balls, and braced myself for frivolity. The room we entered was empty. The sportsmen, whoever they were, were playing in the room beyond. Here there were easy chairs, a table or two, an electric fire and a bar in the far corner, behind which my youthful companion installed himself. I noticed, with misgiving, two enormous urns.

'Coffee or cocoa?' he asked. 'Or do you prefer something cool? I can recommend the orange juice with a splash of soda.'

'I'd like a Scotch,' I said.

He looked distressed. His expression became that of an anxious host whose guest demands fresh strawberries in midwinter.

'I'm frightfully sorry,' he said, 'we none of us touch alcohol. Mac won't have it served, it's one of his things. But of course you can bring your own supply and drink in your room. What a fool I was not to have warned you. We could have stopped at Thirlwall and brought you back a bottle from the Three Cocks.'

His distress was so genuine that I controlled the flood-gates of emotion that threatened to burst from me, and told him I would settle for orange juice. He looked relieved, and splashed the nauseous liquid into a tall glass, deftly sousing it with soda.

I felt the time-had come for further explanation, not only about him, the acolyte, but about the rest of the establishment. Was the Order Benedictine or Franciscan, and at what hour would the bell sound for Vespers and Compline?

'Forgive my ignorance.' I said, 'but my briefing before leaving A.E.L. was somewhat short. I don't know the first thing about Saxmere, or what you do here.'

'Oh, don't worry,' he answered, smiling. 'Mac will explain all that.'

He poured some juice into his own glass and said, 'Cheers.' I ignored the toast and listened to the echo of the ping-pong balls.

'You told me,' I continued, 'that all the work was done in this building where we are now.'

'That's right,' he said.

'But where do all the personnel hang out?' I persisted.

'Personnel?' he echoed, frowning. 'There are no personnel. That's to say, there's only Mac, Robbie, Janus – I suppose you'd count Janus – and myself. And now of course you.'

I put down my glass and stared. Was he having me on? No, he seemed perfectly serious. Tossing down his orange juice like a cup-bearer of the gods quaffing ambrosia, he watched me from behind the bar.

'It's O.K., you know,' he said. 'We're a very happy party.'

I did not doubt it. What with cocoa, ping-pong, and the booming bittern, this team of sportsmen would make the members of a Women's Institute seem like trolls.

My baser instincts made me yearn to prick the youngster's pride.

'And what,' I asked, 'is your position on the staff? Ganymede to the professor's Jove?'

To my intense surprise he laughed, and with an ear cocked to the further room, where the sound of balls had ceased, set two more glasses down upon the bar and filled them both with juice.

'How smart of you to guess,' he answered. 'That's roughly the idea ... to snatch me from this earth to a doubtful heaven. No, seriously, I'm Mac's guinea-pig, along with Janus's daughter and Cerberus the dog.'

At that moment the door opened and two men came into the room.

Instinctively I recognised MacLean. He was fiftyish, craggy, tall, with the pale, rather light blue eyes which I associate with drunkards, criminals and fighter pilots – in my view the three frequently combine. His lightish hair receded from a high forehead, and the prominent nose was matched by a thrusting chin. He wore baggy corduroy trousers and an immense pullover with a turtle neck.

His companion was sallow, bespectacled and squat. Shorts and a baggy shirt gave him a boy scout appearance, nor did the circular sweat stains under his armpits enhance his charm.

MacLean advanced towards me holding out his hand, the broad smile of welcome suggesting I had already become one of his small band of brothers.

'I'm so very glad to see you,' he said. 'I do hope Ken has been looking after you all right. Such a wretched evening for your first glimpse of Saxmere, but we'll do better for you tomorrow, won't we, Robbie?'

His voice, his manner, was that of an old-fashioned host. I might have been a late arrival at a country-house shoot. He put his hand on my shoulder and urged me towards the bar.

'Orange juice for all, please, Ken,' he said, and, turning to me, 'We've heard tremendous things about you from A.E.L. I can't tell you how grateful I am to them – to John in particular – for allowing you to come. And above all to yourself. We'll do everything we can to make your visit memorable. Robbie, Ken, I want you to drink to – it's Stephen, isn't it? Shall we say Steve? – and to the success of our joint efforts.'

I forced a smile, and felt it become a fixture on my face.

Robbie, the boy scout, blinked at me from behind his spectacles.

'Your very good health,' he said. 'I'm the Johannis factotum here. I do everything from exploding gases to taking Ken's temperature, as well as exercising the dog. When in trouble send for me.'

I laughed, then swiftly realised that the falsetto, music-hall comedian voice was in fact his own, and not assumed for the occasion.

We crossed the corridor to a room facing the front, plain and bare like the one we had left, with a table set for four. A long-faced, saturnine fellow, with close-cropped grizzled hair, stood by the sideboard.

'Meet Janus,' Mac said to me. 'I don't know how they feed you at A.E.L., but Janus sees we none of us starve.'

I favoured the steward with a cheerful nod. He replied to it with a grunt, and I instantly doubted his willingness to run errands for me to the Three Cocks. I waited for MacLean to say grace, which would somehow have seemed in character, but none was forthcoming, and Janus set before him an enormous old-fashioned soup tureen shaped like a jerry, from which my new chief ladled a steaming, saffron-coloured brew. It was surprisingly good. The grilled Dover sole that followed was better still, and the cheese soufflé feather-light. The meal took us some fifty minutes to consume, and by the end of it I was ready to make peace with my fellow-men.

Young Ken – whose conversation during dinner had consisted of a series of private jokes with Robbie, while MacLean discoursed on mountain climbing in Crete, the beauty of flamingoes on the wing in the Camargue, and the peculiar composition of Piero della Francesca's 'Flagellation of Christ' – was the first to rise from the table and ask leave to be dismissed.

MacLean nodded. 'Don't read too late,' he said. 'Robbie will turn your light out if you do. Nine-thirty's the limit.'

The youngster smiled, and bade the three of us good-night. I asked whether Ken was in training to race the dog around the marsh and back.

'No,' answered MacLean abruptly, 'but he needs a lot of sleep. Let's to billiards.'

He led the way from the dining-room back to the so-called bar, while I prepared myself for half an hour or so in the room beyond – nothing loath, for I rather fancied myself with a cue – but as we passed through, and I saw nothing but a ping-pong table and a dart-board, Robbie, noticing my puzzled expression, boomed in my ear, 'A quote from Shakespeare, the Serpent of old Nile. Mac means he wants to brief you.' He pushed me gently forward and then vanished. I followed my leader through yet another door, sound-proofed this time, and we entered the chill atmosphere of what appeared to be half-working lab, half-clinic, streamlined and severe. It even had an operating table under a centre light, and instruments and jars behind glass panels on the walls.

'Robbie's department,' said MacLean. 'He can do any-thing here from developing a virus to taking out your tonsils.'

I made no comment, having small desire to offer myself as a potential victim to the boy scout's doubtful ministra-tions, and we passed from the laboratory to the room adjoining.

'You'll feel more at home here,' observed MacLean, and as he switched on the lights I saw that we had reached the electronics department. The first installation to which we came appeared similar to the one we had built for the G.P.O. some years ago – that is to say, a computer cap-able of speech, though its vocabulary was limited and the actual 'voice' was far from perfect. MacLean's box of tricks, however, had various accessories, and I went up to examine them closely.

'He's neat, don't you think?' said MacLean, rather like a proud father showing off his new-born infant. 'I call him Charon 1.'

We all have pet names for our inventions, and Hermes had seemed particularly appropriate for the winged messenger we had developed for the G.P.O. Charon, if I remembered rightly, was the ferryman who conveyed the spirits of the dead across the Styx. I supposed this was MacLean's own brand of humour.

'What does it do?' I asked cautiously.

'It has several functions,' answered MacLean, 'which I'll explain later, but your main concern will be the voice mechanism.'

He went through a starting-up procedure, much as we had done at A.E.L., but the result was very different. The voice reproduction was perfect, and he had got rid of all the hesitation.

'I'm using the computer for certain experiments in the field of hypnosis,' he went on. 'These involve programming it with a series of questions. The answers are then fed back into the computer, and are themselves used to modify the questions that follow. What do you think of that?'

'It's fantastic!' I answered. 'You've gone miles beyond what anybody else is doing.'

I was indeed flabbergasted, and wondered just how he had done it – as well as keeping it all so secret. We thought we had achieved all that could be done in this particular field at A.E.L.

'Yes,' said Mac, 'your experts will hardly improve upon it. Charon 1 will have many uses, especially in the medical world. I won't go into any more details tonight, except to say that it is primarily connected with an experiment I'm working on which the Ministry knows nothing whatever about.'

He smiled, and here we go, I thought, now we're coming to the 'experiments of a dubious nature' which my chief had warned me about. I said nothing, and MacLean moved to a different installation.

'This,' he said, 'is what really concerns the government, and the military chaps in particular. You know, of course, that blast is difficult to control. An aeroplane breaking the sound barrier may shatter windows indiscriminately, but not one particular window, or one particular target. Charon 2 can do just that.' He crossed the room to a cabinet, took out a glass jar, and placed it on the working bench by the wall. Then he threw a switch on his second installation, and the glass shivered to fragments.

'Rather neat, don't you think?' said MacLean. 'But of course the point is the long-range use, should you wish to inflict serious damage on specific objects at a distance. I personally don't – blast doesn't interest me – but the Services would find it effective on occasion. It's just a case of a special method of transmission. But my particular concern is high-frequency response between individuals, and between people and animals. I'm keeping this quiet from my masters, who give me a grant.' He put his fingers on another control on the second installation. 'You won't see anything with this one,' he said. 'It's the call-note with which I control Cerberus. Human beings can't pick it up.'

We waited in silence, and a few minutes later I heard the sound of a dog scratching at the further door. MacLean let him in. 'All right. Good boy. Lie down.' He turned to me, smiling. 'Nothing really in that – he was only the other side of the building – but we've got him to obey orders from long distances. It could be quite useful in an emergency.' He glanced at his watch. 'I wonder if Mrs J. will forgive me,' he murmured. 'It's only a quarter-past nine after all. And I do so enjoy showing off.' His schoolboy grin was suddenly infectious.

'What are you going to do?' I asked.

'Bring her small daughter to the telephone, or wake her up if she's asleep.'

He made another adjustment to the apparatus, and once again we waited. In about two minutes the telephone rang. MacLean crossed the room to answer it. 'Hullo?' he said. 'Sorry, Mrs J. Just an experiment. I'm sorry if I've woken her up. Yes, put her on. Hullo, Niki. No, it's all right. You can go back to bed. Sleep tight.' He replaced the receiver, then bent down to pat Cerberus stretched at his feet.

'Children, like dogs, are particularly easy to train,' he said. 'Or put it this way – their sixth sense, the one that picks up these signals, is highly developed. Niki has her own call-note, just as Cerberus does, and the fact that she suffers from retarded development makes her an excellent subject.'

He patted his box of tricks in much the same fashion that he had patted his dog. Then he glanced up at me and smiled.

'Any questions?'

'Obviously,' I replied. 'The first being, what is the exact object of the exercise? Are you trying to prove that certain high-frequency signals have potentialities not only for destruction but also for controlling the receptive mechanism in an animal, and also the human brain?'

I forced a composure I was far from feeling. If these were the sort of experiments that were going on at Saxmere, small wonder the place had been shrugged aside as a crackpot's paradise.

MacLean looked at me thoughtfully. 'Of course Charon 2 could be said to prove exactly that,' he said, 'though this is not my intention. The Ministry may possibly be very disappointed in consequence. No, I personally am trying to tackle something more far-reaching.' He paused, then put his hand on my shoulder. 'We'll leave Charons 1 and 2 for tonight. Come outside for a breath of air.'

We left by the door which the dog had scratched at. It led to another corridor, and finally to an entrance at the back of the building. MacLean unbolted the door and I followed him through. The rain had ceased and the air was clean and cold, the sky brilliant with stars. In the distance, beyond the line of sand-dunes, I could hear the roar of sea breaking upon shingle.

MacLean inhaled deeply, his face turned seaward. Then he looked upward at the stars. I lit a cigarette and waited for him to speak.

'Have you any experience of poltergeists?' he asked.

'Things that go bump in the night?' I said. 'No, I can't say I have.' I offered him a cigarette, but he shook his head.

'What you watched just now,' said MacLean, 'the glass shivering to pieces, is the same thing. Electrical force, released. Mrs J. had trouble with crashing objects long before I developed Charon. Saucepans, and so on, hurling themselves about at the coastguard's cottage where they live. It was Niki, of course.'

I stared at him, incredulous. 'You mean the child?'

'Yes.'

He thrust his hands in his pockets and began pacing up and down. 'Naturally, she was quite unaware of the fact,' he continued. 'So were her parents. It was only psychic energy exploding, extra strong in her case because her brain is undeveloped, and since she is the only survivor of identical twins the force was doubled.'

This was rather too much to swallow, and I laughed. He swung round and faced me.

'Have you a better solution?' he asked.

'No,' I admitted, 'but surely . . .'

'Exactly,' he interrupted. 'Nobody ever has. There are

hundreds, thousands of cases of these so-called phenomena, and almost every time they are reported there is evidence to show that a child, or someone who is regarded as of sub-standard intelligence, was in the locality at the time.' He resumed his walk and I beside him, the dog at our heels.

'So what?' I said.

'So that,' he went on, 'it suggests we all possess an untapped source of energy within us that awaits release. Call it, if you like, Force Six. It works in the same way as the high-frequency impulse which I released just now from Charon. Here is the explanation of telepathy, precognition, and all the so-called psychic mysteries. The power we develop in any electronic device is the same as the power that the Janus child possesses – with one difference, to date: we can control the one but not the other.'

I saw his meaning, but not where the discussion was leading us. God knows life is complicated enough without seeking to probe the unconscious forces that may lie dormant within man, especially if the connecting link must first be an animal, or an idiot child.

'All right,' I said, 'so you tap this Force Six, as you call it. Not only in Janus's daughter, but in all animals, in backward children, and finally in the human race. You have us breaking glasses, sending saucepans flying, exchanging messages by telepathic communication, and so on and so forth; but wouldn't it add immeasurably to our difficulties, so that we ended up in the complete chaos from which we presumably sprang?'

This time it was MacLean who laughed. Our walk had taken us to a ridge of high ground, and we were looking across the sand-dunes to the sea beyond. The long shingle beach seemed to stretch into eternity, as drear and featureless as the marsh behind it. The sea broke with a monotonous roar, sucking at the dragging stones, only to renew the effort and spend itself once more.

'No doubt it would,' he said, 'but that's not what I'm after. Man will find a proper use for Force Six in his own good time. I want to make it work for him after the body dies.'

I threw my cigarette on to the ground and watched it glow an instant before it flickered to a wet stub.

'What on earth do you mean?' I asked him.

He was looking at me, trying to size up my reaction to his words. I could not make up my mind if he was mad or not, but there was something vaguely endearing about him as he stood there, hunched, speculative, like an overgrown schoolboy in his corduroy bags and his old turtle-necked sweater.

'I'm quite serious,' he said. 'The energy is there, you know, when it leaves the body on the point of death. Think of the appalling wastage through the centuries; all that energy escaping as we die, when it might be used for the benefit of mankind. It's the oldest of theories, of course, that the soul escapes through the nostrils or the mouth – the Greeks believed in it, so do certain African tribes today. You and I are not concerned with souls, and we know that our intelligence dies with our body. But not the vital spark. The life-force continues as energy, uncontrolled, and up to the present . . . useless. It's above us and around us as we stand talking here.'

Once again he threw back his head and looked at the stars, and I wondered what deep inner loneliness had driven him to this vain quest after the intangible. Then I remembered that his wife had died. Doubtless this theoretical bunk had saved him.

'I'm afraid it will take you a lifetime to prove,' I said to him.

'No.' he answered. 'At the most a couple of months. You see, Charon 3, which I didn't show you, has a built-in storage unit, to receive and contain power, or, to be exact, to receive and contain Force Six when it is available.' He paused. The glance he threw at me was curious, speculative. I waited for him to continue. 'The ground work has all been done,' he said. 'We are geared and ready for the great experiment, when Charons 1 and 3 will be used in conjunction, but I need an assistant, fully trained to work both installations, when the moment comes. I'll be perfectly frank with you. Your predecessor here at Saxmere wouldn't co-operate. Oh yes, you had one. I asked your chief at A.E.L. not to tell you – I preferred to tell you myself. Your predecessor refused his cooperation for reasons of conscience which I respect.'

I stared. I was not surprised at the other fellow refusing to co-operate, but I did not see where ethics came into it.

'He was a Catholic,' explained MacLean. 'Believing as he did in the survival of the soul and its sojourn in purgatory, he couldn't stomach any idea of imprisoning the life force and making it work for us here on earth. Which, as I have told you, is my intention.'

He turned away from the sea and began walking back the way we had come. The lights were all extinguished in the low line of pre-fabs where presumably we were to eat, work, sleep and have our being during the eight weeks that lay ahead. Behind them loomed the square tower of the disused radar station, a monument to the ingenuity of man.

'They told me at A.E.L. you had no religious scruples,' went on MacLean. 'Neither have the rest of us at Saxmere, though we like to think of ourselves as dedicated men. As young Ken puts it himself, it comes to the same thing as giving your eyes to a hospital, or your kidneys to cold storage. The problem is ours, not his.'

I had a sudden recollection of the youngster at the bar, pouring out the orange juice and calling himself a guinea-pig.

'What's Ken's part in all this, then?' I asked.

MacLean paused in his walk and looked straight at me.

'The boy has leukaemia,' he said. 'Robbie gives him three months at the outside. There'll be no pain. He has tremendous guts, and believes wholeheartedly in the experiment. It's very possible the attempt may fail. If it fails, we lose nothing – his life is forfeit anyway. If we succeed . . .' He broke off, catching his breath as though swept by a sudden deep emotion. 'If we succeed, you see what it will mean?' he said. 'We shall have the answer at last to the intolerable futility of death.'

When I awoke next morning to a brilliant day and looked from my bedroom window along the asphalt road to the disused radar tower, brooding like a sentinel over empty sheds and rusted metal towards the marsh beyond, I made my decision then and there to go.

I shaved, bathed, and went along to breakfast determined to be courteous to all, and to ask for five minutes alone with MacLean immediately afterwards. I would catch the first available train, and with luck be in London by one o'clock. If there was any unpleasantness with A.E.L. my chief would take the rap for it, not I.

The dining-room was empty except for Robbie, who was attacking an enormous plateful of soused herrings. I bade him a brief good day and helped myself to bacon. I looked round for a morning paper but there was none. Conversation would be forced upon me.

'Fine morning,' I observed.

He did not answer me immediately. He was engaged in dissecting his herring with the finesse of an expert. Then his falsetto voice came at me across the table.

'Are you proposing to back out?' he asked.

His question took me by surprise, and I disliked the note of derision.

'I'm an electronics engineer,' I answered, 'I'm not interested in psychical research.'

'No more were Lister's colleagues concerned with discovering antisepsis,' he rejoined. 'What fools they were made to look later.'

He forked a half-herring into his mouth and proceeded to chew it, watching me from behind his bi-focal specs.

'So you believe all this stuff about Force Six?' I said.

'Don't you?' he parried.

I pushed aside my plate in protest.

'Look here,' I said. 'I can accept this work MacLean has done on sound. He has found the answer to voice production which we failed to do at A.E.L. He has developed a system by which high-frequency waves can be picked up by animals, and also, it seems, by one idiot child. I give him full marks for the first, am doubtful about the potential value of the second, and as to his third project – capturing the life-force, or whatever he calls it, as it leaves the body – if anyone talked to the Ministry about that one, your boss would find himself inside.'

I resumed my bacon feeling I had put Robbie in his place. He finished his herrings, then started on the toast and marmalade.

'Ever watched anyone die?' he asked suddenly.

'As a matter of fact, no,' I answered.

'I'm a doctor, and it's part of my job,' he said, 'in hospitals, in homes, in refugee camps after the war. I suppose I've witnessed scores of deaths during my professional life. It's not a pleasant experience. Here at Saxmere it's become my business to stand by a very plucky, likeable lad, not only during his last hours, but during the few weeks that remain to him. I could do with some help.'

I got up and took my plate to the sideboard. Then I returned and helped myself to coffee.

'I'm sorry,' I said.

He pushed the toast-rack towards me but I shook my head. Breakfast is not my favourite meal, and this morning

I lacked appetite. There was a sound of footsteps outside on the asphalt, and a head looked in at the window. It was Ken.

'Hullo,' he said, with a grin, 'what a wonderful morning. If Mac doesn't need you in the control room I'll show you round. We could take a walk up to the coastguard cottages and over Saxmere cliff. Are you game?' He took my hesitation for assent. 'Splendid! It's no use asking Robbie. He'll spend the morning in the lab gloating over specimens of my blood.'

The head vanished, and I heard him call to Janus through the kitchen window alongside. Neither Robbie nor I spoke. The sound of munching toast became unbearable. I stood up.

'Where will I find MacLean?' I asked.

'In the control room,' he answered, and went on eating.

It was best done at once. I went the way I had been shown the night before, through the swing door to the lab. Somehow the operating table under the centre light held more significance this morning, and I avoided looking at it. I went through the door at the far end, and saw MacLean standing by Charon 1. He beckoned me over.

'There's a slight fault in the processing unit,' he said. 'I noticed it last night. I'm sure you'll be able to fix it.'

This was the moment to express my regrets and tell him I had decided against joining his team and intended to return to London immediately. I did no such thing. Instead I crossed the floor to the computer and stood by while he explained the circuits. Professional pride, professional jealousy, if you will, coupled with intense curiosity to know why this particular apparatus was superior to the one we had built at A.E.L., proved too much for me.

'There are some overalls on the wall,' said MacLean. 'Put 'em on, and we'll fix the fault between us.'

From then onward I was lost, or perhaps it would be

more correct to say that I was won. Not to his lunatic theories, not to any future experiment with life and death; I was conquered by the supreme beauty and efficiency of Charon 1 itself. Beauty, may be an odd word to use where electronics are concerned. I did not find it so. Herein lay all my passion, all my feelings; from my boyhood I had been involved with the creation of these things. This was my life's work. I was not interested in the uses to which the machines I had helped to develop and perfect were ultimately put. My part was to see that they fulfilled the function for which they were designed. Until arriving at Saxmere I had had no other object, no other aim in life, but to do what I was fitted to do, and do it well.

Charon 1 awakened something else in me, an awareness of power. I had only to handle those controls to know that what I wanted now was to have detailed knowledge of all the working parts, and then be given charge of the whole lay-out. Nothing else mattered. By the end of that first morning I had not only located the fault, a minor one, but had set it right. MacLean had become Mac, the shortening of my name to Steve was something that no longer jarred, and the whole fantastic set-up had ceased to irritate or to dismay; I had become one of the team.

Robbie showed no surprise when I turned up at lunch-time, nor did he allude to our conversation at breakfast. In the late afternoon, with Mac's permission, I took my suggested walk with Ken. It was impossible to connect approaching death with this irrepressible youngster, and I put it from my mind. It could be that both Mac and Robbie were wrong about it. Anyway, it was not, thank God, my problem.

He showed no sign of fatigue and led the way, laughing and chatting, across the sand-dunes to the sea. The sun was shining, the air felt cold and clean, even the long stretch of shore that had seemed dreary the night before had now a latent charm. The heavy shingle gave place to sand, crisp under our feet; Cerberus, who accompanied us, bounded ahead. We threw sticks for him to retrieve from the pallid, almost effortless, sea, which gently, without menace, broke beside us as we walked. We did not discuss Saxmere, or anything connected with it; instead Ken regaled me with amusing gossip about the U.S. base at Thirlwall, where he had apparently worked as one of the ground staff before Mac arranged his transfer ten months before.

Suddenly Cerberus, barking puppy-fashion for another stick, turned and stood motionless, ears pricked, head to wind. Then he started loping back the way we had come, his lithe black-and-tan form soon lost to sight against the darker shingle and the dunes beyond.

'He's had a signal from Charon,' said Ken.

The night before, watching Mac at the controls, the dog's scratching at the door seemed natural. Here, some three miles distant on the lonely shore, his swift departure was uncanny.

'Effective, isn't it?' said Ken.

I nodded; but somehow, because of what I'd seen, my spirits left me. Enthusiasm for the walk had waned. It would have been different had I been alone. Now, with the boy beside me, I was, as it were, confronted with the future, the project Mac had in mind, the months ahead.

'Want to turn back?' he asked me.

His words reminded me of Robbie's at breakfast, though he meant them otherwise. 'Just as you like,' I said indifferently.

He swung left and we clambered, slipping and sliding with every step, up the steep slope to the cliffs above the beach. I was breathless when I reached the top. Not Ken. Smiling, he lent a hand to pull me up. Heather and scrub lay all about us, and the wind was in our faces, stronger than it had been below. About a quarter of a mile distant, stark and white against the skyline, stood a row of coastguard cottages, bleak windows all aflame with the setting sun.

'Come and pay your respects to Mrs J.,' suggested Ken.

Reluctantly I followed, detesting unpremeditated visits, no matter where. The unprepossessing Janus household did not attract me. As he drew near I saw that only the far cottage was inhabited. The others had the forlorn, lost look of buildings untenanted for years. Two had their windows broken. Gardens, untended, sprawled. Posts, sagging drunkenly from the damp earth, trailed pieces of barbed wire from their rotting stumps. A small girl was leaning over the gate of the occupied cottage. Dark, straight hair framed her pinched face, her eyes were lustreless, and she was wanting a front tooth.

'Hullo, Niki,' called Ken.

The child stared, then slowly removed herself from the gate. Morosely, she pointed at me. 'Who's that?' she asked.

'His name is Steve,' Ken answered her.

'I don't like his shoes,' said the child.

Ken laughed and opened the gate, and as he did so the child attempted to climb upon him. Gently he put her aside, and walking up the path to the open door called, 'Are you there, Mrs J.?'

A woman appeared, pallid and dark like her child. Her anxious face broke into a smile at the sight of Ken. She bade us enter, apologising for the disarray. I was introduced as Steve, and we hovered uncomfortably in the front room, where the child's toys were strewn about the floor.

'We've had tea,' Ken said, in reply to Mrs J.'s question, but, insisting that the kettle had just boiled, the woman vanished to the adjoining kitchen, to reappear at once with a large brown tea-pot and two cups and saucers. There was nothing for it but to swallow the stuff under her watchful eyes, while the child, edging against Ken all the while, stared balefully at my inoffensive canvas shoes.

I gave full marks to my young companion. He exchanged pleasantries with Mrs Janus, and patted the unendearing Niki. I remained silent throughout, and wondered why the child's likeness, framed in place of honour over the fireplace, should be so much more pleasing than the child herself.

'It's very cold here in the winter, but a bracing cold,' said Mrs Janus, fixing me with her own mournful eyes. 'I always say I prefer the frost to the damp.'

I agreed and shook my head at the offer of more tea. At this moment the child stiffened. She stood rigid a moment, her eyes closed. I wondered if she were going to throw a fit. Then very calmly she announced, 'Mac wants me.'

Mrs Janus, with a murmur of apology, went into the hall and I heard her dial. Ken was watching the child, himself unmoved. I felt slightly sick. In a moment I heard Mrs Janus speaking over the telephone and she called, 'Niki, come here and speak to Mac.'

The child ran from the room, and for the first time since our arrival showed animation. She even laughed. Mrs Janus returned and smiled at Ken.

'I think Mac really wants a word with you,' she said.

Ken got up and went into the hall. Alone with the child's mother, I did not know what to say. At last, in desperation, nodding at the photograph above the fireplace, I said, 'What a good likeness of Niki. Taken a few years ago, I suppose?'

To my dismay, the woman's eyes filled with tears.

'That's not Niki, that's her twin,' she answered. 'That's our Penny. We lost her soon after they had both turned five.'

My awkward apology was cut short by the entrance of the child herself. Ignoring my shoes she came straight to me, put her hand on my knee and announced, 'Mac says Cerberus is back. And you and Ken can go home.'

'Thank you,' I said.

As we walked away from the cottages, over scrub and heather, and took a short cut back to Saxmere through the marsh, I asked Ken whether the call-signal from Charon invariably had the effect I had seen, that of awakening latent intelligence in the child.

'Yes,' he said. 'We don't know why. Robbie thinks the ultra-short-wave may have therapeutic value in itself. Mac doesn't agree. He believes that when he puts out the call it connects Niki with what he calls Force Six, which in her case is doubled because of the dead twin.'

Ken spoke as if this fantastic theory was perfectly natural.

'Do you mean,' I asked, 'that when the call goes through the dead twin somehow takes over?'

Ken laughed. He walked so fast it was hard to keep up with him.

'Ghoulies and ghosties?' he queried. 'Good Lord, no! There's nothing left of poor Penny but electric energy, still attached to her living twin. That's why Niki makes such a useful guinea-pig.'

He glanced across at me, smiling.

'When I go,' he said, 'Mac plans to tap my energy too. Don't ask me how. I just don't know. But he's welcome to have a crack at it.'

We went on walking. The sour smell of stagnant water rose from the marsh on either side of us. The wind strengthened, flattening the reeds. The tower of Saxmere loomed ahead, hard and black against a russet sky.

I had the voice production unit functioning to my satisfaction within the next few days. We fed it with tape, programmed in advance as we had done at A.E.L., but the vocabulary was more extensive, consisting of a call signal 'This is Charon speaking . . . this is Charon speaking . . .'

followed by a series of numbers, spoken with great clarity. Then came questions, most of them quite simple, such as, 'Are you O.K.?' 'Does anything bother you?', proceeding to statements of fact like, 'You are not with us. You are at Thirlwall. It is two years back. Tell us what you see,' and so on. My job was to control the precision of the voice, the programme was Mac's responsibility, and, if the questions and statements appeared inane to me, doubtless they made sound sense to him.

On Friday he told me that he considered Charon was ready for use the next day, and Robbie and Ken were warned for eleven a.m. Mac himself would be at the controls, and I was to watch. In the light of what I had already witnessed, I should have been fully prepared for what happened. Oddly enough, I was not. I took up my station in the adjoining lab, while Ken stretched himself out on the operating-table.

'It's all right,' he said to me with a wink. 'Robbie isn't going to carve me up.'

There was a microphone in position above his head, with a lead going through to Charon 1. A yellow light for 'Stand-by' flashed on the wall. It changed to red. I saw Ken close his eyes. Then a voice came from Charon. 'This is Charon speaking . . . This is Charon speaking.' The series of numbers followed, and, after a pause, the question, 'Are you O.K.?'

When Ken replied, 'Yes, I'm O.K.' I noticed that his voice lacked its usual buoyancy; it was flatter, pitched in a lower key. I glanced at Robbie; he handed me a slip of paper on which were written the words, 'He's under hypnosis'.

The penny dropped, and I realised for the first time the full importance of the sound unit and the reason for perfecting it. Ken had been conditioned to hypnosis by the electronic voice. The questions on the programme were not haphazard, they were taped for him. The implications of this were even more shocking to me than when I had seen the dog and the child obey the call signal from a distance. When Ken, jokingly, had spoken of 'going to work', this was what he had meant.

'Does anything bother you?' asked the voice.

There was a long pause before the answer, and when it came the tone was impatient, almost fretful.

'It's the hanging about. I want it to happen quickly. If it could be over and done with, then I wouldn't give a damn.'

I might have been standing by a confessional, and I understood now why my predecessor had turned in his job. I saw Robbie's eyes upon me; the demonstration had been staged not only to show Ken's co-operation under hypnosis, proved no doubt dozens of times already, but to test my nerve. The ordeal continued. Much of what Ken said made painful hearing. I don't want to repeat it here. It revealed the unconscious strain under which he lived, never outwardly apparent either to us or to himself.

The programme Mac used was not one I had heard before, and it ended with the words, 'You'll be all right, Ken. You aren't alone. We're with you every step of the way. O.K.?'

A faint smile passed over the quiet face.

'O.K.'

Then the numbers were repeated, in swifter sequence, ending with the words 'Wake up, Ken!'

The boy stretched himself, opened his eyes and sat up. He looked first at Robbie, then at me, and grinned.

'Did old Charon do his stuff?' he asked.

'One hundred per cent,' I answered, my voice falsely hearty.

Ken slid off the operating table, his work for the morning done. I went through to Mac, standing by the controls.

'Thanks, Steve,' he said. 'You can appreciate the necessity for Charon 1 now. An electronic voice, plus a planned programme, eliminates emotion on our part, which will be essential when the time comes. That's the reason Ken has been conditioned to the machine. He responds very well. But better, of course, if the child is with him.'

'The child?' I repeated.

'Yes,' he answered. 'Niki is an essential part of the experiment. She is conditioned to the voice too, and the pair of them chat away together as gay as crickets. They know nothing about it afterwards, naturally.' He paused, watching me closely as Robbie had done. 'Ken will almost certainly go into coma at the end. The child will be our only link with him then. Now, I suggest you borrow a car, drive into Thirlwall and buy yourself a drink.'

He turned away, craggy, imperturbable, suggesting a benevolent bird of prey.

I didn't go into Thirlwall. I walked out across the sand-dunes to the sea. There was nothing calm about it today. Turbulent and grey, it sank into troughs before breaking on the shingle with a roar. Miles away along the beach a group of U.S. Air Corps cadets were practising bugle calls. The shrill notes, the discordant sounds, drove towards me down the wind. For no reason at all the half-forgotten lines of a Negro spiritual kept repeating themselves over and over in my mind.

'He has the whole world in his hands,
He has the whole world in his hands . . .'

The demonstration was repeated, with varying programmes, every three days during the weeks that followed. Mac and I took it in turn at the controls. I soon grew accustomed to this, and the bizarre sessions became a matter of routine.

It was, as Mac had said, less painful when the child was present. Her father would bring her to the lab and leave her with us, Ken already in position and under control. The child would sit in a chair beside him, also with a microphone above her head to record her speech. She was told that Ken was asleep. Then, in her turn, she would receive the signal from Charon, and a different series of numbers from Ken's, after which she would be under control. The programme was different when the two were working together. Charon would take Ken back in time, to a period when he was the same age as Niki, saying, 'You are seven years old. Niki has come to play with you. She is your friend,' and a similar message would be given to the child, 'Ken has come to play with you. He is a boy of your age.'

The two would then chat together, without interruption from Charon, with the quite fantastic result – this had been built up during the past months, I gathered – that the pair were now close friends 'in time', hiding nothing from each other, playing imaginary games, exchanging ideas. Niki, backward and morose when conscious, was lively and gay under control. The taped conversations were checked after each session, to record the increasingly closer rapport between the two, and to act as guide for further programmes. Ken, when conscious, looked upon Niki as Janus's backward child, a sad little object of no interest. He was totally ignorant of what happened when under control. I was not so sure about Niki. Intuition seemed to draw her to him. She would hang about him, if given the chance.

I asked Robbie what the Janus parents felt about the sessions.

'They'd do anything for Mac,' he told me, 'and they believe it may help Niki. The other twin was normal, you see.'

'Do they realise about Ken?'

'That he's going to die?' replied Robbie. 'They've been

told, but I doubt if they understand. Who would, looking at him now?'

We were at the bar, and from where we stood we could see Ken and Mac engaged in a game of ping-pong in the room beyond.

Early in December we had a scare. A letter came from the Ministry asking how the Saxmere experiments were going, and could they send someone down to have a look round? We had a consultation, the upshot of which was that I undertook to go up to London to choke them off. By this time I was wholeheartedly behind Mac in all he was doing, and during my brief stay in town I succeeded in satisfying the authorities in question that a visit at this moment would be premature, but we hoped to have something to show them before Christmas. Their interest, of course, lay in Charon 2's potentialities for blast; they knew nothing of Mac's intended project.

When I returned, alighting at Saxmere station in a very different mood from that of three months past, the Morris was waiting for me, but without Ken's cheerful face at the wheel. Janus had replaced him. He was never a talkative bloke, and he answered my question with a shrug.

'Ken's got a cold,' he said. 'Robbie's keeping him in bed as a precaution.'

I went straight to the boy's room on arrival. He looked a bit flushed, but was in his usual spirits, full of protests against Robbie.

'There's absolutely nothing the matter,' he said. 'I got wet feet stalking a bird down in the marsh.'

I sat with him awhile, joking about London and the Ministry, then went to report to Mac.

'Ken has some fever,' he said at once. 'Robbie's done a blood test. It's not too good.' He paused. 'This could be it.'

I felt suddenly chilled. After a moment I told him about London. He nodded briefly.

'Whatever happens,' he said, 'we can't have them here now.'

I found Robbie in the lab, busy with slides and a microscope. He was preoccupied, and hadn't much time for me.

'It's too soon to say yet,' he said. 'Another forty-eight hours should show one way or the other. There's an infection in the right lung. With leukaemia that could be fatal. Go and keep Ken amused.'

I took a portable gramophone along to the boy's bedroom. I suppose I put on about a dozen records, and he seemed quite cheerful. Later he dozed off and I sat there, wondering what to do. My mouth felt dry, and I kept swallowing. Something inside me kept saying, 'Don't let it happen.'

Conversation at dinner was forced. Mac talked about undergraduate days at Cambridge, while Robbie reminisced over past Rugby games – he'd played scrum-half for Guy's. I don't think I talked at all. I went along afterwards to say goodnight to Ken, but he was already asleep. Janus was sitting with him. Back in my room I flung myself on my bed and tried to read, but I couldn't concentrate. There was fog at sea, and every few minutes the fog-horn boomed from the lighthouse along the coast. There was no other sound.

Next morning Mac came to my room at a quarter to eight.

'Ken's worse,' he said. 'Robbie's going to try a blood transfusion. Janus will assist.' Janus was a trained orderly.

'What do you want me to do?' I asked.

'Help me get Charons 1 and 3 ready for action,' he said. 'If Ken doesn't respond, I may decide to put phase one of Operation Styx into effect. Mrs J. has been warned we may need the child.'

As I finished dressing I kept telling myself that this was the moment we had been training for all through the past two and a half months. It didn't help. I swallowed some coffee and went to the control room. The door to the lab was closed. They had Ken in there, giving him the blood transfusion. Mac and I worked over both Charons, seeing that everything functioned perfectly, and that there could be no hitch when the time came. Programmes, tapes, microphones, all were ready. After that it was a matter of standing by until Robbie came through with his report. We got it at about half-past twelve.

'Slight improvement.' They had taken him back to his room. We all had something to eat while Janus continued his watch over Ken. Today there was no question of forced conversation. The work on hand was the concern of all. I felt calmer, steadier. The morning's work had knocked me into shape. Mac proposed a game of ping-pong after lunch, and whereas the night before I would have felt aghast at the suggestion, today it seemed the right thing to do. Looking from the window, between games, I saw Niki wandering up and down with Mrs Janus, a strange, lost-looking little figure, filling a battered doll's pram with sticks and stones. She had been on the premises since ten o'clock.

At half-past four Robbie came into the sports room. I could tell by his face that it was no good. He shook his head when Mac suggested another transfusion. It would be a waste of time, he told us.

'He's conscious?' asked Mac.

'Yes,' answered Robbie. 'I'll bring him through when you're ready.'

Mac and I went back to the control room. Phase two of Operation Styx consisted of bringing the operating table in here, placing it between the three Charons, and connecting up with an oxygen unit alongside. The microphones were already in position. We had done the manoeuvre often before, in practice runs, but today we beat our fastest time by two minutes.

'Good work,' said Mac.

The thought struck me that he had been looking forward to this moment for months, perhaps for years. He pressed the button to signal that we were ready, and in less than four minutes Robbie and Janus arrived with Ken on the trolley, and lifted him on to the table. I hardly recognised him. The eyes, usually so luminous, had almost disappeared into the sunken face. He looked bewildered. Mac quickly attached electrodes, one against each temple and others to his chest and neck, connecting him to Charon 3. Then he bent over the boy.

'It's all right,' he said. 'We've got you in the lab to do a few tests. Just relax, and you'll be fine.'

Ken stared up at Mac, and then he smiled. We all knew that this was the last we should see of his conscious self. It was, in fact, goodbye. Mac looked at me, and I put Charon 1 into operation, the voice ringing clear and true. 'This is Charon calling . . . This is Charon calling . . .' Ken closed his eyes. He was under hypnosis. Robbie stood beside him, finger on pulse. I set the programme in motion. We had numbered it X in the files, because it was different from the others.

'How do you feel, Ken?'

Even with the microphone close to his lips we could barely hear the answer. 'You know damn well how I feel.'

'Where are you, Ken?'

'I'm in the control room. Robbie's turned the heating off. I've got the idea now. It's to freeze me, like butcher's meat. Ask Robbie to bring back the heat . . .' There was a long pause, and then he said, 'I'm standing by a tunnel. It looks like a tunnel. It could be the wrong end of a telescope, the figures look so small . . . Tell Robbie to bring back the heat.'

Mac, who was beside me at the controls, made an adjustment, and we let the programme run without sound until it reached a certain point, when it was amplified once more to reach Ken.

'You are five years old, Ken. Tell us how you feel.'

There was a long pause and then, to my dismay, though I suppose I should have been prepared for it, Ken whimpered, 'I don't feel well. I don't want to play.'

Mac pressed a button, and the door at the far end opened. Janus pushed his daughter into the room, then closed the door again. Mac had her under control with her call-sign at once, and she did not see Ken on the table. She went and sat down in her chair and closed her eyes.

'Tell Ken you are here, Niki.'

I saw the child clutch the arms of her chair.

'Ken's sick,' she said. 'He's crying. He doesn't want to play.'

The voice of Charon went ruthlessly on.

'Make Ken talk, Niki.'

'Ken won't talk,' said the child. 'He's going to say his prayers.'

Ken's voice came faintly through the microphone to the loudspeakers. The words were gabbled, indistinct.

> 'Gen'ral Jesus, mekan mild,
> Look'pon little child,
> Pity my simple city,
> Sofa me to come to thee . . .'

There was a long pause after this. Neither Ken nor Niki said anything. I kept my hands on the controls, ready to continue the programme when Mac nodded. Niki began drumming her feet on the floor. All at once she said, 'I shan't go down the tunnel after Ken. It's too dark.'

Robbie, watching his patient, looked up. 'He's gone into coma,' he said.

Mac signalled to me to set Charon 1 in motion again.

'Go after Ken, Niki,' said the voice.

The child protested. 'It's black in there,' she said. She was nearly crying. She hunched herself in her chair and went through crawling motions. 'I don't want to go.' she said. 'It's too long, and Ken won't wait for me.'

She started to tremble all over. I looked across at Mac. He questioned Robbie with a glance.

'He won't come out of it,' Robbie said. 'It may last hours.'

Mac ordered the oxygen apparatus to be put into operation, and Robbie fixed the mask on Ken. Mac went over to Charon 3 and switched on the monitor display screen. He made some adjustments and nodded at me. 'I'll take over,' he said.

The child was still crying, but the next command from Charon 1 gave her no respite. 'Stay with Ken,' it said. 'Tell us what happens.'

I hoped Mac knew what he was doing. Suppose the child went into a coma too? Could he bring her back? Hunched in her chair, she was as still as Ken, and about as lifeless. Robbie told me to put blankets round her and feel her pulse. It was faint, but steady. Nothing happened for over an hour. We watched the flickering and erratic signals on the screen, as the electrodes transmitted Ken's weakening brain impulses. Still the child did not speak.

Later, much later, she stirred, then moved with a strange twisting motion. She crossed her arms over her breast, humping her knees. Her head dropped forward. I wondered if, like Ken, she was engaged in some childish prayer. Then I realised that her position was that of a foetus before birth. Personality had vanished from her face. She looked wizened, old.

Robbie said, 'He's going.'

Mac beckoned me to the controls, and Robbie bent over Ken with fingers on his pulse. The signals on the screen were fainter, and faltering, but suddenly they surged in a strong upward beat, and in the same instant Robbie said, 'It's all over. He's dead.'

The signal was rising and falling steadily now. Mac disconnected the electrodes and turned back to watch the screen. There was no break in the rhythm of the signal, as it moved up and down, up and down, like a heartbeat, like a pulse.

'We've done it!' said Mac. 'Oh, my God . . . we've done it!'

We stood there, the three of us, watching the signal that never for one instant changed its pattern. It seemed to contain, in its confident movement, the whole of life.

I don't know how long we stayed there – it could have been minutes, hours. At last Robbie said, 'What about the child?'

We had forgotten Niki, just as we had forgotten the quiet, peaceful body that had been Ken. She was still lying in her strange, cramped position, her head bowed to her knees. I went to the controls of Charon 1 to operate the voice, but Mac waved me aside.

'Before we wake her, we'll see what she has to say,' he said.

He put through the call signal very faintly, so as not to shock her to consciousness too soon. I followed with the voice, which repeated the final programme command.

'Stay with Ken. Tell us what happens.'

At first there was no response. Then slowly she uncoiled, her gestures odd, uncouth. Her arms fell to her side. She began to rock backwards and forwards as though following the motion on the screen. When she spoke her voice was sharp, pitched high.

'He wants you to let him go,' she said, 'that's what he wants. Let go . . . let go . . . let go . . .' Still rocking she began to gasp for breath, and, lifting her arms, pummelled the air with her fists.

'Let go . . . let go . . . let go . . . let go . . .'

Robbie said urgently, 'Mac, you've got to wake her.'

On the screen the rhythm of the signal had quickened. The child began to choke. Without waiting for Mac, I set the voice in motion.

'This is Charon speaking . . . This is Charon speaking . . . Wake up, Niki.'

The child shuddered, and the suffused colour drained from her face. Her breathing became normal. She opened her eyes. She stared at each of us in turn in her usual apathetic way, and proceeded to pick her nose.

'I want to go to the toilet,' she said sullenly.

Robbie led her from the room. The signal, which had increased its speed during the child's outburst, resumed its steady rise and fall.

'Why did it alter speed?' I asked.

'If you hadn't panicked and woken her up, we might have found out,' Mac said.

His voice was harsh, quite unlike himself.

'Mac,' I protested, 'that kid was choking to death.'

'No,' he said, 'no, I don't think so.'

He turned and faced me. 'Her movements simulated the shock of birth,' he said. 'Her gasp for air was the first breath of an infant, struggling for life. Ken, in coma, had gone back to that moment, and Niki was with him.'

I knew by this time that almost anything was possible under hypnosis, but I wasn't convinced.

'Mac,' I said, 'Niki's struggle came *after* Ken was dead, *after* the new signal appeared on Charon 3. Ken couldn't have gone back to the moment of birth – he was already dead, don't you see?'

He did not answer at once. 'I just don't know,' he said at last. 'I think we shall have to put her under control again.'

'No,' said Robbie. He had entered the lab while we were talking. 'That child has had enough. I've sent her home, and told her mother to put her to bed.'

I had never heard him speak with authority before. He looked away from the lighted screen back to the still body on the table. 'Doesn't that go for the rest of us?' he said. 'Haven't we all had enough? You've proved your point, Mac. I'll celebrate with you tomorrow, but not tonight.'

He was ready to break. So, I think, were we all. We had barely eaten through the day, and when Janus returned he set about getting us a meal. He had taken the news of Ken's death with his usual calm. The child, he told us, had fallen asleep the moment she was put to bed.

So . . . it was all over. Reaction, exhaustion, numbness of feeling, all three set in, and I yearned, like Niki, for the total release of sleep.

Before dragging myself to bed some impulse, stronger than the aching fatigue that overwhelmed me, urged me back to the control room. Everything was as we had left it. Ken's body lay on the table, covered with a blanket. The screen was lighted still, and the signal was pulsing steadily up and down. I waited a moment, then I bent to the tape-control, setting it to play back that last outburst from the child. I remembered the rocking head, the hands fighting to be free, and switched it on.

'He wants you to let him go,' said the high-pitched voice, 'that's what he wants. Let go . . . let go . . . let go . . .' Then came the gasp for breath, and the words were repeated. 'Let go . . . let go . . . let go . . . let go . . .'

I switched it off. The words did not make sense. The signal was simply electrical energy, trapped at the actual moment of Ken's death. How could the child have translated this into a cry for freedom, unless . . . ?

I looked up. Mac was watching me from the doorway. The dog was with him.

'Cerberus is restless,' he said. 'He keeps padding backwards and forwards in my room. He won't let me sleep.'

'Mac,' I said, 'I've played that recording again. There's something wrong.'

He came and stood beside me. 'What do you mean, something wrong? The recording doesn't affect the issue. Look at the screen. The signal's steady. The experiment has been a hundred per cent successful. We've done what we set out to do. The energy is there.'

'I know it's there,' I replied, 'but is that all?'

I set the recording in motion once again. Together we listened to the child's gasp, and the words 'Let go . . . let go . . .'

'Mac,' I said, 'when the child said that, Ken was already dead. Therefore, there could be no further communication between them.'

'Well?'

'How then, after death, can she still identify herself with his personality – a personality that says 'Let go . . . let go . . .' unless . . .

'Unless what?'

'Unless something has happened that we know to be impossible, and what we can see, imprisoned on the screen, is the essence of Ken himself?'

He stared at me, unbelieving, and together we looked once more at the signal, which suddenly took on new meaning, new significance, and as it did so became the expression of our dawning sense of anguish and fear.

'Mac,' I said, 'what have we done?'

Mrs Janus telephoned in the morning to say that Niki had woken up and was acting strangely. She kept throwing herself backwards and forwards. Mrs Janus had tried to quieten her, but nothing she said did any good. No, she had no temperature, she was not feverish. It was this queer rocking movement all the time. She would not eat any breakfast, she would not speak. Could Mac put through the call signal? It might quieten her.

Janus had answered the phone, and we were in the dining-room when he brought us his wife's message. Robbie got up and went to the telephone. He came back again almost immediately.

'I'll go over,' he said. 'What happened yesterday – I should never have allowed it.'

'You knew, the risk,' answered Mac. 'We've all known the risk from the very start. You always assured me it would do no harm.'

'I was wrong,' said Robbie. 'Oh, not about the experiment . . . God knows you've done what you wanted to do, and it didn't affect poor Ken one way or the other. He's out of it all now. But I was wrong to let that child become involved.'

'We shouldn't have succeeded without her,' replied Mac.

Robbie went out and we heard him start up the car. Mac and I walked along to the control room. Janus and Robbie had been there before us, and had taken Ken's body away. The room was stripped once more to the essentials of normal routine, with one exception. Charon 3, the storage unit, still functioned as it had done the previous day and through the night, the signal keeping up its steady rise and fall. I found myself glancing at it almost furtively, in the irrational hope that it would cease.

Presently the telephone buzzed, and I answered it. It was Robbie.

'I think we ought to get the child away,' he said at once. 'It looks like catatonic schizophrenia, and whether she becomes violent or not Mrs J. can't cope with it. If Mac will say the word, I could take her up myself to the psychiatric ward at Guy's.'

I beckoned to Mac, explaining the situation. He took the receiver from me.

'Look, Robbie,' he said, 'I'm prepared to take the risk of putting Niki under control. It may work, or it may not.'

The argument continued. I could tell from Mac's gesture of frustration that Robbie would not play. He was surely right. Some irreparable damage might have been done to the child's mind already. Yet, if Robbie did take her up to the hospital, what possible explanation could he give?

Mac waved me over to replace him at the telephone.

'Tell Robbie to stand by,' he said.

I was his subordinate, and could not stop him. He went to the transmitter on Charon 2 and set the control. The call signal was in operation. I lifted the receiver and gave Robbie Mac's message. Then I waited.

I heard Robbie shout to Mrs Janus, 'What's the matter?' – then the sound of the receiver being dropped.

Nothing for a moment or two but distant voices, Mrs Janus, I think, pleading, and then an appeal to Robbie, 'Please, let her try . . .'

Mac went over to Charon 1 and made some adjustments. Then he waved to me to bring the telephone as near to him as it would go, and reached out for the receiver.

'Niki,' he said, 'do you hear me? It's Mac.'

I stood beside him, to catch the whisper from the receiver.

'Yes, Mac.'

She sounded bewildered, even frightened.

'Tell me what's wrong, Niki.'

She began to whimper. 'I don't know. There's a clock ticking somewhere. I don't like it.'

'Where's the clock, Niki?'

She did not answer. Mac repeated his question. I could hear Robbie protest. He must have been standing beside her.

'It's all round,' she said at last. 'It's ticking in my head. Penny doesn't like it either.'

Penny. Who was Penny? Then I remembered. The dead twin.

'Why doesn't Penny like it?'

This was intolerable. Robbie was right. Mac should not

put the child through this ordeal. I shook my head at him. He took no notice, but once again repeated his question. I could hear the child burst into tears.

'Penny . . . Ken . . .' she sobbed, 'Penny . . . Ken.'

Instantly Mac switched to the recorded voice of Charon 1 giving the order on yesterday's programme: 'Stay with Ken. Tell us what happens.'

The child gave a piercing cry, and she must have fallen, because I heard Robbie and Mrs Janus exclaim and the telephone crash.

Mac and I looked at the screen. The rhythm was getting faster, the signal moving in quick jerks. Robbie, at his end, picked up the receiver.

'You'll kill her, Mac,' he called. 'For Christ's sake . . .'

'What's she doing?' asked Mac.

'The same as yesterday,' called Robbie. 'Backwards, forwards, rocking all the time. She's suffocating. Wait . . .'

Once again he must have let the receiver go. Mac switched back to the call signal. The pulsing on the screen was steadying. Then, after a long interval, Robbie's voice came through again.

'She wants to speak,' he said.

There was a pause. The child's voice, expressionless and dull, said, 'Let them go.'

'Are you all right now, Niki?' asked Mac.

'Let them go.' she repeated.

Mac deliberately hung up. Together we watched the signal resume its normal speed.

'Well?' I said. 'What does it prove?'

He looked suddenly old, and immeasurably tired, but there was an expression in his eyes that I had never seen before; a curious, baffled incredulity. It was as though everything he possessed, senses, body, brain, protested and denied the thoughts within.

'It could mean you were right,' he said. 'It could mean

survival of intelligence after the body's death. It could mean we've broken through.'

The thought, staggering in its implications, turned us both dumb. Mac recovered first. He went and stood beside Charon 3, his gaze fixed upon the picture.

'You saw it change when the child was speaking,' he said. 'But Niki by herself could not have caused the variation. The power came from Ken's Force Six, and from the dead twin's too. The power is capable of transmission through Niki, but through no one else. Don't you see . . .' He broke off, and swung round to face me, a new excitement dawning. 'Niki is the only link. We must get her here, programme Charon, and put further questions to her. If we really have got intelligence plus power under control . . .'

'Mac,' I interrupted, 'do you want to kill that child, or, worse, condemn her to a mental institution?'

In desperation he looked once more towards the screen. 'I've got to know, Steve,' he said. 'I've got to find out. If intelligence survives, if Force Six can triumph over matter, then it's not just one man who has beaten death but all mankind from the beginning of time. Immortality in some form or other becomes a certainty, the whole meaning of life on earth is changed.'

Yes, I thought, changed forever. The fusion of science and religion in a partnership at first joyous, then the inevitable disenchantment, the scientist realising, and the priest with him, that, with eternity assured, the human being on earth is more easily expendable. Dispatch the maimed, the old, the weak, destroy the very world itself, for what is the point of life if the promise of fulfilment lies elsewhere?

'Mac,' I said. 'you heard what the child said. The words were, "Let them go".'

The telephone rang again. This time it was not Robbie but Janus, from our own extension in the hall. He apologised for disturbing us, but two gentlemen had arrived from the Ministry. He had told them we were in conference, but they said the business was urgent. They had asked to see Mr MacLean at once.

I went into the bar, and the official I had seen in London was standing there with a companion. This first chap expressed apologies, and said the fact was that my predecessor at Saxmere had been to see them, and admitted that his reason for leaving was because he was doubtful of the work MacLean had in progress. There was some experiment going on of which he did not think the Ministry was aware. They wished to speak to MacLean at once.

'He will be with you shortly,' I said. 'In the meantime, if there is anything you want to know, I can brief you.'

They exchanged glances, and then the second chap spoke.

'You're working on vibrations, aren't you,' he asked, 'and their relation to blast? That was what you said in London.'

'We are,' I replied, 'and we have had some success. But, as I warned you, there is still a lot to do.'

'We're here,' he said, 'to be shown what you've achieved.'

'I'm sorry,' I answered, 'the work has been held up since I returned. We've suffered an unfortunate loss on the staff. Nothing to do with the experiment, or the research connected with it. Young Ken Ryan died yesterday from leukaemia.'

Once again there was the swift exchange of glances.

'We heard he was not well,' said the first man. 'Your predecessor told us. In fact, we were given to understand that the experiment in progress was, without the Ministry being informed, connected with this boy's illness.'

'You've been misinformed,' I said. 'His illness had nothing to do with the experiment. The doctor will be back shortly; he can give you the medical details.'

'We should like to see MacLean,' persisted the

second chap, 'and we should like to see the electronics department.'

I went back to the control room. I knew that nothing I had said would prevent them from having their way. We were for it.

MacLean was standing by Charon 2 doing something to the controls. I looked quickly from him to Charon 3 alongside. The screen was still glowing, but the signal had vanished. I did not say anything, I just stared at him.

'Yes,' he said, 'it's dismantled. I've disconnected everything. The force is lost.'

My instantaneous feeling of relief turned to compassion, compassion for the man whose work for months, for years, had gone within five minutes. Destroyed by his own act.

'It isn't finished,' he said, meeting my eyes. 'It's only begun. Oh, one part of it is over. Charon 3 is useless now, and what happened will only be known to the three of us – for Robbie must share our knowledge. We were on the verge of a discovery that no one living would believe. But only on the verge. It could well be that both of us were wrong, that what the child told us last night, and again this morning, was simply some distortion of her unconscious mind – I don't know. I just don't know . . . But, because of what she said, I've released the energy. The child is free. Ken is free. He's gone. Where, to what ultimate destination, we shall probably never know. But – and this includes you, Steve, and Robbie, if he will join us – I am prepared to work to the end of my days to find out.'

Then I told him what the officials from the Ministry had said. He shrugged his shoulders.

'I'll tell them all our experiments have failed,' he said, 'that I want to pack in the job. Henceforth, Steve, we'll be on our own. It's strange – somehow I feel nearer to Ken now than I ever did before. Not only Ken, but everyone who has gone before.' He paused, and turned away. 'The child will be all right,' he said. 'Go to her, will you, and send Robbie to me? I'll deal with those sleuths from the Ministry.'

I slipped out of the door at the back and started walking across the marsh towards the coastguard cottages. Cerberus came with me. He was no longer panting, restless, as he had been the night before, but bounded ahead in tearing spirits, returning now and again to make sure that I was following him.

It seemed to me that I had no feeling left, either for what had happened or for what was yet to come. Mac had destroyed, with his own hands, the single thread of evidence that had brought us, through the whole of yesterday, to this morning's dawn. The ultimate dream of every scientist, to give the first answer to the meaning of death, had belonged to us for a brief few hours. We had captured the energy, the energy had ignited the spark, and from that point on there had appeared to loom world after world of discovery.

Now . . . now, my faith was waning. Perhaps we had been wrong, tricked by our own emotions and the suffering of a frightened, backward child. The ultimate questions would never receive their answer, either from us or from anyone.

The marsh fell back on either side of me, and I climbed the scrubby hill to the coastguard cottages. The dog ran on ahead, barking. Away to the right, outlined on the cliff edge, the damned U.S. cadets were blowing their bugles once again. The raucous, discordant screeches tore the air. They were trying, of all things, to sound the Reveille.

I saw Robbie come out of the Januses' cottage, and the child was with him. She seemed all right. She ran forward to greet the dog. Then she heard the sound of the Reveille, and lifted her arms. As the tempo increased she swayed to the rhythm, and ran out towards the cliffs with her arms above her head, laughing, dancing, the dog barking at her feet. The cadets looked back, laughing with her; and then there was nothing else but the dog barking, the child dancing, and the sound of those thin, high bugles in the air.

POCKET
PENGUINS

1 Emile Zola The Beast Within

2 Willa Cather O Pioneers!

3 Leo Tolstoy The Cossacks *and* Hadji Murat

4 Alfred Russel Wallace The Malay Archipelago

5 Rainer Maria Rilke The Notebooks of Malte Laurids Brigge

6 Virginia Woolf Mrs Dalloway

7 Karen Blixen Out of Africa

8 Franz Kafka Metamorphosis

9 Maxim Gorky My Childhood

10 Emilia Pardo Bazán The House of Ulloa

11 Guy de Maupassant A Parisian Affair

12 Alessandro Manzoni The Betrothed

13 Henry David Thoreau Walden

14 Ivan Turgenev Fathers and Sons

15 D. H. Lawrence The Rainbow

16 H. P. Lovecraft The Call of Cthulhu

17 Joseph Conrad The Secret Agent

18 Jaroslav Hašek The Good Soldier Švejk

19 Henri Alain-Fournier The Lost Estate

20 Mikhail Bulgakov The Master and Margarita

21 Fyodor Dostoevsky The Gambler *and* A Nasty Business

22 Carson McCullers The Heart is a Lonely Hunter

23 H. G. Wells The Island of Doctor Moreau

24 Ernst Jünger Storm of Steel

25 Daphne du Maurier Don't Look Now

26 Suetonius The Twelve Caesars

27 Antoine de Saint-Exupéry Wind, Sand and Stars

28 Natsume Sōseki Sanshirō

29 Arthur Schnitzler Dream Story

30 Jean Rhys Good Morning, Midnight

31 Evelyn Waugh Put Out More Flags

32 Isaac Bashevis Singer The Magician of Lublin

33 Honoré de Balzac Eugénie Grandet

34 Jean-Paul Sartre The Age of Reason

35 Ford Madox Ford The Good Soldier

36 Eileen Chang Lust, Caution

37 Vladimir Nabokov Laughter in the Dark

38 John Reed Ten Days That Shook the World

39 Nikolay Gogol Dead Souls

40 Wu Ch'êng-ên Monkey